BACK IN THE SADDLE

AVENGING ANGELS
BOOK 2

KRISTEN ASHLEY

Back In The Saddle

AVENGING ANGELS SERIES BOOK TWO

AVENGING ANGEL

A ROMANCE NOVEL BY

KRISTEN

NEW YORK TIMES BESTSELLING AUTHOR

ASHLEY

This book is a work of fiction. Any reference to historical events, real people, or real places are used fictitiously. Other names, characters, places, and incidents are products of the author's imagination. Any resemblance to actual events, locales, or persons, living or dead, is coincidental.

Cover Image: Pixel Mischief Design

To all the Homers out here.
Both human and feline.

ONE

CATCH ME IF YOU CAN

It was dark as pitch in the area around the makeshift encampment that sat in the parking lot of an abandoned warehouse, in what had become a kind of no-man's-land just south of the heart of the city.

This darkness might have had to do with the fact it was nearing one in the morning.

It wasn't a great time to do my search, but in the last six months, I'd been hitting up the encampment at random times, day and evening, and always came up empty-handed. But due to safety issues, I'd never gone so late (or early, depending on how you looked at it).

This time, I was giving it a shot precisely because it was so late (also because I was getting desperate).

He had to sleep somewhere, and I was hoping it was here. At the same time, I died a little death thinking it might be.

It was the night before Thanksgiving.

I'd hoped he'd be somewhere with someone on Thanksgiving, even if that someone wasn't me, and, well, that somewhere was here.

I'd learned, and I had the requisite materials with me.

Four bags full of bottles of water (sorry environment) and a backpack stuffed with packs of beef jerky, boxes of protein bars and hydration packets.

Oh yeah, and an empty used sharps container.

Homer shuffled out first, as Homer always did. I wasn't sure Homer slept. I was sure Homer was King of the Homeless Encampment.

I was sure of this because I'd learned something else. I had to make Homer trust me before anyone else did.

This took time.

And lots of bottles of water and packs of beef jerky.

He said nothing as he took two of the bags and the sharps container from me.

Then he mumbled, "Late night."

"Is he here?"

My vision had adjusted to the dark. I'd hit the encampment, and in the dim light that came from the city and various camp lanterns dotting the space, I saw his eyes in his dangerously tanned, leathery, be-whiskered face catch mine.

And I saw my answer.

No.

My brother wasn't there.

"Seen him?" I asked as we began to move through the oddly organized labyrinth of tents, the tarps that created crude shelters, loaded grocery carts and scattering of debris.

"Did you bring clean syringes?"

This wasn't an answer to my question, and sadly my answer to his was, "Not this time."

He nodded, reached into a bag, made a noise, and a hand came out of a tent.

He put a bottle of water in it as I shrugged off the backpack to pull out a bag of jerky.

Homer took that, tossed it into the tent, and we moved on.

We did this at two more tents before I said, "Homer."

That was all I said, but he got me, so he stopped and turned to me.

And he stated it plainly. "You find him, you quit coming."

Oh my God.

On the one hand, it felt good that he trusted me, and him saying that meant he and his brethren appreciated me. I didn't have the resources to give much, and I knew I didn't help their situation at all, but it was nice to understand the little I did meant something.

On the other hand, I needed to find my brother.

"Are you...keeping him from me?" I asked.

He shook his head.

But he said, "Others might."

That meant, since Homer knew everyone and everything, others *were*.

Damn.

I pointed out the obvious. "I've gotta know if he's all right."

Homer gazed around the dismal space that looked bad and smelled worse.

I took his point.

If Jeff was here, he wasn't all right.

Then again, I already knew he wasn't all right.

Just as I knew, the minute Mom kicked him out seven months ago and he didn't do his usual—bunk with one of his buds, then figure his shit out and get back on his meds—I would be doing what I was doing right then.

And there I was, doing what I was doing right then.

We moved through the space, silently handing out waters and protein delivery systems, with me looking closely at faces and trying to peer into tents.

I came up empty.

As usual.

When we were back at Homer's tent, he took the spent plastic bags from me (something else I'd learned: Homer had a thing for plastic bags) but handed me the clattering sharps container.

"It'd be good you bring syringes next time," he said.

With that, he ducked into his tent and disappeared.

I stared at it, the feelings I was feeling balling up inside me, the weight so heavy, the urge was almost overwhelming to open my mouth and shriek my fear and frustration to the skies above Phoenix.

I didn't do that.

I carried that weight with the container and my empty backpack to my car.

Though, I didn't make it to my car.

I stopped dead twenty feet away when I saw Eric Turner, investigator at Nightingale Investigations & Security. The place of business of Eric, Cap (my friend Raye's boyfriend) and a number of other badasses who were all ridiculously attractive.

Yep.

Every.

Single.

One.

His ass was resting on the fender of my black convertible Mini, his long legs stretched out in front of him, ankles crossed, his arms were also crossed on his chest.

He'd been there a while.

Waiting for me.

Okay, one could say, until I met Eric, I hadn't been into older guys.

And he wasn't older, *as such*.

It was just that he belonged to the first generation of the Hot Bunch guys of NI&S (the younger generation, Raye had dubbed the Hottie Squad so we could tell them apart, something that was necessary due to their overall concentrated level of hotness, which was so high, it was immeasurable, so we had to pry them apart somehow).

The first generation were all married (except Eric) and had wives and children (except Eric).

But the minute I clapped eyes on him, I was into him.

That was because he was mega hot.

It was also about other things, which I wasn't in the place to contemplate fully at that moment, seeing as it was now closer to two in the morning, and he had no reason to be leaning against my car at that time—or ever.

Yet there he was.

I restarted walking toward him, and when I arrived, I quipped, "Of all the gin joints."

"I'm not finding anything funny, Jessie," he replied.

Hmm.

One could say we hadn't had very many deep conversations (as in...*none*).

But I'd been around him somewhat frequently, seeing as Raye, one of my three besties, was not only hooked up, but shacked up with Cap. This meant they often came to The Surf Club to have lunch or grab a cup of joe. And The Surf Club was where Raye, my other two besties, Harlow and Luna, and I worked.

Obviously I'd heard his voice, which was normally deep and mellow, but it could get smooth, rich and warm as fudge when he said things like, "Thank you," after I put one of Lucia's (our chef) divine creations in front of him.

Now, it was still deep, though not at all mellow or smooth. Instead, rough and edgy.

In other words...pissed.

"Eric—"

He cut me off. "Have you lost your fuckin' mind?"

"No, I—"

"Wrong," he bit off. "You have. You've lost your fuckin' mind."

Now, hang on a second.

This guy worked with my friend's boyfriend.

No, wait.

Cap was my friend too, so take that degree of separation out, he worked with my friend.

I waited on him a couple of times (right, that was a lie, I'd waited on him multiple times).

And I went out and had wings and beers while watching the Cardinals with that crew once, and he was there.

Other than that, and the mad crush I had on him from not-so-afar, this guy did not factor in my life.

"What I'm doing has nothing to do with you," I told him.

"Wrong again," he retorted.

I was losing patience.

No surprise, since I wasn't the most patient being on the planet, or even in the top ninety-nine percent (and on my bad days, such as now, I occupied more of the lower point-three-percent bracket).

"How do you figure that?" I snapped.

"I take it you haven't read the Rock Chick books either."

The Rock Chick books were novels written about all his buds' courtships (though, not his, obvs).

I know, weird.

But true.

They also apparently stood as warning signals to Raye, Luna, Harlow and me about our futures.

Which would normally lead one to diving right in.

I'd meant to, but what could I say?

I wasn't a reader.

Then again, so far, none of the girls had read them.

Topping that, the one I wanted (the one I was shockingly currently with) didn't want me.

I didn't confirm I hadn't read the books.

I didn't say anything at all.

He hadn't moved from his cool-scary-guy crossed ankles/arms lean against my car (and I hoped his fine ass didn't put a dent in my fender—because he was tall and built, and muscle like his had to have some heft to it), so I mimicked him, without the crossed ankles and leaning parts.

Okay, so I just crossed my arms on my chest.

"We adopt one, we adopt all," he stated. "Raye came into the family, now you're all under our protection."

"That's sweet and all—"

He interrupted me.

Again.

"It's not sweet. We've been through this shit before. It's compulsory."

Compulsory?

Screw that.

I didn't need some hot guy thinking I was an obligatory pain in his ass.

"Consider yourself let off the hook when it comes to me," I offered.

He shook his head. "It doesn't work that way."

Okay.

I'd had a tough night.

And tomorrow was going to be a tough day.

Jeff wasn't there, or they were hiding him from me so I'd continue to bring water, hydration packets, food, clean syringes, bath wipes and the like. My mother was useless (per usual). My father was a piece of garbage (per usual). Therefore, no family Thanksgiving for me, and I loved turkey, and stuffing, and all that shit.

But more, because Mom and Dad were such wastes of space, it was on me to find Jeff.

And the longer it took, the more terrified I got.

So...yeah.

I wasn't in a stellar mood.

And Eric looked delectable, all long, lean, muscled, black-haired hot guy lounging against my Mini.

But I was into him, and a girl could feel vibes, so I knew he wasn't into me (which sucked...*huge*, until very recently, when I was figuring out he could be a dick).

So there was also that.

But straight up, I wasn't doing this.

I started to head to the driver's side door when he said, "The other guys think it's cute. I'm older and I've been through this crap before, and this vigilante shit, it's not cute, Jessie."

That stopped me right in my tracks.

"I'm not being cute," I whispered, my words trembling with my fury.

Because trying to find my missing brother who had significant mental health issues was nowhere near *cute*.

Finally, he pushed off my car and moved to me. I had to tip my head back because the dude towered over me, and I wasn't short.

That said, even though I'd never had a guy that tall, I knew he was the *exact perfect* height to kiss.

Cripes, the hits just kept coming.

"I know," he said, his voice having changed, back to smooth, even gentle. "But what you're doing is dangerous."

I tensed, my head so screwed up with worry about Jeff (and, I couldn't deny, unreciprocated longing for Eric), it hadn't occurred to me to spare a moment to cipher why he just happened to be here.

I felt my eyes narrow. "Do you know what I'm doing?"

"I'd like for you to talk to me about it."

That was both sweet and not an answer to my question, so the second part negated the sweet part.

I abandoned that line of questioning to get things moving so I could go home. In the deep fall and winter, it got cold at night in The Valley, and suddenly, I was freezing.

"Homer looks after me," I asserted.

"Homer?"

"The King of the Encampment."

"And what do you know about Homer?"

"I know he's the King of the Encampment."

"What else?"

"What else do I need to know?"

"Is he addicted to drugs?"

"That's not need to know."

"Is he PTSD?"

"That's not need to know either."

"It will be, when he turns because he can't find his fix and he's going through DTs, or he's having an episode and you're in his space."

"Homer's solid."

"He lives in a homeless encampment."

"He's still solid."

"How do you know that?"

All right.

Enough!

I threw both my arms out and cried, "I just know, all right?"

"Jessie?"

I turned.

And sure enough, about ten feet away, there was Homer and about seven other dudes from the camp.

They seemed menacing in the shadows, but they were scraggly and obviously didn't get regular nutrition.

Though, even if they were healthy, Eric was the kind of guy who could probably best the lot of them.

Another of those reasons why I was into him. It was clear he could take care of himself and any bad business that came his way, so in the end, if you were his, he could take care of you.

No one had ever taken care of me.

Not ever.

In my entire life.

"Everything okay?" Homer asked.

No!

"Yes," I lied. "This is Eric. He's a friend. And he's not a fan of the hour I chose to visit you."

Homer looked to Eric. "You're right. It wasn't smart."

Oh my God!

Really?

"Homer!" I snapped.

He was still looking at Eric. "Make sure she comes when it's safer. And come with her." He jerked his head to the men behind him. "We'll let you in."

With that, he and his bedraggled, improvised posse shuffled back to the tents.

No help there.

"Jessie, look at me."

I tore my gaze from the men who were fading into the mishmash of tents and darkness and looked up at Eric.

Mistake.

There wasn't a lot of light, but the man was so handsome, I could see every delicious angle and delightful hollow of his perfect face.

And how did he get so close without me noticing?

God, I'd never been this close to him.

He smelled like rosemary and cedarwood.

Scrumptious.

And I suddenly got the whole magnetic thing, because even if I was pissed at him and in a crappy mood, I felt the pull of his hotness, and it was almost impossible to resist.

That said, holding a sharps container and being downwind from a not-great smell (though, the rosemary and cedarwood helped) in the middle of the night with a man who wasn't into me but was ticked at me, wasn't conducive to me throwing myself at him.

Then again, I wasn't a throwing-myself-at-a-man type of girl.

I was a catch-me-if-you-can one.

"If you want us to find him, we'll find him," he stated.

Newsflash: I wasn't only impatient, I was stubborn.

Oh, and I could hold a grudge.

So with this shit he was pulling, which was brand-new, it meant he had a whole year before my grudge wore off.

Therefore, instead of taking this supposedly hot-shit investigator up on his offer, I shot back, "I'm no one's obligation."

"I see you took that wrong," he muttered.

"Can we be done with this?" I requested.

"We can, if you promise you'll call me if you ever come back here, so me, or one of the guys, can come with you."

"I've been doing this a while and..."—I held my arms up at my sides, the sharps container dangling from one hand—"here I am, perfectly fine."

Suddenly, the container clattered to the ground and my front was pressed to the side of my car, my legs were kicked wide apart, my arm was twisted behind me, I had a wall of muscle pressed tight to my back, and Eric's mouth was at my ear.

"I make my point about how shit can shift in an instant?" he whispered there.

Even though I was pissed—no, *insanely* pissed—his smooth voice in my ear traveled down the skin of my neck, and I had to fight a shiver.

"Get off me," I whispered.

He didn't get off me, nor did he let me go.

His other arm snaked around my belly and he pulled me tighter to his body.

God, every inch of him felt hard, totally unyielding, and he was very warm.

Lord.

"I make my point?" This time his voice was rougher, almost thick, and I was still insanely pissed, but it did a number on me.

"Please, let me go."

He did, and he didn't.

He let me go enough to whirl me around, then he pressed me back into the car, front to front. He had one arm tight around my waist and the other hand he rested on the soft top beside me.

But, oh crap.

This was worse.

By *a lot.*

"You think I want to be out at two in the morning having a frustrating as fuck conversation with a stubborn woman who knows I'm right?" he asked.

"Fine. Great. I won't ever come here again," I lied.

"You're lying," he called me on it.

I could take no more.

Honestly, could you blame me?

"Can I just go home?" I demanded.

His onyx eyes roamed my face for what seemed like an eternity (and as per the Official Crushing on a Guy Handbook, which I'd recently spent a good deal of time memorizing, in the section where it dealt with unrequited crushes, it was considered an actual eternity) before he let me go and stepped away.

"You have friends," he pointed out, going softly now, because his tone was just that.

Yeah.

I did.

Good ones.

And we'd just gone through a shitstorm with Raye.

I loved them, and I knew they'd take my back.

But this was...personal.

Private.

Family.

"It's a family thing," I told Eric.

Those onyx eyes moved over my face again before he sighed. Heavily.

"Just be smart," he said.

As if I intended to be dumb.

I glared at him.

Something shifted in the way he was looking at me as I did.

Something big and important and consuming.

So much of all of that, it made me stop glaring and start staring, at the same time trying to get a handle on just what that shift was.

He then muttered, like he was talking to himself, "Shit, I'm fucked."

And he had to be talking to himself, because I sure didn't know what he was on about.

He then bent, nabbed the sharps container and sauntered to his truck.

And one could say the man could *saunter*.

Whoa.

I shook my head to get myself together because I'd just learned, no matter how good he could saunter, Eric was a dick (yes, I was ignoring the fact he was out there to talk sense into me, because what I was doing, especially at that hour, truly wasn't all that safe).

It was time to head home.

It was, because, in a few hours I had to get up, alone, and figure out how to roast a turkey breast, make some mashed potatoes and dump a can of soup into some green beans, then pick a movie I could watch that wouldn't make me feel like a total loser because I was all by myself on Thanksgiving.

I PULLED into my parking spot at the Oasis, my apartment complex, and it was only then the SUV, which had Eric's glorious ass in it that followed me all the way home, motored out of the parking lot of my apartment complex and turned right on Seventh.

"Overachiever," I mumbled as I hauled my ass out of my car.

I went through the security gate, and even the courtyard of the Oasis, which was usually lit up with attractive string lights and the pool illuminated—always a cozy welcome home—due to the hour (and the fact the pool was being resurfaced) was dark and forbidding.

Like my mood.

I jogged up the steps, passed Raye and Cap's place, then let myself into mine.

I switched on the light on the table by the door and then let out a small scream.

A very pretty Black woman about my age, wearing a pair of sandy-white satin parachute pants and a stark-white cashmere turtleneck, was sitting on my couch.

This outfit was the shit, and I instantly made a mental note to find those pants, at the same time I prayed they came in black.

I knew immediately who she was, even if, until that moment, I'd never met her.

Her name was Clarice, and she was the middleman for someone Raye and Luna referred to as Arthur.

She was also the wrangler of the Avenging Angels, of which, along with Raye, Luna and Harlow, I was one.

Whoever this Arthur was had given us three cars in three storage units and an array of equipment that ranged from Tasers to handcuffs to white boards in order to conduct our (yes, vigilante) investigations.

When Raye and Luna recruited us, I was all in, mostly because those two were crazy bitches, and they were trying to find missing women.

I honestly didn't think much would come of it. But your girl goes on a mission, and that mission involves her navigating the seedy underbelly of Phoenix? You don't ask questions, you take her back.

Then they actually figured out who took the women, and even found them.

Color me every shade of surprised.

But that was over two months ago, and since, we'd never used those cars, except to go visit our "informants" (who were more like friends we had a burger with every once in a while, who also happened to work the streets as sex workers).

So I kinda figured it was all just a lark.

I mean, your average, everyday server at a funky coffee/cocktail bar (that also served great food, and fabulous drinks (if I did say so myself)) didn't go around cracking cases the cops couldn't figure out.

But here was Clarice, and I couldn't deny the quiver of excitement I felt at finally getting to meet her and what that might mean.

Even if she did break into my pad and scare the crap out of me.

"Not smart," she said before she pushed to her high-heeled, champagne sandaled feet.

I had a feeling she knew where I was that night, but I didn't ask. According to Raye and Luna, this Arthur person knew all, so it stood to reason Clarice would too.

"I take it you're Clarice," I noted as she walked to me.

She then walked right by me, to the door.

She put her hand on the handle and turned back to me.

"It's after two in the morning on Turkey Day," she bitched.

Seriously?

"Sorry, I must have extended your invitation in a fugue state," I retorted. "Hang tight while I pull together a cheese platter."

Slowly, she smiled. "I think I like you."

"I'll notify the papers," I stated. "Why are you here?"

Her smile died and she ordered, "Activate the Angels, Jess." She opened the door and made a move out of it, but looked over her shoulder at me before she was fully out, and she lowered the boom. "Or I will."

The door closed on her, and I heard her heels clicking along the walkway outside.

I stood immobile long after the sound of them faded to nothing.

Only then did the entirety of my night settle on me.

So of course, I muttered to myself, "Well...*shit*."

TWO

NO-FUCKS-TO-GIVING

I was on my gray sectional with my laptop, looking up how to roast a turkey breast (and mash potatoes and make green bean casserole (what could I say? I didn't cook, so I'd forgotten how to do all this since last year). At least the stuffing box had instructions on it.

I was doing this so I wouldn't do what I'd been doing most of the morning: understanding that Eric, and therefore all the Hottie Squad as well as the Hot Bunch, knew about my brother.

Consequently, I was struggling with the many emotions that wrought. From shame that my family was such we didn't look after him. To fear, because the days were ticking by, and no Jeff. To sadness, because it was Thanksgiving, and the only good ones I'd ever had was when Jeff was looking after himself and we shared them together.

I was also enumerating (not for the first time) all the reasons why Eric Turner did it for me.

Of course, there was his extreme good looks. Also, the way he exuded confidence and the manner in which he did, made it clear he knew who he was, and he was down with being that man (seriously, that was all kinds of *hot*). Further, his aforementioned ability to take care of himself and any situation that might befall him, and what that might mean to the people he cared about in his life.

The way he dressed.

The way he walked.

The way he smiled.

The respect the HB and HS showed him, those being men who didn't give that kind of respect unless it was earned.

As usual, I'd forgotten all about roasting turkey and mashing potatoes and was thinking of Eric when there was a knock at the door.

I figured it was one of my neighbors.

Oasis Square was a primo apartment complex just north of downtown Phoenix (primo in the sense it was cool AF, not because it was luxury or anything—no way I could afford luxury, not now, nor, I expected, ever). I'd only recently moved in, but since Raye had been living there for years, I'd hung out with her a lot, and the tenants had rabidly formed a close-knit community, I wasn't exactly a newbie.

So I figured this was some neighbor who'd sniffed out I was alone on a holiday and came to rescue me.

Thus, it was highly likely I was about to be abducted and forced to sit at a table with another person's happy family and gaggle of friends, pretending I was enjoying myself, when all shit like that did was remind me how unhappy my own family was.

Hence, if Jeff wasn't in the picture, me hibernating every Thanksgiving (and Christmas) after weeks of dancing an intricate but practiced dance to avoid getting invited to anyone else's house during a holiday.

I thought about ignoring them, but on the next knock, I was reminded how rabid the Oasis community was, and I didn't want to dis anybody this early in my tenure.

Normally, this friendliness was kickass. It meant parties in the courtyard, and there was always someone who could lend a hand when you ran out of tequila.

Now, I wasn't feeling it.

Even so, I got up, went to the door, and then went solid as I stared out my peephole at Eric Turner.

"What the fuck?" I breathed.

Did I manifest the guy?

Second question, how did he bypass the security gate?

"I can hear you," he called.

Really?

He must have super good hearing or the doors weren't up to snuff.

"Open up, Jessie," he ordered.

Ugh.

I couldn't dis a member of the Hot Bunch either.

I opened the door, stating, "I think I had just about enough of you last night."

Yeah.

I couldn't dis, but I was me, so I could always throw attitude.

I stated that, but I did it shambling back because he was shouldering in, laden with grocery bags from AJ's.

Okay...

What?

I stood, hand still on the door handle, watching him go direct to my kitchen.

He was on this trajectory as he replied, "Tough."

He dumped the bags on my counter.

I closed the door and walked in.

"Turner—"

I stopped speaking when he started sniffing.

He then asked me, "You don't have the bird in the oven yet?"

"The YouTube video said it only takes an hour," I informed him.

"An hour to cook a turkey?" he asked, like I said it took an hour for Beyoncé to prepare to hit the stage.

"Yes," I answered.

"It takes longer than that to roast a chicken."

"Sorry, my man, you missed the turnoff to the Barefoot

Contessa's house on your way here. Just go east for about thirty-five hours and veer north somewhere along the line. Eventually, you should hit Long Island. Be sure to tell Ina and Jeffrey I said, 'hey.'"

He smirked.

It was as hot as everything he did, so I felt that smirk in very private parts of me.

What did I do to deserve this?

Really, tell me.

"The Barefoot Contessa?" he asked.

What could I say?

I was into cooking shows, and hers was the best (according to me).

I just didn't cook.

"Turner, what are you doing here?" I demanded to know.

"You're alone on Thanksgiving, I'm alone on Thanksgiving. So we're having Thanksgiving together."

We were?

Hold on.

Rewind.

"How did you know I was alone on Thanksgiving?"

He stopped pulling stuff out of the bags to lock eyes with me. "You're not at Scott and Louise's with Luna and Raye and that crowd. You're not with Harlow and her family. And your family is a disaster."

Hold on part two.

I barely knew him.

Yes, my family was a disaster. One might even say we were a disaster of epic proportions.

But he didn't get to call them that.

"You don't know anything about my family," I said sharply.

He went back to pulling stuff out of the bags, saying, "Clue in, Wylde."

I moved to the counter opposite him (my pad was one bedroom, it started with a living room that fed into an open kitchen, the two spaces delineated by a bar, then there was a short hall with a laundry closet to one side, a bathroom to the other, and it ended in the bedroom).

I put my hands on the counter and asked, "Clue in to what?"

"What do I do for a living?" he asked in return.

As I suspected…

But worse.

"You investigated me?"

He started folding the paper bags he'd emptied, and there were vegetables and other food-style detritus all over my kitchen bar.

It was a new look for my kitchen, and I would have liked the time to peruse it, but I only had eyes for Eric, and not the usual only-having-eyes-for-him kind.

"We investigated all of you."

Although this confirmed my suspicions about why he was there last night, such was the drama of being confronted by this confirmation, I took a step back and put my hand to my forehead, crying, "Oh my God! I don't know what to do with this. It's so invasive, I can't even process it."

"Get over it," he murmured while moving to my fridge.

Hold on part three.

"How did you know where I was last night?" I demanded. "*Precisely* where I was."

No hesitation, he answered, "Like I said, we've been through this before. We aren't fucking around since it's happening again. So we got trackers on all your cars."

At this information, I waited for my head to explode.

When it didn't…

"Turner—" I began to tell him to get the hell out of my apartment.

"Right. I get it. You got a breast," he muttered into the fridge. "Still gonna take longer than an hour."

"Turner!" I snapped.

He straightened out of my refrigerator and turned to me.

With bad timing, his hot-guyness in my kitchen made its reality known, and since his hot-guyness was off the scales hot, I got flummoxed.

Me.

Jessica Rose Wylde...*flummoxed.*

That said, he had great hair. So black (my favorite non-color), it seemed unreal. It was also thick and had a lot of wave. He wore it longish and it curled around his ears in a way I could write an entire sub-chapter for the unrequited crush section of the Official Crushing on A Guy Handbook about how to cope with curbing your desire to touch something on a man you were crazy about, who was not crazy about you.

I never understood the concept of bedroom eyes, but the fathomless laziness of his inky black gaze sure as hell defined it for me.

Not to mention, his shoulders were very broad, so everything he wore hung on him *just right.* And today, that was a pitch-black thermal that hugged his shoulders and biceps and pecs so lovingly, I was jealous...of a shirt.

To put a fine point on it, there was a lot to be flummoxed about.

Before I could recover, something I didn't know how to do because I'd never in my life been in that state, there was a knock on the door.

I was still attempting recovery, so Eric sauntered out from around the kitchen bar and went to the door.

His sauntering was detrimental to my recovery, as was the way his jeans highlighted his fantastic ass and thick thighs, so I was still standing there speechless when he opened it.

"Whoa!" I heard cried. Then, shyly, "Uh...hi."

"Hey," Eric replied.

Alexis, one of the Oasis tenants, and a particular friend to my crew, looked around Eric, saw me and exclaimed, "Oh my *God*, Jessie! I'm so glad you're home. No one's home!"

She rushed in.

I was still unable to move.

"Please tell me you have flour. I ran out of flour," she babbled. "And Jacob's family and my family are all here...*together*...our first holiday...*together*...and it's super important it goes *without a hitch*... and I *ran out of flour*."

I did not have flour.

In fact, since flour was not required in the mixing of any alcoholic beverage known to man, I'd never actually used flour.

"How much do you need?" Eric asked.

"At least a cup, two if you can spare it," Alexis told him.

He went to the kitchen, commandeered a paper-covered brick and started folding open the top.

"We're having apple crumble for dessert, so yeah, I can give you two cups," he told Alexis.

"You're a star," Alexis gushed.

But hang on.

Apple crumble?

Like that stuff with cinnamony apples covered in gooey, sugary, buttery topping?

We were having that?

"Sooooooooo..." Alexis drew that out, her eyes pinging between me and Eric after she gave him a Stasher for the flour and while he was opening and closing drawers in my kitchen looking for something.

I pulled my shit tight and said, "Right on. First holiday with the joined fams."

Alexis and Jacob were a newish couple.

However new, they were *way* into each other. Practically joined at the hip when in public. And if Oasis gossip was true, literally joined in other ways when they weren't.

Alexis's eyes settled on me. "Jacob's mom is really sweet. His dad is just like him, so obviously, he's awesome. My mom is being a pill, but she's always a pill, so I warned Jacob about that beforehand. And my dad is acting like he always acts with my boyfriends. Like Jacob isn't royalty, prince of someplace or other, so he's not good enough for me. I warned Jacob about that too, but it's still making the day not so fun."

Yikes.

"Will your dad come around?" I asked.

"I don't care," she said in a surly tone that was very un-Alexis. "Jacob is *everything*. I'm the one who's sleeping with him. I'm the one who wakes up beside him. It's my choice who I do that with, Dad doesn't get a vote."

"Speak your truth, sister," I encouraged.

She shot me a nervous smile, which told me she'd spoken her truth, but she was still freaked out about what was happening with her family.

Poor Alexis.

"It's gonna be okay," I assured her, hoping it was.

"Thanks, Jessie," she replied.

"You and Jacob are solid. In the end, that's all that matters, right?" I asked.

Her smile grew sunny, and she did a little hop when she said, "Right."

Eric was there, handing her the Stasher. "That should be about two cups."

She held it to her chest and cooed, "You're a lifesaver."

She then did the eye pinging thing again so Eric held out a hand and said, "I'm Eric. A friend of Jess's."

Hmm.

Was it rude not to introduce a guest you didn't actually ask to be your guest?

"A friend," she mumbled, taking his hand. "Nice to meet you, I'm Alexis." Then she exclaimed, "Right! Have to dash! Have a great Thanksgiving you two!"

After that, she pranced out as only Alexis could prance, considering she was a member of the ballet.

"Hup," I heard.

I turned at this odd sound Eric made and caught the apple he sent flying my way just in time.

"You're on peeling and slicing the apples. We'll get the crumble out of the way. You didn't brine the bird, so that means I gotta get creative."

I stood, holding the apple and glaring at him.

"I'm not making Thanksgiving dinner with you."

"You don't help, you don't eat. So it's gonna be uncomfortable I eat in front of you while we watch *Planes, Trains and Automobiles*."

Damn.

Awesome choice.

I loved that movie. Steve Martin was a comic genius, and John Candy left us far too soon.

It was also the perfect Thanksgiving movie, even if this day was the most painful day (says me) of anyone who had a disaster of a family.

I returned to the counter, put the apple on it and announced, "You don't have to feel sorry for me."

His black eyes came up from something he was doing with some kind of leafy substance on the counter and caught mine.

"I'm used to this," I informed him. "No one ever drove a car through the front door on a holiday," I referenced *The Bear*. "But we'll just say, being at home by myself, burning a turkey breast and making the boxed stuffing soggy, regardless that I followed the instructions to the letter, is something I'm used to, and it's vastly preferable."

"My mom was killed in a car wreck when I was thirteen. It was Christmas Eve. She was bringing home a puppy for my brother and me for Christmas. The puppy died too. Dad was supposed to get the puppy, but he got caught at work. He did that a lot, with Mom covering for him, even though it annoyed her. Especially around the holidays, putting it all on her to do everything, which was probably why she was speeding, because she had so much shit to do. This meant he blamed himself. That lead to him hitting the bottle hard, and since then, he hasn't found his way out of it."

My brows shot up at his relating this brutal honesty even as my heart started hurting at hearing his distressing history.

Eric kept sharing.

"My brother turned into a piece of shit who blames the world for him losing his mom when he was eleven and his dad being a functioning alcoholic by day, a fall-down drunk at night. That's manifested as my brother having three kids by two different women, and he's deadbeat on all of them. He claims disability, even though that doesn't stop him from going hunting or driving one of his buds' jet skis on the lake every weekend, both while wasted. My father doesn't touch base often, but every time he does, I brace for him to tell me Tim shot himself or someone else while hunting deer, or he drowned in the lake."

He paused.

I said nothing mostly because I couldn't find the right words to say.

Eric kept going.

"I haven't been home in ten years, and before that, it was five, but the second time reminded me why I hadn't been home in five, so that's why it's now ten...and counting."

I found a word, it just wasn't the right one, but I couldn't stop it from escaping my lips.

"Whoa," I whispered.

"Yeah," he stated.

"Why aren't you with Mace and Stella or something?" I asked after a his-generation part of the crew who also lived in Phoenix.

"Because I'm here with you."

"Did they ask?"

"Yes. But I'm here with you."

Oh man.

Something weird was happening inside me. I didn't know what it was. I'd never felt it.

But it felt warm.

And...

Gooey.

Gross!

And...

Shit!

"And I'm not here because I feel sorry for you," he went on. "I'm here because we both have fucked-up families, and we get it. Today doesn't have to be about counting our blessings and being grateful our lives are full of love. It can be about food, a funny as fuck movie, then more food and nothing else." He tipped his gorgeous head to the side. "Now, Jessie, are you down? Or do I have to lug all this shit back to my place?"

My mouth made the decision before my mind did.

It said, "I'm a mixologist, so I can slice fruit like nobody's business. But other than that, you're on your own, big guy."

He seemed to relax even though nothing about him physically gave the indication of relaxation.

Then he ordered, "Get your ass over here."

I'd dreamed many a dream of him saying something like that to me, just not in this context.

But the life I lived I'd learned.

You took what you could get.

So I got my ass over there.

We were sitting on stools at my bar, eating the Thanksgiving feast that mostly Eric prepared.

For my part, I was also freaking out.

The thing I was freaking out about was...

Except for when he threw the unopened box of stuffing in my trash, whereupon I snapped, "Dude!" and he shared, "That stuffing is banned in a number of different countries due to the additives in it."

It was?

"Seriously?" I'd asked.

He nabbed a bag of dried bread cubes, held them up and said, "We're doing the real thing."

All right then.

I wasn't going to argue that, so I didn't.

Outside of that exchange, we barely spoke. Most of what was said was Eric telling me what to slice, dice and chop. Therefore, I sliced, diced and chopped while Eric did the rest.

I also concocted an on-the-spot Thanksgiving cocktail of gin, lemon juice, ginger beer and apple slices, which we both sipped as we cooked (I might not have much food in my house, but I had everything on hand to whip up a cocktail).

Oh, and I cleaned up after him when it was clear he was done with a station, leaving only a few bowls and a single pan beside the sink needing to be washed. The rest of the space was neat as a pin. All we needed to do when we were finished eating was rinse our plates and cutlery, put them in the dishwasher, and *boom*, done with the shit of Thanksgiving.

This wasn't what was freaking me out, though.

What was freaking me out was that the silence that had settled between us wasn't weird. It wasn't awkward.

It just...was.

He did his thing. I did my thing. Separate and together. And we just lapsed into it like climbing on a bicycle we hadn't ridden in years and taking off.

I'd never ridden Eric.

Ahem.

But I wasn't that much of a talker, and I could get exhausted around people who needed to fill silence and blabbed all the time.

Sometimes silence was good, and it didn't need to be filled.

It would seem Eric subscribed to that same philosophy.

But right then, I was eating and feeling strange, because making Thanksgiving dinner with Eric felt like we fit. It was natural.

Right.

And...

Safe.

It was only at that moment occurring to me, this wasn't great. I didn't need more things about Eric to feel safe and right. I had enough of those, thanks so very much.

He broke the silence, and it'd gone on so long, I jumped when he did.

"Two questions."

I stopped shoveling his ridiculously delicious mushroom, sausage, and fresh sage stuffing in my mouth and looked to him.

I raised my brows for him to go on.

"You don't cook," he noted.

"That doesn't sound like a question," I replied.

He smiled, and I wished he didn't (yes, his smile was that attractive).

"It wasn't," he agreed. "This is the question. If you don't cook, why are you totally set up in the kitchen?"

Slowly, my head turned toward my kitchen, but I didn't have to look at my shiny counter appliances or the All-Clad pot by the sink. Nor did I have to bring to mind the expensive food processor and juicer I had tucked in a cabinet. I also didn't have to recall how I'd socked away tips and sacrificed on other stuff in order to afford all of it.

Last, I didn't have to cipher why, not only my kitchen, but my whole apartment, every inch, was perfectly perfect, precisely me, my nest, my safe space.

My home.

No, this was last: I wasn't going to share why.

That being, I'd had none of this stuff growing up, so from the moment I moved out at eighteen, and for the last fifteen years, I'd busted my ass to make this just so because I'd never had it.

Instead, I told Eric a little fib, which was only a fib because it wasn't the whole truth, just a small part of it.

"I get wild hairs to take up cooking, or baking, or breadmaking. I buy the shit, but then I get busy and never do it."

"Right," he murmured, and I felt his eyes on me so I looked back at him.

When I did, I saw the depth of his gaze wasn't his resting sexy laziness I could swim in for eternity.

It was searching, acute...uncomfortable.

"What's question two?" I prompted.

"Why no color?"

That one threw me. "What?"

He didn't answer verbally.

He looked over his shoulder at my living room, then to my kitchen, and back to me.

"Oh, you mean the black and white thing?" I queried.

He again didn't answer with words.

He looked down at my black jeans with the ripped knee to my white tee with the black transfer of Debbie Harry's face on it.

"It makes things easy to match," I told him.

Another little fib, because it did, but that wasn't the only reason.

"I can see that with clothes. But Jess, it's everywhere."

I turned to look at my living room, with its crisp gray sectional in the corner. The black toss pillows mixed with the black and white striped ones. The round black coffee table in the middle. The black lamps. The black and white photos that I'd taken and framed with white mattes and black frames, arranging them on a gallery wall above one angle of the couch.

I thought it was the shit.

And it felt like something twisted in me when I looked back at him.

"You don't like it?"

"It's fantastic," he declared. "But I sense there's a story behind it."

I felt such extreme relief he liked it that it tweaked me.

I opened my mouth to say something, but then jumped again, because there was a sharp rap on the picture window behind us.

We both swiveled to see Martha standing there, her hands cupped beside her eyes, looking in.

When she had our attention, she marched toward my door and, without knocking, walked in.

"Thank God you're here!" she exclaimed, still marching, this time to my kitchen.

Of note: Martha was another tenant at the Oasis. She was somewhere in her late fifties, early sixties. She could live elsewhere, she had the means, but she lived here, because she'd lived here in her younger years. Thus, it reminded her of the days before she fell in love then had to spend years helping her husband fight cancer at the same time she raised three boys, and she did this until the boys left the nest, whereupon her beloved husband died from said cancer.

I adored Martha. She had no filter, said what she wanted, did what she wanted, didn't give a shit what anyone thought of her, and by some miracle still managed to be loving no matter how irascible she was. And she was pretty damned irascible.

For me, Martha was goals.

And now was no exception, as both Eric and I watched her opening one of my cupboards, commandeering a glass, slamming the cupboard, going to the cocktail shaker that sat on the bar by Eric and me, then upending it over the glass.

Only a few drops of my Thanksgiving cocktail leaked into the glass, since Eric and I were drinking what had been in it, so she turned the shaker right side up and shook it demandingly at me.

I could take a hint, therefore I slid off my stool and rounded the bar.

I took the shaker from her, snatched up the jigger cups and started doing my thing before I asked, "Everything all right?"

"I love my sons. I love their wives...sort of," she started.

My gaze flew to Eric, who was staring at Martha with an expression I couldn't read, until he felt my attention and looked to me.

I was smiling.

He smiled back.

His packed its usual wallop, so I had to battle to keep mine in place.

Through this, Martha spoke.

Or complained.

"I love my grandchildren. But all of them together? For hours? Those women arranging platters and bowls like a surgeon navigates a chest cavity, and taking pictures of them so they can post it on social media and prove to all their friends they make the best homemade cranberry sauce? *No.*"

I was getting ice when I asked, "Are you all in your apartment?"

She had a one bedroom, like me.

In other words, not a lot of room and no dining room.

"That's the other thing," she stated. "We were going to eat in the courtyard. But by the time everything was ready, Alexis and Jacob were out there with their families, so one of my daughters-in-law said we should just join them. Regrettably, we did. And thus, I learned very quickly Alexis's father is a horse's ass."

Oh shit.

I saw where this was going.

"Martha—" I started.

She threw up her hands in exasperation. "I tried! Honest to Christ, I did. But he's just that much of a horse's ass."

"You said something," I surmised while measuring gin.

"Trust me, Jessica, you would too."

I called them as I saw them as well, so she probably wasn't wrong.

I put the lid on and began shaking the cocktail as I asked, "Why are you up here?"

"For your liquor," she answered.

Huh.

"Spill," I pushed.

She blew out a breath and spilled.

"Well, me laying it out to that horse's ass set Alexis's mother in a tizzy, and *do not ask me how*, it seems the nature of things, but one woman's tizzy set off a chain reaction to other women's tizzies, so we had a table full of women in a tizzy. All except Alexis, who backed me up, and Jacob's mom, who laughed through the whole thing." She nodded her head smartly. "I like that one. She's got her head on straight."

I kept shaking so the chill level would be just right before I slipped off the cap and poured. I topped up with ginger beer and was going for the apple slices for garnish when Martha batted my hand away, snatched up the glass, and I, along with Eric, watched her put it to her lips, tip her head back and down it in one.

She slammed the glass to the counter when she was done, smacked her lips and gusted, "*Ah*."

She then looked at Eric and blinked.

Oh boy.

I opened my mouth again, but Martha was quick on the draw. "Who're you?"

"Martha, this is Eric. He works with Cap," I introduced.

"Of course you do," she stated, not taking her attention from Eric. "I've seen those other boys. Jesus. Are you all recruited from modeling agencies, or what?"

I busted out laughing.

Eric's lips were twitching as he replied, "Not exactly."

"So?" Martha pushed for more info.

"I was in the FBI," Eric shared.

I stopped laughing and stared.

Martha's eyes bugged out. "The Federal Bureau of Investigation?"

"Yup. That FBI," Eric confirmed.

"I'm in no mood to be impressed," Martha declared. "So congratulations, because I'm impressed."

Eric shrugged.

Martha looked at me and squinted. "Are you two a thing?"

I studiously kept my gaze on Martha when I replied, "Just friends."

Martha was still squinting. "Just friends sharing a Thanksgiving *à deux*?"

"Just friends sharing Thanksgiving," I asserted.

She continued squinting.

I fought squirming.

Her squint swung to Eric.

I braced and looked at Eric.

He was taking a sip of his cocktail.

I stopped looking at his face and started obsessing on how his strong throat convulsed during a swallow.

Yum.

"Welp!" Martha cried. "I've gotta head back. Face the music. Explain to my daughters-in-law, once again, that they will one day enter the joyful period of their lives where they'll no longer need the likes on their Instagram posts to validate their existence, and they'll learn life's way too damned short to put up with a horse's ass. They'll disagree with me. Then they'll go home. Still in tizzies. Which means they'll forget to take leftovers. Which works for me. Have fun."

And with that, not waiting for either of us to say anything, she marched right back out.

I held the shaker to Eric. "Ready for another one?"

"Yup," he answered.

I refreshed our cocktails then rounded the bar to resume my seat beside him.

"Is she going to be the last one?" he asked.

"I doubt it," I replied with honesty.

I mean, this *was* the Oasis.

"This seems weirdly familiar," he muttered.

"At least it's entertaining," I remarked.

He shot me a half-smile. "It is that."

"I've neglected to tell you, this is really good." I pointed at my plate.

"I aim to please," he joked.

Even joking, I bet he did.

I shivered.

To fight off that train of thought, I nabbed my highball glass and lifted it his way.

"I also neglected the toast," I declared.

He put his fork down and grabbed his glass.

"Happy No-Fucks-to-Giving," I toasted.

This time, it was Eric who busted out laughing.

I stilled.

I'd never heard him laugh, or saw it, and it…was…*magnificent*.

He was still doing it when he clinked glasses with me and replied, "Happy No-Fucks-to-Giving."

I forced a smile.

We drank.

Then we went back to our plates.

And fortunately…

Silence.

THREE

DARK

I put my spent bowl of apple crumble and ice cream on the coffee table just as the credits rolled on *Planes, Trains and Automobiles*.

Eric, who was indisputably all man, had done what any man would do when we sat down to watch the movie. He'd seized the remote, and as such, right then, he hit pause on the credits.

I tipped my head so I could look at him where his long body was lounged down the longer end of my couch. I was on the shorter end, propped up in the corner, his stocking feet mere inches from me being able to give him a foot massage (which I was not doing, but the urge was there).

I'd always loved my couch.

Seeing Eric stretched out on it, I *adored* it.

"How far will I fall in your estimation if I unbutton my jeans?" I asked.

His lips were curved up. "Not at all. That's the best compliment to the chef you can get."

I snaked a hand under my tee and unbuttoned. I also needed to unzip, or better, go and put on some lounge pants, but the button would have to suffice for now.

"Better," I mumbled.

Eric chuckled before he asked, "I picked the first movie, you get the next."

The next.

I really didn't want to be so happy he wasn't leaving now that dinner, dessert and movie were done, the sun had set, and the day was winding down.

But I was happy.

"I feel like watching Jack sink to the bottom of the Atlantic," I stated.

His lip curve stayed in place, but the feel of him shifted to that strange sensation I sensed last night when he murmured, "Dark."

I shrugged. "That's me."

He said nothing, but I felt approval emanating from him.

Awesome.

And strange.

Not many guys got into my darkness.

Not many chicks did either.

But it seemed Eric did.

"So, what are your thoughts about the door?" I asked.

"The door?" he asked back.

"The door," I repeated. "Do you think Jack could fit on it with Rose?"

His brow furrowed. "Is that a thing?"

"Hotly debated," I verified.

"Why?"

This was a good question.

"I take it from your question, in the spirit of the day, you have no fucks to give about whether Jack could have fit on the door with Rose," I noted.

"I can confirm I have no fucks to give about whether a fictional character could fit on a fictional door in a movie about a fictional story even if it's based on a nonfictional event."

I started laughing.

"Do you care?" he asked.

"Well, perhaps the production team should have made a smaller door so people wouldn't obsess about it for decades after the movie was released. But for the most part, I think there are much larger things in this world to give a shit about. So...no."

"Yeah," he said softly, and I felt that word, and the softness he used, flit over my skin.

To combat the feeling, I remarked, "That said, Jack did try to get on the door. I suppose they could have kept trying, but then Rose might've fallen off. And the impending hypothermia could have taken them both. So, if forced to have an opinion, I think people should just get over it."

"Yeah," he repeated.

"So...*Titanic*?" I prompted.

"Works for me." He tossed the remote my way. "Queue it up. I'm getting more crumble."

He was doing what?

"Are you serious?"

He'd put his feet to the ground in order to get up, but my question stopped him, and his head turned my way. "Yeah, why?"

"How do you maintain that body with extra portions of stuffing and crumble?"

"How do you maintain your body while obviously eating out all the time?"

Did this mean he liked my body?

I didn't ask.

I answered, "I have a job where I'm on my feet nine hours of the day."

"And I have a job where, if I don't keep fit, my ass could be in a sling."

"Are you saying your job is dangerous?"

"I'm saying, if it turned that way and I was out of shape, I'd be shit out of luck. So I prefer to take luck out of the equation."

"So you're saying you don't feel the need to unbutton your pants."

His expression changed, I felt it in my nipples, and his voice flowed over me like velvet when he replied, "Not yet."

Wait.

Was he...

Flirting?

"I take it this discussion means you're a no for more crumble," he noted.

Okay.

Freakout averted.

He wasn't flirting.

Just hopeful thinking.

"Is me switching into lounge pants also a compliment to the chef?"

His black eyes twinkled. "Yeah."

"Spoon it up, big man. I'm gonna go change."

I went to my bedroom and switched out my black jeans for black joggers that had a satiny grosgrain ribbon pinstripe down the side. They were perfect. Warm. Comfy. Cute. And expandable.

I hit the kitchen when Eric was scooping out ice cream.

"Want another cocktail? Or I can make coffee or chai," I offered.

"Coffee," he picked.

I went to my big bowl of Nespresso pods. "Intenso, odacio or stormio? Or are you feeling festive and want pumpkin spice or rich chocolate?"

"Intenso," he ordered.

Seriously, this dude was the man of my dreams.

I started the machine warming and reached for mugs.

This was part of what I did for a living, so when Eric came to the sink in order to lean his hips against it and watch me, I wasn't a huge fan of how unnerved he made me.

I should note, I wasn't surprised.

But I wasn't a fan.

He was offering friendship.

I had good friends. However, I curated them carefully, so they were few.

That said, anyone could use a new friend.

"I got two questions, but you didn't ask any," he said.

I looked to him. "Sorry?"

"At dinner. I asked two personal questions. You didn't ask any."

"Just now I asked about Rose and Jack and the door."

"Does that give you insight into the man I am?"

"Yes."

And it wasn't a lie.

His lips tipped up before he said, "So you get one more."

I felt my brows dip down. "This feels like a test."

"It isn't. We're getting to know each other."

We sure were.

And for the first time since he showed, I wondered why.

"You didn't answer me fully," he pointed out he saw right through my earlier answers. "If I'm not down with what you ask, I'll return the favor."

This was starting to feel like a game.

He wanted to play?

I wanted to know more about him.

So I was in.

The light turned green on the Nespresso machine, so I hit go, turned back to him and asked, "Why'd you leave the FBI?"

"Because we had a mole. Someone who thought money was more important than fighting crime, and worse, keeping his fellow agents alive. I know this, since, due to his shit, one of them died. I made it my mission to ferret out who that fucker was, and I found out it was my partner. My partner, who was also my closest friend. I nailed his ass. He went to prison. He's still in prison. And I got out of the Bureau."

Holy fuck.

This was *a lot.*

"Turner," I whispered.

"It was a while ago."

"That..." I shook my head. "I don't know what to say. That had to be the worst. I'm so fucking sorry that happened. So, *so* sorry you had to do that."

His words were an audible shrug. "It's over."

Those words were also bullshit.

"True, but it's still fucked up."

"It's still fucked up," he agreed.

I was at a loss.

So much, my mouth ran away from me.

"I don't know what to do." I lifted my hands at my sides. "I feel like I should give you a hug or something."

"I'd take a hug," he said quietly, watching me closely.

It was then it hit me.

Not tight with his dad or his brother.

His closest friend, a traitor.

Someone died along the way.

No, a colleague did, and that band of brothers had to be as tight as others like them.

This hit him so hard, he left his career at the FBI, which wasn't like scoring a job at the fryer at McDonald's.

No shade on the fry guys, but it just wasn't.

Had he ever been hugged after he endured this?

Like my mouth, my feet had a mind of their own.

They took the two steps to him, and when I arrived, I fit my body to his, wrapped my arms around him, and rested my cheek on his chest.

His arms curved around me.

Oh yeah.

That felt exactly as good as I thought it would feel.

Exactly.

"Have you talked to anyone about this?" I whispered to his shoulder.

"I just talked to you," he whispered into the top of my hair.

I closed my eyes.

Because he and I were surrounded by good, kind people.

And we were still alone.

I tipped my head back.

He lifted his when I did and looked deep in my eyes.

I was still whispering when I said, "Thanks for saving my No-Fucks-to-Giving."

His eyes got lazy. I felt that lazy in my belly and regions south, and he replied, "Thanks for sharing your No-Fucks-to-Giving with me."

I stood there, holding him, gazing into his eyes.

He stood there, holding me, gazing into mine.

Without warning, it seemed his body relaxed, or mine just melted into it. One of his hands glided up my spine, and it felt so nice, I started rolling up on my toes just as his head started to descend.

And we both jolted when my door crashed open.

For a split second, his arms tightened around me.

And then I was shoved behind his back.

"What the...?"

Hearing Harlow's voice, I peered around Eric's body and saw Harlow, Luna and Raye all standing in my living room, gawping at us.

I might have been wrong, but it seemed like Eric was just about to kiss me.

Therefore, my "Knock much?" was pure acid.

"I...you...uh...we...you see..." Harlow stammered, blinking rapidly, but that was it. She didn't finish a thought.

Luna, as ever, was less unsure of herself.

She planted her hands on her hips and demanded, "What's going on here?"

Raye stepped between them and Eric and me, held a hand up to Luna and said, "No." She turned to me. "Priorities. Excuse me, Jessica Wylde, but *your brother is missing*?"

Well, shit.

Damn you, Clarice.

She didn't even give me a day.

Even a holiday!

"I—" I didn't quite begin.

Because Luna stepped up next to Raye and said, "Yeah. We know. And *hellllooooo*? We found fourteen missing women just two months ago."

Harlow stepped next to Luna. "Yeah," she spat. "*Hellllllloooo.*"

Raye looked to Luna and Harlow in order to state, "I'm not sure she understood the shot of Fireball and pinkie promise."

"Damn straight she didn't," Luna agreed, not taking her glare off me.

Of note at this juncture, when Harlow and I became official Avenging Angels, Raye and Luna made us take a Fireball shot and make a pinkie promise to the cause.

It was girlie-crap bonding, but I'd done it, mostly because Fireball was tasty.

And I dug my chicks.

Apparently, it meant something to them.

Who knew?

"Avenging Angels unite so we can find your brother," Harlow decreed.

Oh shit.

"Word," Raye agreed.

Luna just nodded. Once.

Crap!

"Listen, guys—" I tried.

Raye shook her head. "No. Unh-unh. No way, Jess. This is bullshit."

"This is a family thing," I returned.

Harlow's brows hit her hairline and her voice could shatter glass when she asked, "And we're not family?"

I felt Harlow's offense, because they totally were. Especially

Harlow (they were all my besties, but even with Harlow's cheerleader-on-crack personality, which made us exact opposites, she was the bestest of my besties).

But even if they were, they also weren't.

Fuck!

How to explain?

Eric's hand settled warm and reassuringly on the small of my back at the same time I felt his tall frame take said back.

I very seldom felt warm, and never reassured, so it was highly distracting.

And getting distracted was a mistake.

Raye lifted a hand and pointed at me, then Luna, then Harlow, then herself, and back at me, while saying, "Confab. Tomorrow night. I'll text the deets."

Harlow did the hand lifting thing too and circled it in Eric and my direction, saying, "And during our confab, we're going to be talking about whatever this is."

"You bet your bippy we are," Luna put in.

They gave me a collective glare, and as if they practiced it, they all turned in unison and stormed out.

Luna was the last one through the door, and she slammed it.

"We really need to lock that door," Eric murmured.

I turned to him to find he was, indeed, right there.

I couldn't deal with his proximity right then.

I also couldn't deal with the subtle hints of rosemary and cedarwood wafting my way, a fragrance that had already become an aromatic touchstone to me.

I had other shit to deal with.

"First, they all have keys. Second, I can't have them tramping around Phoenix trying to find Jeff and scaring him off or undoing the work I've been doing for the last six months to get people who might see him to trust me."

"Talk to them. Tell them that."

"Did you just experience what I experienced?"

"Yeah."

"Do you think they're gonna listen?"

He bit his lip in thought.

I thought about how awesome it would be to bite his lip.

Then he answered, "No."

Once again, my body moved without my mind's permission, and this time it did it to plant my forehead on his chest.

He wrapped his hand around the back of my neck.

That was warm and reassuring too.

Gah!

"They did find fourteen women, Jessie," he said gently. "If you're not down with letting me and the men help, maybe they can."

"It's clean," I said quietly.

"Pardon?"

I lifted my head to look at him, but he didn't take his hand away.

"The black and white. It's clean. It's not like I don't like color. I do. But I need clean around me. Uncluttered. Uncomplicated."

"Controlled," he murmured.

I nodded.

He got it.

"Wild stab," he began. "They don't know about your family situation."

I shook my head.

"Do you wanna tell me why?"

"You've laid it all out for me today, and I don't want to be a bitch and not reciprocate that, but honestly, I'm not really sure why."

"Could it be that you seem totally with it, and you actually are, but if you let it out how fucked up growing up was for you, it might be a hit to your cred as a together woman who has it going on?"

He thought I was a together woman who had it going on?

Shit, I was feeling gooey again.

"Maybe," I conceded.

"They're your friends and they won't think anything less of you knowing who you really are. And Jess, you keeping it from them is hiding who you are."

One thing was clear about our most recent intrusion.

I was hiding.

"Our ice cream is melting," I evaded.

"It is," he said.

But he didn't shift away so I could finish the coffees. He wrapped both his big hands around the sides of my neck and dipped his face to mine.

And he kept going.

"Even as shit as it was, your family helped make you. You didn't bow. You certainly didn't break. You became this hip woman with a great apartment, friends who'd go to the mat for her, and neighbors who turn to her in need because you don't hesitate a second to give them what they need. They show because they know that's what you'll do. I don't know it all. I know your brother is missing. I know you reported it to the police. I've read the reports of the cops' visits with your mom and dad about that situation, and I read between the lines at the responses they gave to law enforcement. And I know a lot of people who have two parents who'd give zero shits their schizophrenic son is off his meds and on the streets of Phoenix who would not become the woman you are."

I ignored the glow he created inside me with some (okay, most) of his words and focused on others.

"It was you who gave the flour to Alexis."

"It was you who listened to her when she needed to unload, and encouraged her when she needed someone to remind her to keep her chin up. The flour was incidental. She needed a friend, and that was what you gave her."

He was being awesome.

Or, *more* awesome.

Therefore, I couldn't handle this.

"Can we eat more crumble so I can alternately concentrate on not puking at the same time marvel at James Cameron's moviemaking chops?" I requested. "Because I feel the need to remind you, it's No-Fucks-to-Giving, and it seems to me you're giving a few fucks."

The pads of his fingers pressed into my skin a beat before he sighed and dropped his hands.

"Back to no fucks given," he muttered mildly irritably.

"Thank you," I pushed out, fighting sagging with relief.

"I take a splash of cream, no sugar," he ordered.

"Gotcha." I moved to the coffee.

"Jess?"

I turned to him, liking my name on his tongue.

Damn.

"Your family doesn't reflect on you."

I started to say something, perhaps tell him how wrong he was, but he held up a hand, so I stopped.

"All I'm gonna say."

"Thank you," I repeated.

"I got the crumble. You bring the coffee when it's done."

I nodded.

Eric grabbed the bowls.

I turned to the Nespresso and switched out mugs and pods.

I had no idea what was going on with this guy.

And I wasn't going to think about it.

I wasn't because I knew two things for certain in this world.

If you wanted something, you worked for it.

And...

No matter how hard you worked for it, what would be was going to be, and whatever that was, you had no choice but to deal.

What was going on with Eric was going on.

And whatever it was, I would deal.

SOMETHING lovely slid across my cheek.

I opened my eyes and Eric Turner's beautiful face was close to mine.

"Hey," his beautiful voice whispered. "Sorry to wake you, but I'm leaving."

Oh shit.

It was the end of No-Fucks-to-Giving.

"You need to lock up after me," he said.

He was right. I did.

I struggled with my lethargy and the blanket on top of me to get up.

I didn't struggle long. He demonstrated his broad shoulders weren't simply aesthetically pleasing, because he used them, and his arms, to scoop me off the couch and set me on my feet.

Like *literally* scoop me up and set me down.

Just like that.

He didn't even grunt.

I started teetering, and it wasn't because I'd just been awakened. Nor was it because I'd had an emotional juggernaut of a day: good, mixed with bad, mixed with great, mixed with uncertain, mixed with just plain weird.

Eric steadied me, then he took my hand and led me to the door.

He'd wisely locked it before *Titanic*.

I fell asleep somewhere in the middle of *Snakes on a Plane* (yep, Eric had exceptional taste in movies, along with everything else that was exceptional about Eric, the newly learned items on this list including his cooking, his listening abilities, his sharing abilities and the dual purpose of his shoulders).

He stood in my open door, holding my hand.

I stood in my open door, having my hand held, liking my hand held and staring up at him.

"I know I shouldn't give a fuck, but it's been a great day," he stated.

I slipped out of my What Will Be, Will Be Mentality and wondered what in *the fuck* was going on here.

"It has," I agreed.

He squeezed my hand. "Go to bed, Jess."

"Text me when you get home."

"Pardon?"

Shit!

I needed to learn to control my mouth around him.

That was something I'd say to Harlow, Luna, Raye (though the last two lived at the Oasis, and Harlow was moving in December first, still).

Also Jeff.

In other words, people I loved.

I shook my head, pulled my hand from his, and waved my other one between us.

"No. Sorry. You're a big boy. You don't have to do that. I'm sure you'll get home just fine."

"I don't have your number."

"Seriously, it's okay if you—"

"Jessica, give me your number."

Gazing into his eyes, I rattled it off by rote.

So much for learning to control my mouth.

"Got it," he replied.

"Just like that?"

"In my line of business, you make a point to remember important things."

Totally out of my What Will Be, Will Be Mentality.

Because, what the fuck was that?

"Go to bed," he ordered. "I'll see you later."

"Right," I mumbled. "Later."

He chucked me under the chin.

Chucked me under the chin.

Again...

The fuck?

Was this...*something*?

Or was I like some little sister he was adopting because I was alone and fucked up?

"'Night," he murmured.

Then he was gone.

I stared at the space he used to be in until I heard him call from down the walkway, "Close the door and lock it, Jessie."

I closed the door and locked it.

I then woodenly turned to look at my apartment.

The TV was off.

The black-and-white-striped throw Eric had pulled over him was folded on the edge of the couch (the diagonal stripe one I was using was in a bunch on the floor).

There were no bowls or mugs lying around.

I wandered to my kitchen.

I heard the dishwasher whirring and saw that our crumble bowls and coffee mugs were nowhere to be seen.

"What's happening?" I asked my sink.

The sink had no answers.

I needed a pet.

Pets had no answers either, but at least you didn't feel like a moron when you talked to them.

I went to the bathroom, brushed my teeth, washed my face, moisturized and pulled my dark hair up into a ponytail.

I then went to my bedroom, turned on a light beside my bed and donned my pajamas (yes, black leopards crawling over a white background, drawstring sleep shorts and a long-sleeved pajama top—when I sought control of my surroundings, I didn't mess around).

I went back out and checked the lock on the door I'd locked maybe five minutes before, grabbed my phone, extinguished the lights and headed back to the bedroom.

I was sitting with my back to my headboard, zebra print comforter tucked to my lap, flicking through TikToks to kill time, when it came in.

Home.

The text from Eric.

I programmed him into my phone, then sent, *Good. Thanks for starting the dishwasher.*

No problem.

This did not say, "I don't want the day to end either, keep me engaged."

I nibbled the side of my thumb, trying to decide if I should text something else.

He didn't send another text while I was deciding.

Which decided for me.

It also reminded me I wasn't that girl. I didn't wait up to get a text when I was sleepy, and I didn't obsess about whether a guy was into me or not.

With that reminder of who I was, I put my phone down on the charge pad, turned out the light and settled in, ignoring the fact I felt empty and very alone in that bed. Both feelings I was used to, so for the most part ignored. Neither feeling boded well, making themselves known in a manner I couldn't ignore after spending the day with Eric Turner.

I was pulling the covers up to my shoulder when a text coming in illuminated the area of my nightstand.

It would have been embarrassing if anyone saw how fast my hand moved to grab my phone.

Sleep well, Jess.

It was from Eric.

The empty feeling evened out, the alone feeling remained, but wasn't as sharp, and I replied, *You too, Turner.*

He dropped a thumbs-up on my text.

I smiled, put the phone back on the charge pad.

And slipped right to sleep.

FOUR

BURRITOS

At 10:57 the next morning, I swung my Mini into a parking spot at the back of The Surf Club.

I then grabbed the cherry Icee I'd picked up at QuikTrip, scrunched up the wrapper of the corndog I'd consumed as a late breakfast on the way to work, and got out of my car.

One could say I was in a foul mood.

I'd like to consider myself a pretty chill chick, for the most part.

Though, I was human.

I wasn't immune to the occasional foul mood.

But this foul mood was unusual in the sense it had several levels.

The first level was that I knew what I was about to face with my friends at work. They were pissed at me (rightly...*maybe*), and I felt that they deserved an explanation. At the same time, I thought what was private was private, and I shouldn't have to offer an explanation.

The second level was that I'd heard nothing from Eric all morning, and I'd lamentably had time to give no small amount of consideration to the day we'd spent together yesterday.

Something I tried not to do, but as had become my usual when it came to Eric Turner, I did.

And although it would be a weird first date...

It still felt like a first date.

Smiles. Laughter. Movies. Food. Deep sharing, which frankly, upon contemplation, I decided from what was offered up, particularly from Eric, took us significantly into seventh or eighth date territory.

And I swear, before the girls had stormed in, he was *this close* to kissing me.

Sure, he chucked me under the chin before he left (huh).

But seriously, his mouth was coming toward mine, and since we were already hugging, there was no reason for it to do that except to claim it.

Even so.

No text, no phone call, no nothing.

Maybe he was playing games. Maybe this was that stupid standoff thing boys and girls did to make sure the other one didn't think they were too into them in order to save face or gain the upper hand.

If it was, he had to be a decade older than me, so definitely past this immature bullshit, surely.

If it wasn't, then yesterday was all about something else. Eric developing a platonic-type thing between us, which would be torture since I wanted to jump the man's bones and maybe someday give him babies.

And, again, he was old enough to know, or at least sense, where my head was at with him, so why would he torture me like that?

The third level of my bad mood had to do with the fact that I had to figure out a way to get the girls to back off about finding Jeff, and I had no clue how to do that.

Sure.

I got it.

That was what friends were for.

Especially good friends.

And they weren't good friends.

They were great ones.

Still.

I pushed into the back entrance of SC and was immediately confronted with Harlow, who was tying a server's apron around her waist.

She was wearing a cute lace dress with a high halter neck and a short swing skirt that was a sure tip inducer from the straight male and lesbian crowds.

It was also just her style.

Harlow was all girl, all the time, and proud of it.

Contradictory to her normal sunshiny outlook on life in general, she was also wearing a scowl that was pointed my way.

"Harlow—" I began.

She gave me The Hand and clipped, "Later. We're meeting at the storage units tonight at eight. You can tell me then all about how you didn't trust me to share your brother was missing, even after all that went down with Raye and her sister."

Quick debrief: Tragically, Raye's sister had been snatched at a playground nearly two decades ago. Also tragically, just two months ago, the men of Nightingale Investigations & Security had located her remains and obtained a confession from the man who abducted and murdered her, even though law enforcement was unable to solve the crime for nineteen years.

See what I mean about these guys (including Eric) being able to take care of themselves and the ones they cared about?

With what they did for Raye and her dad, it seemed like they could do anything.

And one might want to admit that this happening was the perfect segue to sharing about Jeff.

It also wasn't (says me, though I was finding myself in the minority).

"Raye was going through a lot," I pointed out.

"Yes, but *I* wasn't," Harlow clapped back.

She then flounced out.

Crap.

She was right.

But I thought she was also wrong.

I didn't wear a server apron. It would mess with the line of pretty much any ensemble I put together (today, a fitted, black muscle shirt, black cropped cords and black fisherman sandals).

So I dumped my bag in my locker and headed out to the front of The Surf Club.

Clearly, there was no real surf to The Surf Club, considering Phoenix was landlocked.

Even so, SC was the hippest, chillest, awesomest hang in The Valley.

Case in point: the colorful mural at the back. The plants all around. The mismatched tables and lamps and seating areas and beanbags. Lucia's excellent fusion food. My fabulous cocktails.

And then there was Tito, our boss and the owner, a man who knew the art of silence, because he didn't talk much, but even so, he often had a lot to say.

He also looked like a diminutive Santa, but one who wore Panama hats, shorts, Hawaiian shirts and flip flops. The hat might change to a fedora, or a bandana. The flip flops might be slides worn with tube socks or red Keds. The shorts veered between madras to Bermudas, or, if he was feeling sassy, board shorts.

But always, a pair of shades covered his eyes.

Even at night.

There was no denying Tito was a weird guy, but I embraced weird. The minute I met him—when he recruited me from the speakeasy I worked at downtown—I hadn't even seen The Surf Club, but I knew I wanted to work for him.

In the years since, my instinct proved right.

When I made it behind the bar, I got a chilly reception from Luna, who was there making someone a coffee. I also got a frosty glance from Raye, who was out, dropping some of Lucia's Mexican hot chocolate French toast on a table.

This vibe permeating the air meant I also had Tito's attention from where he sat, in what I considered his "office." This was the back corner booth by the massive plate glass window that spanned the wall and afforded a view of the raised beds, which contained Lucia's herb garden, and our paloverde-adorned parking lot.

Tucked with his plethora of books, journals, and holding his ever-present iPad, Tito didn't move, even after I lifted my chin in greeting to him when I caught his eyes.

He just watched me.

Tito might be quiet, and for the most part unobtrusive, but he didn't miss anything.

And he was the most generous man I'd ever met.

Even though tips were good, he paid over minimum wage, for one. He offered great insurance as well as contributed to a 401(k), for another. And if you were in a jam, he somehow always intuited it, even if you didn't tell him, and extra would be in your pay envelope... in cash.

This had never happened for me, because I'd never needed it, but I knew it happened.

In other words, the crew at SC didn't change much because Tito was loyal to us, so we were loyal to Tito.

I turned from Tito to Luna.

"If you give me The Hand, I'll shoot you," I warned.

"If you don't understand why Harlow, specifically, but all of us collectively are hurt by you not sharing, you aren't the person I thought you were, Jess."

Ouch.

Luna was much like me, calling 'em as she saw 'em.

But that was below the belt.

She turned from me to put a latte in front of a woman sitting at the polished-ash bar.

When Raye came back and stabbed an order into the computer like she wanted to put her finger straight through the screen, I decided to let them stew.

I didn't keep myself to myself to hurt them, and if they didn't already know that, then, well...they weren't the people I thought they were either.

I made coffees, took orders, dropped food, bussed tables and shook the occasional noontime cocktail through the lunch rush, and things were just calming down, when Lucia did the unimaginable.

She left the sanctuary of her creative palace (aka: the kitchen), and with a strange look on her face, she approached Tito in his office.

I was filling a customer's water glass as she spoke to him.

I almost overfilled it, because when she was done, he got up and followed her to the kitchen.

Peculiar.

Raye was passing me, so I asked, "What's that about?"

"Obviously, I have no idea," she answered coolly.

No thaw there, then.

Whatever.

I was throwing some dirty plates in the bus bin when Tito's voice came at me, making me jump.

"If you could follow me, Jessie," he requested.

I looked to him.

I looked to the girls who were all in the vicinity, watching us.

I turned back to him and nodded.

We went through the kitchen to the staff room and then the back door.

Tito opened it and walked out. I followed and stopped in my tracks.

Homer was loitering at the door, and he was with a scruffy, youngish (about my age, maybe a bit older (I was thirty-three)) Black man who was shifting foot to foot.

"Homer," I greeted, shocked. "How did you get here?"

"Walked," Homer replied.

I quickly had to get over the fact they'd walked probably a good ten miles to get to the back door of The Surf Club, because Homer was sunken into himself. Not in his safe space, exposed, vulnerable.

The King of the Encampment was a memory. Although I recognized him visually, everything else about him had changed.

My heart crunched, and I offered, "Let's go sit in the garden."

He shook his head curtly and said, "General Grant has something to tell you."

"General Grant?" I asked.

"Ulysses S. Grant," the Black guy said, jerking a thumb at himself.

My heart crunched more at a Black man referring to himself by a dead white president's name, because I seriously doubted at his age that was his real name.

"Hey, Mr. Grant," I said.

"*General* Grant," he corrected.

Totally not his real name.

"Sorry," I mumbled.

Tito said nothing, but remained close and got closer when Homer did.

"Iraq," Homer muttered. "Afghanistan," he went on. "Decorated sniper. Now...this," he finished.

My ticker couldn't take much more as I turned to a veteran of this great country wearing filthy clothes, sporting nappy hair and dancing foot to foot.

Homer looked to Tito. "You need to leave, or he won't talk. She's ours. You're not ours. But she's safe with us. None of us would harm Jessie."

Tito tipped his head to look up at me through his shades, and I saw his bushy white eyebrows rise over the frames.

"I'm good," I assured.

Tito hesitated.

"Promise," I said.

Tito nodded once, but I could tell he didn't like it even if I couldn't see his eyes, before he went in the back door.

Once it closed, I returned my attention to Homer and the General.

"You can tell her," Homer urged the General.

"Gotta get back to Mary," the General stated.

"We'll go back, once you tell her," Homer replied.

"Mary's all alone," the General returned.

"Mary?" I whispered to Homer.

"She's new," Homer whispered back. "General Grant looks after the new ones."

Of course he did.

"Boomer's looking after Mary," Homer reminded the General. "But you're right. We gotta head back so you can look in on her, which means now, you gotta talk to Jessie."

The General moved foot to foot then his body jolted, and he looked behind him.

I looked behind him.

At nothing.

God, this guy was killing me.

"General," Homer called him back to us.

The General turned to me. "Street Warrior."

That was all he said.

Therefore, I asked, "Sorry?"

"Street Warrior," the General repeated. "He's one of 'em. Keeps the darkness back. Keeps it back."

I wasn't liking this—at all—even if I didn't get it.

At all.

I looked to Homer to see if he could offer any illumination.

Homer's whiskered lips were pressed tight.

"What's a street warrior?" I asked him.

He didn't answer because the General was moving quickly toward the side of the building.

Homer followed.

I followed.

The General checked the side of the building, then he looked at Homer and said, "Mary."

I peered around the corner and saw no woman, just a direct shot to the traffic on Indian School.

"We'll head back," Homer promised him.

"I'll take you back," I offered.

Homer's faded blue eyes shot to me in surprise just as the General jumped alarmingly when the back door opened.

Harlow and Raye came out, each carrying a thick, foil-wrapped burrito in one hand and our largest lidded paper cup in the other.

"They're my friends," I said hurriedly as the women made their approach. "Harlow and Raye. Good friends. You can trust them."

The girls glanced quickly between the two men before Raye said to Homer, "Tito thought you might want something to eat and drink."

To my shock, the General went right up to Harlow, took the burrito and said, "Thank you kindly, ma'am."

Harlow offered the drink as the General peeled back the foil and paper. "Water," she told him. "But I can get you a soda or something if you'd like."

He munched into the burrito and took the drink, shaking his head. Not even swallowing, he munched more.

While this happened, Homer extricated a plastic bag from his pocket and wrapped it around the burrito Raye was holding out to him.

"Obliged," he murmured. Using the plastic bag to shield his fingers from the foil and paper, he peeled it back. He unearthed another plastic bag, shoved his free hand in it like it was a glove, and only then took the drink from her. After he got his beverage, he munched too.

Divested of their offerings, neither of my chicks left the scene.

No surprise.

I had a low buzz humming through me that there was an imminent breakthrough about Jeff, so I gave the guys a few minutes to put some food in their stomachs and tried to ignore Harlow and Raye lingering before I pushed, "Homer, what's a street warrior?"

"They're us," Homer told me.

I clenched my teeth, reaching for patience, because that gave me nothing. Or, at least, not anything I understood.

When I got a lid on it, I urged, "Can you share more?"

"What he said. They keep the darkness out."

"Homer, I really need you to explain this to me," I begged.

"Shadow soldiers," Homer said.

And that was all he said.

God!

That didn't give me any more!

I was about to press him further, but he took a step back, the General took five, and this was because a shiny, black Denali rolled up beside the herb garden and stopped.

The cavalry had arrived.

Damn.

I was back to clenching my teeth as I watched Cap swing out of the passenger seat.

And more clenching as Eric angled out from behind the wheel.

I didn't know who called them. There were four viable culprits (including Tito), but I'd deal with that later.

Now, if these two badasses scared away my informants when I was on the verge of learning something about my brother, I was going to lose my shit.

What happened next was unexpected.

Cap and Eric strolled up, the General's empty wrapper fluttered to the ground, his partially sipped water thumped to it, he took two strides forward, stood at attention, saluted, left his hand at his forehead and grunted to Cap, "Colonel." Then to Eric, "General."

Without missing a beat, Eric replied, "At ease, soldier."

The General widened his stance and caught his hands behind his back.

Oh fuck.

I was going to cry.

Harlow made a noise that told me she was feeling the same thing.

Raye's fingers closed around mine.

"We hear you need transport," Cap said to the General.

"Yessir. Back to barracks, sir," the General replied.

Shit!

"We're not done," I said quickly to Eric.

"Does this lady have everything she needs?" Cap asked the General.

Smartly, he turned to me and shared, "Street Warrior. Your brother is a Street Warrior. You won't find him. But we'll put the word down, and he'll find you."

My stomach squeezed so tightly with hope, it came out wheezy when I requested, "Will you do that? Put the word down?"

A smart nod. "Yes, ma'am."

"Thank you," I said.

The back door opened and Luna came out carrying a milk crate filled to the brim with foil wrapped burritos. Hunter, one of our coffee cubby guys, was beside her holding a bread tray filled with lidded cups with straws stuck in them.

More tears threatened.

Told you Tito was generous.

"Provisions," the General said, excitement in his voice.

"Let's load 'em up," Cap told him.

They moved to the back of the Denali.

"Homer, you wanna climb in?" Eric invited.

"I don't have enough plastic bags for the seats," Homer told him.

"We don't mind," Eric replied.

I squeezed Raye's hand before I let it go, sidled close to Eric and murmured, "It's not about that. He needs plastic bags for the seats or he won't sit in your car. It's rare he touches anything without a plastic bag between him and it, unless that something comes from a plastic bag."

"On it," Raye said and dashed in the back door.

"We'll get you covered," Eric said to Homer.

Homer nodded, glanced at me, dipped his chin, then moved to the passenger door on the driver's side.

"I'll help look for bags," Harlow mumbled and went inside.

This left me with Eric.

"Who called you?" I asked.

"Tonight," was his bizarre, uninformative reply.

"What?"

"I gotta get these guys back, and Cap and I were in the middle of something. We'll talk tonight."

We would?

"Later, Jess," he said and started to move away.

Just like that.

No further info.

No "Hey, great day yesterday. Let's do it again sometime."

He was just walking away.

Whatever.

Though, we weren't done.

I caught his forearm, and he stopped. "Do you know what a Street Warrior is?"

He shook his head, then said, "Never heard of it. And don't give me any shit. I know you wanted to go this alone, but that cat is way the fuck out of the bag, so it's gonna happen. With that I mean, I'm gonna find out."

I narrowed my eyes at him. "Are you pissed?"

"They walked right to your place of business, Jess."

Oh shit.

They had. I hadn't thought of that.

I also hadn't ever mentioned where I worked.

But...they *had*.

They'd walked miles, just to give me a little information about Jeff.

Damn.

I was about to cry again.

Eric saved me from that emotion.

"Please tell me you didn't share that intel," Eric demanded.

"Of course not," I replied, openly affronted.

"Someone did," he stated.

Shit!

"Tonight," he grunted, and with that, he pulled his arm gently out of my hold and walked to the Denali.

Raye and Harlow showed with some plastic bags, and I helped Homer spread them, including holding one against the seat so he could settle back and hit the bag.

Once he was good, the General was already beside him, Cap was in, Eric was in and had turned the ignition, so I had no choice but to smile at Homer and the General, thank them, close Homer's door, step back and watch Eric reverse and drive away.

He didn't even flick his fingers to me, like Cap did to Raye (and he added a sweet smile with his goodbye).

Ugh.

Me and my girls stood outside the back door, a soft breeze fanning the scent of cilantro, basil, mint and thyme in our direction, and even though we were supposed to be waiting tables, nobody moved.

Street Warrior.

My brother was a Street Warrior.

I whirled on them and stated, "My brother's name is Jeff. When he was seventeen, he was diagnosed with schizophrenia. Mom and Dad were divorced long before then, mostly because Dad couldn't quit fucking around, but also because Mom was a nag, the worst housekeeper alive, and a shit mother who considered her children and husband severe impediments to attaining her ultimate goal in life. That being acting like a teenager looking for a drunken good time until the day she dies."

My chicks said nothing, though their eyes didn't leave me.

So I kept talking.

"Dad was a shit housekeeper too, and jokingly called all of us his 'balls and chains,' even though he said it so often, it was clear it wasn't a joke."

"Jessie," Harlow whispered sadly.

I couldn't deal with her sad.

I had to get this out, or I'd never share it with them.

So I kept going.

"Needless to say, having a son with significant mental health needs was not something they'd signed up for. Though they did the deed and got the result of two kids, they acted like they didn't sign up for parenthood either. To wit, I've taken care of Jeff for as long as I can remember, and when he got old enough, he returned the favor. It was the two of us surviving in a barren world of neglect and indifference. We weren't beaten, but it was clear we were unwanted responsibilities, and the minute we could look after ourselves, they left us to it."

I took in a deep breath, and none of them spoke, so I continued sharing.

"Jeff's meds work relatively well. He's usually good about taking them. The thing is, he also needs therapy. Behavioral. Cognitive. And there will always be triggers. Stress. If he starts drinking. Shit like that. He needs constants in his life. We're tight, so even if I offered, he refuses to saddle me with him. And 'saddle' is his word. Not mine. Usually, he lives with Mom or Dad or one of his buds. One of his buds is good. They care so they look after him. Mom or Dad is bad, because they don't give a shit and get on his ass to do things like pay rent and fix stuff around their houses. He can do that, no sweat, the thing is, the constant yammering from them is a stress trigger, and then things go south."

I drew in a big breath and went on.

"Jeff being Jeff, he feels like a weight on his friends, so he doesn't stay with them very often either. That's why he's with Mom or Dad most of the time. This isn't the first time he's been triggered, went off his meds and disappeared. But he has places he goes. It's easy to find him. This time, I can't find him. And Mom and Dad aren't helping, because first, they don't care. And second, they make it clear it's a relief when he's gone, because they don't want him around in the first place."

"Jesus, babe," Luna whispered miserably.

"Why didn't you tell us?" Raye asked carefully.

I shrugged. "I honestly don't really know."

"Jessie," Luna warned.

Fuck.

"Maybe it's because I'm embarrassed," I explained. "Not about Jeff. He can't help it. And Jeff is awesome. The best baby bro in history. About my parents, who can."

"You aren't your parents," Harlow pointed out.

"I know that. But I don't like to think of them. I try not to see them. I don't ever instigate talking to them. And the kicker to that is, they're all the way down with that."

"You still could have told us about them," Harlow pushed.

"Really?" I asked sharply. "Why? What's the purpose of you knowing my parents are useless wastes of space, not only when it comes to parenthood, but all around?"

"Because we know and love you," Harlow shot back.

"And what will that help?" I retorted.

Harlow's head ticked with insult, so I dialed it back.

"I don't mean it like that, Lolo," I said quietly. "I mean, you guys are the good parts. You guys are the rewards after growing up like that, and then getting out of it. You guys are normal and caring and good. You guys are where I can be, and where I don't have to be back with them, mentally or physically. So if I stay with you physically, that means I don't have to go back to them mentally."

Harlow's face got soft with understanding.

Well...

Shoo!

Raye took us out of that, thankfully, by asking, "What did you just learn from those guys that came here?"

I turned to Raye. "What you heard. That's it. They told me Jeff is a Street Warrior. And before you ask, I don't know what that is. But obviously, I have to find out."

They nodded and Luna turned to Raye, "I'll call Jinx. Maybe she or one of the girls has heard of them."

"Awesome," Raye replied. "And tonight, maybe a run by Mr. Shithead's place of business. We can bribe him with fresh porno mags and maybe he's got some intel."

"Good plan," Luna said.

I knew they wouldn't let me fight it, so I didn't.

And if I was honest with myself, now that we were here, it felt all kinds of nice that they were so in to take my back.

But more, Jeff's.

"Right. Now...Eric," Harlow prompted.

Crap.

To buy time, I looked at Raye and asked, "Did you know NI and S investigated all of us and track our cars?"

Her eyes got big, and she answered, "Cap told me they did that to me, but...all of you?"

I nodded.

"No shit?" Luna asked.

"Oh, how sweet. They're looking out for us," Harlow cooed.

Blech.

"It's incredibly invasive," I noted.

"I can have a chat with him," Raye said in a voice that told me what was coming next. And then it came. "But I don't think it'll make a difference. The last time they went through this, people were shot. Yes, plural. Shot at, and that's plural too. Stella Gunn's apartment was exploded by grenades—"

"No shit?" Luna asked.

"None at all," Raye answered, then she recommenced her litany of what befell the Rock Chicks. "There were a slew of kidnappings, at least one car bomb, several car chases, arson, stalkers—"

"Stop," I begged.

"I'm okay with a tracker on my car now," Luna mumbled.

"Totally," Harlow agreed.

I was too.

Totally.

It was then Luna's gaze sharpened on me. "You didn't answer the question about Eric."

"Well, I would, if I had any freaking clue what was going on," I told her.

"You were making out when we showed yesterday," Raye pointed out.

"We weren't. It *seemed* like he was about to kiss me, but when he left at the end of the night, he chucked me under the chin."

Raye and Luna winced. Harlow actually flinched.

Yeah, that was what I was sayin'.

"I have a massive crush on him," I announced. "And I think he regards me as a little sister."

That time, all of them flinched.

"You have a crush on him?" Harlow asked.

I nodded.

"He's crush-worthy, that's for sure," Luna stated.

I nodded again, but more heartily that time.

Then I shared, "He told me about his family, none of it good. I'm not going to tell you because it isn't mine to tell. He also told me why he left the FBI, which wasn't good either."

"He was in the FBI?" Harlow breathed.

Both Raye and I nodded at that, which meant Cap had shared at least that part with her.

"That's a whole lotta sharin' goin' on when you're informally adopting a lil' sis," Luna noted.

She had that right.

As such, the mindfuck Eric left me with.

"Are you sure it's a little sister thing?" Harlow queried.

"He chucked me under the chin, Lolo," I reminded her.

She scrunched her nose.

Mm-hmm.

"He's all lazy bedroom eyes and good movie choices, but it seems that's just him," I groused. "I don't think he knows he's a big tease, but he definitely is."

"Lazy bedroom eyes?" Luna asked.

"Yeah," I confirmed.

"He has great eyes, but I wouldn't call them lazy or bedroom," Luna stated.

Then she hadn't looked at him close enough.

"Me either. He's nice, like all the other guys, but he's more standoffish," Harlow put in.

I noticed then that Raye seemed intent on inventorying the pocket of her server apron.

"What?" I asked her.

Her head came up with a fake *Who? Me?* expression on her face.

"Oh my God," Luna snapped at Raye. "You know something."

Raye shook her head. "I don't know anything."

"Cap told you something," Luna pushed. "Spill it, bitch."

"Honestly," Raye said heatedly. "I don't know anything." Her gaze wandered to me. "Except..."

She trailed off.

"*What?*" Harlow's word was nearly a shriek.

"Eric does have bedroom eyes," Raye stated.

"Puh," Luna blew out. "I don't know what your issue is. It's not like Cap doesn't know you're all about him and there are other hotties out in the wild. He's not gonna be ticked you think a man has bedroom eyes. To end, you don't have to be weird about admitting you think Eric has bedroom eyes."

"Um, it isn't that he has bedroom eyes all the time. Just, uh... when he's looking at Jess," Raye said.

My head jerked and my lungs seized.

Slowly, Luna and Harlow turned to look at me.

"And just to say," Raye continued. "Lucia told us what was going down, and I called Cap, just in case we needed backup. He was with Eric, and within seconds of Cap reporting to Eric what was happening, they were in the middle of something, but Eric said they were aborting and heading to SC."

Oh my God, I thought.

"*Oh my God*," Harlow breathed.

"I think he's, um...into you," Raye finished.

"Oh my God!" Harlow cried happily.

"He chucked me under the chin," I reiterated.

"I can't explain that," Raye muttered.

"Okay, we gotta get back to work or Tito's gonna be forced to do something Tito avoids like the plague, be a boss and tell us to get our asses back to work," Luna began. "But, you know, Eric isn't Hottie Squad. Eric is Hot Bunch. He's OG. He's got experience with bitches like us. So maybe he's into Jess but isn't all the way down with being into Jess, considering she's an Avenging Angel, and he isn't all fired up to deal with stalkers and car bombs. So he's gonna take shit slow and see how it plays out."

Harlow latched onto that instantly. "That makes sense."

"I hope we don't have any car bomb action happening," Raye decreed.

"I'm not too thrilled about the stalker stuff," Luna put in.

"It's the grenades that scare me. Especially if it happens at the Oasis," Harlow said. "I can't wait to move in. I've been trolling Target and Home Goods for weeks. I'm going for a whole new aesthetic. And it's gonna be *pimp*. I don't want to get it all set up and then it explodes."

These freaking women.

Loved them to their bones.

But...

"Bitches!" I snapped.

They all looked at me.

"Whatever this is with Eric is what it is. I can't obsess about it. I have to find my brother," I stated.

They all nodded in agreement.

"So, plan. Luna calls Jinx. And tonight, after Harlow and I are off work, we head by the motel to talk to Mr. Shithead," I concluded.

"It's a Merc night," Luna declared.

"I say we roll in the Sportage," Harlow contradicted. "And it's my turn to drive."

"I'm driving," Raye said.

"You never let me drive," Harlow retorted.

"That's because you drive like a granny," Luna said.

Harlow gasped. "I do not. I drive safe. There's a difference."

"No, there isn't," Luna returned.

"Road rage is an epidemic," Harlow shot back. "And I'm not getting caught in someone's rage. They want to cut me off or pull out in front of me or drive thirty miles over the speed limit in the city, they can go for it. I'm going to get where I'm going all in one piece, thank you very much."

"Granny," Luna mumbled.

Harlow's face got red.

I sighed.

The back door to The Surf Club opened, and Tito stood in it silently.

Well then.

Time to get back to work.

We all trooped in with Harlow muttering under her breath, "Sportage. I drive."

And Luna replying, "Merc. I'm at the wheel."

I looked to Raye who was looking at me.

When she caught my eye, she winked encouragingly.

The last half an hour had been bizarre to say the least.

But whether it be in the Mercedes Arthur gave us, or the Sportage that Arthur also gave us, it didn't matter.

I was rolling with my girls that night.

And I finally had a lead.

So, even though the feeling wasn't overwhelming.

I was encouraged.

FIVE

SMOKES & SUCH

That night, Harlow came by the Oasis, and we all met up at Luna's to head to the storage units to switch out our car and roll.

When I arrived at Luna's and Raye was already there, I saw immediately that we were all getting with the program, this trumped when Harlow showed.

Last time we hit the town on Angels' business, we looked like four girls having a girls' night.

That was part of our ruse to case a strip joint.

But it didn't say, *We mean business!*

And tonight, we needed to mean business.

So, now, I was in my outfit for the day, since it fit our activities of the night, but I switched out to some black Old Skool Vans and threw on a black bomber jacket.

The bomber jacket was satin, but what could I say? I was an Angel. We swung it out there in style.

Further making my case, Luna was wearing a black, slim-fitting, merino wool turtleneck, black chinos and black suede Pumas. Raye was in dark-wash jeans with a black tee covered in a cropped black cardigan, black leather, white-soled Alexander McQueen kicks (Raye was a designer whore, even on a budget, and the woman worked it).

And when Harlow showed, she wore black crop pants, a puff-sleeved black sweater and black Nikes.

Okay, so my satin bomber and the puff-sleeved sweater were pushing it, but at least, if any of us had to run, we were wearing the appropriate footgear.

We didn't say much as we got into Luna's Prius and headed to the units.

But once on our way, Raye filled us in.

"Okay, Cap shared that he and Eric talked to Homer and General Grant—"

"The General," I corrected.

"I thought he referred to himself as—"

"Girl, no," I said low.

"Right. Gotcha," she replied. "So, Homer and the General, precisely the General, said that your brother told him where you worked."

My chest tightened.

That meant the General actually talked to Jeff.

That meant, at least for now, my brother was okay.

"Why would he do that?" Luna asked.

This was a good question.

"Maybe he thought they'd get word to her," Harlow suggested. "And they did."

"Any news on the Street Warriors thing?" I inquired.

Raye shook her head as she twisted to peer at me from the front seat. "Not yet. They're sniffing around, though."

"I hope we beat them in figuring it out," Luna muttered.

Luna could be competitive.

I didn't care who figured it out first.

My brother was a handyman savant. He could fix anything going. He had some schooling and experience as an apprentice pipefitter, but for unsurprising reasons, he was never able to complete his training.

That said, Mom and Dad both worked to live, then they lived as large as their meagre wages would allow, in other words, making sure faucets didn't leak, thermostats continued to work and ice makers made ice were not priorities to them.

This necessitated Jeff figuring shit out.

And honest to God, he started doing that when he was around eleven.

Necessity for sure was the mother of invention.

Nevertheless, my brother was no warrior.

He was about three inches taller than me, which put him at five eleven. He had Dad's body, which was bulky, and for Dad, soft and came with a beer gut. For Jeff, it was solid because he found regular workouts helped him deal with stress, so when he was himself, he didn't miss one.

This meant he was fit. And could probably take care of himself in, say, a bar fight.

But beating "darkness" back (whatever that meant), I was thinking...no.

"That said, I got an email into Arthur," Luna went on. "We'll see if he's heard anything about these Street Warrior people."

That was a good idea.

I forgot all about Arthur.

"I've been pondering this all afternoon," I told them. "And if you're in, maybe tomorrow we could do the rounds to all of Jeff's buds. I've done that already, checking in frequently, and no word. Also, none of them would keep something from me. They're as worried about Jeff as I am. But maybe, if he's getting word to me through the General, he's also started communicating to them."

"I'm in," Raye said.

"Me too," Luna added.

"Totally." Harlow rounded it out.

This felt weird, and I wasn't sure if it was a good weird, or bad.

Of course, having my girls with me was good.

But having anyone help felt alien. Like a new outfit that didn't fit.

Maybe I'd get used to it.

Maybe it would chafe.

Time would tell.

We hit the storage units and Luna parked in front of numbers eleven and twelve, the units that held the Accord and the Mercedes.

Raye opened number thirteen, where the Sportage sat.

She flipped on the lights and went to the back of the unit where she nabbed a dry erase marker at the base of the whiteboard that Arthur had mounted there to aid in our investigations (all the units had them, we also had a laser pointer, which, according to Raye, made us official).

We all stood around and watched as she wrote on one side of the whiteboard, *Jeff Wylde*, and under that, *Street Warrior*, then under that, *???*. And on the other, she listed in a column, *Mr. Shithead, Jinx, Jeff's Friends, Other?*

This reminded me.

"Did you hear from Jinx?" I asked Luna.

"She didn't answer or return my voicemails," Luna told me. No worries on that. There was nothing unusual about it. She worked nights, so she slept days. "Hopefully, she's in her office tonight."

Considering Jinx's occupation, her office was a patch of sidewalk across the street from the Sun Valley Motor Lodge, where Mr. Shithead, a recalcitrant informant, worked nights in reception.

Hopefully a double bang for our buck that night.

"Did someone buy some dirty magazines?" Harlow asked.

We all looked at each other.

No one piped up.

Shit.

"I don't actually know where to buy dirty magazines," Raye admitted.

"Me neither," Luna said.

"Maybe they have them at one of those racy lingerie and sex toy places?" Harlow suggested.

"Maybe we just forget the pornos, whip out our Tasers and ask him questions, like Raye did when he spilled the last time," Luna said.

"I think we need to develop him as a willing informant," Raye put in. "You catch more bees with honey."

"Gross," Harlow mumbled.

"Oh, for fuck's sake. Give me the keys. I'm driving," I declared.

"But—" Harlow began.

"I'm driving," I stated firmly.

She stuck her lower lip out in a pout.

Raye handed me a set of keys.

We climbed in the Sportage. I backed out. Raye jumped out to turn out the lights, pull down the door and lock it.

And we rolled.

I then drove us directly to a seedy strip mall on Indian School, angled in a spot and parked.

The girls stared at the store in front of us.

"You vape?" Raye asked.

"No," I answered.

"You smoke?" Luna queried, her voice pitched high with surprise.

"No," I repeated.

"Um...." Harlow hummed.

I got out.

My chicks got out with me.

And with them following, I pushed into a business that was named "Smokes & Such" but its better title was "The Place to Maybe Get Murdered & Smokes & Such."

It was a long, narrow space stuffed full of wares. Concrete floors. Cinderblock walls. Dark lighting.

The back section was replete with a dizzying variety of bongs on display, but it was so dark back there, it seemed like a cavern, and I couldn't imagine how anyone could see the bongs. More, I fancied it'd be the perfect place to stab someone since nobody would see you do it, and the victim might not be discovered for weeks.

The front space was only slightly more illuminated. It had a glass cabinet filled with one-hitters, rolling papers, vapes, vape cartridges and vape liquid. Behind it there was a long display on the wall of disposable vaping devices and a cornucopia of tobacco products from cigarettes and cigars to chew.

There were also racks and racks of pornographic magazines and DVDs.

There was a guy standing in the deep shadows at the back staring at the bongs, his face blank, his upper body swaying, stating plainly he'd already overly imbibed.

There was also a couple at the cash register: the very petite, waif-like girl flicking at some cheap keychains exhibited on a stand, the equally short, waif-like guy with her paying for something.

Their size told me they were around thirteen, when they were not.

Their faces and affects told me they were addicted to meth.

The clerk was female, probably in her early twenties, but with an expression on her face that was of a much older person. One who survived the Depression, the Dust Bowl, three wars and various other military skirmishes, a bankruptcy or two, and around four cheating husbands.

She was new. I'd never seen her when I'd been there.

Then again, Smokes & Such had a massive turnover as far as I could tell.

My chicks huddled around me about five feet in from the door, like we'd just entered a haunted house and they'd nonverbally elected me the leader to get them through unscathed.

"How did you know this place existed?" Raye whispered.

At this juncture, I had to add a caveat to an earlier assertion.

I didn't read.

But I read porn comic books.

"I read porn comics," I told them.

Harlow reared back.

Luna smirked.

Raye's eyes bugged out.

The door opened, the bell ringing, and all of them jumped, but not me.

They did this before we watched a woman who had to be in her mid-seventies strut in like she owned the joint.

She was wearing white skinny jeans on her stick-like legs, and a supple, beautifully constructed caffe latte leather jacket over a smooth white shell.

At her neck, ears, fingers and wrists were what I'd approximate as tens of thousands of dollars in gold and diamonds.

Her hair was a perfection of blonde swooped into a dramatic updo.

She wore fancy, gold-rimmed sunglasses like Tito, meaning even if it was night.

Her clinically-filled lips were perfectly lined and swiped with a nude combo that looked made for her.

And her face was Botoxed to the max, and so tan, I wished I had a leaflet on the causes of melanoma to hand to her.

Last, she was carrying a handbag I knew cost over seven thousand dollars.

It appeared Scottsdale Mama was out for her smokes before a martini-soaked evening with her girls.

With varying awestruck expressions on our faces, our heads moved with her as she clickity-clacked on her gold high heels to the cash register.

The girl was still flicking at the keychains as the guy with her seemed to be having trouble shoving his change into his jeans pocket.

Scottsdale Mama allowed this to go on for approximately point two five seconds before she cleared her throat imperiously.

The guy's head shot up in surprise that anyone else was in his vicinity (or maybe that anyone else existed on the planet). He tagged the sleeve of his girl and they shunted out.

Scottsdale Mama stepped up to the register and husked, "Marlboro Lights."

Without a word, the clerk turned, grabbed the smokes and plopped them in front of Scottsdale Mama.

With delicate movements, the better to show off her exquisite manicure of long, rounded, blush nails, she pulled a Prada wallet out of her bag and handed over some money. Even if she could afford it, she didn't drop the change in the tip jar. She meticulously put it back in her wallet and tucked billfold and smokes into her bag. Then, no mention of thanks, or anything else, she lifted her nose, clickety-clacked back through the store and pushed open the door.

It was at this juncture we saw a white Mercedes coupe with a tan soft top double parked behind the cars at the front of the store, not only blocking them in, but also blocking the thoroughfare. We witnessed this before the door swung closed.

She matched her clothes to her car.

Impressive.

"I'm not sure whether to claim her as goals, or rant on social media about the behavior of the privileged," Luna declared.

"Goals," Harlow stated.

"Rant," Raye said.

"Let's get this done," I said.

We moved to the clerk.

"Um...is he okay?" Harlow asked her, jerking her head toward the man among the bongs who still hadn't moved.

The clerk looked to the man.

She then looked back to Harlow and demanded in a bored tone, "What can I get you?"

Harlow squared her shoulders, psyching herself up.

Ah, there was my girl.

"We need porn," Harlow announced.

I smiled.

I was so proud.

The clerk made no move and said no words, just stared at Harlow.

Harlow turned to me. "You do this. What do we ask for?"

"What are our choices?" I asked the clerk.

"DVD or print?" she intoned.

"Print," I said.

"Comics or pictures?" she asked.

"Pictures," I answered.

"Generic? BDSM? Role-play? And then what type of role-play? Like secretary or school girl? Or school marm or bad bitch boss? Spanking, him or her—?" the clerk recited.

"Spanking," Luna cut in. "Him by a her."

"You think?" Raye asked her.

Luna shot her a look.

"I see that," Raye mumbled.

The clerk meandered to the porn display.

"All you have, uh...in the spanking genre," Raye called to her. "And throw in something else, just for shits and grins."

She grabbed five magazines, walked back to us and plopped them on the counter.

She rang us up. We had a five-minute, highly irritating conversation about who was going to pay, seeing as we all knew Arthur would eventually reimburse the expense. I ended this by shouldering them out of the way and handing over some cash. I dropped the change in the tip jar. The clerk stared into the distance, dismissing us.

Luna grabbed the mags and we walked out.

We were in the Sportage, Luna and Raye in the back, Harlow beside me in the front, when Harlow remarked, "I feel like I need a shower."

"I'm at odds about porn," Luna put in. "I mean, I think there's some that's empowering. It's consensual. The women do it because they want to. But I also think there's an element that's very bad. How do you know which is which?"

"My guess is, that's why you buy comics," Raye drawled.

I didn't bite.

"Well?" Harlow pressed me.

What the hell.

"The dudes have massive cocks, they fuck each other, the positions are wild, it's not real, so even if it gets rough, which it almost always does, no one gets hurt. Oh, and it's totally *hot*," I said.

"You read gay porn comics?" Luna asked.

"I'll lend you one. You can thank me later," I told her.

"You're on," Luna said.

The cab lapsed into silence, all of us considering my gay comic porn fetish, I was sure, as we drove the rest of the way to Sun Valley Lodge.

The bad news: Jinx wasn't on her patch.

The good-ish news: Mr. Shithead was behind the reception desk.

The ish part of that was, when he saw us fold out of the Sportage, even from across the parking lot, we could see him roll his eyes.

He then stood and pretended to shoot himself under his chin. He did a dramatic flourish with his hands behind his head to mimic his brains blowing out and collapsed to the floor.

"He's upped the ante on drama," Luna noted.

"I think I might be starting to like him," Raye replied.

We pushed in.

"Get up, my man," Luna called, leaning way over the counter to get eyes on the guy still on the floor. "We're not going away and we bring gifts."

I peered over too and saw he'd pried one eye open.

"Spank porn," I supplied, then took the mags from Luna and sifted through them before I added, "And school marm, naughty boy shit."

He popped up to his feet, saying, "She's in room twenty-one."

"Who?" Raye asked.

"You lookin' for Jinx?" he asked back.

Well then.

Part two of our night was set. We just had to wait until her service was completed.

"Actually, we had some questions," Raye told him.

He snatched the mags out of my hands, flitted through them, then looked at Raye. "This buys you one question."

"Oh, please. Five mags, five questions," Raye bartered.

"Two," he returned.

"Five." Raye didn't back down.

"Three," he tried.

"Five," Raye repeated.

"FFS," I grunted. "Have you heard of the Street Warriors?"

"What?" he asked me.

"Street Warriors," I reiterated.

"Is that a porn movie?" he asked.

The dude had a one-track mind.

I sighed.

"No. We believe they protect homeless people," Luna informed him.

"What do I know about homeless people?" he asked, hugging the magazines to his chest protectively, like we'd take them away if he didn't have anything good to give us.

"So you haven't heard of them," Harlow murmured, disheartened.

"No," Mr. Shithead said to her tits.

I sighed again, which was what I needed to do instead of slapping his gaze into another dimension.

"If you hear of them, would you call us?" Raye asked, slipping a business card across the counter to him.

He stared at it like it would grow a hundred legs and start crawling.

"Yo!" I called.

His eyes shot to me.

"She asked, if you hear of them, will you call us?" I restated.

"What do I get if I do?" he retorted.

"More dirty magazines?" Harlow offered shyly.

"I want you all to show me your tits," he returned.

Harlow gasped as she drew back.

I grabbed Harlow's sleeve and said, "Byeeeee," as I dragged her toward the door, Raye and Luna following.

"No! Wait!" he called. We all stopped, turned and looked back. "Mags are good. Films are better."

"Spanking?" I queried.

He didn't quite meet my eyes. "Whatever."

It was spanking.

"You got it," I agreed.

We then walked out the door.

We'd taken positions, leaning in a line on one side of the Sportage, to wait for Jinx, when Luna decreed, "I've decided. Only comic porn for me. Because he's just...*gross*."

"Word on that, sister," Raye replied.

"Ulk," Harlow gagged.

I didn't know if her gag was about porn in general, or the clear evidence we'd just witnessed from Mr. Shithead about how it felt skeevy he got off on it, no matter how consensual it was, and women got paid (hopefully) a fair wage to do it.

I also didn't ask.

I put the sole of one of my Vans up to the side of the SUV, crossed my arms and aimed my eyes at the top deck of the motel, at room twenty-one.

There was general chitchat that I didn't participate in, mostly because I had my mind on other things.

Primarily the fact that Eric had said, "Tonight."

However, it was Raye who told me Homer had shared how he and the General knew where I worked. And as with the rest of the day, outside of him rolling up to The Surf Club to give Homer and the General a ride back to the camp, I'd heard not a thing from him.

Was he playing games?

Or was he busy?

"Heads up," Raye said low.

I focused and saw a white guy, maybe mid-forties, dressed in nice jeans and still tucking in a button down that he wore under a sweater into his jeans, hustling out of room twenty-one.

He wore glasses and looked like a mild-mannered accountant, and he wasn't unattractive, so he could totally score and not pay for it.

Unless he was married and getting his kicks elsewhere, but he wasn't wearing a wedding band.

The world always surprised me, and usually it wasn't in awesome ways.

By the time he made it to the ground level, he had eyes on us, and he didn't take them away.

Maybe because we were all staring at him.

He pulled out in a well-maintained BMW (totally an accountant) and was idling at the entrance, his left turn signal on, when Jinx sashayed out in platform heels, a leather jacket she had tugged closed at the front, and a stretch micro-mini covering her ass.

Also, she had sex hair.

Then again, Jinx always had sex hair, both by design...and by profession.

She did a massive eye roll they could probably see from space when she spotted us before she took her time strolling down the walkway, the steps, and across the parking lot to where we'd pushed away from the Sportage to gather and wait for her arrival.

"You *gringas* are bad for business," she griped in greeting.

"Was he a regular?" Raye asked.

"Not yet. But I hope he will be since he's gotta be new, 'cause I charged him ten bucks more than the usual and he didn't blink." She paused before she finished, "And he gave me a big tip and he has a big dick."

"*Nice*," Luna drawled.

"What you bitches doin' here?" Jinx asked.

"I called," Luna told her.

"I know. The night's been busy. This is good. I can get done before it gets too cold," Jinx replied.

"Right then, we won't take a lot of your time," I said.

"*Excelente*," Jinx muttered.

"Have you heard of the Street Warriors?" I asked.

She tipped her head to the side. "Is that a gang?"

God, I hoped my brother didn't join a gang.

"I don't think so," I told her.

"Why you askin'?" she queried.

"My brother is missing. I'm worried he's sleeping rough. He has mental health issues," I shared.

Jinx tried to hide it, but the flash of compassion showed in her face before she nodded curtly.

"And I got some information he's a Street Warrior," I went on.

"Never heard of them, *linda*," she said quietly.

That was a gift. Right on display.

Jinx was a tough nut.

But still.

She liked us.

And there was the evidence.

No matter the stereotype of women in her profession, the truth of it was, under that street smart exterior, lay a heart of gold.

Alternately, the Rolex Raye scored for her on our last case bought a shit ton of loyalty.

"Can you ask around?" Luna requested.

"My ass on the line if I do?" Jinx returned.

"We honestly have no idea," Raye admitted. "We think maybe they look after homeless people."

Jinx nodded. "I'll be careful, and I'll ask. I find something, you buy me a burger."

"Deal," I agreed.

She did a finger wave, clutched her jacket back around her bosoms, and strutted off.

We climbed into the Sportage.

I pulled out as Raye announced, "Okay, we have feelers out. What time do you want to head out tomorrow?"

It was college football season, so unless my brother's friends went to a bar to watch the games, our audience was captive.

"Say, ten o'clock brunch at Brunch Snob, then we roll out?" I suggested.

"In," Raye said.

"In," Luna parroted.

Harlow reached out and gave my thigh a reassuring squeeze, because we had feelers, but the night was a bust.

And then she said, "In."

There it was.

I put it on and it didn't feel like it fit.

But I was wrong.

Rolling with my girls.

It fit like a dream.

SIX

TWO QUESTIONS

When we got back to the Oasis, Raye went straight to her pad and her hot guy, and Luna came with me to my place to borrow some porn.

As for Harlow, she went right home because it was past her bedtime.

My best chick was an early to bed, early to rise type of girl, even if her shift didn't start until eleven.

This was because, if she didn't go to bed at 9:00, she wouldn't wake up at 5:00 or 6:00, allowing her time to journal, make a complicated and highly nutritional smoothie, hit an early yoga or Pilates class, or that shit women did when they were trussed up to bungee cords and they bounced around a studio. Then she'd go home, make herself some oatmeal with berries or overnight oats with other healthy shit in it, tidy her house or clean a room, take a shower, perform makeup miracles, pick the perfect cute outfit, and hit SC. Always on time.

That was Harlow.

And it was awesome.

But knowing Harlow's parents, particularly her ballbuster of a mother, it was also something else.

As for Luna, whose shift started at 7:00 a.m., so she had to be up super early just to make it in, it was totally her, when I offered a cocktail after she hit my pad, she accepted and settled in to gab with me until her glass was empty.

She then took her comics and boogied.

This left me cleaning glasses and thinking that Eric still hadn't touched base.

"Fuck this noise," I muttered, snatched up my phone and pulled up my texts.

He was a big boy. It was late, but if he was incommunicado for the night, he'd silence his notifications.

But I wasn't playing this game.

Therefore, I texted, *What happened to "tonight?"*

The whoosh barely sounded on the sent text before my phone was vibrating with a call.

It was Eric.

Whoa.

That was quick.

While I answered, my heart started beating hard, not only because Eric was connecting, but what it said he did it so quickly.

"Hey."

"You home?" he asked.

Oh.

Well then.

He didn't get in touch because he knew me and the girls were rolling that night, as he would, since Cap undoubtedly told him.

"I thought you tracked my car."

"Your car has been sitting at the Oasis all night."

Right.

Whoops!

He continued, "Cap said you took off in Luna's ride then took the Kia. He hasn't reported you're back."

Seemed Cap and Raye got busy when she arrived home.

Also seemed the Nightingale team knew about our storage unit setup and tracked those vehicles as well, because I hadn't noticed Raye use her phone all night to report to Cap.

I was not mad about this.

Never hurt to have a badass (or better, half a dozen of them) keep an eye, especially when you were a totally untrained, amateur sleuth in a satin bomber jacket out interrogating skeeves.

"We're back," I pointed out the obvious.

"That didn't last long."

"We didn't get much," I informed him. "What about you?"

"We've asked around. Nothing yet. This is a hole in our operations here in Phoenix," he shared work stuff, surprisingly openly. "We've known about it since we started setting up. None of our men are locals. It takes years to develop an information network in a city, and we've only had months. We need a local guy. We're just having issues recruiting one who fits with the team."

Supreme badass skills derived from time in the military or law enforcement or some other kickass former occupation, plus insane good looks, plus ridiculous sex appeal, plus complete confidence in their abilities, plus melding perfectly with the unit...

Yeah.

I could see that'd be hard to recruit.

"Raye told me the General told you that Jeff shared where I work," I said.

His voice was sweet when he noted, "Means he's good for now, Jess."

My voice was quiet when I replied, "Yeah."

More sweet when he repeated my, "Yeah."

Man, I had to get us out of this sweet or I'd have an orgasm just talking to the guy.

"Everything go okay getting Homer and the General to the camp?" I asked.

"Nope," he answered.

Oh shit.

"What happened?"

"The General twisted Cap up in a big way."

Cap used to be in the Army, so I could see this. I'd never been in the Army, and he twisted me up.

"Something I've learned since I started this gig, Turner," I began. "I don't have the skills to deal with the myriad of issues they face. It sucks and sometimes it kills, but you gotta treat them like humans and turn the rest off."

"We don't operate that way, Jess," Eric replied. "No way Cap was going to sit on his hands about the General. But meeting Mary kicked it over the edge."

"Mary?"

"Mary. She's an eighty-two-year-old great grandma who's been on the streets about a month because she was kicked out of her apartment for not being able to make rent. She has a small retirement, and social security, it just didn't stretch that far. She's also got a finely honed stubborn streak and didn't tell her kids her situation was fucked."

I was stunned. "She'd rather live on the street than tell her children she was being evicted?"

"She doesn't want to be a burden. The impression is, none of them are rolling in it, and they got mouths to feed. If they also had to look after her, things that are tight would get out of hand."

"So what are you going to do?"

"Cap and Mace are looking into veterans' services to see if we can get the General into a facility that will help bring him back to himself. Cap's also gonna get in touch with Scott and Louise to see if they can find accommodations for Mary."

Scott and Louise, Luna's parents, worked together at a non-profit that dealt with affordable housing and unhoused initiatives.

I'd been keeping them in my back pocket, obviously not ready to share what I was doing. But when I found Jeff, I was going to go to them and see if they could help me get him set up someplace where he didn't have to deal with Mom and Dad, and he didn't have to feel like a drain on me and his buds.

Eric kept talking.

"In the meantime, we gotta get Mary and her cat off the street. She risks exposure in the winter, but if she makes it through, a summer in Phoenix might end her. The men are gonna get her in a long-term hotel until something more permanent can be arranged."

Right, the things Eric was saying were giving me that gooey feeling again, and that feeling was bad, because it felt really freaking good.

"How're you doin' with all this?" he asked.

"I have hope for the first time in months that my brother is okay," I answered.

"Right," he said, sensing I wasn't done.

Because I wasn't. "But he didn't finish his pipefitter training. He's not a warrior. He's not a shadow soldier. When he's experiencing an episode, he isolates himself. He gets confused easily. Once he holes up somewhere, sometimes he gets so stuck in his head, he gets so listless, he doesn't even eat. When he talks, he doesn't make a lot of sense. And if it's really bad, he has hallucinations. In other words, I don't even know what this Street Warrior thing is, but I know Jeff's got no business being one."

"We'll figure it out, and we'll get him some help," Eric assured.

I wanted to be assured, but something was creeping up inside.

I knew what that something was, and I could not be in a conversation with Eric when I gave it free reign. When that happened, I had to be alone.

Because it never failed to devastate me.

"Jess?" Eric called.

I needed a second.

Actually, I needed to get off the phone so I could deal.

Before I could do that, Eric said, "Two questions."

"What?" I whispered.

"Two questions. You start. Whatever you ask, I have to answer, no bullshit, no evading. Then I get two, and the same."

Oh God.

I really wanted my two questions.

And I was terrified of his.

"Deal?" he pressed.

"Okay," I said.

See?

I *really* wanted my two questions.

"Hit me," he invited.

"Why didn't you ever get married?" I asked something, in all his hotness, and coolness, that had been bugging me since I met him.

"Who told you I've never been married?" he answered.

Uh...

"No one," I said. "I just assumed."

"I was married for six years to a woman I met in LA. Her name's Savannah. She was the executive chef at a hot-shit restaurant. She wanted to start her own, and I backed that play. She loved what she did and she was really good at it. I just had no idea what kind of time it would require of her, which was pretty much every hour she was awake."

"I know something about this," I said carefully. "Lucia, our chef at SC, used to be like that. I wasn't there when it happened, but I've heard she and her husband Mario had some issues and it got rocky there for a while."

"Yeah," Eric confirmed, his tone weighty. "Rocky."

Cripes.

When he didn't keep talking, I did.

"Lucia and Mario made a deal. She comes in at six to do the prep work and start cooking, but she leaves at three. Period, dot. Though, as a family, she and Mario and their kids tend her herb garden."

"Well, Savannah wasn't into making a deal like that. I understood in the beginning it was going to take some concentration, commitment and a lot of work. But four years into it, and her restaurant was a commercial and critical success, I wasn't feeling her being dead to the world when I got up and took off for work, and having her wake me up at two so I could fuck her before she passed out when she got home."

Well, that was honest.

"Yeah, that doesn't sound like a fulfilling relationship," I muttered.

"It wasn't."

"She wasn't willing to compromise?"

"When I broached it, she told me that I was trying to force a double standard on her. I didn't have a nine to five job, why did I expect that of her? She's right. I didn't have a nine to five job. But I also didn't work sixteen-hour days, not pick up calls and completely ignore texts."

"Yikes."

"Mm," he hummed.

"I shouldn't have asked that question, Turner," I said, feeling shit I'd made him talk about this.

"Why?"

"Well...I feel like shit I made you talk about it."

"It isn't a secret, Jess. It got messy. Then it got ugly. Then it was done."

I shouldn't ask.

I really shouldn't.

I asked.

"How did it get messy?"

Again, no hesitation from Eric.

"She wanted kids. I wanted kids too. But, when I pointed out her life couldn't be about the restaurant if we had a family, she'd get pissed. It went without saying she thought she could have our children and they'd get as much of Mom as I got from my wife. I wasn't going to do that to my kids. She was furious, spouting all this shit about how men felt women needed to be the caregivers. Her answer to her schedule, as well as mine, was for us to get a live-in nanny. It's the way of the world to need daycare or help at home with two working parents, but I didn't want some person who wasn't blood essentially raising our kids. I also didn't feel like doing it on my own when I was married to their mother."

"I can see that."

"Yeah. The writing was on the wall. I asked for a divorce. She refused. I moved out and filed for divorce. Honest to fuck, she was shocked. Like she didn't understand we had integral problems with our marriage."

This was such deep denial, or narcissism, I couldn't think of anything else to say but, "Whoa."

"Yup," he agreed. "She wanted to give it another go. She suggested counseling. I loved her, so I took her up on it. She went to two meetings, missed the next three because of restaurant shit, and then it was over."

"God, Eric, I'm so sorry."

"I'm not. She was smart, funny, talented. When it was good, it was fantastic. When it got bad, I got out."

"You don't feel like you wasted six years?"

"None of us have a crystal ball, Jess. We take the hand we're dealt and cope."

That was the truth of it.

"I don't regret the time I had with her," he continued. "I loved her, so I'd regret it if I didn't give it a shot. In the end, it didn't work out, but it worked out the way it should."

That was aggressively adjusted.

"I think I got about fifteen questions with that," I noted, bracing for his to come at me.

"Right," he said softly.

"So it's your turn to hit me."

"Do you want kids?"

Something lovely and warm shifted in my belly, because that was not a you're-my-new-lil'-sis type of question.

"Honestly? The concept scares me. I didn't have great role models. But yeah," I shared. "I do."

"You'll be a good mom," he stated.

"How do you know?"

"Maybe you forgot, just two days ago when you strutted out of a homeless camp at two in the morning on the mission of finding your brother."

That lovely warm thing shifted again, feeling lovelier and warmer.

I attempted to ignore it (impossible!) and prompted, "Question two."

"What were you thinking when I lost you ten minutes ago?"

Oh shit.

I said nothing.

"Jess, we had a deal. No bullshit. No evading," he pushed.

It was gentle.

But he was pushing.

And we'd made a deal.

Fuck!

"He'd be you," I forced out.

"Pardon?"

"Or Cap. Or Knox. Or Liam." I referred to other members of the NI&S team. "If Jeff didn't have his illness, he'd be like you. He'd be strong and fit and confident. And he'd do things to help people. He'd have a job that was about honor. Respect. And he can't do that. He can't be all he should be. So he has to live with this illness, and live knowing he can't have that. Instead, he lives thinking he's a burden to—"

I cut myself off with a painful gulp.

"Jessie?" Eric called.

"I gotta go. Talk to you later," I blurted.

And then I hung up.

It was rude. But I couldn't stop myself from doing it.

Just like I couldn't stop myself from turning off all my lights, flipping off my Vans, crawling into bed, and curling myself into the gloom.

It'd pass, this darkness. I knew that because it always did.

It had to.

Life went on, and I had to get on with it.

But I'd learned through the years to just let it happen. To feel it, not bury it, so I could get on with it.

I loved my brother. I wanted everything for him. And the reality of it was, he'd never have that.

And it was a bottomless pit of how much that sucked.

I didn't know how much time had passed before I heard my front door open.

Great.

Eric had called Cap to tell Raye to look in on me.

Fabulous.

I could deal with my girls having my back.

I couldn't deal with anyone when I was like this.

I waited for her to call out.

She didn't call out.

Getting a sinking feeling that it might not be Raye and instead it was someone who shouldn't be in my place, my mind racing as to whether I'd locked the door when Luna left (I hadn't), I was about to get up and grab my Taser when a shadow filled the doorway.

I'd know that shadow anywhere.

It was Eric.

I suddenly couldn't breathe.

He didn't say a word.

He just walked into my room, scooped me up out of bed like he did when he picked me up from the couch, but this time, he didn't put me to my feet.

He got in my bed...

Yes!

He got in my bed!

Then he settled me in his lap, tucked my head under his chin, wrapped his arms around me, and they went tight.

Oh man.

This felt awesome. Way better than just hugging him, and that felt *great.*

"You didn't have to come here," I said huskily.

"Yeah, I did."

I didn't know what to say to that.

"You're not crying," he noted quietly.

"No," I agreed, still huskily.

"You need to cry."

"I'm not a crier."

"I don't have to tell you, you're dealing with a lot," he remarked.

"No, you don't have to tell me that."

"And it's clear you have been for a long time."

"Yep."

"Babe, you need an outlet."

Babe.

Did you call your adopted little sister "babe?"

Did you haul your ass over to her house after eleven at night to comfort her?

Did you hold her in your lap against your chest in her bed?

God, I wanted him so bad, *so fucking bad*, I *needed* to ask what was going on here.

But I couldn't because I was scared shitless about his answer.

"Do you cry when you're upset?" I asked.

"I cried when my mom died."

"You were thirteen."

"It didn't happen at the time, but when I got home and I was alone, I cried because my father showed up at my graduation from the FBI Academy so drunk out of his brain, he had to be ejected."

Oh god.

I hated that for him.

The only way I could express the depths of that hatred was to mumble, "Yuck."

Lame.

But there it was.

"They were angry tears, and they didn't last long," he carried on. "But I shed a few when one of Tim's baby mommas called me, asking me if I knew where he was and telling me he was behind six thousand dollars in child support. This was more of an issue than it normally simply was, because my nephew just got out of the hospital after getting his tonsils out, and not only did Tim not pitch up to visit his kid, she didn't have the money to pay the co-pay."

"I'd cry about that too," I noted. "Let me guess, you sent her the money."

"Of course."

Of course.

"I'm not the kind of girl who schleps around, pissed about shit I have no control over," I informed him.

"That doesn't mean you aren't allowed to have a reaction when that shit bites you in the ass," he returned.

"True," I mumbled.

Eric started stroking my back.

It felt like...

Everything.

Man, I was in trouble.

"Tell me about him," he murmured.

"He's funny. He's sharp. It's weird, because he's kinda like Harlow. When things are going well, he's always in a good mood. Life did him dirty, and still, that's Jeff."

"Look forward to meeting him."

The idea of Jeff meeting Eric...

Shit, Jeff would totally dig Eric.

He'd dig all the guys.

Most especially, he'd dig knowing I had this capable crew in my life.

On these thoughts, I turned my head and shoved my face in his throat.

Eric tangled his long fingers in my hair.

"It's really cool you came, but you don't have to be here," I said into his skin.

"Something else you should know about Jack and Rose."

I tensed at this intro, but prompted, "What?" when he said no more.

"Jack did the right thing. Not because he was a guy, and she was a woman. But because he cared about her, and he gave everything just for a shot that she'd make it out alive."

Oh fuck.

That did it.

A painful hiccup surged up my throat, I pressed my face deep into his neck, and the tears came.

Eric untangled his hand from my hair, wrapped his arm around my shoulders, and both of them held me close and tight.

He didn't say a word. No murmurs of encouragement to get it out. No statements that it was going to be all right.

He was silent.

And very, very *there.*

Even when I quit crying, and nestled into him, my cheek to his chest, he didn't say anything.

I really wanted to know what he was about, what was happening with us.

But in that moment, he felt so good, and it felt so good, having someone close, having someone hold me, specifically having *him* there, I couldn't break that moment. I couldn't mess it up.

I'd never had it, but I knew I needed it.

Especially from him.

So I went with it.

I fell asleep with it, just like that, held close in Eric Turner's strong arms, cocooned in his long body.

But around eight hours later, in my bed, the covers tucked tight around me, I woke up alone.

SEVEN

WORTH IT

I'd texted the girls I was running late and told them I'd meet them at Brunch Snob.

Along the way, I did my best, but my best wasn't good enough.

So when I finally arrived and swung into my seat in the kickass establishment (my chair having the word CUTIE on the back, others had TASTY, SEXY, NAUGHTY, QUEEN and the like, the décor part of why Brunch Snob was the greatest, the fabulous food and drinks did the rest), I knew I hadn't tamped down my shit mood that Eric had taken off...*again*...leaving me high and dry and totally confused.

I knew this, because the instant Luna got a load of me, she remarked, "Methinks someone didn't sleep so great."

The server showed, and I said, "Latte. Hot. Full fat. And your poutine."

I hadn't even looked at the menu.

But that day was a poutine day, for certain.

The girls all had drinks, but they ordered food when I did, and the server took off.

I launched in.

"Eric told me we'd talk last night, but I heard nothing from him. I thought he was playing games, and that's bullshit. So I texted him."

"He didn't text back?" Harlow asked, looking and sounding deflated.

"No. My text barely took off before he phoned me."

Harlow's face lit up with a bright smile.

"We then got into the heavy, as seems our usual," I went on. "We talked about Eric's ex-wife—"

"Eric's been married?" Luna asked, and she was looking and sounding shocked.

I nodded. "Big time chef. And crazy bitch. She didn't want to lose him. But she also didn't want a healthy marriage. She wanted him hanging in the wings while she worked on her professional dreams every waking hour of the day, not even connecting with him by replying to his texts. And she expected they'd hire a nanny when she popped out his kids. Eric wasn't down with that, so he ended it before they had any kids."

"She *is* a crazy bitch," Luna agreed. "I mean, I get being into your career, but is the woman blind?"

Eric was a lot more than just gorgeous.

A *whole* lot.

Which was part of my current shitty mood.

"Then we got to talking about Jeff," I continued.

They all leaned in to hear me share more about my beloved brother who I'd never shared much about.

I couldn't freak out about that. I had to get the Eric shit out of the way so I could focus on finding said beloved brother.

"And I got overwhelmed by it. I didn't want to share that with him, so I hung up on him."

"Oh, Jessie," Harlow murmured.

"Nope," I said. "That's not the bad part. The bad part is, I went into my zone so I could deal and get to the other side of it. And while I was doing it, Eric showed at my place."

"Oh, Jessie," Harlow chirped on an audible happy-clap.

"He picked me up, got in bed with me and held me, and we got even deeper about Jeff and life. And I started crying when he told me Jack did right by Rose in sacrificing himself for the chance she'd survive."

"Holy shit," Raye whispered.

"Yeah, that was when I started crying," I stated.

"I didn't think you were a crier," Luna noted.

"I'm not. But, bitch, when I told him he didn't have to come all the way over to my pad to be with me in my shitty zone, he said Jack did right by Rose in sacrificing himself. What was I supposed to do with that?"

"I'm not a crier either, and that'd make me cry," Luna replied.

"It doesn't make me cry. Jack totally could have gotten on the door with her," Harlow said huffily. "I mean, they barely even *tried*."

I ignored Harlow. She was totally a happily-ever-after-at-all-costs girl.

"Right," I agreed with Luna. "So, he's open, has no trouble sharing, doesn't regret his divorce because he loved his wife, and said he'd regret not giving it a shot with a woman he loved. He listens. He's great with silence. And I fell asleep in his arms in my bed."

"Awesome," Harlow whispered, over her slight tiff about the door, her dark-brown eyes were shining bright and happy.

"Then I woke up and he was gone. No note. No text. And I've been awake for two and half hours. Still no text or call." I threw up my hands. "I mean, what the fuck is going on with this guy?"

"Have you, per chance, *asked*?" Raye queried hesitantly.

"No, because then he might tell me we're just friends," I returned.

"Which means, you asking puts your ass out there that you want more, only for him to say he doesn't," Luna added.

"Exactly!" I cried. At this point, the server put my latte down, and I didn't look at her as I said a heartfelt, "*Thank you*," picked it up and took about seven sips.

In other words, I was in such a tizzy all morning, I hadn't bothered making myself a mug o' joe.

"Maybe she needs a mimosa," Raye suggested, eyeing me.

I put my mug in its saucer. "I don't need a mimosa. I need my senses sharp when we talk to Jeff's buds."

The server took off.

"You want me to ask Cap to feel Eric out?" Raye offered.

"No. I don't want Cap in the middle of this," I refused.

Translation: I didn't want Cap to know I had it bad for his colleague. That would be embarrassing. And it'd suck. Because then I'd have to start avoiding Eric, and Cap, and all of them, which would mean I'd need a new job because they all showed at SC on the regular.

Raye read my translation so she remarked, "This isn't high school, Jess. You aren't fifteen, neither is Eric. You can both survive knowing where you stand and sharing the same friends and eventually getting over it."

"Thanks so very much, Ms. I-Got-My-Hot-Guy-So-I'm-Never-Gonna-Be-In-That-Kind-Of-Shit-Place-Again," I retorted.

"It *is* a yucky place," Harlow asserted. "I mean, sure, they'd both get over it. But it wouldn't be fun until that happened."

"You're in a mood, so I hesitate to say this, but it has to be said," Luna began.

I swung narrowed, warning, indeed-I-*am*-in-no-mood eyes at her.

She ignored my narrowed, warning, indeed-I-*am*-in-no-mood eyes and kept going.

"Has it occurred to you that it's you playing games by talking about all this deep shit with this guy you like, who seems to find a lot of excuses to be in your space, but not asking pertinent questions, like, 'Are you into me?'"

"I didn't want to say it, but...yeah," Harlow switched teams and whispered her accord with Luna's assessment.

"I mean, the man is hardly giving off mixed signals," Luna remarked. "And, babe, love you, you know it. But *you* are."

Wait.

What?

"I am?"

"Kinda...*totally*," Raye put in.

I looked to Harlow, and she didn't verbally confirm. She stretched her lips out and turned them down. Which was nonverbal confirmation.

"Women get into this place where they think the man has to do all the work," Luna declared. "Like, he has to be the one who texts. He's gotta be the one who swings his ass out there. When, you know, he's human too, and it doesn't matter if you've got a vulva or a dick, getting shot down is no fun. The thing is, he keeps putting himself out there, and you're not shooting him down, but you also don't seem to be letting him in. I mean, on Thanksgiving, you said he was about to kiss you. When he left for the night and chucked you under the chin, before he did that, did you make it clear you wanted a goodnight kiss?"

"I was sleepy, he'd woken me up so I could lock up after him," I defended.

"So that's a no," Raye remarked.

"I have to be giving off a vibe he can read," I asserted.

"Jess, again, love you, you know it, but you've got resting 'fuck off' vibes," Luna replied. "Eric's got it going on. But I'm still surprised he had the balls to make a play in the first place."

"You kinda do. With the ef off vibes," Harlow said cautiously. "It's only when you let people in where you realize how amazing you are." She continued hurriedly, "I get it. With your folks. Guarding your heart and being careful who you let in. But I never got it before, you know, until yesterday when you gave us the full skinny about them. You'd always just told me your relationship with them was difficult. You never gave me the full story."

Now she looked hurt.

Because I'd hurt her.

And she was right to be hurt.

They all were.

Crap, I'd built walls around myself, even with my besties, when there was absolutely zero reason to keep them out.

Damn.

"I'm sorry, Lolo," I muttered. "It's hard to talk about it. And it's hard to explain. It wasn't like they were abusive or anything. They just didn't care."

"That's abusive, Jess," Harlow countered.

"Others have it a lot worse," I replied.

"I'm not best friends with others," she shot back. "I'm best friends with you. And how you grew up stinks. And I don't like it. But I get you now more than I ever did." She smiled, it was a bit trembly, but she did it. "I just thought you were a kickass bee-yotch. And I'd always wanted to be friends with a kickass bee-yotch, and you're the most kickass bee-yotch there is."

Did people say "bee-yotch" anymore?

I didn't ask that.

It went against the grain, but I knew it would mean something to her, and she meant everything to me, so I twisted in my seat, pulled her into my arms and hugged her.

"We are witnessing growth right this very instant, folks, and I'm here for it," Raye joked.

I let Harlow go and shot a look at Raye, at the same time I pulled out my phone and dared, "Wanna see growth?"

"Hit us with it," Luna invited.

I pulled up my contacts, found Eric, and disregarded my finger was shaky when I hit go on his number.

I put my phone to my ear.

It rang once (once!), and he greeted, "Hey, Jess. You good?"

"Hey. Yeah. I'm fine. Out for brunch with the girls, but I wanted to say thanks for coming over last night."

"Not a problem."

"It, uh...meant a lot."

"Really not a problem, babe. Happy to do it."

Shit.

Shit.

Fuck.

"I also wanted to know if you have plans for tonight?" I asked.

"I don't know. Do I?" he asked back.

Why was that answer sexy AF?

"On No-Fucks-to-Giving, you got two movie picks, and I only got one. So I thought I'd order a pizza and we could even things out and watch *Joy Ride*."

"How about you come to my place, and I'll make us pizza, and we'll watch *Joy Ride*?"

Oh my God.

He was into me.

My clit started tingling, my heart started hammering, and I suddenly turned all girlie and shot big, happy eyes at my chicks.

Harlow lifted her hands and did the clapping motion without clapping so it wouldn't make noise.

Raye and Luna just smiled at me.

"Jess? You there?" Eric called.

Oh shit.

"Yeah. I'm here. Sorry, our food was served," I lied.

Raye snorted. Luna rolled her eyes. Harlow kept clapping silently.

"But that'd be good. What time?" I asked.

"Six work?"

"Yeah."

"Great, babe. I'll text my address."

"Can I bring anything?"

"Just you. I'll have us covered."

Just me.

Oh man, that gooey feeling was coming back.

"Okay. Good. Awesome. Fantastic. Looking forward to it." Must...stop...mouth! "See you then."

"See you then, Jessie," he purred.

Purred!

Jesus Christ.

He was totally into me!

"Bye," I pushed out.

"Later, Jess."

I hung up and gusted like I'd just run a hundred-yard dash, "That's the hardest thing I've ever done *in my life*."

"Worth it though, yeah?" Raye asked.

We would have to see.

I still nodded.

"What's No-Fucks-to-Giving?" Harlow asked.

Maybe it was what I'd just done, and all it'd taken me to do it. Maybe it was all the emotion about Jeff and my parents surfacing. Maybe it was the fact I'd learned that I hadn't been as good of a friend as I should be to the best friends you could have.

But when Harlow asked that, I busted out laughing.

Harlow was smiling tentatively when I was done, and I told her, "It's what people with shit families call Thanksgiving."

"Do you get turkey?" she asked.

I nodded. "And stuffing, and all the other good stuff that makes you need to unbutton your pants when you're done shoving food in your face."

"Oh my God, did you unbutton your pants in front of Eric?" Raye asked.

"He said it was a compliment to the chef."

"And *again*, love you, you know it, but you really, really, *really* have had your head up your ass about this guy," Luna remarked.

I couldn't get pissed at her.

Because I had.

And I had a date with him that night.

So I was no longer in any mood to be pissed.

I was in the mood to hit up my brothers' friends, hopefully find out something that would settle my mind, then go home and be more of a girl by picking out the perfect outfit, doing the perfect makeup, going and buying the perfect bottle of wine.

And having an at-his-house-for-pizza-and-a-movie date with a hot guy.

"I'M JUST GONNA SAY, you know, you might have Eric, after tonight, if things keep going good," Harlow started as we drove from Jeff's bud number three, David, to Jeff's bud number four, the last bud on my list, Joshua.

Newsflash: so far, none of them had heard from my brother.

"But if you find yourself in the zone again, you know, the bad one you mentioned at brunch, and you want company, you can call me," Harlow finished.

"Me too. I'm just a couple of doors down," Raye said. "I could be there in a jiffy."

"Me three, I'm just across the courtyard," Luna put in.

I would feel like a real asshole at how I'd kept these guys out if it didn't feel so great having them in.

"Thanks, bitches," I muttered as I pulled up in front of Joshua's house.

I'd saved the best for last.

Joshua was Jeff's longest-standing friend, and his closest one. If memory served, they'd been that to each other since they were twelve. Jeff was Joshua's best man. Joshua's wife, Katelyn, was super cool. She loved Jeff almost as much as Joshua did.

Most wives of husbands with friends who had troubles like Jeff wouldn't be down to let him crash in their guest room for however long he needed.

But Katelyn was a nurse. Jeff did his best when he was with them because she helped him stay on top of his meds, she was careful about avoiding triggers, she also educated Joshua on that, and she busted her hump to make him feel welcome.

Even though Jeff resolutely stayed employed, no matter what shit jobs he had to take, and he insisted on paying rent, eventually, Jeff always decided he'd worn out his welcome, and I got that. I'd feel the same, obviously, since I very recently realized I hadn't even allowed myself to unload the weight of my family issues on my chicks.

But in the end, if there was anyone Jeff would reach out to when he was in the wind, it'd be Joshua and Katelyn.

We trooped up to their cookie cutter, tile-roofed, xeriscaped, two-story house in Litchfield Park, and I rang the doorbell.

It took a while (the college games were on), but Joshua answered.

Instead of his face splitting into a grin, his usual response to seeing me, it curved into a cagey smile, something that told me Jeff was in contact with him.

But he didn't want me to know.

"Hey, Jess! Wow! What a surprise!" He faked happiness.

"Hey, Joshua." I turned and used my hand in a sweeping motion to the chicks, but I didn't take my eyes off him. "Sorry to show without calling. These are my girls, Harlow, Luna and Raye. And we got some info about Jeff yesterday, so we're out seeing if he's checked in with anybody."

"You got info from Jeff?" He faked not having his own info from Jeff.

"Yeah."

"What's that? Is he okay?" He faked not knowing Jeff was okay, or not, whatever the case might be.

I looked beyond him into his house. "Is Kat around?"

Katelyn would give me the skinny.

He didn't move, which meant she wasn't, and he told me why. "She's at work."

"Right, so, you haven't heard from him?" I pushed.

He shook his head. "No. Not in a while. Still totally worried. Sucks you had to come all the way out here. You should have called."

"Well, we were at David's so..." I let that hang.

"Did you call David?" He was making a point.

"No. I just figured you'd all be in, you know, because of the football."

"That's what I'm doing. Watching U of A get their asses kicked."

"Bummer," I muttered.

"I'd ask you in, but..." It was his turn to let his words hang, probably because he had no excuse not to let us in, outside of us being totally rude and showing at his house unannounced, that was.

"Oh, we don't want to bother you." I could lie too. "I just...I have to ask. The thing I heard was that Jeff was something called a Street Warrior. Have you heard of that?"

His face paled (shit!), and he lied right back, "No. Never. What the hell is that?"

"I don't know." *But you do! And you don't like it!* "I'm trying to find out. Because, you know, if Jeff isn't taking his meds, he's not really in any shape for much of anything. He needs seeing to."

Joshua caught himself stretching his neck to release tension before he suggested, "Maybe, I don't know, he got back on his meds or something."

That meant Jeff was back on his meds.

I couldn't deny that was a massive relief. Especially if Katelyn oversaw that situation.

Even so.

"Joshua, I really need to know where my brother is."

"Jess, I really would tell you if I knew where he was," Joshua replied.

I couldn't read that.

Did it mean he actually didn't know where Jeff was, even if Jeff was in communication?

Or was he still lying, and he did know where he was, and for some screwed up reason, he wouldn't tell me?

I looked away and said as a veiled threat, "Maybe I should call Katelyn."

"No," Joshua stated firmly. "Kat doesn't know where he is either."

"Okay, Joshua, straight up, it feels like you're keeping something from me."

Shocking me, because Joshua was a good guy, I'd always liked him, he'd always liked me, and I'd never seen him do it before, nothing close, I watched his face harden.

He then replied, "Okay, Jessica, straight up. If Jeff needed me to do something for him, you know I'd do it for him, and you know I wouldn't ask questions or deviate from his wishes. Even for you. But honest to Christ, I don't know where he is. But if shit wasn't right, you also know I'd tell you."

I felt a modicum of relief that Joshua thought shit with Jeff was right.

On the other hand, they'd gotten kicked out of a bowling alley once for "human bowling" during which they wore helmets, and frankly, even though my brother had explained it to me, I still couldn't comprehend how they tossed each other down the lanes into the pins.

I just knew they got kicked out for trying, and I knew that particular shenanigan was Joshua's idea.

"Do you know about this Street Warrior business?" I pushed.

He clamped his mouth shut and glowered at me.

So no more lying, because I called him on it, just no more talking.

Right.

"When you talk to him again, you tell him I'm looking for him, and it'd be nice he checked in with his big sis since I've been worried sick about him," I snapped.

"Will do," he clipped, glanced beyond me and said, "Ladies."

He then shut the door in my face.

The gall!

Fuck him.

I was *so totally* contacting Katelyn.

I saw the error of my ways in that moment. I should have bypassed Joshua and went right to her.

I wouldn't make that mistake again.

Though, if she was on shift, I wouldn't bother her. She worked twelve-hour shifts and dealt with enough shit during it, she didn't need mine.

I'd text her tomorrow and hope she wasn't working.

We all trooped back to my Mini and squeezed in.

"I know you're pissed, and I know this is heavy stuff, but if Harlow's sister came looking for her, and Harlow told you not to say anything, you wouldn't say anything," Raye pointed out before I turned on the ignition.

"Harlow doesn't have a sister," I reminded her, purposefully being obtuse because I was pissed and frustrated, though not in equal measure at that juncture.

Harlow, by the by, only had a Golden Boy older brother who I really tried to like the few times I'd met him, but he was such an arrogant shithead, it was hard.

"You get what I'm saying," Raye went on.

"Huh," I grunted, then fired up my baby and set us motoring.

"Okay, the day wasn't a bust. My guess from what we just heard is that Jeff is back to taking care of himself," Harlow noted.

"Yeah." I was still grunting.

"And he's in touch with someone, so not in the wind," Harlow kept searching for the silver lining.

"Yeah," I repeated.

"And that guy will probably tell him to contact you, so maybe he will." Harlow was a dog with a bone with her damned positivity.

"He knows what this Street Warrior gig is, and he didn't share, which doesn't say good things to me," I announced.

"Yeah. Dude got real freaked when that came up," Luna mumbled from the back seat.

"This doesn't give me fuzzy, happy vibes," I stated.

No one said anything.

"I'm texting Katelyn tomorrow. She's the shit. She'll give me the skinny," I announced.

"I think that's a good plan," Raye said.

"And remember. We heard back from Arthur, and he's looking into it too. So between the Angels, the Hottie Squad and Arthur, we'll crack it," Luna put in.

I hoped so.

"Not that what we're discussing isn't important," Harlow said. "But we're in suburbia and they have a lot of shops. Do you know what you're wearing to Eric's tonight? Or do you need to go shopping?"

"I'm wearing my white shorts, black men's-style button-down, my silver belt and my silver sandals," I stated.

"The short shorts?" Harlow whispered, agog.

"The short shorts," I confirmed.

"The silver flat sandals? Or the silver high, platform wedges?" Raye asked.

"Duh. Wedges," I answered.

"Oh my God. That's like the best, at-home-for-pizza-and-a-movie-please-God-feel-me-up-when-we-eventually-make-out outfit *ever*," Luna gushed.

Luna wasn't a gusher.

Which meant I was smiling when I said, "You got that right, sister."

Harlow giggled.

Raye chuckled.

Luna patted me on the shoulder then shoved a thumb's up beside my face from the back.

I turned onto the ramp for I-10.

It was nearing three. It took about half an hour to get back to the city.

This meant I'd have about two and a half hours to spruce up, find a great bottle, and make it to Eric's house in the Biltmore area.

Perfect timing.

I was nervous AF.

And I couldn't wait.

EIGHT

TEASE

Okay, I couldn't do this.

I'd just pulled into the driveway of Eric's sprawling ranch-style house in one of Phoenix's toniest neighborhoods, and even if my outfit kicked ass, I was back to wondering if I was wrong about the signals, because friends could make pizza together and watch a movie.

But my outfit did not say friend.

With my newfound openness with my chicks, I wanted to text one of them for a quick pep talk.

But I was sitting in his double driveway, staring at his long-ass house, and it would've seemed weird if I sat there for ten minutes getting my shit sharp.

"Now or never, Wylde," I muttered to myself, threw my door open, my leg out, and I grabbed the bottle, my black crossbody and exited the car.

I pulled the thin strap of the crossbody over my head and walked to the door, liking the color green it was painted when the rest of the house was a soft yellow with white trim, though the shutters on the windows were black.

I hit the doorbell, and I could understand why it took Eric a few beats to get to it, considering if he was in the back, it'd take a while to make it to the door.

I didn't think the FBI paid for a pad this killer, so NI&S must remunerate really well.

The door opened, and I jolted because I was in my thoughts about his house, but also, he stood there wearing an untucked, white linen shirt that made the tan of his skin all the tanner, supremely faded jeans that hung on him just right, his feet were bare, and his black hair was messy, like he'd just gotten up from a nap.

A hot nap where he had hot dreams about doing nasty things to a hot chick, one like me.

"Hey," I forced out, doing it while realizing his eyes were not on my face.

They were taking their sweet time traveling down my body.

They got to my shoes, the tip of his tongue came out to wet his lower lip, my vagina shuddered, and I kept forcing myself to speak.

"I brought wine. I hope you like red."

His eyes sped up to mine, the look in them not one you'd ever give a little sister. My vagina pulsed a whole lot stronger, then I let out a squeak because his arm was around my waist, pulling me inside.

He had to do some lifting since there was a step up.

This he did.

It was *amazing.*

All of it.

Then the door slammed, I was pressed against it, Eric was pressed against me, and that was so much more amazing, I forgot how to breathe.

"Those shorts and shoes," he said in a thick voice that, yes, caused further reactions in my nether regions. "This mean I'm finally out of your friend zone?"

"I thought I was in *your* friend zone," I whispered.

"I'm a good guy, honey, but I don't pull out my mom's recipe for mushroom sage stuffing for a woman I consider a friend."

Oh man.

He made me his mom's recipe.

That didn't have a nether region reaction.

That reaction I felt in my heart.

"Good to know," I breathed.

His face was so close, our foreheads were almost touching.

Which meant his mouth was so close, we were almost kissing.

And I was surrounded by the smell of cedarwood (back to the nether region reaction).

But he didn't kiss me.

"Are you…gonna…kiss me?" I pushed out.

"Oh no," he murmured. "You put me through two months of not clueing in, now you wait for the good stuff."

What?

It had been two days.

"Two months?"

"Jess, I've been waiting for an in from you since you made me your dragon fruit refresher. Which, I'll confirm, is better than Starbucks."

I was pleased with the compliment.

But…

Was he serious?

I slapped his arm. "Why didn't you make it more clear?"

"You're my friend's girlfriend's girlfriend. Staring at your ass and showing up at your place of business for lunch nearly every fuckin' day made my point. I couldn't come on stronger than that. You had to clue in and make your move."

"The other guys do too, though, not the staring at my ass part. I didn't even notice you staring at my ass."

"That's good, because I didn't want you to see that part. And they don't."

"They do."

"Cap does. I do. The other guys don't."

I thought about that.

And...

Shit!

They didn't.

Sure, they'd come.

But Eric and Cap came the most.

Because Cap wanted to see Raye.

And...

I was *such* a dufus.

Eric came to SC because he wanted to see me.

"Then I showed up at two in the morning at a homeless camp to ream your sweet ass," Eric reminded me.

Yeah, that was above the call of duty.

A friend would do that, for certain.

But a guy acquaintance you only kinda, sorta knew?

Not unless he was into you.

Total dufus.

"And I hauled most of the makings of a Thanksgiving dinner to your house, and cooked for you," Eric kept on.

Okay.

Maybe I was beyond a dufus.

"I could continue," he stated.

He could.

"I'm a dufus," I mumbled.

His tone went from teasing to gentle. "You had other shit on your mind."

"I thought you liked Lucia's cooking."

"I do. I like your ass better."

Not the most flowery of compliments, but I was pretty proud of my ass. It was awesome. I was thrilled he noticed.

"Okay, if you're not going to kiss me, can you stop pressing me against the door so I can have wine? Suddenly I need it. *Bad.*"

He grinned.

It was a sexy wicked grin.

He didn't end it kissing me.

So I frowned.

That made his grin broader, and his head came in, I braced for the goodness, but he dipped at the last minute and ran his nose along the side of my neck.

I shivered.

"You smell good," he murmured there.

"So do you," I murmured to his thick, curling hair.

Abruptly, he lifted up, pulled away, grabbed my hand, and tugged me into his house.

Okay, so I knew where we stood.

The man was still a tease.

The problem with that was, it was fantastic.

Which totally blew.

Once I recovered from the pressed-to-the-door antics, and he had me in his kitchen and took the paper bag of wine out of my hand, I looked around.

Massive, open great room that included the most humongous, attractive, three-sided sectional I'd ever seen. The seats were deep. The couch was facing a built-in unit, in which was an enormous eighty-inch flat screen, as well as shelves with a lot of books, some photo frames, and a few mementos I made a mental note to peruse later.

Behind that was a seating area that held more attractive furniture, including a big double-wide chair and ottoman with a sloping lamp over it where, if one were to read, it would be the perfect reading spot.

All of this was surrounded by windows that gave a view to his backyard, which looked like a straight-up resort. Amazing landscaping. An interesting shaped pool. A pergola on one side that looked covered in something like wisteria. A built-in grill. Great patio furniture. And a fabulous high-top outside table with six stools around it.

Rounding out the inside was a dark wood oval dining room table just inside the front door with a striking gold and globe chandelier.

And the huge-ass kitchen where we were.

Eric was pulling down wide-bowled, gleaming wineglasses from a glass-fronted cabinet.

"I take it the PI business is lucrative," I remarked, and his black eyes came to me. "Not being rude, but it's hard not to notice your place is the absolute shit."

His lips curved and he murmured, "Thanks, Jess. Glad you like it."

He set the glasses down, pulled the wine out of the bag, looked at the label and whistled.

This meant he knew good wine.

Probably not a surprise, considering his tenure in California.

"Honey, you didn't have to do this," he said softly, holding the wine my way.

"Turner, I did. You've been super cool with me through some pretty tough shit," I replied.

He leaned in.

I held my breath.

He kissed my nose.

I frowned.

He pulled back, caught my frown, and started laughing.

"You're a tease," I accused.

"Takes one to know one," he muttered, opening a drawer to nab a wine key.

"I'm not a tease," I retorted.

He aimed his eyes to the vicinity of my shorts, legs and shoes.

Okay.

Point taken.

I smirked.

He started laughing again, but it abruptly stopped when his phone on the kitchen island clattered.

I saw the screen light up and caught the name *Savannah*, before he reached out and swiped the text notification to clear it.

"I can't pretend I didn't see her name," I said quietly. "Is everything cool?"

"No, since you're finally here, in those shorts, bringing good wine, and she's pulling her usual shit."

Oh man.

"Ummmm..." I drew that out, because he was normally open, and we'd cleared a big hurdle, but we were in no place for me to expect things that weren't yet mine to have.

He popped the cork and went right to pouring, not bothering with the aerator I saw in the drawer where he got the wine key (because that vintage didn't need it, so he really did know wine), and he did this being the Eric I was coming to know.

He shared.

"Our divorce was final two years ago. She's in regular contact."

"Okay."

He put the bottle down, picked up a glass and handed it to me. He then picked up his own but neither of us drank.

Instead, he lowered the boom.

"Found out this morning, she's in town. Phoenix. She's scouting a location to open another restaurant."

"Holy shit," I whispered. "Is she...moving here?"

"According to the conversation I had with her this morning, that's the threat," he murmured.

"Threat?"

"Jessie." He sighed.

And one could say it was a wallop of a sigh.

He carried on and explained why it was such a wallop of a sigh.

"I don't want to sound like a dick. I also don't want to be talking about this. But we are, because Savannah is Savannah, and no fuckin' way I want you to see her name on my phone and wonder."

"You really don't have to tell me," I promised.

"I really do because I think you finally get I'm interested in you. I want to get to know you better. And to do that, I want to spend time with you, and that time shouldn't have you wondering why my ex is texting me."

Oh man.

That felt *great.*

"So you need to know, she and I are over," he continued. "I don't want her here. She's no longer in my life. I don't want an antagonistic relationship with her. In the beginning, I was good with adapting to friends. She wasn't. She wanted me back. She is where she is in her profession because she doesn't give up. But I'm not a recipe to perfect or a critic to win over, and she isn't getting that. So now, I'd prefer no relationship at all." He grinned. "And I finally got this woman at my house I've been hoping would get her head out of her ass about me. So I really don't want her a part of tonight."

There was no denying my head had been firmly up my ass, so I let that slide.

"I can assume with the honesty you share with me, which is awesome by the way..."

His lips quirked, and he inclined his head to accept the compliment.

I kept speaking.

"...that you're as honest with her."

Eric nodded. "I am. And her response is to open a restaurant where I moved. And just to say, we have a branch of NI&S in LA. I had a nice house there too. A life. Friends. My closest being Darius, who now manages that branch since Mace moved here. And his wife, Malia, is my second closest. But I moved here to get away from Savannah."

Whoa.

That put this in a whole new category.

Like, stalker category.

Because I didn't feel I could share that (yet), I let my, "Cripes," offer my thoughts.

He lifted his glass. "That about says it."

I reached out and wrapped my fingers around his wrist.

"We're not toasting to that. We're toasting to heads being out of asses."

He chuckled. "That's something I'll be down to toast to."

I let his wrist go, we clinked glasses and sipped.

The wine was yum.

Yeah.

I done good.

"Excellent." He was purring again, and physically being with him when he did it was oh so much better.

"My poutine wore off about an hour ago, so we need to make pizza," I informed him.

"Where did you get poutine?"

"Brunch Snob."

"You'll have to take me there," he murmured, putting his glass down and turning to a bowl with a towel over it.

I *so* was taking him to Brunch Snob.

He flipped the towel, and there was a perfect ball of pizza dough rising in it.

I bit my lip, because I doubted his mom taught him how to make pizza dough.

Maybe.

But doubtful.

"Fuck," he whispered.

"What?" I asked.

He came to me, rested the sides of his hands on my neck and tipped my head back with his thumbs at my jaw.

Nice move.

"Yes," he said quietly. "She taught me how to cook. That was part of the good times we had. But once she gave me that, it became mine, Jess. Okay?"

I nodded.

"Can we be done with her?" he requested.

I nodded more fervently.

He smiled. "Great."

It was the perfect time for a kiss.

He didn't kiss me.

He took his hands from me, moved to some canisters, and ordered, "Grab the red sauce from the stove."

I let my disappointment at no kiss go, put my glass down and headed toward his massive six-burner Wolf stove.

They said delayed gratification was a thing.

Though I hoped it wasn't too delayed before I could be the judge of that.

For your edification, getting my head out of my ass might not earn me a kiss from Eric Turner.

But it did significantly alter how we watched a movie together.

That being, after we ate his delicious homemade prosciutto and fig pizza topped with mounds of arugula, I'd seated myself on one side of the couch. He'd come up to me, bent, caught my leg behind my knee, lifted it so my wedge was in his stomach, and then with a few tugs and a flick, the strap was released, and the shoe was gone.

He repeated that with my other shoe.

And then he put his hands under my arms, lifted me up, and stretched us out across the long back side of the couch, me tucked to his front.

Once he had us situated, he leaned into me to grab the remote from the coffee table but left his arm draped around my waist after he fired up his TV.

I wasn't given the option of a different seating arrangement.

But no way in hell was I complaining.

He murmured, "Need anything before we start?"

He'd emptied the last of the wine in our glasses before we headed to the couch, but mine was on the other end of the coffee table now.

"Just a sec," I said as I started to push up to reach for it.

But he growled, "Hold."

I was so stunned by his growling, and his word, I held as he pushed up and nabbed my glass.

He put it in reach and settled back behind me.

I didn't know how to respond to this.

"I can reach for my glass, Turner," I told him.

"I know," he replied. "Though, now that reach is easier."

It definitely was.

Though, I still didn't know what to do with a man who was so attentive, he wouldn't allow me to execute about a second's worth of effort to grab a wineglass.

As noted, I'd never had anyone look after for me, certainly not someone who would growl at me so he could retrieve my glass.

He was the kind of man who, in a different time, would throw his mantle over a puddle so a woman wouldn't get her shoes wet.

Or knock the shit out of his opponent with his lance in a joust to earn the ribbon from her hair.

I felt this settle, surprisingly easily, into the space around my heart, as he asked, "All good now?"

"Yeah," I answered in an understatement.

He started up the movie and rested his head on some toss pillows he bunched there.

I rested my head on his biceps.

They weren't fluffy.

But they felt *nice*.

Halfway through the movie, he shifted to his back, sliding me on top of him. His head was still on the pillows, and mine was on his chest, the rest of my body covering the length of him, and his hand at the small of my back. This was *so much better*.

Not only because he felt good and smelled good, but also because, when he laughed, which he did, a lot (the movie was funny, and I was glad he thought so), I heard it *and* felt it.

When the credits were rolling, I lifted my head and looked down at his profile since his head was turned on the pillows to see the TV.

It wasn't as good as full face, but it was still gorgeous.

He turned to look at me.

Yeah. The profile was fantastic.

But this was better.

"Did you by chance make dessert?" I asked.

"No, but I scored a quart of Lotus cookie ice cream from Frost."

I was a kickass bee-yotch. Not the kind of woman to let my eyes go happy round with excitement over yummy ice cream.

But I knew with the satisfied smile he had on his face, I'd let my eyes go happy round with excitement.

What was not exciting was, when he angled up, taking me with him, he was no longer my couch. Instead, I was on my feet, my hand held, being pulled to the kitchen.

Why did I ask about dessert?

Why?

He grabbed the gelato and put it in the microwave for twenty seconds to soften it (full approval) as I asked, "Bowls?"

"Cabinet above the dishwasher."

I headed there, grabbed the bowls and came back.

I put the bowls down where he was standing with the gelato quart, and he'd managed to unearth an ice cream scoop during my long (and it was long) trek across his huge-ass kitchen.

He looked at the bowls.

He looked at me. "Those are pasta bowls."

"Your point?"

He busted out laughing, dropping the scoop and taking hold of me.

I was plastered to his front, one of his arms around my waist, the other hand entwined in my hair. So, obviously, I had to wind my arms around his shoulders.

"It's only a quart," he murmured.

"File it away for future reference, big man, I'm a my-own-quart kind of woman."

"You really want a kiss, don't you?" he whispered, eyes aimed at my lips.

"Yes," I whispered back, eyes aimed to his.

His head was descending.

I was rolling up on my toes.

And his doorbell chimed.

"Fucking *shit*," he bit out. He kissed my nose again and said, "Hold that thought."

He let me go and walked to the door.

There was a line of windows at the top, I couldn't see outside from my angle, but I saw his entire body language change before he opened it.

"Jesus Christ," he said.

"I could see you through the door," a woman replied.

"Then why'd you ring the damned bell?" he asked. Before she answered, he said, "Strike that. I don't give a shit. I'm not doing this, Savannah."

Oh fuck.

"Who is she?" his ex-wife asked.

"Go," Eric said as answer.

"You're not answering my texts."

"Take a hint."

"I leave town tomorrow night, and we need to talk."

"Did you hear me say I'm not doing this?"

Eric made a move to shut the door, and she snapped, "Don't you shut that door on me, Eric!"

He shut the door on her.

She knocked on it.

Loudly.

He came back to me and started scooping ice cream.

I waited for another knock. There wasn't one, but now I could see the top of a brunette's head in the window because she got close. And not only that, her eyes were aimed at us in the kitchen.

Yikes.

"Uh..." I didn't quite start.

"Don't," Eric grunted.

He finished doling out the entire quart, put a spoon in each bowl, handed one to me, took the other, and grabbed my hand.

He then walked me down to the very end of the longest hall I'd ever traversed, where there was a massive bedroom that had a seating area at the front, opened doors to a dreamy walk-in closet, and a double wide opening to an even dreamier bathroom with a soaking tub being the star of the show, this set in front of a glass block wall.

He didn't take me to the bathroom or the handsome couch by the fireplace at the front of the massive room.

He took me to the king-size bed at the back wall, pulled me into it, uncovered a remote from a bedside table and flicked on another huge TV mounted to the side wall but swung out to face the bed.

He queued up *The Nice Guys*.

Seriously primo taste in film.

"Do you wanna talk about it?" I offered quietly.

He looked me dead in the eye. "That my ex is borderline stalking me?"

I gave him Harlow's stretched-and-turned-down-lips face.

He looked at it, it seemed to lighten his mood, then his mood took a hit when he leaned forward, pulled his phone out of his back pocket and scowled at it.

He did some things to the screen with his thumb and put it to his ear.

I didn't know if she said anything, I just knew he spoke pretty quickly upon putting the phone to his ear, and what he said was, "My next step is a protective order. Not sure your rep will take that hit when it gets out. And I promise you, it'll get out. Your choice. And you know that's not an empty threat." He then tossed his phone on the bedside table and said to me, "Your gelato is melting."

I spooned some up and told him, "Your bedroom is da bomb."

"Da bomb?"

"Da bomb," I confirmed.

His lips twitched, and he spooned up his own ice cream.

"Though I now get why you're so fit, because I think your living room is in Phoenix, but your bedroom is in Hawaii," I quipped.

He started laughing.

Good.

I made him laugh.

"That's the longest hall in history," I kept going for it. "If he was alive, Louis the Fourteenth would be jealous as all hell."

He shoved pillows behind him, rested against his headboard, yanked my back against his chest, stretched his legs out, and said, "Shut up, Jess."

He then started the movie.

I shut up, and somehow we both managed to eat ice cream in his bed with me using him as my cushion (I saw how he did it, he held his bowl in the hand with the arm around me, and used his free one to dip into the creamy deliciousness, performing a minor miracle by not dripping any on him...or me).

When we were finished, he put the bowls aside, and I was pleased beyond measure when he relaxed against me and started laughing at the movie.

It was such a good choice, my selection of *21 Jump Street* after didn't compare, but Eric didn't complain.

Though I fell asleep, curled into his side, my head on his chest, my arm around his abs, in his bed, about halfway through it.

And Eric didn't wake me to send me home.

NINE

TINKERBELL

My eyes opened, only to take in a slate-gray pillowcase.

My pillowcases were white.

I sat up and realized I was in Eric's bed, in his killer bedroom that was decorated in navy, gray and black with touches of hunter green. I wasn't under the covers, but a super soft throw was covering me.

And Eric wasn't there.

I checked his smart home unit on his nightstand and saw it was around my normal waking-up time, ten to eight.

Eric being an early riser (as I categorized anyone who woke up before me) wasn't a surprise.

Fortunately, he couldn't vanish like he had before since I was at his house.

Time to find him.

First things first, I got out of bed and hit his bathroom.

After I took care of business and moved to the double basin decked out with a black marble countertop, I saw beside the unused basin a new electric toothbrush head, the toothbrush upstanding beside it, some toothpaste, and last, a tube of cleanser and tub of moisturizer that were a brand so far out of my price range, it wasn't funny.

There was also a note.

I washed my hands, dried them and nabbed the note.

J-
Sadie forgot to take these after she and Hector stayed with me.
If you need them, I don't think she'll mind.
X

I didn't think that "X" was a riff on a signature.

I thought it was a kiss.

Or I decided I was going to take it as a kiss.

And it was good to know he didn't have expensive facial products hanging around for all his babes who fell asleep watching movies with him (or other). But instead, this was Sadie's (by the by, she was a Rock Chick, and Hector was OG Hot Bunch, they lived in Denver).

It was better to know that he knew a girl who slept in her makeup would think it was priority one to get rid of it when she woke up.

Of course, he'd been married.

But it meant he paid attention to the stuff that might seem small to him, but was important to a woman.

The gooey feeling was back, I was still uncertain about it, but my teeth and face were not uncertain about being brushed, cleansed and moisturized.

That accomplished, I wandered down the hall, already seeing him sitting on a stool at his island at the end of it.

Since he was watching me walk to him, and he looked hot wearing blue lounge pants and a gray long-sleeved shirt that hugged his torso in all the right places, I couldn't tear my eyes from him in order to assuage my curiosity and peruse the abundance of rooms that sat along this hall.

He swiveled my way when I got close, his bare feet resting on a rung, his long legs spread wide.

I decided to take that as an invitation.

Therefore, I walked right between his legs, felt his hands settle on my hips, watched him tip his head back, and he was so damned beautiful, I decided tease time was over.

I finally got my fingers in that thick, soft hair, dropped my mouth to his, and I kissed him.

He opened for me instantly.

Nice.

My tongue swept inside, and I tasted coffee and warmth and man musk.

I tasted Eric.

And as suspected, he was sheer *perfection.*

I pressed closer and went for more.

When I did, Eric decided to taste me, and he did this by moving his hands to my ass, lifting me up while standing. He then twisted, planting me on his kitchen island.

This was such a smooth move, I was still recovering from it so he was free to angle his head and take over.

And thus commenced him plundering my mouth.

God, he mastered a kiss.

Absolutely...*delicious.*

And as a first kiss?

Best I ever had.

By far.

No other came close.

Eventually, and regrettably, he broke the snog, and I wasn't breathing right because of it, but also, he might have lifted his head, though we were still pressed crotch to crotch, chest to chest.

So there was that.

And one could say I very much liked that.

"Good morning," I wheezed.

His face grew warm, but his lips curved in that wicked, sexy smile, and he kissed me again.

We went at it, but disappointingly, he broke it again.

Such a damned tease.

"Good morning," he belatedly replied.

Tease or no, starting my day like that, I couldn't be in a bad mood (in fact, my mood was so good, it could last the rest of the year), so I smiled at him.

His fingers at my hips pressed in.

"Want coffee?" he asked.

"Please."

"A bagel?"

"Sure."

"Wanna spend the day together?"

Oh God.

There was no confusing it anymore, no denying.

This amazing man *liked me*.

And I *loved* that.

"Yes," I whispered.

There was a shift to the expression on his face that made my heart skip a beat, because I knew he knew how glad I was we were where we were (finally), and even better, he wasn't hiding he was just as glad.

He punctuated all of that by running his knuckles gently along my jaw.

No man had ever touched me like that. No person had touched me with that kind of gentleness.

It was the sweetest touch I'd ever felt *in my life*.

With perfect timing, because all I was feeling for him was suddenly overwhelming, he pulled slightly away and asked, "Great. Do you hike?"

Suddenly, an unfamiliar feeling took hold of me.

Not true. It wasn't unfamiliar. I'd had it before in other things, but not with guys.

So I knew what it was.

Panic.

Nope.

Sheer panic.

"Jess?" Eric called.

"I don't hike," I replied.

"Okay," he said slowly, studying my face.

"And I, um..." I couldn't finish that.

"You what?" he prompted.

Shit.

"Well, I don't read," I said quickly.

His head quirked in surprise, which made sense, considering I wasn't making any.

But, for reasons unknown to me, I didn't stop talking.

"And I don't cook. I don't go to the gym or exercise in any formal way. I can shop, but the mood has to strike me, something it doesn't do very often. I don't go to concerts or festivals, because people are rude, and they bug the crap out of me, so if there are a lot of people in one place, it bugs the *absolute* crap out of me. I like to go to movies, but I prefer to watch them at home. I like going out to eat, because I like food, but mostly I do it so I can check out their cocktail menu to keep sharp. I also go to bars, but I'm not a barfly, it's usually also for professional research. Or to hang with my girls. I like taking photos of stuff, but it's not like I think I'm some great master. I just see things that interest me, and I want to get an angle on them and leech the color to black and white because I think the subtlety of that, the shadows and light, is more interesting."

I took in a massive breath and finished my litany.

"Mostly, when I have time off, and don't have plans with the girls, I clean my house, pay my bills and hang in front of the TV."

"Okay," he repeated slowly.

I was talking slowly too when I admitted, "In other words, I just figured out, I'm kinda...*boring*."

For a beat he looked utterly stunned.

Then he busted out laughing.

I was plastered to his front, his face shoved in the side of my neck, still laughing, when I asked, "You think me being boring is funny?"

He raised his head to look down at me. "You think you're boring?"

"I spend most of my free time watching TV."

"So do the vast majority of Americans."

"You're a former FBI agent and current badass private investigator. You make pizza dough from scratch and top it with figs and shit, not pepperoni. Your first thought on what to do to spend the day together is hike. No shade on hikers, and I'd probably get some good photos along the way, but huffing and puffing my way up Camelback Mountain, getting sweaty and gross, is not exciting to me."

"So we won't hike."

"Okay. But so far, mostly what we do when we're together is watch TV and talk deep shit about our lives, and make no mistake, I love learning about you. But I think we could both use a break from deep shit."

His was smirking sexily when he said, "Agreed."

"And I'm not sure I'm up for a day of watching more movies."

"Same. Do you travel?"

"Sorry?"

"We could take a day trip to Prescott or Sedona."

I relaxed.

Maybe I wasn't totally boring.

"I love Prescott *and* Sedona," I told him.

"Then I'll make you coffee and a bagel and get dressed while you chill with some breakfast. I'll take you to your place so you can get ready. And we'll head out. Is that a plan?"

"It's a total plan."

He tipped his head to the side. "So, do you travel?"

I nodded eagerly. "It's not like I head out and discover Arizona every weekend, and I wish Bisbee wasn't too far away. That's definitely an overnighter trip, but if you haven't been there, you have to go. Though, I hit Sedona to peace out or Prescott to chill out. They've got totally different vibes, but they're both awesome."

"Right, babe, but do you *travel*?"

His stress on the word "travel" had me tensing again.

"I'm not exactly financially in a position to jet to Paris," I noted.

"Do you want to jet to Paris?" he asked.

There were a lot of things in life I wanted that I'd learned a long time ago I couldn't have.

As such, this was threatening to get us into deep territory, so I answered, "I never really thought about it."

"Paris is the first thing you mentioned when you talked about traveling," he noted.

Oh shit.

"Honey,"—his hands gave me a squeeze—"we're real. We share. That's the deal. You don't have to bare all. If you don't feel like talking about this because it leads you to a place you don't want to be right now, we won't. But just tell me that. Don't hide from me. Yeah?"

"I've never really had the money to go far, but I've been to Anaheim, four times. And Orlando, twice," I blurted.

He blinked.

Oh God.

He liked me.

I liked him.

I wanted this.

I wanted him.

His ex might be an issue, but…whatever.

He wouldn't even let me stretch to get my own wineglass.

And he wouldn't let me be alone in my gloom.

I had to give it to him.

If this worked, he'd find out eventually.

So I squared my shoulders and informed him, "Eric, I'm a Disney chick."

He blinked again.

And then a repeat of him busting out laughing.

I shoved at his chest in affront.

He rocked back maybe half an inch before I was plastered to him again with his face in my neck.

"Holy fuck," he said there, still laughing, and his next vibrated with it, "Disney."

"A lot of people like Disney," I defended. "There are millions of us."

He pulled his face out of my neck to look down at me. "There are big crowds at those amusement parks."

I didn't meet his eyes. "It's impossible to get pissed at rude people in one of the Magic Kingdoms. That's the magic part of the kingdom. Among other magic they offer there."

He chuckled. Loudly.

I huffed.

He framed my face in his hands and whispered, "I honestly didn't think you could be cute. But you are. Adorable."

"I hate to rain on your cuteness parade, but the go-to for neglectful parents is to park their children in front of kids' movies, and some of my only good memories growing up were watching *The Little Mermaid, Beauty and the Beast* and *Mulan*."

That wiped the amusement off his face, and...*damn*.

I wished I'd kept my mouth shut.

"Honey," he murmured.

"Jeff loved *Robin Hood*. My favorite was *Peter Pan*."

He wrapped his hands warmly around the sides of my neck. "That tracks."

Jeff: right wrongs and be a hero.

Check.

Me: escape to a magical world that didn't have adults.

Check again.

"I feel like I've bummed you out, and I'm sorry," I mumbled.

"Jessie, sweetheart, don't be. The reason why you dig Disney sucks, but that's part of why Walt built what he did. So all kids, no matter what kind of lives they had, could have some joy. And you needing to turn to that to find joy doesn't make it any less adorable you still dig it enough to get your Disney on."

I said nothing, but what he said made me calm down.

Though, I could tell I wouldn't like what came next when the teasing light hit his black eyes.

"Do you have ears?"

I looked over his shoulder.

"Fucking hell." His words were vibrating with amusement again. "What kind?"

I crossed my arms on my chest and muttered, "Not telling."

He stroked my jaw with his thumbs, urging, "Jessie."

Ugh.

I looked at him. "Ursula, Maleficent, and I bought some Tinkerbell ones off Etsy. Okay? Happy?"

He sounded like he was choking when he asked, "Tinkerbell?"

It was verbal when I grunted, "Ugh!"

I pushed him again, but he didn't sway this time.

Nope.

Not an inch.

He kissed me again.

So obviously, I got over my tiff real quick.

When he lifted his head, he swept his thumb along my lower lip and whispered, "That's why Paris came to mind."

He was correct.

I'd done Disneyland. I'd done Disneyworld, Animal Kingdom and Epcot.

I had not done Euro Disney.

"Bucket list," I whispered back.

His eyes warmed so much, the look he was giving me was downright tender.

I was trying to cope with the beauty of that when he gave me more beauty and brushed his lips against mine.

After that, he moved away and pulled me off the counter to set me on my feet.

"Grab a seat, babe. I'll get you set up then go take a shower."

I slid onto the stool he vacated and saw he'd been reading the paper.

An actual newspaper.

"You read an actual newspaper?" I asked, looking to him at his Nespresso machine.

"Only the Sunday edition. It's a tradition."

My gaze wandered back to the paper.

I knew there was more to it, but I'd just survived confessing my Disney side. I wasn't sure I could take him sharing the only time he spent with his ex was when they shared the Sunday paper (or something).

"Being in the FBI is no joke."

I focused on him. He'd moved to the island and was leaning into his forearms across from me.

"Working for Mace was no joke either," he continued. "The same with my current position. And I *do* workout. I hike. I like to be outside. I have a housecleaner, but I take care of my own yard. I'm a busy guy. I learned early in my FBI days that whatever shit I'd face on the job that I couldn't work out when I trained my body, I could let go if I made Sunday mornings with coffee, a bagel and the paper sacrosanct. I could catch up on the news. Read the comics. Check out the sports section. Do my best with the crossword. And just be."

"That's pretty cool," I said.

He pushed up and gestured to the paper. "Help yourself. I got my fix."

"Thanks," I replied.

He did my coffee, spread the perfect amount of shmear on my bagel, and kissed the side of my head before he muttered, "I won't be long."

I lifted my cup at him as I turned the page on the *New York Times*.

Yeah, he got *The Times*.

Even his Sunday paper was classy.

I heard the shower go on from afar, right before I heard a vibrating noise coming from my cross body that was sitting on the island not far from me.

Getting a text was good. It took my mind off Eric in the shower.

Eric, naked and wet in the shower.

Eric, naked, wet, and in the shower just down a long-ass hall from me.

I might not exercise, but I bet I could sprint down that hall. I might be winded at the end of it, but I had a feeling once I got there Eric would be up for doing all the work.

Pushing these lovely thoughts aside (with no small amount of difficulty), I set my mug down, reached for my bag, pulled my phone out, engaged the screen, and stared in shock at the number of texts I had.

Three from Luna. Two from Raye. Two from Harlow.

And five from Katelyn as well as a voicemail from her.

I didn't know where to begin, since I was freaking out about what all this could be because it had to be about Jeff.

I started with the voicemail.

Katelyn said, "Hey, Jess. Joshua said you came by yesterday asking about Jeff and I *cannot believe* he didn't tell you what's going on. First, Jeff's okay. Second, we got him back on his meds. The rest, it's too much for a voicemail. *Call me.*"

I then went to her text string and saw the following:

First: *Joshua is in sooooo muuuuuch trouble!*

Second: *Jeff's fine. He's been in touch. We've seen him. We got him back on track.*

Third: *I still cannot believe my husband didn't tell you your brother is okay.*

Fourth: *There's more you need to know.*

Fifth: *Screw it, I'm calling you.*

I then went to Luna's text string.

First: *How'd the date go?*

Second: *OMG, bitch! Arthur emailed.*

Third: *Call me!!!!!*

I hit up Harlow and Raye's texts, and they both started with asking about the date, and ended with demanding I call Luna.

I called Luna.

She answered with, "Oh my God. Thank fuck. Your car's not in its spot, even so, I've gone to hammer on your door five times. Are you still at Eric's?"

"Yes. What did Arthur say?"

"Wow. You're still at Eric's?"

I loved her, but...

"Yes! Luna, tell me what Arthur said."

She shook off her nosiness and stated, "We need a confab. Like... immediately."

"Just tell me what he said."

"Honestly, Jess, you need to come home. This needs to be face-to-face."

It felt like my throat closed so I had to shove out, "I'll be home in a few."

"Come to mine. See you then."

We hung up, and I raced down the hall, into Eric's room and then his bathroom.

It hadn't occurred to me I should give him a head's up I was coming in. At that juncture, nothing was occurring to me, except getting home and hearing what Arthur had to say then connecting with Katelyn.

But a lot occurred to me when I saw Eric in nothing but a dark gray towel, leaning over his sink, shaving.

His eyes came to me.

My eyes went to his chest.

Holy, mother of—

"Jessie, what is it?" he asked.

I tore my eyes from his ridiculously gorgeous, perfectly hairy chest and said, "First, remember when I told you over pizza last night that I thought one of Jeff's friends knew something about Jeff?"

Some shave cream still on his face (hot), he straightened to me and nodded.

"Well, Joshua's wife called and texted. I was right. Jeff's been in touch. And whatever else they have to tell me, she said was too much for voicemail, so I have to call."

"Did you call?"

I was swaying side to side on my feet, anxious on the whole, mostly anxious to get to Luna.

"No, because Luna left a text saying Arthur had been in contact, and so I called her, and she said whatever Arthur had to say I had to hear face to face."

"Arthur?"

"He's our Charlie."

"Charlie?"

I was losing it, so my voice pitched high when I explained, "As in…Angels."

"Right," he murmured.

"I've gotta go."

"Hang tight, I'm driving you."

"Eric—"

He moved to me, caught me behind my neck, pulled me to his bare chest (oh my God, why did this happen when I didn't have either the time or headspace to enjoy it?), and said, "You're in a state. You're not driving in this state. I'll be five minutes, tops. Swear. Go get your shoes on."

I nodded.

He touched his mouth to mine, swiped off the lather he left there, then let me go and went back to the sink.

I hustled down his long-ass hall to my shoes, and I was standing in them with my bag across my body when I discovered Eric didn't lie.

In less than five minutes, he was walking down the hall toward me.

His hair was wet, but curling. His face was shaved. And he had on a faded Foo Fighter tee, equally faded jeans and running shoes, and he didn't waste any time grabbing my hand and tugging me to the door to the garage.

He led me to the passenger side of his humongous, spiffy blue Tahoe and spotted me getting up.

He slammed my door, crossed the hood, angled in and hit the garage door opener.

It took some maneuvering, but he skirted my Mini as he backed out.

And we were on our way.

TEN

ONE OF THEM

To say the ride to the Oasis was tense was an understatement. And all the tension was coming from me.

There was so much of it, Eric couldn't miss it.

And he didn't.

I knew this when he grabbed my hand, squeezed it tight and held it to his thigh.

I wasn't a virgin (far from it), and I wasn't inexperienced with relationships.

I'd even had two long-term ones.

One lasted a year, then the guy moved to Michigan for a job. He'd asked me to come. But as a native Phoenician, no way in hell I was headed to cold and snow six months of the year, humidity the other six.

So that told us both how I felt about him down deep.

The other one was the biggie.

Braydon.

We were together for nearly four years and lived together for over two.

Then one day, he came home, and he'd been acting weird for a while, so I was sure he was going to propose.

And I was going to say yes.

He didn't.

He sat me down and shared that my having no ambition, other than to be a kickass mixologist, troubled him. He then confessed he'd been waiting for me to change my mind and exhibit some kind of loftier life goal. But he'd learned that wasn't going to happen, and even though he felt deeply for me, he couldn't waste any more time with a woman like me.

I'd been destroyed.

I'd loved him. Saw a future with him. Wanted to have his kids. And I didn't see his betrayal to who I was—the woman he'd spent four years with—coming.

No, I thought he was going to produce a ring.

In other words, he'd totally blindsided me.

It would take a long time for me to understand he was a snob. That his issue with me had no teeth.

I made okay money. I was very good at what I did. I loved my job and the people I worked with (and for) and brought home zero stress, which was as good as a trunk full of gold. Especially in the life I'd lived with my parents (a life Braydon knew all about, he'd even met them), and then after Jeff started having symptoms, and got diagnosed, where every day was stress, until I struck out on my own and finally found SC.

But I'd still been heartbroken at Braydon's personality betrayal.

Now, I could see how huge a bullet I'd dodged.

Braydon could hold hands, sure.

But if he was in this situation, he'd be urging me to calm down or telling me I was overreacting.

Wait.

No.

He wouldn't rush to shave and dress so I didn't drive when I was fretting and my mind was messed up.

He'd say, "Let me know how it goes," and turn on the NFL pregame.

On these thoughts, I tightened my fingers around Eric's and said, "Thank you for driving me."

His response was to lift my hand and touch his lips to my fingers.

Totally dodged a bullet.

He swung into the Oasis lot and parked in my spot.

We hit the courtyard to see my fellow tenants Patsy, Shanti, Bill and Zach putting up holiday decorations.

Shanti, by the by, was a new addition to The Surf Club. When Tito started sniffing around that he needed extra help during the final shift, Raye recruited her. She worked the evenings. She was around the age of my posse, and I'd been meaning to connect with her to get to know her better, because, from what I already knew, she was the shit.

"Heya, Jess!" Patsy called.

Shanti had straightened from organizing fake evergreen boughs, and she was staring at Eric.

Zach was organizing red bows at the outdoor table while his partner, Bill, was in a corner of the courtyard arranging massive Christmas baubles that came up to his waist that were red and green plaid.

They'd also stopped doing what they were doing and were staring at Eric.

It was rude, but I didn't stop to introduce them to Eric.

And it told you where my head was at that I also didn't stop and ask where the hell they stored all that shit. We all had small storage units that came with our apartments. But no way in hell those baubles would fit in one, much less that humongous pile of boughs.

We were again holding hands, and I was tugging Eric toward the stairs to Luna's place, when I called back, "Hey, guys."

We made it to Luna's door, and I only got one knock in, my hand raised to keep doing it, when the door was pulled open by Harlow.

"Oh my God!" she cried. "Get in here!"

She then tugged my free hand, and I was in there.

Since Eric was attached to me, he was in too.

"Oh, uh...hey there, Eric," she greeted timidly.

"Hey, Harlow," he replied.

Luna's pad was a study of Urban Outfitters with CB2 and West Elm thrown in. She had much the same UO design aesthetic as Raye, but Raye's coordinating stores were Anthropologie and Z Gallerie.

And now, shoved into her pad were Luna, Harlow, Raye, along with Cap, and oddly, Knox (Cap and Knox's inclusion didn't give me warm fuzzies), me and Eric.

It was a lot of people for not a lot of space.

More, there was Jacques, Luna's French bulldog, who usually adored me.

But he was sitting on Cap's lap when we arrived, and he jumped off and made a bee-line not to me, but to Eric.

I watched Eric pick him up, and I watched Eric scratch his ears as Jacques bathed Eric's freshly shaved jaw with his tongue.

Now I was jealous of a dog.

"Sit down." Luna took me out of my covetous thoughts by shoving me in a deco-inspired, russet velvet tufted swivel chair.

"She didn't finish her coffee," Eric murmured to Luna, but his gaze was shifting from Knox to Cap.

Oh yeah.

He didn't have warm fuzzies either.

Though, a weak one fluttered in me that he noticed I didn't finish my coffee.

"Got it," Raye jumped up.

"You guys are freaking me out," I informed them.

"We got confirmation on this intel too," Cap told Eric.

"What intel?" Eric asked.

"Yeah, what intel?" I demanded.

"Hurry up with that coffee," Luna ordered.

"Coming, coming," Raye called from the kitchen.

"Just tell me!" I almost shouted.

Cap sat in Luna's mod curve, yellow couch at the end closest to me. He angled his body my way and leaned his elbows into his knees.

With his posture, still no warm fuzzies.

"Okay, Jess, there's some shit going down in a few of the homeless camps."

Oh God.

Oh no.

"What kind of shit?"

"People going missing," Cap said.

Oh God!

Oh no!

"I..." I didn't even know what to ask.

"And they're not going into shelters or other facilities. They're just...disappearing," Cap went on.

Raye shoved a mug of coffee at me. I took it and looked up at her.

"Trafficking again?" I asked.

She shook her head. "We don't know."

Cap kept at it. "As you know, the people in those camps aren't big on sharing with outsiders."

I nodded.

"Even so, they have a manner of taking care of their own."

I nodded again.

"And if there was an issue, they'd share it." There was a meaningful pause. "With one of their own."

I had a feeling I knew where this was going.

"Jeff," I whispered.

"No. A guy that goes by the street name Mountain," Cap told me.

I was confused. "Who?"

"We've heard about this guy a lot," Knox put in at this juncture. "People who don't get scared of shit, they get petrified of this guy."

"Is he like, big as a mountain or something?" I asked.

"We don't know that either. None of our team has ever seen him. The stories about him make him out to be larger than life," Knox said.

"What we do know is that he doesn't hesitate to take care of business, even if he has to get dirty doing it."

"What kind of business?" I pushed.

"The kind of business where, he gets wind someone is trolling homeless camps and snatching humans for whatever reason, he rallies his crew, they patrol the camps and deal with these fuckers if they run across them," Knox shared.

Oh, Jeff.

What are you doing?

"Your brother," Cap brought my attention to him, "we believe, is a member of his crew."

"Why do you believe that?" I asked in a small, terrified voice, even though I knew he was because the General told me.

"Because, we've just learned, they refer to themselves as Shadow Soldiers," Cap said.

I closed my eyes and slouched in the chair.

I opened them when I felt a strong hand wrap around the back of my neck and saw Eric had seated his ass on the arm of my chair, therefore it was his hand there.

Jacques remembered my existence at this juncture and jumped into my lap.

Eric made to grab him, but I cuddled him to me because I needed some doggie love. Nothing in life was certain, but in that moment, my need for doggie love was.

I got a jaw bath, and, fortified, I looked to Cap.

"What else do these Shadow Soldiers do?" I asked.

"Clear dealers from doing their business around schools. After the shit you women dealt with a couple of months ago, they started offering presence on patches where sex workers do their business." Cap took a big breath, which spoke volumes even before he laid it on me. "And we believe they go undercover in criminal organizations so they can anonymously pass information to the police."

I lost Eric's hand when I stood and snapped, "Oh my God!"

Jacques barked in solidarity.

"Your brother is young, fit," Knox stated. "We think Mountain saw him sleeping rough, noted his potential, helped him get his shit together, and folded him into his operation."

I put my coffee down on Luna's coffee table and started pacing, taking Jacques along for the ride, something he enjoyed if his happy panting was anything to go by.

I looked among the women. "We need to find this Mountain guy."

Eric was suddenly in my space.

Jacques made a lunge for him and Eric caught him easily, tucked him under his arm and spoke to me.

"Honey, look at me."

I tipped my gaze from pup to him.

"I didn't know Jeff was involved with Mountain. Now that I do, I gotta ask you to let us take this from here," Eric requested.

Yep.

You guessed it.

Now even *less* warm fuzzies, and when there were none to begin with, the negative ratio of warm fuzzies was a sensation I never wanted to feel again.

"Why?" I asked.

"Because this guy is serious," Eric answered. "And his crew is serious."

He drew breath into his nose, and I braced.

"This is blood pact shit, Jessie," he said carefully. "This is, you're in it until you die. They get ink. They take oaths. It's like being in a gang, or a motorcycle club. You aren't inducted unless they know you're one of them, and when you're inducted, everything you used to be is gone, and all you are is one of them."

I took this in, grabbed my mug, sat back down and sipped coffee.

Everyone stared at me.

I kept sipping coffee.

After about my fifth sip, I set the mug aside and dug my phone out of my bag.

I pulled up the number and hit go on Katelyn.

"Oh my God, I'm so glad you phoned," Katelyn said by way of greeting.

"My brother joined a gang," I replied dully.

"Wait. Did Jeff get hold of you?" she asked.

Confirmation.

"No. I'm friends with some PIs," I told her.

"Oh," was her only reply.

"Jeff isn't answering his phone," I noted.

"Jeff has a new phone," she told me.

Out with the old, in with the new, I guessed.

"Can you give me that number?" I requested.

"I can't, because I don't know it. Only Joshua has it, and he won't give it to me. He also didn't lie to you yesterday, Jess. We don't know where Jeff is. But we do know he's doing okay. I mean, this group that he's in, it's not a gang. They're good people. They look out for each other. They look out for him."

"Is he undercover in some criminal organization?"

"What? No! Or, I don't think so. Why would you ask that? Is that...is that what these people do?"

I didn't answer her question.

I said, "Please reiterate to Joshua what I asked him yesterday, and that is, to contact Jeff and tell him I need to speak to him."

"I've seen him, Jess, and I wouldn't lie. You know me. I wouldn't lie. And I honestly can say, whoever these people are, he's the best he's ever been with them. He seems bright. Clear-headed."

"Of course he is. He has a purpose."

"He does seem to have that," Katelyn mumbled.

"Please, Kat, just ask Joshua to ask Jeff to call."

"I will, Jess. But you're worrying me. You don't sound good."

Because my schizophrenic brother is being seen to by street vigilantes! Of course I don't sound good!

"I'm fine. Just still worried. I don't know these people."

"I'm overseeing his medications, if that helps. And they got him into some cognitive and behavior therapy. He does one or the other on alternating weeks."

Fabulous.

Street vigilantes with therapeutic connections.

I wondered what kind of doctors enrolled in their plans.

"It really seems to be helping," she continued.

"Right."

"I don't mean for you to take this wrong. I know you're worried. I know it was on you for a long time to look after him. But he's a grown man now, Jess. And he's found a way to take care of himself. I can tell his confidence has boosted. I wish Joshua had told you all of this yesterday so you didn't have to worry. But like I said, he's the best I've ever seen him. And I think part of it is that he doesn't have to depend on you, or anyone. Not anymore."

"Kat, you're a nurse. Having decent people around him doesn't cure his psychosis. If it did, he'd have been cured long ago."

"Jess, please know, I hear you. I understand you. And again, I beg you, don't take this the wrong way. But helicoptering your adult younger brother doesn't help manage it either."

Yes, I one hundred percent checked in with my brother frequently.

Yes, I often pleaded with him to move in with me so I'd know he was safe, but more, he'd feel that.

Yes, when he had an episode, I stopped at nothing to find him under one of his two favorite overpasses or camped by the dumpster behind that Mexican restaurant where the owner had a soft heart and gave him stuff other people didn't eat at closing time.

And clearly, Jeff thought I was over-mothering him.

So Jeff bitched to Joshua.

Joshua shared with Katelyn.

And now this.

"Right," I said shortly. "Thanks for letting me know I don't have to worry anymore. Time to plan my vacation to Euro Disney. I'll be in touch."

"Jess, don't be like that."

"Your brother was a running back for the Sun Devils and is finishing his residency," I retorted. "My brother has a new family I haven't met, a new phone number I don't have, and he's in contact with his bud, but he hasn't bothered to get in touch with me to tell me everything is hunky-dory. Don't tell me how to be."

She gave me healthcare-professional speak. "I hear you and understand your issues."

I knew she did.

I knew I was being a bitch.

But my brother was tight with some dude called Mountain and was a Shadow Soldier, maybe undercover with some bad guys, and stress was a trigger.

What happened when shit went south, and he started hearing voices?

What then?

Fuck!

"I'm sorry. I'm being a bitch," I said on a sigh. "But I do want to talk to him."

"I'll push Joshua."

"Great."

"Try not to worry, Jess," she urged.

"I will," I lied, and it wasn't a lie because I wouldn't try. It was a lie because I knew it'd be impossible, so why try? "Take care."

"I will."

I hung up.

Eric (with Jacques still in his hold) immediately crouched in front of me.

"You gonna give us this?" he asked.

He meant, was I going to let the NI&S team find my brother?

Abso-fucking-lutely.

"Yes."

His face changed.

And damn it all to hell.

Seeing that expression on it, determination and pride and tenderness and worry for me, all mixed up with his normal handsomeness, I fell in love with him on the spot.

We'd had several non-official dates, one official one, and I hadn't even fucked him yet!

He pushed up from his crouch only enough to move in and press his lips hard to mine (Jacques swiped at both of our jaws at the same time and succeeded in a double puppy kiss).

He pulled back, locked eyes with me, and asked, "Is this day gonna end at your place or mine?"

Even if I knew this meant we weren't spending the day together, the fact he was saying we'd end it together, well...

That was the best question I'd ever been asked.

He had a bigger TV.

And a bigger bed.

"Yours."

"I'll get you a remote and key."

With that, he straightened, handed Jacques to Luna, looked to Knox and Cap and ordered, "Let's roll."

In the time it took for Cap to drop a kiss on Raye's lips, they rolled.

The door closed on Knox not with a slam, but it was firm.

Men on a mission.

My chicks gathered around me.

"Are we really gonna let them have it?" Luna asked.

"Yes, and no," I answered. "We asked the wrong question of Jinx. We need to know if she's heard of this Mountain guy or the Shadow Soldiers."

"Got it," Luna said, getting up and moving away to grab her phone.

I looked between Harlow and Raye. "Either of you have memberships at Costco?"

Both of them shook their heads.

Well then.

"We have to hit Fry's. Then we have to go talk to Homer, and if we can, the General."

"I'm gonna dash back to my pad and put on tennies," Raye murmured.

She jumped up, gave me a stand-up (her), sit-down (me) hug, and she was out the door.

I needed to change clothes too.

But Harlow took her seat, which was where Cap had been sitting.

"You spent the night with Eric?" she asked.

I nodded. "We fell asleep watching movies. Or I did. We were going to spend the day together. But not now."

"So I take it, it was a good date."

"I fear his ex might be a narcissistic stalker. But overall, it was fantastic."

Her brows hit her hairline. "Narcissistic stalker?"

"It's a long story. I don't have it in me right now to explain. But Eric has it in hand, so whatever she does, it'll be okay."

"Okay. So, um, did you...*do it*?"

Do it.

Only Harlow could make me smile right now.

"No. But he's an unbelievably good kisser."

She sat back. "Wow. You guys act like you did it."

That was a strange thing to say.

"What does acting like we did it entail?" I asked, curious.

She shrugged. "I don't know. You've had, like, one official date, and you're super comfortable with each other. Like you know each other, you know, as in *know each other*. You know?"

I kinda did.

"Well, I've slept with him twice. We just didn't have sex either time," I noted.

"Maybe that's it," she said. "I mean, Raye and Cap were like you and Eric before Raye and Cap did it. But they slept together too, before they went all the way. So that makes sense."

Only Harlow would be twenty-nine years old and refer to fucking as "going all the way."

God, I loved my chick.

"They'll find him or we'll find him, Jessie," she said softly. "I'm not going to tell you not to worry. But I think you'll see him soon."

Oh, I'd see him soon.

The NI&S team solved a nineteen-year-old mystery of a kidnapped girl in about two weeks.

After Jeff being missing six months, I'd see my brother soon.

The question now was, how was I going to keep my cool when I did?

Because Katelyn was right.

Jeff was a grown-ass man, and his life decisions should be his own.

But he was also my baby brother.

And what it seemed he was doing scared the living daylights out of me.

ELEVEN

KEEP UP APPEARANCES

I'd taken a quick shower, changed, and we'd hit the storage units to get the Sportage. We swung by Fry's but took a detour on our way to the homeless camp because we got a text from Jinx, who told us to meet her at the diner.

Since the diner was maybe a five-minute drive from the encampment, and I was all in for any information I could get, not to mention, I hadn't taken bite one of my bagel and I was starved, we swung by there first.

We trooped in to see Persia, Skyla and Divinity were with Jinx.

This extra company was nothing to worry about.

Persia was sporting an electric blue wig today, and although she worked it, I preferred the pink.

They shared the same occupation as Jinx, and since our last case, we'd all grown tight.

Seats were taken and greetings were exchanged (these centered around a bunch of cheek touches and "Yo, bitches").

They already had sodas.

After we sat, the server came, and I ordered a Diet Coke and the perfect accouterment to a said beverage: a double, bacon cheeseburger with cheesy tots, and I asked her to bring my chocolate malt up the rear.

The rest of them put their orders in and the server walked away.

"Shit, bitch, how do you stay so skinny eating like that?" Persia asked.

Jeff looked like dad, though we both had Mom's healthy, thick, chestnut hair and blue eyes, and I got Mom's body, which was no tits, long legs, and lots of ass. My flat belly was impervious to what I fed it, except for the occasional overconsumption that required me to unbutton my pants. And trust me, as the unbuttoning corroborated, I'd tested it.

Nevertheless, for understandable reasons, I didn't want to answer "good genes."

"Mad luck?' I asked as answer.

Persia rolled her eyes.

"Not to dispense with the pleasantries," Luna said, then she dispensed with the pleasantries. "But Nat is a little freaked about this sitch, and we have another errand to run, so can we get down to it?"

Important note: They had street names, we had code names. I was Natalie (as in Natalie Cook, next generation *Charlie's Angels*). Harlow was Dylan (ditto next gen). And Raye and Luna were Kelly and Jill, respectively (they were named after OG Angels).

Persia looked to Jinx. Jinx looked to Skyla. Skyla looked to Divinity.

Divinity had eyes on me, a straw between her lips, and she was slurping on her drink.

"Can somebody start?" I requested.

"Okay, just to be sure, you bitches aren't gonna try to shut Mountain down or anything like that, right?" Skyla asked.

Persia snorted. "Like this crew could shut him down."

"I'd take a shot at shuttin' him down," Jinx muttered.

"Mm-hmm," Divinity hummed around her straw.

"No, we're not shutting him down," I said. "I just want to talk to my brother, and we think he's working with them."

"Ooo, is he the new one?" Skyla asked.

My blood pressure ticked up a notch.

Persia eyed me. "I see it. The hair."

"And eyes," Divinity put in around her straw. "They both got the same pretty blue eyes."

And again.

Confirmation.

I exchanged glances with my chicks.

"They got trouble," Jinx remarked. "The cops don't like Mountain and his boys showin' 'em up."

"Mm-hmm," Divinity again hummed around her straw.

"They gotta be like, more shadowy than their normal shadows," Skyla put in.

"Is there a way to get word to them?" Raye asked.

Jinx shook her head. "They be where they be, *gringa*. And you never know where that's gonna be."

"Isn't there like, an underground communication system?" Harlow inquired.

All the girls looked to Harlow, clearly trying not to laugh.

But only Jinx spoke. "She so cute."

That was a no on the underground communication system.

"What's this about trouble from the police?" Luna asked.

"Tryin' to round 'em up," Jinx told her. "Like maybe they should focus on the dealers and car thieves and gangbangers."

"Yeah, they should focus on them," Divinity said, then blew bubbles in her soda.

Oh shit.

"Like, arresting them?" I asked.

"The Soldiers mean business, you hear?" Persia asked. "I mean, there's a law to bein' on the street, but they *are* the law on the street."

"And they don't carry handcuffs," Skyla put in. "If they tell you to do something, and you don't do it, they deliver the message another way. One you got a lot of time to contemplate during your hospital stay."

I was pretty sure I was cruising to a panic attack that only a bacon double cheeseburger could contain (but barely, thus I was glad I ordered the tots), so I craned my neck to look for our server.

"He tight, Natalie," Jinx said to me, watching me closely. "Mountain, I mean. He looks out for his crew."

"I'm sure it means a lot for my brother to be a part of this kind of thing." It took a great deal out of me to say my next, instead of what I wanted to say. That I wanted Jeff out of this mess. "I just want to talk to him. See him. Make sure he's all right."

"Well, if we see him or one of the boys, we'll get that message to them," Skyla said as the server put down our drinks, but the food wasn't up yet, which would be a miracle if it was in that time, but it was still a bummer.

"I'd appreciate it," I replied, grabbing my DC.

I took a hit of it and noticed Jinx, Raye and Luna giving each other looks.

"What?" I asked into this.

"Nothin'," Jinx said.

"Really, please tell me," I replied quietly, not to mention desperately.

Jinx looked at Raye and Luna again, and when she got nods from both, she turned to me.

"Not sure you're seein' the whole picture," Jinx said. "The cops don't like the Shadows, but the bad guys don't like 'em a whole lot more."

God damn it.

I sucked anxiously on my straw.

"Does anyone know the story of this Mountain guy, or his name?" Raye asked.

"No name, but he street," Jinx told us. "To his bones."

"And that means?" I pushed.

"Never shared a burger with *el guapo*, so he hasn't told me his life story," Jinx began. "But it's known wide he grew up in a tent with his *mamá*."

"Like, homeless?" Harlow breathed.

"His whole life?" Luna added.

"Not sure about his whole life. Heard word his *mamá* ain't all there. She ain't on the street no more, though. He got big and strong, he took care of her," Jinx said on a firm nod.

"Is he known as *el guapo* as well as Mountain?" Harlow asked.

All the ladies smiled big.

"No, but he *guapo, chica. Muy guapo,*" Jinx shared.

"Good looking?" Harlow requested confirmation.

"Tom Hardy is good looking," Skyla put in. "Mountain is *guapo.*" And she put a whole lotta emphasis on *guapo.*

"Hardy do it for you?" Persia asked Skyla.

"He doesn't do it for you?" Skyla asked Persia.

"I'd give him a freebie, for certain. Did you read that letter he wrote to his dead dog?" Persia asked Skyla.

Skyla put both hands to her chest. "Ohmigod! Melt!"

That letter was sweet and all.

But…

I really needed my burger.

Raye reined it in. "Okay, let's move on to the situation with the people going missing from the homeless camps."

Jinx shook her head. "Heard nothin' about that."

Persia shook her head too. "Me either."

Skyla just shook her head.

Divinity sucked up some drink, and after she swallowed it, around her straw, she said, "That's sad, though. They got enough problems without someone cruisin' in and pickin' 'em off."

She was right about that.

"You'll keep your ear to the ground?" Luna asked.

Jinx lifted a hand and circled a finger at the table. "You pickin' up this bill?"

They'd ordered food too.

"Yes," Luna said.

"Definitely," Raye said.

"For sure," Harlow said.

"It's on me," I said.

"Then, yeah," Jinx said.

I knew the girls would keep their ears to the ground even if we didn't buy them lunch.

But everyone needed to keep up appearances.

This was their version of that.

No skin off our noses.

In the end, it was Arthur who'd pick up the tab.

We'd learned he was good at reimbursement.

I'D BEEN THERE enough times, I knew before we even stopped at the camp, shit was not right.

What I hoped was that it didn't have anything to do with the line of shiny black Denalis at the curb.

Or, more precisely, the work vehicles of the NI&S team.

We got out of the Sportage and immediately heard shouted, "Help! Help! They're kidnapping me! Help!"

Thus, we all, as a unit, reached back into the car to nab our Tasers.

And then we all, as a unit, raced into the encampment.

Last, we all, as a unit, skidded to a halt when we got to the screaming old lady who was surrounded by a semi-circle of hot guys standing with feet planted and hands on their hips.

Eric, Cap and Knox had been joined by Mace, Roam, Gabe, Liam and Brady.

The whole Phoenix crew vs. one old lady.

Overkill, but even so, it looked like the old lady, huddled on top of a milk crate, clutching a scrawny tiger cat who had to be a hundred years old, was winning.

Homer and a bevy of other men from the camp had fanned out behind the lady.

A lady I assumed was Mary.

I pushed through the guys and demanded, "What's going on here?"

Homer and all his buds looked at my Taser.

Mary pointed a bony finger at Mace and shouted, "He's trying to kidnap me!"

I turned to Mace, who actually wasn't very near Mary, and I processed the hit his extreme good looks dealt me (I had practice with this, I'd been doing it with all of them for months—as such, at that juncture, I knew not to take them all in at once, or I might not be able to function for days).

Having Mace's attention, I asked, "What's happening?"

"We've explained to her three times that we have temporary accommodation sorted for her until we can find something permanent," Mace explained.

"I'm not getting in a car with a stranger, I don't care how good looking he is," the lady declared. I turned to her, and she finished, "I know what happens after that."

She drew a line across her neck.

"Are you Mary?" I queried.

She squinted her eyes at me.

"She's ours, Mary," Homer mumbled. "This is Jessie."

Mary stopped squinting, and her mouth dropped open.

She explained her reaction. "You're a lot prettier than I thought you'd be. All the do-gooders got big butts, wear tie-dye, and don't believe in deodorant." She did a top to toe on me. "I take that back about your big butt. Still, you're pretty. And no tie-dye."

"Here we are!" I heard cried from behind us in a voice I knew.

I turned to see Luna's parents, Scott and Louise, pushing through the hot guy arc.

And shit.

Louise was wearing tie-dye.

And I wasn't that kind of sister, but there was no denying her vegetarian lifestyle didn't quite keep her ass tight.

Last, Louise was definitely a do-gooder.

"Well, hi, sugar bun," she said, kissing Luna's cheek. "Sweet pea!" she cried and bussed Harlow. "Hey there, pumpkin." And Raye got the treatment. "Aw. There you are, poppet." That was for me.

Louise had a gift with endearments, and it was the kind that kept on giving.

She turned and smiled at Mary. "You must be Mary."

Mary eyed Louise then looked at me. "See?"

Louise appeared confused and turned my way. "See what?"

Fortunately, Scott came forward and handed Mary a card. "We're here to make sure you have everything as we relocate you and settle you in."

Mary squinted at the card.

She then looked to Scott and waved it in the air. "This looks official."

"That's because it is," Scott replied.

"You're not taking me to a lab to experiment on me?" Mary asked.

God, I hoped they weren't doing that to the people who'd gone missing.

"No. We're relocating you to a long-stay hotel until a unit opens up at one of our affordable housing complexes," Scott said.

Mary did a loop with the card to indicate the entire camp. "Are you gonna take everybody?"

The posse at her back shuffled several steps away from her.

Yeah.

Some people were on the street and didn't want to be.

Some people, their home was the street.

"We've only made arrangements for you," Scott said. "But if anyone else wants us to assist, we can make a list and start the ball rolling."

No one piped up.

Mary squinted again. "Who's payin' for this hotel?"

"We have an anonymous benefactor for emergencies," Scott

semi-lied in so far as they weren't exactly anonymous, since they were all standing right there.

Mary tapped his card on her lips in thought.

Louise stared at her daughter. "Why are you carrying a gun?"

Shit.

Raye, Harlow and me quickly shoved our Tasers in our back waistbands.

"It's not a gun, it's a Taser," Luna replied.

"Why are you carrying a Taser?" Louise asked. Then went on, "Where did you even get one of those?"

Shit!

Needless to say, Scott nor Louise knew anything about the Angels. Even if they did, they were card-carrying progressive liberals (that tie-dye did double duty for Louise), and as such, they frowned on things like straws not made out of avocado pits, not taking your own bags to the grocery story, the man-spread...and Tasers.

Eric stepped forward, pulled mine out of my waistband and shoved it in his by his hip.

Oh, and he also looked mega hot doing it.

"They're ours, Louise." Now, he was totally lying. "The ladies just wanted to see them."

Raye was handing hers to Cap with an *I better get that back* look on her face. Harlow gave hers to Gabe. Luna handed hers to Knox.

It was then I noticed Knox was the only one who'd broken ranks and was standing super close to Luna.

Interesting.

He'd also been at her pad that morning.

Interesting part two.

"You don't need to come in armed with the unhoused," Louise chided Eric.

"We always come prepared," Mace said in a steely voice.

"Well, whatever," Louise mumbled, bobbling her head, rolling her eyes and still mumbling, "I mean, *really*."

"They aren't dumb," Mary decreed, then whipped out a wicked chef's knife so fast, we all jumped back a step.

Except the Hottie Squad. They all took a step forward with Liam grabbing my waist and shoving me behind him.

"Even I'm packin'," Mary continued. "Can't be too careful."

"Oh my goodness, please put that away," Louise begged.

As Mary resheathed her knife, I looked around, because somewhere through this, I'd lost track of Eric.

I saw him with Cap not too far away, their heads bent in conversation with the General.

I had a few things to ask the General myself.

"Excuse me," I murmured, but got not a step in before Brady had his hand at my chest, stopping me.

The instant I stopped, he took his hand from my chest.

"You need to stay here," he told me.

I braved the further depletion of my resources to process his dark-haired, russet-bearded, lumberjack hotness and looked at him.

"In case you didn't know this, these people trust me."

"That conversation is between a soldier and his superiors," Brady returned. "The spell is cast. You can't break the spell, or they won't get anything."

Crap!

He was right.

Whatever.

Eric would fill me in.

I turned back to the matter at hand, specifically, I looked at Homer.

"We have some things in the car. Before we start packing up Mary, can you and a couple of the guys help us bring it in?" I requested.

I got nothing but a nod, though Homer and a couple of the men followed me and my chicks to the car.

"Are they gonna see to General Grant?" Homer asked on the way.

"They're looking into programs to help him, yes," I answered.

"Good. He doesn't belong here," Homer mumbled.

This wasn't a dis.

Like I said, there were people whose home was the street, and people whose circumstances put them there.

We both knew which camp the General fell into.

Raye opened the back hatch of the Sportage, and the men moved in to grab the plastic-wrapped, cardboard bottomed cases of bottled water and bags of bath wipes, mondo bottles of generic aspirin, Slim Jims, breakfast bars and packets of dried fruit and nuts.

Homer had his arms laden with two cases of water when he looked at me.

"They won't like that team being here," he announced.

"Who won't?" I asked.

"You know," he said.

The Shadow Soldiers.

I didn't want to ask him if he knew what Jeff had been doing all along. I didn't want to put him on the spot or do anything to shake the trust he had in me, which I knew was fragile and always would be.

But it still stung that I suspected he knew who Jeff was with and what he was doing.

"Those men are my friends," I said. "They're here to help Mary and the General."

"I know, they still won't like it."

He said no more, and I could say no more, because he walked away.

My chicks didn't gather around me.

They didn't because they huddled nearby to watch, seeing as Eric was sauntering toward me.

And *man.*

Seriously.

The dude could saunter.

Considering my reserves were depleted, I was unable to process how good he looked walking my way, so I just stood there waiting for him and tipped my head back to look at him when he arrived and came in close.

It was only then I noted he seemed mildly peeved.

He explained his peevishness. "I take it you being here means you're not gonna let us find your brother."

"No. I'm totally gonna let you find my brother. Though, that doesn't mean me and the Angels aren't gonna nose around ourselves."

I wasn't sure that appeased him, however, the big breath he let out would communicate it didn't.

"Did it take all of you to come get Mary?" I asked.

"No. It took all of us to come get a lay of the land, be seen and understood we're no threat, so maybe in future, if they need anything, or we need anything, we can return."

"So you're multi-tasking to create informants?"

"In our business, you need to be known on the streets. Trusted by the people who need to trust us, and acknowledged as the threats we are by the people who don't. I mentioned before this takes years to accomplish. We're doing what we can to fast track that. But the multi-tasking part is getting Mary out of here, making inroads with the General so when the time comes to relocate him, he's on board, and if we can find out anything about Mountain and his soldiers, that's a bonus. Men who do his kind of work leave traces."

Fascinating.

"What kind of traces?" I asked.

"Tags to claim territory or notify other members of their team that someone's been here recently and checked things out. Or tech, so they can keep an eye and roll in if there's trouble."

"Tech? Like...cameras?"

"Like cameras."

Fascinating.

"Have you found any?" I queried.

"We were only here five minutes before you got here so...no. Not yet."

"Maybe I should let you carry on."

That set the peevishness on its hike, I knew, because his fabulous lips quirked.

"Maybe," he murmured.

"Just so you know, we talked with our informants and came up empty, except for the fact it seems all of them would give Mountain a freebie if he wanted. Though, if you find him, don't tell him that. It's theirs to offer. Not ours."

Now he was full-on smiling. "I'll keep it confidential."

"They also shared that the cops aren't the Shadows' biggest fans."

"We've heard that too."

Hmm.

Since there was nothing else to talk to him about, sadly, I had to let him go.

"Well, I should let you get to it."

"One sec," he said, grabbing my hand, taking me to a Denali, opening the driver's side door and reaching in.

He came out with his garage remote and a key.

As he was putting both in my hand, he whirled me, pressed me into the car, pressed himself into me, and he laid a hot, wet one on me.

I was surfacing from this (with some difficulty) when he said, "Now, you can let me go."

I narrowed my eyes at him.

"You are *such* a tease."

He grinned, ignored what I said, and stated, "I'll text when I'm on my way home."

"Right."

"It might be a long day, so we'll order something to eat when I get there."

Oh no we wouldn't.

I didn't say that.

I said, "Okay."

"Try to stay out of trouble," he ordered.

"We've depleted our leads. I have no choice."

At that, he looked relieved.

It was my turn to ignore something.

I rolled up to my toes, touched my mouth to his, and said, "Later, Turner."

I scooted out from in front of him and made sure I put a lot of sass in my sashay as I made my way back to the girls.

"Just to confirm, he watched your ass the entire way here," Luna informed me when I arrived. "Only when you stopped moving did he start back to the camp."

Mission accomplished.

"Also to confirm, that kiss was hot," Raye stated.

She didn't have to confirm that. I already knew all about that.

"We should help Scott and Louise with Mary, but after that, what next?" Harlow asked.

"We have to hit a bookstore, then a grocery store," I declared.

"Why?" Harlow inquired.

"Because Eric is spending the day finding my brother, and I'm gonna make it worth it."

"That says trashy lingerie and sex store, not bookstore and grocery store," Luna remarked.

She was right.

She was also wrong.

"I've got a point to make," I told her, but didn't elucidate, and my chicks didn't push me. They were awesome like that.

"We've got a plan. Let's hit it," Raye said. "Angels on the move."

And then the Angels were on the move.

TWELVE

PASTITSIO

I slid into full freakout mode when I heard the garage door going up.

Eric had texted fifteen minutes ago to tell me he'd be home in fifteen, but that was already way sooner than I expected him, so I wasn't done doing what I needed to get done in time for his arrival.

I did one final swipe of the counter, tossed the sponge in the sink, shoved the book I'd been using in the first drawer available, then raced across the room, threw myself over the back of his couch, crossed my legs under me and nabbed the remote.

I had just enough time to switch on the TV, but not enough time to change the channel, so it appeared I was kicked back, watching a monster truck rally, when Eric strolled in from the garage.

"Hey," I said, trying not to sound breathless.

He looked from me, to the kitchen, to the TV, back to the kitchen, returned to the TV, his brow lifted as a monster truck crunched over a triple-deep pile of cars, and he ended on me.

He then walked to me, took my hand, pulled me out of the couch and to the sink in the kitchen.

Once there, he turned me to face him and then he used his thumb to swipe at something on my cheek.

He swiped twice.

After he did that, he threaded his fingers into the right side of my hair, and I thought we were going somewhere I very much wanted to be, only for him to shake his fingers through it.

I looked down at my shoulder.

Flour dusted my tee.

I looked back at him when he turned on the faucet at the sink, grabbed a dishtowel, wet the end of it, turned off the faucet, and rubbed at some sauce on my shirt.

Okay, so maybe I didn't communicate my superpower of being a super sleuth by day, and a super bitch who could bring home the bacon (or in this case, ground beef) and fry it up in a pan by night, being able to do all this like it was sleight of hand.

Whatever.

He threw the towel by the sink and asked, "What's for dinner?"

"I whipped up some pastitsio."

"You *whipped up* some pastitsio?"

I understood the emphasis.

The recipe had about five thousand ingredients, and making the béchamel produced a level of angst in me I never wanted to feel again.

But I thought I cracked it.

Only time would tell.

"Yeah," I said breezily. "I put it in the oven when you texted. We have about an hour before we can eat. I'll make the salad closer to."

I read the look on his face and addressed it immediately.

"I'm not competing with her. And I could tell by your reaction to my assertion this morning that you don't think I'm boring. But first, you and your boys were out dealing with my brother on a Sunday, and I can't show my appreciation to all of them, but I'm damn well gonna show it to you. And second, I realized today that *I* think I'm boring. I need to shake shit up. Learn new things. Grow. And if what's baking in the oven isn't total crap after all the effort I put into it, I'm starting with cooking."

"You're a member of a group of women who have storage units full of cars and a mysterious benefactor to help you solve crimes. And you had lunch with a crew of informants today."

I shrugged. "We're only on our second case. And it doesn't seem like this one is going as well."

"Raye worked that last one for a year. And once you pulled them in, you women figured out your brother was a Shadow Soldier in less than three days. I think your skills are progressing."

Whoa.

He was right.

We did.

Go us!

"Yeah. Looks like we're getting better at this gig," I agreed.

"You own Tinkerbell Disney ears," he kept at it.

I planted a hand on my hip. "As much as I can conceive of a life that's all Disney, all the time, since I don't live in Cinderella's palace...*yet*, I'm diversifying."

"Jesus, fuck," he muttered.

I didn't understand that reaction.

Then both his hands threaded in the hair on either side of my head, he turned us to press me against the sink, and held my head steady for the onslaught of his mouth.

I held myself steady by grabbing fistfuls of his tee at his back.

He didn't end this kiss too soon this time.

Oh no.

We made out in the kitchen until his big hands were up my shirt at my back, covering a lot of territory, and I was enjoying his perusal. That said, most of my attention was on the delightful machinations of his tongue and the fact I had my hands up his tee at his back and was covering my own territory, all of it swells and ridges and heat and hardness.

Total *yum*.

Finally, he lifted his head.

I sucked in breath because I needed it.

Make no mistake, I was happy to expire from lack of oxygen when Eric's mouth was on mine. But since he gave me the opening to extend my survival, mostly so I could get a shot at another one of his kisses (and other things he might give me), I took it.

"Sucks," he muttered. "I wanna take this further. But what I wanna do to you is gonna take time, I'm hungry, and I don't want the pastitsio to burn."

I didn't want it to either. It had been touch and go about ten times while I was making it, and all that effort wasted would be a bummer.

However, my hands were still on his back, and my curiosity was seriously piqued about precisely what he wanted to do to me, so I was down to make the sacrifice.

"We need to talk anyway," he said.

That doused some cold water over me.

"About what?" I asked, though I knew.

The ever-present Jeff.

If he'd found him, he would have already told me, so I didn't reckon the news he had to share was earth-shattering.

Still, I needed to have it.

"First, I know this is just starting to happen with us, but I also think you should know I liked pulling in next to your car in my garage."

What a way to start.

I'd worried about that, wondering if I should take the liberty.

He was right. This thing with us was just beginning. Not that any guys I'd dated had garages, but if they did, I couldn't think of one of them I'd take that chance with this early in our relationship.

So I loved it that he was down with that version of intimacy.

"I'm glad," I said softly. "I worried it was too soon."

"I hope I've confirmed it's not too soon."

I shot him a smile, and even though I couldn't see it, I knew it was dazzling.

Eric smiled back. His was a different kind of dazzling, and as such, I was dazzled.

He then asked, "Did you get wine?"

I did.

Though I also discovered he had a wine fridge for white and sparkling, and a hefty stock of red in the pantry situated off his kitchen, which looked more like a display alcove offering the most exclusive wares in a fine food grocery store.

That wasn't the only thing I discovered.

In retrospect, one could say I should have started cooking earlier, but my curiosity got the better of me, and without Eric taking my attention, I gave myself a leisurely tour of his house (but not a gross one, as in intrusive, like I didn't rifle through his drawers and medicine cabinets or anything).

I found his long hall was taken up by two rather large guest rooms, both completely kitted out (and no wonder Sadie and Hector stayed with him, they were pimp), a full bath, which was damned sweet, and another bedroom he'd converted into a workout room, and that was sweet too (or, for people who did that sort of thing I knew it would be).

I also discovered his book collection was almost completely thrillers. And his framed pictures shared he did indeed like to hike, as well as do shit on boats in lakes and on the ocean. During time spent doing the latter, he'd caught an amazing shot of a whale breaching the surface of a clear blue sea.

Last, on the other side of the garage—and you could only get to it through a door in the garage— I happened onto his man cave.

It had two recliners I was pretty sure he bought when he was twenty-one, a TV that was so big, I didn't know they made them that big, and a wall of DVDs that explained why he was so good at picking movies. Across the back wall there was a small kitchenette-type area with a beverage fridge, a microwave, a sink, and the pièce de résistance, a countertop-size, professional kettle-pop popcorn machine. His cave also had a complicated stereo system with turntable, which was what he used to enjoy his CDs and vinyl that filled the other wall. This, and the TV, were hooked up to a seriously boss surround sound system.

No, there wasn't a game console in sight, or hidden anywhere (I checked).

And yes, you guessed it.

All of this made me like him even more.

"Or do you want me to pull a bottle?" he finished on the topic of wine.

"I got wine," I said.

He slid his hands out of my shirt, which woefully meant I had to do the same.

He went to the glasses.

I went to the pantry to get the wine.

He took it from me when I got back and started on the cork.

"So, what did you learn today?" I asked.

"They got tech. It's impressive. We didn't touch it, but we did leave a message to get in touch."

"How did you do that?"

"We wrote 'get in touch' and our office number on a piece of paper and held it up to the camera."

This was disappointing. I was hoping there was some kind of commando code or street sign language they used.

"Is that it?" I pressed.

"That and a confirmation of what we already knew. Pretty much anyone on the street would face torture before they'd give up Mountain or any Shadow Soldier."

"Surely that can't be true," I said quietly, even though the girls at the diner gave much the same impression.

"It's probably not, but Mountain is smart enough to steer clear of any weak links."

I would think this Mountain was pretty awesome, if he hadn't involved my brother in his operations.

Right, moving on to another lead.

"Did the General give you anything?"

Eric shook his head. "Except, in the short time since we saw him, he seems to be spiraling. He kept asking us who his target is, couldn't concentrate on anything else, and any time we tried to bring him into the present, his confusion was extreme, so we had to quit trying."

God.

The General.

"Damn," I whispered.

"Yeah," he agreed. "Mary's settled, and even though veterans' affairs aren't Scott and Louise's expertise, they have connections. So they've made it their mission to get him someplace where he can get the help he needs."

"That's good," I mumbled.

"Yeah," he repeated.

"So in the end, we got nothing," I remarked.

Eric handed me a filled wineglass. "Not nothing, honey. If your brother loves you half as much as you love him, he now knows from a variety of sources you're keen to talk to him. The ball is in his court, and I figure he'll run with it. In the meantime, we'll keep looking."

"Thanks," I mumbled before taking a sip.

"One more thing I gotta update you on, and one thing, with your car in my garage and your pastitsio in my oven, we're in a place now that you need to know."

Oh boy.

Although I was all the way down to be in that place with him, neither of these sounded like things I wanted to discuss.

But better to get them out of the way so we could eat, then he could do the things he wanted to do to me.

Therefore, I asked, "What are those?"

"Savannah texted seven times today."

Brilliant.

I shot him a scrunchy face.

"My thoughts exactly," he said when he took it in. "I didn't reply, and after number seven, I blocked her."

"So there could be twelve."

He shook his head. "It doesn't matter. We checked. She was on her flight. She's in LA now. And with her blocked, there's not much she can do to get to me."

I nodded because this was true.

Though it was interesting to know their resources extended to being able to check if someone was on a flight.

I filed that in my *To Discuss with Turner Later* folder, and was mentally photocopying it to add to my *Ask Arthur if He Can Do This Too* file, when he kept speaking.

"I understand what happened, Jess," he stated.

"Sorry?"

"The intensity of how we got together. The way she seemed totally into me. It's taken me a while to figure out I fell for it, and process how I felt because I did. And I still believe there are a lot of good things about Savannah, particularly her talent and ambition. It isn't easy to make a go of it in her business. And she didn't just make a go of it. She's a star on the LA scene, she's won awards and has been written up in magazines. And even if her behavior had an ulterior motive, we had good times. But she did everything just right in the beginning. She made me think I was the most important thing in her life. So when I wasn't, it was a blow. And I didn't realize until much later that all her behavior in the beginning was to set me up so I'd be hobbled by my feelings for her, which would allow her to get away with however she wanted to behave. Her shock that I wasn't sticking to the program was another signal to what was going on."

"Love bombing," I said.

"Yes, that," he agreed. "Then gaslighting, manipulative language and denial."

"I obviously don't know her, but she kinda seems like she thinks the world revolves around her."

"That's what narcissists do."

So, he knew she was a narcissist too.

I said nothing.

"Jessie," he said softly. "I don't want every conversation we have to include her, but I do want you to know I understand how she's operating. It isn't lost on me. So I also want you to know I'm gonna handle it."

"I didn't think you wouldn't."

"If you were me, wouldn't you want to assure me?"

I totally would.

I slid closer to him and put my hand on his chest. "I get it, Turner. I'm not worried about her."

"Good."

"And I also know you've got to process the shit happening with her."

"It doesn't have to be with you."

"I'm not in this just for your mushroom sage stuffing, baby," I said quietly.

His eyes warmed, and he came in for a brush of his lips.

I really loved it when he did that.

When he lifted away, I asked, "So what's the thing I need to know?"

He took in a breath.

I braced.

He let it out and said, "Shit gets around. Your crew and my crew are interlocking. So I want you to hear it from me before someone else tells you."

"Tells me what?"

"That my introduction to this crew was when I was undercover for the FBI. I was assigned to Stella. She wasn't doing anything illegal, but a really bad guy had targeted someone in her circle. I decided dating her was the way to get close to her. I did this. It was unexpected, but not inexplicable, I developed feelings for her while I did. But we were never intimate. She and Mace had been together before I met her, and they'd broken up. She was hung up on him, and shortly into that op, they got back together. It was a little dicey between Mace and me for a while. But years have passed. Weddings.

Kids. It's not an issue now. However, I didn't want you to hear about it and think it was."

Stella, by the by, was not only Mace's wife, and the mother of his two children, she was also the award-winning, multi-platinum lead guitar and front woman for the kickass rock band, the Blue Moon Gypsies.

Oh yeah.

And she was gorgeous.

Oh yeah to the yeah.

Although the only time I'd spent in her presence was during Raye's little sister's funeral, and she seemed lovely, Raye had spent a lot of time with her. She'd even been over to Stella and Mace's house more than once for dinner, and she confirmed the super-rock star was also super sweet.

"Okay," I replied to Eric. "Thanks for telling me."

"That's it?" he asked, his brow furrowed in confusion.

"Yeah," I answered, confused at his confusion.

"You don't have any questions?"

"Like what? Like why you'd pick dating as your cover then fall for a beautiful, mega rock star? Puh," I puffed out. "It's hardly surprising, Turner."

Delivering that, I took a sip of my wine.

He was eyeing me.

So I eyed him.

Oh man.

"Let me guess, the ex wasn't a big fan of this intel," I surmised.

"Savannah hated Stella."

"Mm..."

"No more about her."

"Mm!"

He grinned.

"My turn," I stated.

He took a sip of his wine, then circled it at me to lay it on him.

And lay it on him I had to, considering he admired Savannah's talent and ambition.

"Okay, so I have an ex too," I began.

I stopped talking, because I suddenly became uber fascinated with the way his long, muscled body went completely alert at this information.

I didn't know if it was possessiveness, or protectiveness at thinking Braydon was still a part of my life and being a pain, or a bit of both.

But either way, it did a number on me in the sense that I didn't care what way it was.

I just liked it.

Still.

"He's not a problem, Turner," I assured him. "He's history."

Wait.

That wasn't strictly true.

"Okay, sometimes he comes into SC to grab a coffee and check in on me, because we did adapt to friends," I admitted. "Well, he did. I think he's a dick. But for the most part, he's history."

His body being alert didn't change.

I sallied forth anyway.

"We were together for four years. Living together for two. I thought he was going to propose. He didn't. Me being a bartender wasn't his idea of the kind of wife he wanted or the mother he wanted for his kids. He wanted someone with more drive, bigger goals in life than mixing drinks. So he ended it."

Eric said nothing and didn't move.

Thus, I carried on. "The thing is, you should know that's still me. One thing my parents taught me that was good, I work to live, not the other way around. I love my job. I think you know I love the people I work with. I *do* have goals. To craft original cocktail sensations that will knock people's socks off...and keep doing that. But I don't go out with my camera expecting to one day be in a gallery. And I doubt I'll suddenly get a wild hair to go to law school or something. And you should know that about me."

I would find, even though what I just said was important to me, Eric was stuck on an earlier part.

"He still comes into The Surf Club?"

"Occasionally. But that's not a big—"

"What's occasionally?"

I had to think about this.

Then I said, "Two, three times a month, maybe. Maybe more."

"So maybe once a week?"

I shrugged. "We have good coffee, and the place is popular."

"I haven't been to Savannah's restaurant once since I moved out of the house we shared. And her place is very popular."

Oh man.

This was definitely a point to ponder.

"He's not coming because of the coffee or because it's a cool place," Eric stated. "He's coming to see you."

"I'm not really sure—"

"Babe, I got a dick. I'm looking right at you. We just finished making out. You gave me a show earlier walking away from me that fucked with my head all day, just as you intended. You've demonstrated to me repeatedly your capacity for love and your loyalty is unending. You've cried in my arms. You've let me in. So trust me. *He's coming to see you.*"

I got a happy quiver, but it wasn't about Braydon.

"My sashay fucked with your head all day?"

"Jessica," he growled.

Oo.

A growl!

And another happy quiver.

I hid it and kept focused.

"He dumped me because I was a bartender, Turner, and I thought he was on the verge of giving me a ring," I reminded him. "And you're kind of an overachiever, so, since we're doing our usual and sharing the deep honesty, I'd really like to talk to you about that and make sure me not wanting to be a neurosurgeon or something isn't gonna turn you off one day."

"I want the woman in my life to be happy. That's it. I don't care what you do to be that way, just as long as I'm a part of it. Now, back to this fuckin' guy."

We didn't go back to that fuckin' guy.

Due to his answer, and how much I liked it, I put my glass down and threw myself at him.

Eric caught me.

We went at it awhile, and it was even better because I got my hands on his tight ass, and he got his hands on my not-so-tight one.

Then my phone timer went, telling me I needed to get started on the salad.

Our mouths unmeshed, but Eric didn't let me go very far, and he did this by catching the back of my head in his hand as I angled it away.

Mm.

My guy had all the smooth moves.

"We're not done talking about that guy," he warned.

"He doesn't matter."

"When were you over?"

"I don't know for sure, but at least two years ago."

"So the wuss-ass knows he fucked it, and he's such a wuss-ass, he can't figure out how to unfuck it, and he's staying in your orbit, hoping you'll do the unfucking for him."

"He doesn't give off that vibe, Eric."

"How long did it take you to catch *my* vibe?"

Oof!

Another point to ponder.

I bit my lip.

He watched me bite my lip and whispered, "Yeah."

"I need to make salad. There's lots to chop and slice. So I need to get on that and reset the timer for the pastitsio."

There wasn't a lot to chop and slice. Just an onion and a cucumber. I didn't like tomatoes, so I got those baby ones because I knew from his food orders at SC that Eric did like them. But with the baby ones, I could eat around them without any of their slimy juice wrecking my Greek salad jam.

But I did need to reset the timer for the pastitsio.

"Not my place to say, but you should make things clear to him, Jess," Eric advised.

"It isn't your place to say?" I asked.

"Are we there?" he asked back.

Did that mean he thought we weren't, or that he just didn't know if we were?

I mean, my car was in his garage, and he liked it there.

"Did you pack a bag?" he asked.

"Yes," I answered.

"Then we're there. So it is my place to say. As such, I'd appreciate it if you made it clear to him next time he comes in, Jess."

I had warm fuzzies it was his place to say, so I smiled and said, "All righty then."

"Stop being cute, or the pastitsio is gonna burn," he warned.

I had to take a second to consider how committed I was to the perfection of the first dish I ever created.

I was leaning toward not fully committed at all when Eric spoke again.

"Babe, I'm hungry."

There was humor in those three words.

Just as I liked it.

"You wanna help with the salad?" I asked.

"Yup," he answered.

"I know how to slice and chop, so I need to practice my dressing chops. Can you slice and chop?"

"I can do that."

I nabbed my wine, socked back a gulp, and said, "Let's do this."

He just grinned at me.

I went to the fridge.

FYI: in the end, the pastitsio was perfect.

But the only reason pursuing my new hobby of cooking solidified in my mind was seeing Eric's face when he took the first bite.

So I decided I was going to make the Barefoot Contessa's mocha icebox cake next.

And by next, I meant tomorrow.

The day after that, it was going to be her fettucine with mushrooms and truffle butter.

I had no earthly clue where to score truffle butter.

But as God was my witness, it was going to happen.

THIRTEEN

WHITE SHOE POLISH

"Honey."

My hip was moving.

My eyes opened.

Barely.

"Hate to do this, your little snore is cute as fuck, but I don't wanna sleep in my clothes for the third night in a row."

I forgot I snored.

Braydon had thought it was cute too.

He said I sounded like a bunny.

I had these thoughts as I slithered out of bed and dragged my ass to my bag on Eric's couch.

Once there, I pulled out the nightie I packed. Black, of course. Made of lace. Deep plunge that even made my small tits look good. Little bows at the spaghetti straps. A bigger one at the bottom of the plunge. So short, it barely covered my ass.

I stood there and chucked my clothes.

I pulled on the nightie.

Then I shuffled to his bed, pulled the covers back, slipped in and collapsed against his awesome pillows.

I was nearly asleep again when the bed moved with Eric getting in it.

He slid an arm around my waist and pulled me into his body.

Oo.

Warm.

I nuzzled deep.

I thought I heard him mutter, "And you think I'm a tease."

But I couldn't be sure.

Because I was back to sleep.

My hip was moving.

"Honey."

I opened my eyes to dark.

Eric's shadowed face was close.

"Whas goin' on?" I mumbled.

"I have to go to work."

"Now?"

"Yes."

"Why?"

"Because it's time to go to work."

I squinted at his clock.

It told me it was 6:45.

I squinted at him. "Your commute is fifteen minutes."

"I know. That's why I need to leave for work."

I glanced around in confusion.

Oh fuck.

I looked back to him.

"Did I fall asleep in front of the TV again?"

"You're right. You need to quit TV. It's valium to you."

I wasn't sure it was the TV.

It was probably more my second helping of pastitsio (okay, full disclosure, it was my third helping).

We could just say I had to unbutton my pants again, which could be why Eric didn't instigate anything. I was in no shape for physical exertion.

"You didn't get to do all the things you wanted to do to me," I noted.

"No kidding," he replied, his voice vibrating with laughter. "And I was okay with that, until you stripped and showed me your sweet body only to put on a nightie that might get me shot since I can't get it out of my head, doing this before you fell right back to sleep."

I couldn't help it.

I was still kinda asleep.

But I smirked.

"Don't get shot today," I said.

"Don't put that nightie in the laundry."

"Oh, there's more where this comes from, big man."

He grinned, and it was so wicked and wolfish, I had a mini-orgasm.

Then he swooped in for his now-patented lip brush before he asked, "What time do I need to set the alarm?"

I snuggled down into the pillow, deciding to sleep in. "Nine."

He told his unit to wake me at nine with soft rock, came in to kiss my temple. That felt so soothing after my mini-orgasm, I closed my eyes, then Eric was gone, and I was back to sleep.

I SAT in my car in the suicide lane waiting for an opening to take the turn and staring at The Surf Club, a thrill of excitement racing through me.

This was because the front window had been defaced with white shoe polish, and it said, TODAY'S TEX SPECIAL, SUGAR COOKIE PEPPERMINT MOCHA. A hook-type thing was drawn next to it that I suspected was supposed to be a candy cane, but it looked like a weapon.

This meant Tex was back!

Tex was part of the Denver crew, much older, kind of the beloved uncle of the Rock Chicks, who proved worthy of that title by being able to take a bullet for you (this he'd done) and getting clobbered over the head while guarding you (this he'd also done) and getting kidnapped for you (and ditto with him doing this).

He'd been around a few months ago when Raye first got with Cap, coming down to check Raye out. He'd also passed his time by making coffee in our coffee cubby (don't ask, I still didn't understand why he'd horned in to do that).

He'd proved to be incredibly popular, regardless of how unrelentingly rude he was to customers.

But his coffees were *insane.*

So there was that.

He was humongous, had a long-ass beard, wild-ass hair, and a wardrobe of nothing but jeans and flannel shirts.

And I fell in love with him at first sight.

I knew he'd come back for Thanksgiving, and I'd received news since from Raye and Luna that he and his wife had decided to retire in Phoenix.

I just didn't know he was still in The Valley.

Or he'd be back at SC.

This meant, once I hit the parking lot, I hightailed it in, dumped my bag, and made a beeline for the coffee cubby (not only to say "hey" but to get a sugar cookie peppermint mocha—sometimes something was too much of a good thing, but I reckoned that creation wrought by the hands of Tex was gonna be stellar).

I made it into the main room to hear Luna say "Hey." I vaguely noticed Harlow making an approach with an empty tray, but I skidded to a halt when I saw the two women sitting at the bar.

One was Shirleen, Cap's mom.

He was adopted, which explained why he was white, and she was Black. She was also gorgeous, she had a killer wardrobe, shoe collection, and the biggest, finest Afro I'd ever seen.

The other was *Daisy*.

I'd met *Daisy* (emphasis earned by all that was *Daisy*) at Raye's little sister's funeral.

And I fell in love with her at first sight too.

I moved to her, clasped my hands in front of me, and gushed as a joke, "Oh my God, you're my favorite recording artist of all time!"

People turned to look.

Strike that.

People were already looking (such was *Daisy*), now they were staring.

She laughed a tinkly-bell laugh.

"Well, that'd be sweet, sugar, if I was who you think I am. But don't worry, it's a compliment you think I'm her."

This was a joke, and it wasn't, because she looked exactly like Dolly Parton except younger: huge rack, big, blonde hair and plethora of rhinestones on her stonewashed denim jacket with its saucy peplum, opened at the chest for maximum cleavage potential, and a thick line of more rhinestones acting as a pinstripe down the sides of her skintight, stonewashed skinny jeans.

Her platform stripper shoes had a Lucite sole and pink line of marabou feathers across the top of her foot and at her ankle.

See?

Totally love-at-first-sight worthy.

She kept her narrow ass on her stool and threw out both arms, at the end of which were fingers, at the end of which were nails sporting long, lethal, almond-shapes that were entirely crusted in pink sequins.

"Give me some love, Jessie."

I moved in for a hug. "So good to see you again, and better circumstances this time," I said in her ear.

"You too, sugar bunches of love."

Seemed Louise was going to have competition with the endearments.

I let Daisy go and turned to Shirleen.

"Heya, Shirleen."

"Hey there, child," she said softly and opened her arms too.

Oh man.

Someone told her about Jeff. I knew it just looking at her face.

Still, I'd had a hug from Shirleen before (yes, at the funeral), and learned they were very good, so I went in for another one.

I remembered correctly. They were very good.

The news on Shirleen, by the by, was that she and her husband Moses were moving to Phoenix as well.

Then again, Cap wasn't her only adopted son. Roam, another member of the team, was too, with designs to move down, something it appeared he didn't mess around in doing, seeing as I'd noticed just yesterday, he'd already been folded into the crew.

So, of course she'd want to be where her boys were.

"I'm so glad you're moving to town," I told her.

"I'm not," Daisy chimed in as I stepped out of Shirleen's embrace.

"You could move too," Shirleen stated. "You been outside. Did you feel that? Eighty-four degrees. And it's almost December."

"I ain't leavin' my castle," Daisy fired back.

Castle?

"Have Marcus move it for you," Shirleen replied.

Move a castle?

"My babies are still in school," Daisy retorted. "Annamae would never forgive me if I moved her at her age."

"How old is she?" I asked.

"Ten."

I winced. "Yeah. She'll be forming her posse by now."

"You got that right, sister," Daisy replied.

"So, are you just here to visit?" I asked.

"Nope," she turned and picked up a paper coffee cup from the bar, which meant she got it from the cubby, not from the restaurant. In other words, Tex made it, not one of the girls. She took a sip and said, "I'm here to help Shirleen with house huntin'."

"Rad," I drawled.

"We don't need help," Shirleen asserted. "My Moses isn't gonna be outside, mowing a lawn in a hundred and twenty-degree heat."

I heard that.

Though, it brought to mind that Eric liked yardwork, and he hadn't lived in town for more than a few months, so he'd only experienced the dying breaths of a Phoenix summer.

I wondered how long it'd take before he hired a yard crew.

"So we're gonna buy the condo in that high-rise Raye showed me on that website," Shirleen concluded.

"You haven't even seen it in person," Daisy said.

"I don't need to see it," Shirleen returned. "It's got a rooftop pool for me. It's got a nice gym, for Moses. And it's got valet parking, also for me."

"And it's also got seventy neighbors living right on top of each other," Daisy pointed out.

Yeah.

Unless you scored a joint like the Oasis, that could be bad.

"We're in Phoenix," Shirleen replied. "At that price range, they're all gonna be old as dirt, wadin' in the rooftop pool, waiting to die. They're not gonna throw wild parties. And they'll all be retired, so they'll be in good moods all the time. Alternately, they'll be on the Phoenix Suns, and I'll get to ride the elevators with a slew of fine-lookin' Black men. Moses won't mind. We're allowed to look. Just not touch."

This made sense.

I knew it did to Daisy too when, instead of conceding the point, she screwed up her pretty face so hard, I thought a false eyelash would pop off.

Raye sidled up, and she asked, "Did Shirleen show you pictures of her kickass high-rise condo yet?"

"We're getting there," I replied as I watched Shirleen take the hint and dig (also with perfect, lethal, almond-shaped but grape-colored nails) into her bag.

"No!" we heard boomed. "I can't take the sugar cookie part out!

You get a sugar cookie peppermint mocha, or you don't get anything, sucka!"

Oh yeah.

I loved Tex.

"Excuse me while you pull that up," I said to the ladies. "I'll be right back."

I then dashed to the coffee cubby at the front of SC to say hey to Tex.

When Otis saw me, he beamed.

He loved Tex too, mostly because Tex meant his busy load was halved, and by association, he didn't have to be nice to customers either.

Tex saw me, threw out his hand, and I squealed and jumped out of the way since he was holding a fully-loaded portafilter, and all the sloppy, wet grounds flew my way, almost hitting me.

"We need a meeting!" he kept booming (all Tex could do was boom, I know it sounds strange, but it was part of his charm).

"A meeting about what?" I asked.

"I gotta lay down the rules. Two o'clock in the morning, and you're by yourself on the mean streets looking for your brother?"

Shit.

Eric had blabbed.

Or Eric had shared and Cap had blabbed.

"Tex—"

"Nope!" he bellowed. "Shut it, woman. Don't wanna hear it."

"I was okay," I told him.

"Because Turner was on your ass," he told me.

"No, I was okay before that."

"Zip it!" he hollered. "At the meeting." He then looked at one of the crowd standing before him (Otis's coffee was popular, but with this throng, it was clear I wasn't the only one who noticed the white shoe polish), and he demanded, "Now, you gonna whine at me about sugar cookie syrup, or are you gonna suck it up?"

"I'm gonna suck it up, sir," the Gen Zer, who probably had shown zero respect to any adult in his life, said to Tex.

"Damn straight you are," Tex grumbled (but his grumble was also loud).

"Can you make one of those for me?" I requested.

Tex's head came up so fast, his beard nearly flipped into his face, and he narrowed his eyes at me.

I lifted my hands and pressed them down as I backed away.

I returned to Shirleen, Daisy and Raye, and now Luna was hanging with them on the other side of the bar.

"I sure hope Tito hires him," I announced when I arrived.

No one looked at me like I was crazy I'd want a big, loud man shouting at me in my place of business.

Then again, I was among Angels and Rock Chicks, so they wouldn't.

Shirleen showed me the listing for her condo, and as I scrolled through all the pictures, I whistled.

"Dope," I said.

Shirleen jerked a thumb at me. "See?"

"We *will* see at the showin' this afternoon," Daisy replied.

"*Aaaaaaargh!*"

We all turned at the loud shout to see Byron, a regular, slip on the spent coffee grounds on the floor and fall on his ass.

Whoops.

Probably should have seen to those so Tito wouldn't face a lawsuit.

Raye and I raced to him.

"God, sorry," I said. "I forgot to wipe them up."

Byron was on his feet and dusting wet grounds off the ass of his jeans. "How did they get there?"

"Tex," Raye told him.

"Oh. Right then. Whatever," Byron said, then he walked to his regular booth at the back, across the club from Tito, and he sat back down at his laptop.

I was a little surprised at this, since we'd learned (the hard way) Tex didn't make tea, so Byron got his dirty chais from the bar.

But I guessed that was part of the magic of Tex.

Luna bent over the grounds with a dishtowel and swiped them up.

Tex came out from behind the cubby, right at me, and shoved a paper cup in my hand.

He then lumbered away without a word.

I tasted my sugar cookie peppermint mocha.

And yeah.

Tex had magic.

Sublime.

It was late in the lunch hour when it happened.

A triple threat to a great day.

Shirleen and Daisy hadn't left yet (the showing was at 3:00), which was awesome, because I wanted the shot to get to know them better, and since I spent a lot of my time behind the bar, mixing lunchtime cocktails, I could hang with them.

Tex was now with Hunter in the coffee cubby.

And I was making a Jessita Mojita (a regular mojito but with spiced rum, a dash of Cointreau, and a hint of passionfruit syrup) when part one of the triple threat strolled in.

Dream, Luna's sister.

Luna tried to avoid her sister.

Raye tried to hide she didn't like Luna's sister.

Harlow said that Luna's sister had issues we didn't understand, so we should try to have patience with Luna's sister.

I loathed Luna's sister.

She was a granola hippie mooch with a chip on her shoulder who treated Luna like garbage, didn't treat Scott or Louise much better, and the only thing she had going for her was that she adored the two kids she'd already popped out by two different guys (with another bun in the oven—yeah, by an entirely different guy).

All that was enough.

But I'd had more than my fill of parents who brought kids into the world, then thought the world owed them the favor of raising those kids for them.

Yes, at least Dream loved her kids.

But she often dumped them on Luna, and Raye, and her parents, and went off to do her own thing like she didn't take on the most important job on the planet when she pushed them out.

However, she *did*.

I hadn't seen her in a while. She'd come to the funeral too. But just prior to that, at Luna's birthday party, Cap had torn her a new asshole when Dream was being Dream and sucking all the joy out of Luna's big night, so since then, she'd made herself scarce.

Now she was back with a kid strapped to her front over a slightly protruding belly, and one to her back.

She gave Shirleen a nod as she moved toward the bar, Daisy a once-over, whereupon she wrinkled her nose before she forced a smile (they'd met at the funeral, obvs).

And then she gave them a wide berth in an obvious effort not to engage with them, heading straight to the other side of the bar where Luna was.

I was already pissed at the nose wrinkle, the wide berth only made me more so. Therefore, I quickly finished my mojitos, put them on the server station for Harlow to pick up and slunk toward Luna to step in if shit went south.

"I know I'm not supposed to bother you at work, but I was driving by," she started.

Raye got close too, and began polishing an already cleared table to a high shine.

"And I know you don't want to help me with the kids," Dream went on. "But I have an interview at a daycare center on Thursday,

Mom and Dad are working, and I was hoping you could help me out."

"I never said I didn't want to help you with the kids—" Luna began, but she stopped when Dream gave her The Hand.

And yep.

At that, I was more pissed.

"We don't need to go over it," Dream said snottily. "I just need to know if you can watch them on Thursday."

"I work Thursdays, Dream."

Dream glanced over her shoulder. "Maybe Tito..."

She let that hang, and I didn't know if she was asking if Tito would give Luna the time off, or if Tito would watch her kids for her.

She didn't clarify.

I was so intent on this, I heard, "Hey, baby," coming at me before I saw him walk up to the bar.

I knew that voice, and that "baby," and...damn.

I really needed to click into a man's vibe.

And his schedule.

Because I'd just talked about the guy last night, and it didn't occur to me a visit was imminent.

In other words, Braydon was there.

He also was gorgeous, but he wasn't anywhere near the ballpark where Eric's gorgeous resided.

"Hey, Braydon," I replied, and felt Luna's attention, Dream's, Raye's, and now Harlow had found something to do close by.

Yeah.

They'd sensed his mission.

And I totally missed the vibe.

He slid on a stool in front of me. "How's things?"

Right, except for my boyfriend who moved to Michigan (and that was easy, I just had to say, "No, I don't want to go with you"), I'd never had to let a guy down.

Either my edginess, darkness, or lack of ambition (huh) sent them packing. Or if I wasn't feeling it, I ghosted them.

How did a chick do this?

I moved to stand across from him at the bar. "Things are good, Braydon."

He smiled widely at me.

"I thought she was with Eric," Daisy whispered loudly.

"Shush!" Shirleen shushed her.

But Braydon heard them.

"Are they talking about you?" he asked.

Why was this hard?

This shouldn't be hard.

He broke my heart.

No, he put me down *while* breaking my heart.

I hadn't given him that first indication I was considering reconciliation. I'd been friendly, in the way an employee was friendly to any customer, but in no way could he construe I was pining for him.

Because I wasn't.

With that in mind, I asked, "What can I get you?"

"Are you seeing someone?" he asked.

"Sorry?"

"Are. You. *Seeing*. Someone?" he enunciated very clearly.

"Not to be rude, Bray, but that really isn't your business."

His face flushed, and he moved quickly to cover, "I'm just interested, Jess. We have a history. History like ours doesn't just die."

"It did for me," I returned.

His chin went into his neck.

"Oowee," Shirleen whispered.

"Now do you want a drink or a menu?" I inquired.

He opened his mouth, but Shirleen whispered, "*Oowee*," again with a lot more weight, which took my attention to her.

And thus, the third part of the triple threat happened when I saw Eric sauntering in all his sauntering lusciousness my way.

He came up right beside Braydon, smiling at me in all his smiling lusciousness.

"Hey, honey," he greeted.

"Hey," I greeted back.

"Mouth," he ordered.

Oh man.

I leaned all the way across the stainless-steel barback to get his brush of the lips.

He caught me by the chin before I could move away and said, "Please, fuck, tell me Lucia has pulled pork burritos on the menu today."

Braydon made a strangling noise.

Eric heard it, let me go and turned to him with concern, like he'd need to be ready to jump into action with the Heimlich maneuver.

"*Oooooweeee*," Shirleen said again.

Daisy's bell laugh sounded, but there was a tinge of nervousness to it, and I didn't get a good feeling about that.

"Braydon, Eric," I introduced. "Eric, Braydon is my ex. Braydon, Eric is my—"

"Man," Eric grunted.

Well, even with the deep honesty, my car in his garage, and all of that, I wasn't sure we were there this soon in our relationship, but at his indication we were...

Nice.

Braydon's flush turned beet red.

Eric turned to me. "Did you have a word with him?"

"What word?" Braydon choked out.

"Um, kinda," I said.

"How kinda?" Eric asked.

"White boy would have to have bricks for brains not to get her 'kinda,'" Shirleen said *sotto voce*.

That got another tinkly giggle from Daisy.

Braydon slid off his seat and moved away from Eric a step. "She made things clear."

Eric locked eyes with him. "Good."

Braydon looked at me. "I won't bother you again."

I didn't know what to say.

It was neither here nor there to me if he showed at SC again.

I decided to say nothing.

Braydon marched out.

I noted Cap was standing with Raye watching this, and I was about to tell Eric that he was out of luck with the pulled pork burritos, but the pulled chicken nachos were up for grabs, when Dream chimed in.

"I see how it goes," she said snidely. "Gross."

I felt Cap's displeasure cresting in like a killer wave, but I had other things take my attention, because, slowly, Eric turned to her.

"Are you speaking to me?" he asked.

"No," she answered.

"You're looking at me," he pointed out.

"Forget I said anything," she returned.

"Eric, I'm not sure you met her at the funeral. This is Dream, Luna's sister," I introduced.

Eric couldn't hide his surprise.

That answered that.

They didn't meet at the funeral.

Dream looked at Luna. "Forget it. I'll just miss the interview."

"I thought you were going to take kids in at your house," Luna noted.

"This place has insurance, they say I can enroll my babies for a huge discount, and they don't mind I'm knocked up," Dream replied.

"What time is the interview?" Luna asked.

"Don't worry. I won't disturb your important work with the care of my children," Dream retorted.

Luna sighed.

Cap held Raye back.

Harlow's cheeks turned an angry pink.

I spoke.

"What's your problem?"

"I'm sorry, was I talking to you?" Dream asked in return.

"You were talking to one of my best friends, coming in, asking for a favor and being a bitch doing it," I fired back.

"I don't need this," Dream muttered, making a move to leave.

"No, actually, Luna doesn't. But you don't hesitate to bring it on," I stated.

"Babe," Eric said quietly.

Yeah, I should just let it go. She wasn't worth it.

I grabbed one of today's menus and put it in front of him.

Dream remarked, "You think you can tell me off when you're the kind of woman where some man says one word and you obey?"

"Not that I need to explain myself to you," I began. "But I didn't obey. He pointed out with one word you weren't worth it. I'd forgotten that for a second. He reminded me. I was done with you. That's what partners do. They check each other and make sure the person they care about doesn't expend unneeded emotion on someone who doesn't deserve it."

Dream threw up both hands. "Why do I even come here?"

"Good question," Luna stated. "Because I would have found a way to help you out. Even if you weren't nice when you asked, you're my sister, and I want what's best for you, so I'd have figured it out. But you turned nasty and didn't even give me a chance to work it out with you. It's like you came here not wanting my help, instead just to piss all over my day."

Dream put a hand to her daughter's head at her chest. "I need a babysitter. I just don't want to ask you to do it because you get so shitty about it," Dream returned. "But I had no choice."

"How hard would it have been to even *fake* being nice when you asked, and then not put your two cents in to other shit that's going on around you when you don't even know what you're talking about?" Luna demanded.

Dream pointed at me and opened her mouth.

"Put your fuckin' hand down," Eric growled.

That growl was hot too, as ever, but this time it was also mega freaking scary.

She put her hand down but asserted, "He said 'babe,' and Jess, your take-no-shit friend, took his shit, did what he told her to do and shut up."

"Actually, I don't think Jess was right about what Eric was saying," Luna stated. "I think he said 'babe' to share that this shit is between you and me as sisters and to remind her she should butt out. And in normal circumstances, he'd be right. Except Jess is more of a sister to me than you ever were, so it's the other way around."

Ouch!

"These bitches actually *take no shit*," I heard Shirleen murmur.

"I like it," Daisy murmured back.

Dream, however, looked like she'd been slapped, and verbally she had.

"I guess I know where I stand," she said.

"I would hope so, since you put yourself there," Luna shot back.

That was definitely a score, and Dream knew it, which was why she turned on her foot and semi-waddled out.

For my part, I turned to Luna. "I'm sorry, Loon. It wasn't my place to intervene, and I made it worse."

"You know," Luna replied, "I think half her problem with me is that I have you, and Raye, and Harlow, and she doesn't have anybody, and she's jealous as fuck."

I'd say this was a good bet.

Harlow had gotten close and she asked, "What's the other half?"

"No flipping clue," Luna said.

Raye was also there. "You okay?"

"Par for the course," Luna mumbled.

It was then, Tito was there, behind the bar with Luna and me.

"You haven't had lunch, Luna," he noted.

"It's been busy," she muttered.

"Lucia has set up a chef's table in the kitchen." He held his hand out to her. "Come."

She took his hand, shot a look at all of us, and Tito led her out from behind the bar to the kitchen.

"I wasn't sure about the Santa guy," I heard Daisy whisper. "He looked like a gangster at the funeral, and he looks like a Jimmy Buffet impersonator now. But I think I like him."

"I hear that," Shirleen replied. Then she said, "Excuse me," got up and walked right into the kitchen.

"Should I go get her?" Cap asked Raye.

"Not on your life," Raye said to Cap.

Cap smiled at his woman.

I turned my attention to Eric and smiled at him.

Then I tapped the menu and asked, "What can I get for you, baby?"

Eric took a stool.

Cap took the one beside him.

Daisy scooched over.

And we heard Tex bellow from the cubby, "Can't anyone read in this town or has the sun fried your brains? It says *sugar cookie peppermint mocha* and *I...don't...deviate!*"

Which made Daisy laugh her amazing bell laugh.

But the rest of our laughs were just normal.

FOURTEEN

GENERALISSIMO HOT GUY

It was a little after 7:00, our shift was over, so Harlow and I were walking to our cars.

I had a lot on my mind.

The least of which was that, when she came on shift, I'd quizzed Shanti about the Oasis Christmas decorations.

She'd told me that Bill and Zach (our self-appointed community organizers and Oasis shared-space decorators) had asked Dreamweaver Inc. (our landlord) if they could put up holiday decorations.

Dreamweaver had answered by giving them a budget and the number to a storage unit where they could haul the stuff they bought when the holiday was over.

Yeah.

It sounded crazy, but our landlord was just that awesome.

As much as I could still marvel at how awesome our landlord was, again, that was the least of what was on my mind.

The majority was twofold.

First, that morning I hadn't done what I promised myself I would do. Jump out of bed, hit the grocery store, then go back to Eric's and make the mocha icebox cake so it had plenty of time to ferment (or whatever) by that evening, so Eric and I could eat it.

The second was, Eric had come to lunch, but I hadn't heard from him since, and before he left from lunch, we hadn't made plans for that night.

Things had been intense, and we'd been pretty up in each other's space even before I got my head out of my ass. So maybe he needed a break.

But I thought he'd been pretty taken by my nightie, my copious pastitsio consumption interrupted his plans for me (and I would be remiss not to note that Eric had three helpings too), and I'd gotten the impression that morning he was all in to get back on track with those plans, ASAFP.

Despite wanting to see him, if he needed space, I could give him space. It'd give me time to get to the grocery store to get the cake ingredients and throw that baby together.

Man, I sure was glad I owned a springform pan, even if I'd never used it.

Until now.

Eric and I could have some time apart, then I could ask him over for dinner tomorrow and manage our consumption of the cake so neither of us passed out, and then we could have wild, sweaty, awesome, delayed-gratification sex.

We could have more cake after shared orgasms.

This was my thought when I heard Harlow cry out.

My heart stopped at the sound, I whirled, and just caught her being dragged away by a shadowy figure.

I started to take off after them, but then I saw nothing because a hood was thrown over my head, one of my hands was yanked behind my back, then the other, and I heard the zip ties zip on my wrists...

And in my ear, an ultra-deep, rough man's voice said, "Be good, Angel."

Oh...

Shit.

After the guy shoved me into a car, we took off, and I realized Harlow wasn't with us (because I heard no whimpering, sobbing or my bestie calling out "Jess, are you there?"), I asked, "What did you do with my friend?"

And got the answer, "She's fine. We only want you."

Terrific.

That was when I decided to keep quiet, expend my energy in not freaking out and save as much of it as I could to handle whatever was about to befall me.

I had no idea what this was or who was behind it. It could be we missed some of the human traffickers the Angels and the Hottie Squad took down a few months ago, and the ones we missed were after payback. It could be the bad guys who were abducting people from the homeless camp somehow got a lock on me, and for some reason, targeted me.

I just knew it wasn't a random assault because he'd called me Angel.

But why only me?

Whatever it was, I had to have my head together to handle it.

My crossbody was vibrating like crazy against my hip, probably Harlow frantically calling if they did let her go, but since my hands were zip-tied behind my back, and I could feel someone was sitting beside me in the car, I could do nothing about it.

The vibrating pretty much didn't stop the entire short drive to wherever we went, so I had a feeling Harlow got in touch with somebody else, or somebodies plural, and now several of my loved ones were trying to get hold of me, probably scared out of their brains.

So, if the hood over my head and the zip ties biting into my wrists didn't piss me off enough (and, mark my words, they seriously *pissed me off*), the people I loved being freaked on my behalf did.

The car stopped, I was pulled out by my arm, and I heard the car drive away as I was marched somewhere. I knew when we went inside, even if I didn't hear a door open.

Though, I heard it close.

Shit.

I was shoved down in a chair that was surprisingly comfy and plush. It felt like an armchair.

"Lean forward," the ultra-deep, rough voice ordered.

I wasn't sure if I should do what he said, and in my hesitation, he curled his fingers around my shoulder and pressed me forward.

It wasn't violent and it didn't hurt. It was actually kind of gentle, which threw me.

Then I heard a snap, and my wrists were freed. One hand was seized, though, but only for me to hear another snap, and the tie was off. Ditto on my other wrist.

And then the hood was yanked away, my hair went flying, but the instant I oriented myself, I saw my brother sitting on the end of a coffee table right in front of me.

He looked good. Healthy. His hair was a bit longer, but he worked it. In fact, his shoulders were a bit wider too. And his forearms, that I could see since the long sleeves of his black thermal were pushed up, were all thick and wiry and veined.

And there was a tattoo I'd never seen on one of them.

Even so.

"The fuck?" I whispered.

"Could ask you the same thing, *Angel*," Jeff clipped. He then kept talking. Irately. "Have you lost your mind? Tangling with sex traffickers?"

Was he...?

Was I...?

Did he just...?

I surged to my feet, shouting, "Are you freaking *kidding me*?"

He surged to his too and got in my face.

"Calm down and sit down, Jess," he ordered.

"Oh no. That ship has sailed, baby bro." I got in *his* face. "I've been looking for you for *six months*!"

"Brother. Time," I heard murmured, and I jerked my attention to our audience.

Or, I should say, I jerked my attention up, up and then *up* to the only other person there.

He was tall, taller than Mace, and Mace was super tall (with Brady and Knox being the second tallest, both maybe an inch shorter than Mace, Roam being the third—yes, I could call out the order of their tallness, and their hotness, Eric was *numero uno* hottie (obvs), but he was in the Cap zone in tallness, in other words, around six one).

Though, this guy had bulk Mace did not have, all of it muscle, which Mace did have, just not as much of it.

He was also spectacularly good looking. Like, take your breath away. There was maybe some Latino in him; his hair was dark, his skin was olive, and his eyes were a crystalline amber that almost didn't seem real.

If I wasn't saving my nighties for Eric, I'd so totally go there.

"I take it you're Mountain," I sniped.

He grinned, big and white, and no one but me would ever know, because I was never going to breathe a word, but that grin was so good, no matter the shitty mood I was in, my clitoris tingled.

"My friends call me Javi," he shared.

So I was right about the Latino.

"I have a bone to pick with you," I declared.

Jeff stepped between us and stated, "No, you don't."

I looked to my brother. "I know you're not hiding anything from him, so you can just step aside while I have a few words with Generalissimo Hot Guy here."

Javi chuckled.

Hang on a second.

He thought I was *amusing*?

I glared at him.

"I'm fine, Jess," Jeff asserted, and my attention shifted back to him. "So you don't have to worry."

"Well, thanks so much for sharing that info after I searched high and low for you for six months, talked to the police, badgered your friends, forged a friendship with Homer, the King of the Homeless Camp, and yeah..." I saved the best for last. "I was forced to have several conversations with Mom and Dad."

He knew how much that sucked, but he didn't even flinch.

He just said, "I'm not five. I can look after myself."

Here we go.

"And you're here because I have a few things to say to you," Jeff went on.

"Lay it on me," I invited, but I wasn't done. "So you can get over it, and I can share the not-so-few things I have to say to you."

"You have to stop with the Angels business," he decreed.

"Oh yeah? I'll one up you. *You* have to stop with this Shadow Soldier business," I retorted.

Jeff shook his head. "I've been trained. I know what I'm doing. I have men around me who know what they're doing. You have none of that shit," he shot back.

"No offense," I said to Javi, then to Jeff, "but my concern remains unassuaged that some vigilante street gang trained you in their vigilante street law missions."

"No offense taken," Javi murmured, still sounding amused.

I shot him another glare.

I moved it to Jeff when he started talking.

"We know what we're doing," Jeff retorted.

"I've heard. Mad respect," I aimed that last at Javi, then I went back to Jeff. "But lest we forget, you have a certain *issue* that makes this kind of shit dangerous for you. Or, more dangerous than it already just is."

"It's managed."

Could a head actually explode?

"Managed?" I whispered. "*Managed?*" I shouted.

"Keep your voice down," Jeff hissed.

"Fuck that, fuck this, and fuck your hood and zip ties. I mean, what the hell was that?" I demanded.

"I asked Javi to do that so you'd see how vulnerable you are."

"Sorry to disappoint you, but it didn't make me feel vulnerable. It pissed me off."

"Only you could get pissed when someone kidnaps you from a parking lot," Jeff muttered.

"Jeff, let's try to focus here," I suggested impatiently.

"I am focused, Jess. I got your message." He put his hands out to his sides. "As you can see, I'm fine. Stop worrying. Stop trawling homeless camps in the middle of the fucking night. Stop hanging with hookers—"

Boy, they'd been watching us, for certain.

"Sex workers," I corrected.

"Whatever," he replied.

"Not whatever. They're my friends. And I'm older than you, and all grown up, so you can't tell me what I can and can't do."

"I'm all grown up too, Jessie, not that you ever noticed."

I snapped my mouth shut, wounded.

My brother didn't seem to realize he'd cut me.

He asked, "Can you imagine what it feels like to have everyone fucking taking care of you all the fucking time? Especially you. Your whole life, all you seemed to be about is getting in my shit. You live and breathe to take care of me like I'm still a kid, and you need to get the fuck over it."

I swayed back at the power of that blow.

"Brother," Javi said in a low, *dude, uncool* voice.

Jeff visibly reined it in.

But the damage was done.

Because, I'll remind you, I was stubborn and could hold a grudge.

And this grudge was fixing to last the rest of my days.

I looked beyond him to Javi. "Am I free to leave?"

"They're comin' for you," he replied, and to Jeff. "Means we gotta bounce, man."

"Who's coming for me?" I asked.

"The Nightingale men," Javi said. "They track your car. They also track your phone."

My phone?

"It's a good neighborhood, they'll find you in here, but you can wait on the sidewalk," Javi continued as he and Jeff made a move toward the door.

Jeff turned back, so Javi did too.

"Jess—" my brother began.

"Save it," I bit off. "I don't get it, because I don't have it, but I can empathize that your illness sucks."

"Yeah, you don't get—"

I cut him off.

"But I'll leave you with this. My life isn't about you, Jeff. It's clear your head is so far up your own ass, you don't realize that. That said, when you disappear for six months, and I'm looking under overpasses and behind dumpsters and spending money I can't afford on bottled water to earn the trust of a community of people who don't have a lot of trust left in them, it's because I love you. It's because you're my brother. It's because you were the only solid thing I had my entire fucking life, and I don't know what I'd do if I lost you. I know the man you are. I know you're smart and capable. You aren't the only one who has issues, you just have a particular one that needs managing. And yeah, I worry about that. Not about you managing it, just about you needing to cope with it. What you've been so fucking selfish you didn't see was, I have issues too. And they don't always involve you."

With that, I pushed through them and got to an open-air breezeway of an apartment complex.

I was stopped when Jeff caught my arm.

I looked at my brother's handsome face, and it almost broke me, because I loved him so much, and he'd just laid me out. Fortunately, being as insanely pissed as I was held me together.

"I just wanted to give you a break from me," he said quietly.

"I didn't need a break from you," I replied. "But I guess now I need to figure out what to do after losing you."

"You haven't lost me, Jessie," he whispered.

"Let me rephrase. Now *you* need to figure out what to do after throwing me away."

Jeff sure flinched at that.

Even Javi grunted at the weight of my blow.

I was so angry and hurt, I was beyond caring.

I yanked my arm from his hold, slid my gaze through Javi, who was sporting an open look of concern that made his male beauty exponentially more beautiful, and he had it aimed at me, and then I turned and jogged in the direction I was brought in.

I hit the sidewalk, stood there and pulled my phone out of my bag to call an Uber.

And yeah.

I had seventeen missed calls and not a small amount of texts.

I was about to hit go on a ride, then start phoning people to tell them I was okay, when a line of Denalis sped down the block and came to a dramatic halt opposite me.

The men rolled out, and they did "as a unit" a whole lot better than us Angels did (for your information, "the men" were Mace, Cap, Roam, Knox, Liam...and Eric).

The first ones formed a huddle around me.

Eric got in my space, cupped my face in both hands and dipped close to me, his eyes roaming everywhere.

"You okay?" he asked.

"So you do track my phone."

"Answer me, babe."

"I'm fine. They didn't hurt me. It was my brother. By the way, I believe Mountain's first name is Javier, since he goes by Javi."

A quick glance over my head, then back to me. "They were here?"

"Yep."

All the men but Eric took off.

I pulled out of Eric's hold, turned to look over my shoulder, and called after them, "You won't find them!"

This had no effect. They kept motoring, or, I should say, they took off so fast, I couldn't see any of them, so I turned back to Eric.

"Are you okay?" he repeated.

"Apparently, I was a pain in my brother's ass, which he decided to interpret as needing to give me a break from him. Though, he made it clear that mostly his vanishing was about me being a pain in his ass."

Eric's mouth tightened.

"I really want to go home, Turner," I stated.

He slid an arm around my shoulders, came to my side so he could tuck me into his, and murmured, "Then let's get you home."

Eric didn't take me to my Mini that was still at The Surf Club.

He took me to the Oasis.

He did the arm around my shoulders thing to the security gate, whereupon he punched the code in.

"You know the code?" I asked.

"All the men know the code," he answered.

Cars tracked. Phones tracked. Security codes disseminated.

Well, tonight proved it was good they kept an eye on us. Because if that situation had been about someone with an unhappy (for me) message to deliver, they wouldn't have had the time to alter the course of my life and mental health in delivering it before the guys got there.

We walked in, and I stopped dead at the holiday display before me.

There were illuminated, fake evergreen boughs looped the entirety of the upper walkway. At the top of each loop at each post on the railing, there was a big, red velvet bow.

The annual flowers in the planters had been switched out to poinsettias or baby pine trees, and those had Christmas lights too.

The green and red plaid, giganto baubles in one corner of the courtyard were mimicked by giganto red-and-green striped baubles in the other. These were illuminated from the inside.

There were elegant, life-sized white deer positioned here and there, and they had lights in their antlers.

There were lit wreathes with red bows attached to all the standing light fixtures.

In the big trees that shaded the place, there was an abundance of Christmas lights, and even if the trees were tall, the lights were *everywhere*, trunk to tip.

There was also a massive Christmas tree—seriously, it had to be at least sixteen feet tall—festooned with white lights, red baubles and red berries with fat, cascading red ribbons waving down from the huge-ass bow at top, towering over the north side of the pool.

And down one side, there was a gold Menorah that had to be at least three feet high, five feet wide, with none of the candles lit because Hanukkah hadn't started yet.

It was a holiday wonderland, Phoenician style.

Man, Bill and Zach could *work it*.

I saw the renos on the pool had begun again after the Thanksgiving break, and the pebble finish had been sprayed that day. So once that cured, and the cool deck was installed, we'd have our pool back.

Last, at one of our new, fancy outdoor tables sat Luna, Raye, Harlow, Martha, Alexis, Daisy, Shirleen, and gracing us with her megastar presence was Stella Gunn.

Oh, and Jacob was pacing angrily.

They all stood at our approach, and we barely made it to them before Jacob clipped, "What are you women into?"

But Harlow hit me like a rocket.

I went back on a foot, but luckily didn't go down before I wrapped my arms around her.

"Are you okay?" I asked.

She leaned back but didn't let me go. "Are you?"

No.

I was not.

My brother was a dick.

"It was my brother. He was trying to teach me a lesson in vulnerability."

She screwed up her face in anger, and totally. Jinx was right.

She cute.

Shirleen got to me, and with a hand at my back, she led me to the table, murmuring, "Come sit down, child. Linda's bringing hot chocolate."

"I'll go tell her to make an extra couple mugs," Alexis said, and dashed toward Linda's door.

I sat down, assuring them all, "I'm fine." I looked among my girls. "And the bitches are right. Mountain is *muy guapo*."

"Oh my God, you met him?" Luna asked.

"Yep," I answered, my attention having been taken by Eric, who'd left me and was having a seemingly intense conversation with Stella by the plaid Christmas baubles.

"Who's Mountain?" Daisy asked.

"He's a street vigilante," I told her.

"Ah," she said, entirely unaffected by this information.

"Jesus Christ," Jacob bit off, then tramped to where Eric was with Stella, probably to ask what Eric was doing about my insane life, rather than asking me, seeing as it was my insane life.

Men.

"I'm thinking there's something we don't know about you girls," Martha stated, her eyes pinging indignantly between all of us.

No one said anything.

Martha harrumphed, but surprisingly didn't push it.

Guess there were advantages to being abducted.

My eyes strayed back to Eric and Stella.

Jacob was striding toward Linda's apartment, but Eric and Stella were still at it.

"Don't you worry, sugar bunches of oats," Daisy said, reaching out to pat my hand.

"Worry about what?" I asked.

She jerked her blonde coif toward Eric and Stella, it trembled seismically, and she said, "Ain't nothin' but a thing."

"What are you talking about?" Luna asked Daisy.

Raye had her lips sealed tight, which meant Cap had told her about Eric and Stella's history.

"Eric and Stella used to date," I announced.

Harlow gasped.

Luna shot wide eyes to me.

"Your man used to date a rock star?" Martha asked.

I decided against telling them the undercover part and just shrugged.

Daisy waved a bedazzled-tipped hand in front of her enormous bosoms. "It was *eons* ago." She leaned into the table. "Stella's havin' flashbacks. The least fun part of the Rock Chick ride was getting kidnapped." She paused to consider. "Also nearly crashing over a bridge onto a highway during a high-speed chase. That wasn't a barrel of laughs."

Martha stared at her and did the sign of the cross, and as far as I knew, she wasn't Catholic.

Linda, with Alexis and Jacob in tow, showed with a tray of hot chocolate.

Linda was a retired schoolteacher, the oldest Oasis resident, both in her time spent renting there and her age, and she was a sweetheart.

I adored Linda, and not just because she spooned a mound of marshmallow fluff on the top of her hot chocolate.

But in that moment, I etched that particular trait high on my list of why I adored her.

"Oh, Jessie, I'm glad you're okay. Getting snatched in a parking lot. What on earth?" Linda asked as she put her tray down.

I reached for a mug and was about to say something to make her feel better when the security gate slammed back on the fence, making a loud bang.

We all turned to see Tex plodding toward us, a man on a mission.

"I...you...I..." he blathered in a boom after he reached the table. "*We haven't even had our meeting yet!*"

"Tex, I'm okay."

He glowered at me, then leaned into me, reached beyond me, snatched up a mug, and I watched as he did a slurp (the fluff) then dropped his head back, downing the hot drink in one.

He slammed the mug down, pounded a fist on his chest, and declared, "I'm unprepared. This trip, I forgot to bring my grenades with me to Phoenix."

At this, Jacob took a mug, handed it to Alexis, took another one, then grabbed Alexis's hand and dragged her to his apartment.

On the way, she waved her mug at us and called, "'Night all! Glad you're okay, Jessie!"

Jacob slammed the door behind them, and I heard the locks go.

"He's a Hot Bunch boy without bein' a Hot Bunch boy, that one is," Daisy decreed.

Eric and Stella joined us.

"Glad to see you're okay, Jess," Stella said.

"Thanks, Stella," I replied, shot her a smile and then took a sip of my cocoa.

"Were you kidnapped?" Luna asked Stella.

"I never thought I'd say this to a living soul, but you girls really need to read those books," Stella replied.

I was thinking I should.

I would look at it as a form of training.

"You all good?" Eric asked the table at large.

"With what?" Luna asked back.

"With knowing Jess is all right," Eric explained.

"I'm good," Luna said.

"Me too," Raye put in.

"It wasn't fun, but it's over"—Harlow lifted her mug—"and we have cocoa."

"You got cocoa, and you're downright *loco*," Martha decreed.

Shirleen looked to Daisy. "I forgot how crazy this all seems in the beginning."

"I'm havin' a flashback too, since I was introduced to it when my Marcus kidnapped Jet," Daisy replied.

"I forgot about that," Shirleen murmured in her mug.

Eric took my hand and pulled me out of my chair.

He then pulled me toward the stairs.

I waved my mug behind me and called, "I'll bring this back clean, Linda."

"I'm not worried, hon," Linda called back.

"'Night, everybody!" I kept calling when we got to the stairs.

"'Night!" everybody called back.

Eric dragged me to my door while I took in the glow of the lights and the holiday setting from above.

And seriously.

Zach and Bill had vision.

"Key," Eric grunted.

He let my hand go so I could pull out my key.

He took it from me to open the door while I said, "I need to go get my car, Turner."

He looked at me, looked at my keychain, pulled off the fob, went to the railing and whistled.

Tex tipped his head toward us and bellowed, "Yo!"

Eric tossed the fob down, Tex caught it, and Eric yelled, "Someone needs to get Jess's car."

Tex raised a hand to his forehead in a salute.

I took that as Tex's version of *Gotcha*!

Eric pulled me into my apartment.

And uh-oh.

He also slammed the door.

FIFTEEN

ICEBOX CAKE

I watched as Eric prowled around my tiny pad turning on lamps.

When he was done and focused on me, I asked, "Are you mad?"

He didn't answer verbally.

He stalked to me, took my hand, lifted it, then rubbed his thumb lightly along the red marks there.

Okay, he was mad.

Truth, I'd been ignoring how my wrists stung from the zip ties, though, the good news was, none of the skin was broken.

"Yeah, my brother is a dick," I agreed with his nonverbal assertion.

"He couldn't approach you in the parking lot and say 'hey'?"

I'd never heard Eric's voice rumble like that. It was low. It was abrasive.

And it was hot.

"He was teaching me a lesson about my vulnerability as an Angel," I informed him.

"He couldn't let you be who you are, do what you need to do, and just look after your ass like my crew does?"

Right.

I parked my car in his garage. He proclaimed himself my "man." He rolled out to rescue me.

But we were still only days in.

Even so.

I didn't know the distinction. I already knew I was in love with him, in that first blush, he's gorgeous, he's a great kisser, he won't let me reach too far for my wine, he'll go out and spend his Sunday looking for my selfish, ungrateful brother, kind of way.

But I was still actively falling for this guy.

I wasn't sure how that worked. Maybe, if Eric and I went the distance, I'd spend a lifetime constantly falling deeper and deeper for him.

And in that moment, that sounded like a good life plan to me.

"He thinks I'm over-protective," I shared.

A muscle jumped up his cheek.

Mm.

That was hot too.

"I can't say I enjoyed tonight's activities," I told him. "But at least I know he's okay, I got confirmation Mountain is impressive, I know where I stand." I lifted my mug. "And I got cocoa."

"Where do you stand?"

"Far out of my brother's space."

"Jess," he growled.

FYI: I was falling deeper and deeper in love with his growl too.

Even so, I sighed.

"On the one hand, I see how he thinks my looking after him infantilizes him. On the other, he could just tell me that, not disappear for months only to arrange for me to be kidnapped and act like a dick."

That muscle jumped again (and yes, this sitch was running rampant, because I was falling in love with that muscle jumping as well, especially since it indicated how he felt about me being jacked around, something I obviously wasn't a huge fan of, and it felt uber-freaking-nice to have someone I cared about so openly giving a shit about me).

"Tell me about Mountain," he ordered.

"He's taller than Mace, bigger than any of you, and it's all muscle, and he didn't talk much. And I'll repeat, he impressed me, and that wasn't entirely about his muscles." I thought about it and said, "There were at least two guys with him when he snatched me, one who dealt with Harlow, one who drove the car. I think Mountain sat beside me. Also, there was Jeff, obviously, who I don't think was with them, but I couldn't tell, because I was hooded."

His black eyes suddenly blazed hellfire.

Yikes!

Wrong thing to say.

To tamp down the blaze, I hurried it along, starting with a question. "Didn't Harlow say anything about them?"

"She reported she didn't even get a first look. He pulled her away, and then he was smoke. Vaporized into the shadows. She said it lasted maybe ten, fifteen seconds, and in that time, she was neutralized, he was gone, and so were you."

Okay, so maybe the Shadow Soldiers *did* know what they were doing.

At the very least, they had clean kidnappings down pat.

I returned to my report.

"I didn't see the car, or either of the other guys. Just Jeff and Javi. Though, important to remind you, somehow they know I'm an Angel. I also was involved in my convo with my brother, so I stupidly didn't take time to check out the apartment they took me to."

"That apartment is Javier Montoya's ex-girlfriend's place."

My brows rose. "Javier Montoya?"

"I didn't connect with you this afternoon because we got a lock on someone who was willing to talk. Montoya is the product of an NFL offensive lineman's affair with a woman who was not his wife. Because the man's a motherfucker, he demanded a paternity test and probably breathed a sigh of a relief when the woman and her son started dropping on and off the grid when Montoya was six, and he no longer had an address to send child support to. Since the age of six, Montoya grew up either in shelters, or unhoused. CPS tried to take him from his mother several times, not only due to their living situation, but also because she has significant mental health issues. But he always ran away from his foster homes and found her. And twice, in his teens, he sprung her from state-run facilities that were nightmares and took care of her himself. In the end, they couldn't find him, and it's probably because he hid them both so they wouldn't. Now his mother is in an expensive live-in facility with five-star amenities up in Flag courtesy of Montoya hunting down and then threatening his dad."

I'd sensed I liked that guy. Good to know I had decent instincts.

Though, his life was heartbreaking.

"And he knows you're an Angel because he knows everything that goes down on the street," Eric finished.

Ah.

I slurped some cocoa.

Eric watched, and after I swallowed, he asked, "Have you eaten?

"Harlow and I shared some of Lucia's nachos. Have you?"

"Grabbed a burger at Protein House."

He was still holding my hand, but he'd stopped talking, I stopped talking, and this went on so long, it felt weird.

"Is something else up?" I asked.

"I didn't connect with you because I was talking with an informant."

"Okay."

"Now's the time when you share why you didn't connect with me."

Oh.

"Well, first, I was working. Then I was abducted."

"Jessica," he whispered.

"I thought you wanted space," I said.

"If I want space, I'll tell you I want space. If you want space, it'd be cool you return the favor."

Hmm.

"Somewhere between gathering intel and getting a burger you could have dropped a line, Turner," I pointed out. "We were both working that whole time."

"I did drop a line. I texted you around the time you got off. That being five minutes before Harlow called Raye, who called Cap who was with me, and then we tracked your phone and went after you."

"Whoops," I muttered. "I haven't had a sec to check my texts."

"I gathered that."

"What did you text?" I asked curiously.

"Did you want to come to mine, or did you want a night on your own? Also, that we got a lock on Mountain."

"I would have gone to yours, because I had nachos, but I learned recently, as in, right about now, there's always room for leftover pastitsio. But just to say, I was going to text you when I had the chance. However, my plan was to hit the grocery store because I'm making us mocha icebox cake next. It's probably too late for that now, but even if it isn't, I'm finding a kidnapping kills the cooking mood."

That muscle jumped again.

So noted.

Don't joke about the kidnapping.

Yet.

"Is Stella okay?" I asked. "Daisy says she's having Rock Chick flashbacks."

"It's her opinion I should try to talk you out of being an Angel."

Well!

From what I knew of them, that didn't seem very Rock Chickian.

"She got shot in the beginning of her Rock Chick gig," Eric explained. "A graze, but it was deep. She and Mace were then shot at onstage. That time, they missed. And I could go on. She thinks you women are cool, but she also thinks you're nuts."

Well, again!

Eric read my affront.

"In the end, her apartment exploded, and she was holed up in a warzone that was the house where her apartment was located while she, Mace and Mace's dad were all under heavy fire. They survived that, only for Mace's dad to be picked off by the bad guy right in front of her eyes. He took that bullet for her. Which meant he died for her, and he did it in her arms."

Holy *fuck.*

"So, yeah, she thinks you women are nuts," Eric concluded.

I'd let her have that.

And I decided again I wasn't reading those books.

Because...

Cripes!

"We are nuts, just not the bad kind," I told Eric just in case he was worried.

His gaze hyper-focused on me. "You okay about your brother?"

I was not.

"Jeff has never been a dick to me. He's obviously been harboring shitty feelings for a long time. I think he's transferring. He is what he's always wanted to be now, and I don't know. I'm not in his head. I've never done anything but care. Maybe how I did that was too much for him, but we both speak the English language, so I have no clue why he couldn't just tell me to back off. But I honestly don't think it's that. I don't know how this shit got twisted up for him, and why it all landed on me, but that's not my problem."

I took another sip of cocoa while I watched the banked fire continue to burn in Eric's eyes.

Then I kept sharing.

"Did what he say hurt me? Yes. Was the abduction way over the top? Yes. Am I still worried about him? Yes. Am I going to back right the fuck off? Yes again. Something else to know about me in our deep sharing, you get to hurt me once. Then I'm done with you. I'll always love him. And I might get over it. But right now, I'm done with him."

"I sensed that about you with the unemotional kill shot you

delivered your ex. He waited two very long seconds for you to stop him from leaving, and you just stared at him. Then he left and you didn't even watch him go."

"You were right. I wasn't catching his vibe. I'm glad you pointed that out because he needs to move on."

"And the way you laid into Luna's sister."

My lips turned down. "That was wrong."

"So you know, both you and Luna were right about what I was communicating. I thought it was Luna's battle, not yours, and you needed to butt out. But also, the woman was obviously begging for a confrontation. She dresses like a hippie, but she's a drama queen. She feeds off negative attention. It's her drug of choice. You were giving her her fix, so I was also telling you to chill out. She wasn't worth it."

"Whoa," I breathed at this revelation. "She *is* a drama queen. How did I not see that? It's always about the drama with Dream."

"Shocked as shit that woman is Scott and Louise's daughter, and Luna's sister."

"Do you have a take on that?" I asked.

"On what?"

"Why she's so different from all of them? You're also right about the negative attention. Which is weird. It's not like Scott, Louise and Luna are always rays of sunshine like Harlow." I reconsidered. "Well, Louise is. But none of them are like Dream."

He shrugged. "Could be she feels left out because they're tight. But she's a grown-ass woman, so she should learn to deal with her feelings without lashing out."

"No truer words spoken."

And he had a point about Dream maybe feeling left out.

But I knew for certain Scott and Louise loved both their girls and showed it.

So I reckoned it was more about Dream being jealous of her sister.

"Going back," Eric took me out of my reverie. "You weren't

wrong calling her on her shit. It's never wrong to stand up for someone who's getting beaten down by a bully."

Aw.

I loved that he thought that.

I grinned at him.

Then I took another sip of my cocoa.

"What's this about mocha icebox cake?" he asked.

"I'm not sure it's an actual cake. It's some mocha mascarpone cream thing sandwiched with chocolate chip cookies that you chill for a long-ass time then eat."

Eric swiped my mug out of my hand and put it on the coffee table.

"Hey! I wasn't done with that," I snapped as he dragged me to the door. When we were out of it, I asked, "Where are we going?"

"To the grocery store."

I grinned again.

So...totally...and perhaps it would be constantly...*falling for this guy*.

My hip was moving.

I opened my eyes.

Eric's face was close to mine.

"Hey," I mumbled. "Headed to work?"

"Yeah."

Catching you up, we didn't do it. Apparently, getting kidnapped and having your brother be an asshole to you killed your have-wild-sweaty-sex-for-the-first-time-with-your-new-hot-guy vibe.

But that was okay.

Eric and I made the icebox cake. Then I showed him the Barefoot Contessa episode where she made it. Then, although he didn't confirm he shared this urge, we both struggled with not going and attacking the cake we made before it was fully chilled. I gave him a toothbrush head for my pad. He stripped to his boxer briefs. I took some time to recover from seeing his chest again before I put on my third sexiest nightie (I didn't want to be a bitch), and we went to bed.

And that brings us to now.

"I'll cook tonight," he said.

Dig it!

We had plans!

That said...

"No. I'm on a roll. But in your day's meanderings, if you run into truffle butter, give me a shout. I'm making mushroom, truffle fettucine."

"I think my gut needs you to stop watching Ina Garten."

Like he had a gut. I'd seen those ridges. And the hip dents.

Delicious.

And nice. My have-sex-for-the-first-time-with-your-new-hot-guy vibe was coming back.

He came in to brush his lips to mine, but when he moved away, he advised, "It was fucked up how they went about it, but the lesson to be learned is keep sharp. You women are out there. Get rid of that little bag and take your Taser with you."

Good advice.

I nodded.

He did the lip brush again, and this time murmured, "Go back to sleep."

Then he was out of my vision, and not long later, I heard the front door close, so I knew he was out of my apartment.

I was about to fall back to sleep when a thought occurred to me.

No.

An idea occurred to me.

No!

A *brilliant* idea occurred to me, so my eyes popped right open.

It was such a good one, I threw the covers back and hauled ass out of bed.

I hit the Nespresso, then I hit the toothbrush then I hit the shower.

AJ's Fine Foods was probably already open. I'd get my shopping done. Then I'd get to work. There, I'd talk to the girls and get my plan in motion.

THE WHITE SHOE polish said Tex's special that day was Gingerbread Rum Raisin.

The drawing was a gingerbread man who looked very angry, and possibly homicidal.

Gingerbread, I could do.

Rum, I could also do (very much).

Raisin, I could do in an oatmeal cookie (maybe).

So I'd skip that today.

I swung into the back door, dropped my bag (my bigger one, with Taser, something Eric returned by leaving it on my kitchen counter that morning) in my locker and announced to the room at large when I hit the main area, "Angels Confab!"

Raye, serving someone a mug of coffee, looked at me.

Harlow, taking an order, looked at me.

Luna, at the espresso machine steaming milk, looked at me.

Tito glanced at me, then he returned to and poked at the screen of his iPad.

I headed behind the bar.

Raye and Harlow joined me and Luna.

I opened my mouth.

I shut it when Tex joined us, his bulk making the space back there, which wasn't minimal, seem stifling.

"Hey, Tex," I greeted.

"Yo," he mini-boomed.

"Um..." I circled a finger among the girls. "We're having confab."

"Right," he said and didn't move.

Okay.

Tex was going to be in on our confab.

I looked to the chicks.

But Harlow spoke. "Are you okay after last night?"

"Yeah," I replied.

"Where did you and Eric go after you went in and came out of your apartment?" Luna asked.

"To the grocery store for the ingredients to an icebox cake."

The chicks stared at each other.

"Are we doin' boy-girl stuff, 'cause I'm out if we are," Tex announced.

Since he wasn't an Angel, I considered lying and telling him we were.

Then I said, "No. I had a great idea this morning to catch whoever is grabbing people from the camps."

"What's that?" Raye asked, her eyes lighting.

She started this shit and was our unofficial ringleader, so they would.

"One of us go undercover in a camp," I announced grandly.

All the women made faces, and I got that, because it wasn't a super glamorous undercover mission, but Tex leaned back and shared, "Boys already thought a' that. They're gettin' me kitted. And Duke's flyin' down. I'm goin' in tomorrow at your camp, Duke's going into another one where people have been snatched."

I blinked at him, and my blink wasn't about the fact I had no clue who this Duke person was.

Okay, bummed my bright idea was already thought of by the Hottie Squad.

But one could say Tex would definitely melt into that world a lot better than me or any of the girls.

And I'd really like to see what he'd do to someone who tried to snatch him.

Everybody gazed expectantly back at me.

I lifted my hands. "That's all I had."

"I have a thought," Harlow said timidly.

We turned to her.

She bit her lip, took a big breath into her nose and said, "Okay. So, Jess has been hitting these encampments regularly for a while now. And, I mean, before you commit a crime somewhere, you case the joint. Yeah?"

How could she still be adorable when she said shit like "case the joint?"

It was just the way of Harlow O'Neill.

"Yes," Raye encouraged her to go on.

"So, the bad guys probably keep an eye. They've probably seen Jess. They might not know what she's doing, maybe they think she's a do-gooder, like Mary did," Harlow went on.

"Yeah?" Luna prompted.

"So, two things. One, the people in the camp trust Jess, and the baddies have maybe seen her, so they won't think anything of Jess showing. So maybe she could go in, with us going with her, and ask a few questions. Even the Hottie Squad can't get them to talk, but maybe Raye could, and maybe they've seen something. Something that will give us leads," Harlow suggested.

And it was a good suggestion.

"Eric and I are having truffle fettucine tonight, but I can be in to do that tomorrow night," I said.

"Truffle fettucine?" Raye asked.

"It's all in the truffle butter," I told her like I knew what I was talking about, when I really didn't, but I suspected it was a good guess.

"That sounds awesome. I need to share that with Cap. Do you have a recipe?" Raye asked.

"Sure," I said.

"Focus," Tex grunted.

Right.

Focus.

"Maybe we should wait for a weekend," Luna remarked. "Do it

during daylight hours. When are more of them around?" she asked me.

"At night."

"Okay then, we do night," Luna stated.

"What's your other idea?" Raye asked Harlow.

"Well, it'll be boring, but a stakeout."

Oh yeah.

I liked this idea.

We could get corn nuts and corn dogs, and rounding out the theme, corn chips and salsa and drink lots of coffee to keep us awake and have concentrated girl time before we catch the bad guys in the act.

I was feeling this.

"Cap told me the Shadow Soldiers have cameras on the camp," Raye noted.

Shit.

There went my corn-snack theme stakeout.

"Cameras aren't being right there, seeing shit going down and being in a place to intervene," Luna pointed out. "We don't have to go up against these guys, but if they grab someone, we can follow them, so we know where they're taking them, and call the Hottie Squad or the cops to move in. Or at least we could get license plate numbers, so we'll have a lead."

Right on!

My corn-snack theme stakeout was still on the table.

"We'd have to find a place, like high ground," Harlow continued planning. "Where we could maybe watch the bad guys watching the camp. If something goes down, we might not be in position to follow, but if we see anything, maybe we could take pictures so we can show the Hottie Squad and the police, and of course, get license plate numbers. We'll need to ask Arthur for stakeout equipment, but he's never denied a request, so we should be set."

We all jumped, Harlow especially for obvious reasons, when Tex dropped his big mitt on the top of her head and said, "I thought you were a grown-up cheerleader. Like, an airhead."

I winced.

Raye winced.

Luna's eyes narrowed on Tex.

Harlow stared up at Tex with his hand still on her head and her mouth hanging open.

"You aren't. You got chops, Peewee," Tex concluded.

Peewee?

She wasn't short.

But she was the shortest of us, and way shorter than Tex, so I could see that.

He took his hand from her head and looked between all of us, ordering, "Go out in twos or more. Always. Get army knives and carry them in your back pockets. That way, you get zip tied, you can get it out and cut yourself loose. Then, you get the opportunity, run. You get in a physical skirmish, go for the gonads, hard as you can. You don't got an opening, the instep or the butt of your hand to their windpipe. Then, again, run like hell. Fuck it. I'll get you the knives." He looked at Harlow. "They got 'em in pink. You want just pink, or pink camo?"

"Just pink," she whispered.

"I'll take pink camo," Raye said.

"Do they have them in orange?" Luna asked.

"Fuck if I know," Tex answered. "I'll look. Second choice?"

"Camo, any camo, just not pink," Luna told him.

Tex looked at me.

"Black," I said.

He grinned.

I couldn't tell if his grin was slightly terrifying, mostly lovable, or slightly lovable and mostly terrifying.

He trundled out from behind the bar before I could decide.

Raye closed in. "After our shifts, Luna and me will scout locations to see if we can find someplace where we can watch without people who might be watching the camp knowing we're watching."

That was kinda confusing, but I got her.

"Rad," I said.

"We'll reconvene tomorrow to figure out schedules," Raye went on.

"Awesome," Luna said.

Raye put her hand in the middle of our huddle.

Luna put hers on top.

I put mine on top of theirs.

Harlow came up the rear.

"Angels unite," Harlow whispered excitedly.

I fought rolling my eyes.

We bounced our hands and broke.

"You women done with whatever the hell you're up to now?" Byron asked from the other side of the bar.

"Dirty chai refill?" I asked back.

He gave me a *Duh!* expression and headed back to his booth.

I hit the espresso machine.

SIXTEEN

QUIET NIGHT

That evening after work, I came in my apartment door, saw Eric in my kitchen slicing mushrooms, and suddenly understood why many women hankered after that white dress and big cake day.

If this vision before me was what I got for a lifetime after going through those motions, I'd put up with all the overblown hoopla to get it.

That said, I was me so I had to shovel shit.

"What? Did you pick the locks?"

He smiled at me.

That hoopla was looking better.

Then he answered, "Yup."

Fascinating.

Though, mental note. Give the guy a key.

"You found truffle butter," he said as I closed the door behind me.

"I totally did," I replied.

I tossed my bag on the couch and went to him.

He twisted from the counter, but not fully, though he did fully circle me with his arm, pull me up against his side and drop down to give me a quick kiss.

Oh yeah.

Official.

I'd go through that hoopla.

When he lifted away, he said, "I know you wanted to cook, but I haven't eaten since lunch, so I got started."

Since I hadn't eaten since lunch, and it was after seven, I was glad he got a head start.

I looked down at my cutting board that had some chopped chives and a bunch of sliced mushrooms on it.

I returned my gaze to him. "You know I'm already good at the slicing and chopping parts. I want to get into the meaty stuff."

"Then hurry, honey, your man is hungry."

"Can you wait two point five minutes for me to change clothes?"

"Absolutely."

I smiled, rolled up for my own lip touch then dashed to my room to switch out from the clothes I worked in all day to a pair of black wide-leg lounge pants with a white racing stripe down the side and a tight white tank. That accomplished, I pulled my long hair up into a messy bun.

When I came back out, Eric sent a glance my way, almost turned back to the mushrooms but instead did a double take.

Yeah, I had nice arms, a nice ass, and I rocked a lounge outfit.

But I especially rocked a tank.

Seemed someone was feeling his have-sex-for-the-first-time-with-your-new-hot-chick vibe.

I smirked.

"If you ever call me a tease again, I'm shooting you," he muttered to mushrooms.

I smirked harder.

Then I clapped my hands and said, "Let's get this puppy going."

I moved to the Barefoot Contessa cookbook I'd bought at the bookstore a couple of days ago to start my new hobby. It was where I left it, on the kitchen counter, opened to the recipe.

And that was when I saw the box with a flier resting on top of it, sitting on the counter next to the cookbook.

"Did you grab my packages from downstairs?" I asked.

"No. All of that was on your mat at your door. I just brought it in."

That was weird.

Was our postal chick delivering right to the door now?

"I didn't order anything. Can you hold another minute while I look at this?" I requested.

"Sure," he said. "I'll get the pasta water going."

That wasn't a meaty part of the recipe (in truth, this recipe wasn't hard, and there were only nine ingredients, two of them salt and pepper, so this wasn't the spectacle the pastitsio was, but it sounded yummy), so I let him have at it.

I grabbed the flier, turned it over and saw:

Oasis Holiday Extravaganza!!!!!!!!!
When: December 12, starting at 7:00 p.m.
Where: Oasis Courtyard
What: Glitter and Potluck
Dress: Get your holiday on!
(We're dressing up.)
RSVP: Bill and Zach

Fill out the OASIS HOLIDAY EXTRAVAGANZA!!!!!!!! Google form sent to your email to share what you're bringing (Raye, your only acceptable contribution is your pudding, Jess, you're on a signature cocktail, make it a good one!)

Anyone coming must give Bill or Zach $20 by December 10 to fund the bar.

Anyone wanting to participate in the Secret Santa,

FILL OUT THAT GOOGLE FORM IN THE SAME EMAIL.

IF YOU COME IN JEANS, WE WON'T THROW SHADE, BUT THIS IS ABOUT GLITZ AND GLAMOR AND HOLIDAY CHEER. SO FIND A SEQUIN OR TWO OR PUT ON A BLAZER. IT WON'T KILL YOU.

HOSTS: BILL AND ZACH!

"Do you think we'll still be together on December twelfth?" I asked Eric.

"Yes," he answered immediately.

I smirked again, though that was on the outside. On the inside, that gooey feeling was back.

I waved the flier and inquired, "Wanna be my date to a glitz and glamor holiday extravaganza in the courtyard?"

"Yes," he repeated.

"Feel like being in on the Oasis Secret Santa?" I kept at him.

"No."

I laughed.

Just what I thought he'd say.

But I was totally getting in on the Secret Santa. I killed at Secret Santa stuff.

It wasn't hard, just buy a good bottle of booze.

"I don't think you have to wear a tux, but you might have to wear a suit," I warned him.

"I'm not allergic to suits, honey," he told me. "What are you wearing?"

I thought about the sleeveless, black lace dress with the deep, to-the-midriff vee bodice and flirty, understated ruffles at the shoulders and on the long skirt that I scored on sale to go to a friend's black-and-white wedding. Only to have said friend call off her wedding three weeks before it was supposed to happen because she figured out she was more in love with the best man than her groom.

An aside: I was no longer her friend. That wasn't the first time she was a total flake in the worst way. I'd liked her fiancé, he was a good guy, so after that, I was out.

Another aside: since then, I'd heard she eloped with the best man.

The last aside: their marriage lasted four months before the new groom filed for divorce.

Wait, no, this was the last aside: the other last aside was no surprise to anyone.

To answer Eric's question, I simply said, "I think you'll like it."

"I bet I will," he murmured while getting out a sauté pan.

I set the flier down and reached for the box.

There was an envelope resting on top that had my name on it in handwriting I'd never seen before.

I slit open the envelope and pulled out a piece of notepaper. I unfolded it. It was from one of those freebie notepads you got at hotels.

And it said,

Jess,
Don't give up on him.
He's working through some shit.
He took it too far. You were right to be pissed.
I didn't know he was going to go there with you.
I'll give him time and have a word.
Sorry about the hood and zip ties.
Also the kidnapping.
Be careful out there,
~~Javi

"Oh my God," I breathed.

"What is it?" Eric asked.

I handed him the note, folded open the unsecured flaps on the box and peered in.

I couldn't help it.

I gasped.

"What?" Eric was right at my side, peering in with me. "Well... damn," he muttered.

Damn was an understatement.

With reverence, I unearthed the sleek, stainless-steel cocktail shaker with copper accents. Then I pulled out the set of bar tools in their stand that included muddler, double jigger, tongs, spoon, bottle opener and strainer. More stainless-steel with copper accents, but the muddler was a phenomenal, polished walnut and had a marble tip.

"This is insane," I whispered reverently.

"Seems the man's got class as well as an over-honed sense of justice," Eric stated.

I looked up at him. "Over-honed sense of justice?"

"Babe, this is the Wild West. Denver was Candyland compared to the trip that was LA. But this place, I've never experienced anything like it. It's touch and go just driving from one place to another. I learned fast when I hit The Valley, anything goes. And Javier Montoya is the gunslinging marshal who put the star on his own chest."

I didn't travel much.

But I always knew my city of birth *rocked.*

"Do you think Javi extorted money out of his deadbeat dad to buy me this primo bar set?" I asked.

"I think if Javier Montoya wants to do something, he finds a way to get it done."

And there it was again.

I knew I liked the guy.

"Since he put this on my welcome mat, I'm thinking our security gate doesn't know it has the word 'security' in its description," I remarked.

"Don't worry, babe. Your gate is solid. Again, if Montoya wants something, he'll get it done."

Hmm.

I could think on it no longer. I had to feed my man, so I dragged the cookbook closer to me, gave the recipe a once over, then turned to the stove.

"So...my day," I began as I started to melt the butter and olive oil. "The girls and I are gonna head into the camp tomorrow after Harlow and I get off work. We're gonna ask some questions and see if anyone saw anything. We're also going to set up surveillance. And get this, after Raye and Luna scouted out a good place to keep watch in that abandoned warehouse across from the camp, Raye asked, and Arthur is going to kit us out with communication equipment, binoculars and a camera with an extreme telephoto lens."

Eric slid his hand along the small of my back (nice) as he moved from my one side to the other to open the packet of fresh fettucine I bought.

After he did this, he said, "I know. Raye told Cap. Cap told me. I sat down with Mace. The men are going to do the surveillance with you."

My head twisted from the oil in the pan to him. "You are?"

He shrugged. "It's a good idea. We'll have men undercover in the camps, and they'll have comms so they can communicate. But Mace and Lee have been uneasy about Tex and Duke being in there without backup close. If we take shifts with the Angels, we can keep a better eye on them."

Lee was the managing partner of the Denver branch of NI&S. He was also the hero of one of the Rock Chick books, seeing as he married a Rock Chick. To end, his last name was Nightingale, so he's the one who started the whole thing, literally, as his book was also the first book.

I dumped the mushrooms in the pan and stirred them around before I said, "Two important questions."

"Hit me."

"One, who's Duke?"

"Duke's a friend in Denver. He's around Tex's age. He's a biker, so we can make him look like he's been sleeping rough. He's also sharp as a whip. And he's got a few years on him, but he can take care of himself. Though, normally, he works at Indy's bookstore."

Indy, by the by, was Lee's Rock Chick wife (I met both of them at the funeral, she was gorgeous and very sweet, he was the requisite *hot*).

"What's question two?" Eric prompted.

I gave it to him. "You need to tell the boys they need to be all in for my corn nut, corn dog, corn chip and salsa theme for stakeouts. I'm not sitting around for hours, staring at a bunch of people who are just living their lives, hoping for the bad guys to show up, without the appropriate snacks available."

Eric smiled. "I see stakeouts with the Angels are gonna be a whole fuckuva lot better than the ones we do on our own."

"What are your snack themes?"

He started laughing. "We don't have snack themes. So already your stakeouts are better."

I shot him a smile and turned back to the mushrooms to give them a swizzle.

I did this asking, "So, how was your day?"

"It was a day."

I thought he was blowing me off, but he continued.

"We have an established rep in Denver and LA. But as I mentioned to you before, we're starting from scratch here. Things have been slow. However, our rep in those other places is such, they weren't that slow. That said, now shit's sparking off. Since we're picky with recruiting, there's gonna be a lot of shuffling of staff until we can get another couple people on the payroll. This isn't going to be easy. All the men in Denver have families they don't want to be away from for very long. All the men in LA primarily do security details, and they can't get away. It's good Roam is moving down. That'll help."

"I thought Roam just made the decision to move. Is he fully down already?"

"He's gotta move his shit, but he's staying with Mace and Stella while he looks for a place and meshes with the team. Soon as he finds a place, he'll go get his shit."

"Right."

"Also, we're bracing for a showdown at the office because Shirleen has decided she's going to be the firm's Operating Manager with her base here, but Mace had just talked the woman who worked with us in LA into moving to Phoenix, so we don't know how that's gonna go."

I turned to him again as he continued talking.

"They're both spitfires, so unless we can figure that out, it's gonna spark off too."

"That doesn't sound good," I noted.

He shook his head. "Shirleen manages the entire operation of NI and S. Payroll. Billing. Accounts receivable. Bookkeeping and accounting. Marjorie, who has already retired, twice, the second time when Mace and Stella moved to Phoenix, would only manage Phoenix operations, which means local staffing, case reporting, filing, receptionist functions and acting as a personal assistant to Mace."

"So they won't clash," I remarked.

"No. They'll clash. Shirleen has a laissez-faire work ethic. She gets it done and done well, but if she feels the need to take an afternoon off to go shopping, she'll go. Marjorie has a Puritanical work ethic. She's there on time. She's highly organized. She's obsessively professional. The only thing they have in common is that they're both ballbusters. If they work together, shit will undoubtedly get real."

"Well, at least it'll make the office interesting."

His eyes twinkled, and I noted how good of a look it was for him, before he said, "Yeah. And fortunately for me, I don't have to be in the office very often."

I kept stirring the mushrooms, thinking that this recipe was kind of boring (though, it was gonna taste amazing), when I offered, "I was born here, and I know a lot of people. No one springs to mind as a badass, but what are you looking for in recruiting?"

"Cap and I think Jacob might be a fit for the team."

I looked at him yet again, this time with surprise.

Not *surprise* surprise, because it appeared the most important aspect of having a job with that team was to be built and ludicrously good-looking, and Jacob was that.

But still, surprise.

"Jacob?"

"He's in excellent shape. He works with his hands. He seems to have good instincts. He's protective of those he cares about, and we have to know what we're doing, but we have to do it having the backs of the people we work with. He'll need a lot of training, but we think he'd be a fit."

"Have you talked to him about it?"

He smiled at me. "No, since he's pissed I'm not talking you out of 'whatever that fool shit is' you're doing. And to make it clear, the 'fool shit' part of that were his words."

I knew he'd gone to Eric to talk to him about my insane life.

"Once he calms down, we'll talk to him," Eric concluded.

"How many people are you looking for?"

"At least two for fieldwork. An additional two for full time in the surveillance room. And we need someone who can manage the surveillance room. All of the junior members of the team work that room, Brady, Knox, Gabe. But with that, we're seriously short-staffed, and we need people who take that on as their primary job."

"Surveillance room?"

"We also provide security, so the surveillance room is operational twenty-four-seven to keep an eye on client properties. But we have cases where we need to install cameras to keep an eye on other things."

"Your job is so rad," I muttered to the mushrooms.

I felt warmth coming from him at my comment, but he didn't reply to it.

"Want me to grate the cheese?" he asked. "Or is that a skill you want some practice with?"

Grating cheese did not sound like something I had a desperate desire to do at that moment (though I'd want practice at a later date).

However, what I did have a desperate desire to do was feed my man, so I told him, "You can do that."

He shot me a smile, then he got on the cheese.

We cooked the rest of the meal together in that comfortable silence we shared during our No-Fucks-to-Giving.

And as we did, I enjoyed not only having this synchronicity with Eric, but also having this time of normal where it wasn't about Jeff or my head being up my ass or anything. It was just about winding down from the day, being normal and getting chill.

I peeked at the icebox cake in an effort to curtail my need to shove my entire face in the bowl of fettucine (it smelled so good!) before we sat down on the stools at my kitchen bar after we dished up.

Eric had cut the fresh loaf of bread I'd bought to add carbs to our heaping bowl of carbs, as well as put butter out on a plate that he'd nuked for ten seconds to soften it.

He went for that.

I swirled my fork in the fettucine and shoved a huge bite into my mouth, a part of my anatomy I'd positioned to hovering over the bowl (*God*, so good!) when he said softly, "Thanks for asking about my day."

Face still hovering over my bowl, mouth munching the simple but rich and decadent pasta, I turned to him.

His eyes were on me, and his teeth were sliding into a piece of buttered bread.

First, how he could go for the bread before the pasta would forever remain a mystery.

Second, I couldn't wait for those teeth to bite into me.

I had to concentrate on those thoughts, because last, I was getting the impression from what he said that his ex didn't bother to pull herself out of the world she thought revolved around her to ask after what was happening in her husband's world.

Of course, according to Eric, she was never home to do so. But it would seem, even if she was, she didn't.

And that pissed me off.

Therefore, it was angrily I finished munching. Still angrily, I swallowed.

And yes, *still* angrily, I asked, "Let me guess. Savannah didn't have a lot of interest in how your day went."

Eric shook his head. "I don't wanna talk about her, sweetheart. But I do want you to know that I appreciate us having a quiet night and all the conversation isn't about what's happening with you. I'll grant, what's going on with you is a lot. So it means something to me you can find your way out of it to think about me."

Translation: No. The bitch didn't bother to pull herself out of her world to see to the man she'd vowed to share that world with.

I forked (mm-hmm, still angrily) into a mushroom and shoved it in my mouth.

Eric chuckled.

I turned to glare at him.

His chuckle became a laugh.

I reached for some bread and the butter, and one could say my swipes on the unoffending bread were somewhat violent.

"There's something to be said about not having it all that great, then finding something great, so you know to appreciate it. Yeah?" Eric asked.

I glared at him again. "Don't be sweet when I'm in the mood to cut a bitch."

At that, he busted out laughing.

I took a bite of my bread.

It was good and all, but the fettucine was far superior.

Thus, I put my bread down and returned to my pasta.

Eric put his hand on my back and leaned in close.

"And it means a lot that you'd get so angry on my behalf."

"You're still being sweet," I warned around a mouth full of fettucine.

He was grinning largely as he sat back and went after his own pasta.

I'd managed to remind myself that Savannah was history, Eric was sitting beside me, we were having a quiet night, and the portion I'd served up for myself wasn't gut-busting—which should lead to wild, sweaty sex for the first time with my new hot guy—when Eric leaned forward to pull his phone out of his back pocket, muttering, "Goddammit."

"What?" I asked.

"I'm on a case that's close to breaking," he said while reading the screen of his phone, "and I worried this would happen."

"What?" I repeated.

He sent a text flying and then circled more fettucine on his fork. "The case is breaking. I gotta eat up, babe, and roll."

Shit.

"You're leaving?"

When he turned his eyes to me, he didn't need to say words. I could see he was maybe even less happy about it than I was.

Still, I was tremendously unhappy about it.

"So I take it tonight is not the night for wild, sweaty sex for the first time with my new hot guy," I remarked.

He suddenly caught me behind my head, pressed his mouth tight to mine, pulled back and replied, "If I slide in bed beside you tonight and you're wearing something that even minorly resembles the last two nighties I've seen you in, prepare to get your ass woken up before it gets tagged."

God, I wished I hadn't wasted my best nightie on my first sleepover at Eric's house when nothing happened.

It was then, I remembered a red number I had, which wasn't in my normal color rotation (red was strictly accent), which was why I'd forgotten about it. I only bought it because the style was so hot, and it didn't come in black, but I had to have it.

I'd never worn it.

Now Eric was going to get it.

My smile to him was slow.

Eric watched it, muttering, "Fuck."

"Be safe," I bid.

His eyes came up to mine. "Don't dig into that cake. I'll cut us a slice after we break this fuckin' seal."

Oh yeah.

He was as frustrated as I was that seal hadn't been broken yet.

I saluted him with my fork. "Righty ho, big man."

He pressed his lips to mine again, turned to his fettucine, downed a couple more bites, and I got another lip touch before he buttered another piece of bread and took off with bread in hand.

I took my time eating, and then I took my time cleaning up.

While I did the latter, I washed and polished my new bar set, stashed the old one I had, which wasn't near as nice (or as expensive), and put the new one on my bar cart.

It looked amazing.

Staring at it, I didn't want to be reassured that it was clear Jeff had cast his lot with a really good guy.

But Javi's present, and his note, were so thoughtful, I couldn't help but be reassured.

SEVENTEEN

AN ANGEL WILL DO PERFECTLY

My hip was moving.

When I opened my eyes, I saw weak light coming in from outside and a hot guy leaning over me in bed.

With a bleary gaze, I glanced at the clock and noted it was ten to eight.

I pushed up to rest on a hand in the mattress and looked back at Eric. "Are you just getting home?"

Eric was checking out my body, or more to the point, my nightie, but he raised his gaze to mine when he said, "No. I got home at around three. I didn't expect it to go that long, but what went down required us to make a report to the police, which always drags shit out. When I got back, you were dead to the world, and I was wiped. So I grabbed a couple hours of sleep. Now I gotta hit the office."

I turned my head and saw both pillows disturbed.

I went back to him, and with no small amount of shock, asked, "You got in bed beside me, and I didn't wake up?"

He shook his head. "Nope. You were dead to the world."

Argh!

I wasted my second-best nightie!

Okay, don't panic.

Maybe I could salvage things.

"If you work late, don't you get to go to work later in the morning?" I tried.

"I am going to work later in the morning," he answered.

"By...an hour."

He seemed to be struggling with a smile, when I didn't think anything was funny, because, *again*, we hadn't broken the seal.

"I have some more bad news," he announced.

I'd barely been awake five minutes. I was already not thrilled with what I was processing. I wasn't sure I could take more bad news.

"Fabulous," I muttered.

"I gotta take a shift in the surveillance room tonight. I won't be relieved until late. So I probably won't see you until tomorrow."

"Wait. I thought only the junior investigators did that."

"They would only do it if we had the appropriate staff hired to man that room. Now, we all have to kick in."

"But you worked late last night," I pointed out.

"Taking my turn is part of that 'taking your brothers' backs' I was talking about last night."

God!

Why did he have to be so responsible and dedicated to teamwork?

"So we're not gonna break the seal on wild, sweaty sex until, earliest, *tomorrow*?"

I barely got the last word out before I had an arm around my waist, I was flying through the air only to hit a hard wall of muscle, and then I was being kissed.

Hard. Deep. Wet.

And delicious.

I had my hands in his hair. Eric had jacked up my nightie at the back, so I also had his hand cupping one cheek of my ass inside my panties, skin to skin. Their first introduction. And they liked each other a whole lot.

This made me think he was going to be irresponsible and go even later to work.

I was in for that.

All in.

But he set me on my knees in bed, slid his hand out of my panties and the pad of the thumb of his other hand ran along my lower lip.

"I couldn't help it," he murmured, watching his thumb move. "It was the nightie. But that was a mistake."

"I take it that means you're going," I noted.

"Sorry, honey," he whispered.

"Do not *even* say I'm the bigger tease, *ever again*."

He smiled at me, kissed my nose, and ordered, "Don't dive into that icebox cake. We'll have it tomorrow."

And then he was gone.

Gah!

I fell back on the bed.

And I was Jessica Rose Wylde. I didn't do what I did next.

Ever.

But I did it then.

Because I couldn't help it.

No Eric.

No icebox cake.

Thus, I pouted.

For a very long time.

One could say I was *not* in a better mood by the time I swung into work later that morning.

I knew I wasn't hiding it when Harlow, behind the bar shooting Diet Coke into a glass, turned to look at me, her eyes got big, and she said, "I can tell something's wrong, but with that look on your face, I'm scared to ask what it is."

Raye came back with some empty mugs while I explained, "Eric was called out last night in the middle of dinner because one of the cases he was working broke. He didn't get home until late. He was wiped, and I was out, so I only saw him this morning long enough for him to tell me he's working the surveillance room tonight, so I won't see him until tomorrow. Oh, and he laid a hot kiss on me, leaving me wet and frustrated, before he went to work. And just FYI, I don't have any awesome memories of sticky, delectable sex with Eric to tide me over, because we haven't *done it* yet."

Harlow scrunched up her face in disappointment for me.

Raye grimaced.

She then said ruefully, "Just so you know, Cap was working that case with Eric so he was out until all hours too. And it happens, Jess. A lot. Probably two, three times a week. He gets home late as well." Her gaze on me became intense. "It's important to understand, babe, these are not nine to five guys."

"I can tell he loves his job," I retorted. "That's not the issue. The issue is, I've gone through the top three of my four sexiest nighties, and they saw *no action*. I've got one left, then I'm down to the dregs. Sure,"—I flipped out a hand—"those dregs are top-notch. I don't do anything but. They just aren't my best. Now we have this situation with these abductions, and we have questions to ask and stakeouts to do, which means I don't have time to run to the mall to find even better ones to mark the occasion."

At this point, I realized we had an audience, so I turned to the bar to see Byron standing there.

"Do you need another dirty chai?" Harlow asked him.

"Yes. But carry on with your conversation. I can wait until you're finished," Byron answered.

Byron was always hyper-caffeinated, which meant hyper about always having caffeine. It was only four women discussing sexy nighties that slowed his roll with that.

Thus, I shot him a side eye.

Raye got started on his dirty chai.

Harlow took my hand and walked me away from Byron.

She kept hold of it as she said sweetly, "I think he'll be worth the wait. And today is nearly halfway done, so tomorrow will be here before you know it."

"I'm falling for this guy, Lolo," I whispered.

Her eyes lit with happiness and her hand squeezed mine tight. "He's a good guy. And he's really into you. I love how he looks at you."

My breath was coming funny when I asked, "How does he look at me?"

"Like you're the most beautiful woman he's ever seen, and he can't believe his luck."

What?

Really?

Eric did that?

Super gorgeous Eric, ex-FBI guy, current generally badass PI?

Wow.

"Totally how he looks at you," Luna confirmed as she squeezed by us to punch an order into the computer.

"See?" Harlow asked. "So it's totally going to be worth the wait."

No man kissed that well when he didn't fuck just as well.

Okay. I didn't know that for certain, because I'd never been kissed anywhere near as consummately as Eric kissed me.

I was just connecting the dots.

So, yeah.

I had a feeling I knew what was to come, and the wait seemed like torture.

But Harlow was right.

This was Eric.

We were building something, something pretty damned beautiful.

It'd be worth the wait.

Had I said how much I loved my besties?

Just to reiterate, I seriously loved my besties.

I gave Harlow's hand a squeeze back and said, "Thanks, babe."

Everyone jumped when we heard shouted, "Where's the crazy coffee guy?"

We all turned in the direction of the shout, and I saw the guy who Tex snapped at about the sugar cookie syrup a couple of days before standing just in from the coffee cubby.

"He's not here!" the guy yelled. He then stabbed a finger toward the coffee cubby. "That guy's good, but he's not the crazy coffee guy. No offense!" he shouted toward the cubby.

"None taken!" Otis shouted back.

The guy kept yelling. "But you can't give him to us, take him away, give him *back* and then *take him away again*!"

"Chill, dude," I ordered.

"*You chill!*" he screeched. "I want the crazy coffee guy back!"

"He's moving to Phoenix. He has a wife, cats. They all need somewhere to lay their heads. He's house hunting," I lied. "Give him a chance to settle in, man. Yeesh."

"So he's gonna be back?" the guy asked.

I had no idea.

Though, I hoped so.

"Yes," I told him.

"Promise?" he pushed.

"Promise," Raye cut in. "Now go get your coffee from Otis. Tex will be back soon."

"When?" the guy asked.

"Soon!" Luna snapped. "Go back to Otis. Get your coffee. And chill, sucka!"

The "sucka" was a good touch, and it worked.

The guy hung his head and moped back to the coffee cubby.

I moved to Raye. "Is Tex coming back?"

She nodded, a happy light glinting in her eye.

"Tito officially hired him. Though, he gets to make his own schedule, you know, just in case he has to go undercover at a moment's notice," Raye replied, then, in an afterthought, she added,

"Or clandestinely meet with his arms dealers to replenish his supply of grenades."

My day brightened.

I turned to Tito to see how he reacted to these goings-on, but he had his nose stuck in a book.

It was a Rock Chick book with a light-purple cover.

Not surprising, Tito had always had a quiet way with keeping his finger on the pulse.

Anyway, somebody needed to do the research, and I was back and forth on it. But when it came to those books, I was leaning toward that somebody not being me.

I got to work, and it was just after the lunch rush when they walked in.

Daisy.

With Stella Gunn.

Stella showing caused more than a mild sensation, and for once, it wasn't because of the addition of Daisy. Even if Daisy was wearing a track suit comprised of shimmery, pale-pink velour joggers and a matching cropped jacket that was unzipped to the point Mr. Shithead might give us a limitless number of questions he'd answer for an entire year just for a glance. This was bedazzled with diamante around the waistband of the joggers and at the wrists of the jacket.

Oh, she also had sequined, pink and purple platform sneakers on her feet.

But Stella outshone her because Stella was mega-famous, and it didn't hurt she was also mega-gorgeous.

Totally got why Eric decided to date her as his cover.

One didn't normally hang at a kickass coffee/cocktail/fusion food joint and have one of the most celebrated musicians in history casually stroll in.

Therefore, I, along with everyone in the joint, only had eyes for Stella.

On my part, it was for more than just the fact that she seemed to be an uber famous chick wandering out in the wild without a bodyguard.

I kept my gaze on her as Daisy took a stool at one end of the bar and Stella approached where I was standing at the other end.

She slid onto a stool there and greeted, "Hey, Jess."

I moved to her and put my hands on the bar. "Hey, Stella. Want a coffee? Or are you here to eat? Lucia's got an awesome chorizo toad-in-the-hole with cayenne-garlic mashed potatoes and green chile gravy on the menu today. Trust me, it'll rock your world."

"Although that sounds fantastic, I already ate."

She shifted on her stool, and to me, it seemed like it was nervously.

Terrific.

This wasn't a fun getting-to-know-the-new-girls-visit.

"Listen," she went on. "I know you're working, but Mace told me you girls were going to be busy for a while in your off hours, and I just wanted to..."

She didn't finish that.

I didn't know her well enough (say, at all) to fill in the blank, so I waited patiently, hoping she wasn't there to try to talk me out of being an Angel.

Since her Rock Chick Ride was as bumpy as Eric said, I got why she'd be concerned about us.

But I had no problem with what we were doing. And the girls had no problem with it. And Eric had no issue with it.

So, no shade, but I didn't see why Stella should have a problem with it.

"I just wanted to make sure we got off on the right foot," she announced.

Now I was confused.

"Do you think we haven't?" I asked.

She spread her hands out in front of her in supplication, something that was both sweet, coming from a mega-famous person, and weird, considering our conversation didn't seem to warrant it.

"Eric is a member of my family," she declared. "And he told me that he told you we had a history. I just wanted you to know that it was, um...*history* and—"

Ah.

Right.

I held up my hand, and she stopped talking.

I did this because this was about Savannah.

And it made me even more pissed at the bitch because I could see Stella was uncomfortable, which meant Savannah made her feel that way.

I dropped my hand. "I appreciate you coming in. But like you said, it's history. And that's the end of that."

Her shoulders slumped with relief.

"God, was she that bad?" I asked.

"Eric's told you about her?" Stella asked back.

"Yes," I answered. "Including the fact she wasn't a fan of this history."

"She really wasn't." This was uttered in a way I knew it was a vast understatement.

And yep.

I got more pissed.

"What a pill," I bitched.

"You don't have to worry," Stella informed me. "She'll forget he exists. As shocking as it is with the man he is, she's good at that. This whole thing with demanding a second chance is about her being unable to admit she failed. The more she pursues him, the longer he resists, in her head, she can say she tried, and he refused to try with her, so the end of the marriage was all his fault."

"This woman is a fuckin' trip," I mumbled irately.

"He deserved a Rock Chick," she stated.

My attention laser focused on her.

She kept talking.

"He also needed one. He needs a woman who will understand his commitment to his work and the team, who won't be worried about it and make him feel guilty for doing it. One who'll understand his training and experience and the men who he does it with means they know what they're doing. A woman who'll complement his life, is his partner in it, the way he'll give the same to her because she has a life of her own, and they fit together that way. And a woman he can't steamroll, though he'd sniff that out right away and he'd never go there, because that really isn't his thing."

She took a breath.

Then finished it.

"But mostly, since he'll be all about her, she needs to be all about him too. And he needs to know that, be shown it, be told it, and then be allowed to live it." Her voice lowered when she concluded, "There weren't any Rock Chicks left. But I'm seeing an Angel will do perfectly."

Oh my God!

What a nice thing to say!

"I don't want to overshare," I told her. "But it hasn't even been a week, and I'm a little freaked how into him I am."

"I'm going to repeat something I never thought I'd say in the first place. You need to read those books."

My eyes wandered to Titto, who was engrossed in what he was reading, then I returned to Stella.

"I think your stories are scarier than ours."

"Give it time," she muttered, but even in a mutter, it was authoritative.

It was the authoritative part that made my body give a little shudder.

"Are you out without a bodyguard?" I asked.

"I have a stun gun," she said breezily. "And so does Daisy. And Kai knows I don't like to be shadowed. Which is why Gabe is lurking in the parking lot. Because Kai saw my car leave the house and sent Gabe after me. I pretend I don't know I have a detail. Gabe pretends he doesn't know we made him. Kai pretends he isn't ticked that Gabe got made." She smiled. "Works beautifully."

I smiled back.

Sensing the hard part was over, Daisy slid onto the stool by her side.

"I know we only had lunch two hours ago, but Harlow told me what toad-in-the-hole is and now I'm feelin' peckish. Wanna share a plate?" she asked Stella.

Stella looked at her watch and then asked me, "I have to go get Tallulah from school and Walsh from daycare in an hour and a half. Do we have time?"

"I'll fast track it," I said.

"That'd be awesome."

I dashed into the kitchen to give Lucia the VIP order, telling her who that VIP was, and in pure Lucia style, she simply nodded and pulled a metal pan of oil out of the oven. She poured some thin batter into it. It started sizzling immediately.

I watched in fascination as she plopped some sausages in it, slid it back into the oven, and with no further ado, got back to work on the order she'd been preparing when I showed.

Okay.

Maybe she wasn't into rock and roll.

Okay part two.

I was totally making toad-in-the-hole for Eric.

By the time I made it back to the bar, Harlow, Luna and Raye were huddled close to Stella and Daisy.

They were looking at a piece of paper on the bar.

I approached and Raye said, "Glad you're here. We finally have a lull, so I wanted to go over the stakeout schedule with you guys." She tapped a finger on the paper. "Cap said that all the people who have been snatched were snatched when it was dark. So we only have to cover sunset to sunrise. Cap cleared this with Mace and the team this morning, and then dropped it by."

I looked down at the paper.

It said:

5:30–9:00 *Luna & Knox*
9:00–12:30 *Harlow and Brady*
12:30–4:00 *Raye and Cap*
4:00–7:30 *Jess and Eric*

Although these pairings didn't say multi-tasking corn-themed snacks girlie time while nailing the bad guys, I was pretty danged thrilled I got to do my stakeout with Eric.

Thus, the schedule seemed perfect to me (I could share my corn theme with Eric). It'd give Harlow some time to chill a bit after work, but plenty of time to get some sleep. It'd give me time to get some shut-eye before I had to head out. And Luna and Raye could get to work on time.

In fact, only Raye and Cap's allotment sucked.

"We should do a rotation of Raye and Cap's slot, because it sucks," I noted.

"Yeah. That's the worst one," Harlow agreed.

"Aw, you guys are sweet," Raye said.

"Why am I with Knox?" Luna demanded.

We all looked at her, though Daisy did it with a mini tinkly bell laugh.

"Why not Knox?" Raye asked, and she did this suspiciously.

"Why not Liam? Or Gabe?" Luna retorted, I will note, without allaying Raye's suspicions.

"Because Liam is managing the surveillance room since they haven't found someone to do that," Raye explained. "And because Gabe is Stella's officially unofficial detail."

"Roam then," Luna kept at it.

"Roam needs to find a house to live in," Raye retorted. "And get his legs under him here in Phoenix. He's only been here days. The others have been here months."

"Then why can't I have Brady?" Luna didn't let it go.

"Do you *want* Brady?" Harlow asked leadingly.

Another mini trill from Daisy.

"No, I don't *want* Brady," Luna returned weirdly heatedly.

"Let's go back to why you don't want Knox," Raye stated.

"I just don't, okay?" Luna didn't quite answer.

"Are you keeping something from us?" Raye demanded.

I stared in surprise as pink hit Luna's cheeks (she wasn't one to blush) before she narrowed her eyes on Raye and totally lied, "No."

Now we were all staring at her.

"If I was fifteen years younger and my Marcus didn't exist in this universe or any other, I'd want Knox," Daisy said under her breath to Stella.

"Don't tell Kai, or he'll pull him from my detail, but I'd pick Gabe. He's got those Luke vibes going on," Stella replied.

"It's in the blood," Daisy noted.

"It sure is," Stella responded. "Who would have guessed there was more Stark goodness floating out there? You'd think we'd sense it simply because we have uteruses."

Another update: Gabe was the second cousin to one of the OG Hot Bunch, Luke Stark. I'd met Luke at the funeral too. And there was more than a mere family resemblance. In a number of ways.

"Luke do it for you?" Daisy asked Stella in surprise.

"The question should be, which one doesn't?" Stella answered. "And the answer is, none. Though, the caveat is the same, with Kai not existing in this universe or any other."

"I hear you, sister," Daisy mumbled.

"We should get back to work," Luna decreed.

"Don't think you're off the hook on this," Raye called to her back as she left the bar.

Luna ignored her and kept motoring.

This reminded me to ask a question I hadn't thought to ask earlier (no, not the one about why Knox was at Luna's apartment Sunday morning, that'd have to wait until later since she plainly wasn't feeling talkative about the subject, and equally plainly, Raye nor Harlow knew what was going on with those two either). My actual question needed to be asked, particularly to Eric, someone I couldn't ask at that moment, because he wasn't there.

So I asked Raye.

"These guys are expending a lot of resources on a case that isn't theirs. What's up with that?"

Stella made a noise.

Daisy murmured, "Mm-hmm."

I looked to them then back to Raye when she spoke.

"Cap explained that they do this kind of thing."

"They sure do." Daisy was still murmuring.

"Do what kind of thing?" Harlow asked.

It was Stella who answered. "Watching your asses, so you don't get exploded by a car bomb."

Cripes!

She continued, "Along with working cases they lose money on so stuff the cops don't have the time and resources to focus on can get sorted a whole lot faster so innocent people stop vanishing." She threw out a hand and finished, "And the like."

I ignored the car bomb mention and said to Stella, "Like pro bono avenger type stuff?"

Stella smiled. "Yes. But in this case, there's also the fact they can't have you girls showing them up."

I didn't think it was that.

I thought it would be easy just to keep an eye on us and let us do our thing without members of their team being up all night, helping us do our thing.

I thought instead they were doing it because, just like us, they didn't want anyone else to go missing, and if they were still around to be found, they wanted to locate the ones that were already gone.

I also thought this was tremendously awesome.

"What time are we starting tonight?" I asked Raye.

"Right after work, if you two are game," Raye answered.

Harlow and I nodded our heads.

"Cap suggested we start with swinging by the hotel to talk to

Mary. She wasn't around for very long, but she was there when someone was taken," Raye told us.

"That's a plan," I confirmed.

"Luna can just get over it. Knox will be at the stakeout spot at 5:30. She can join him when we're done," Raye stated.

Harlow inched closer, so Raye and I inched with her, and Daisy and Stella both came up to their forearms on the bar so they could listen in too.

"What do you think that's about?" Harlow queried.

There it was.

I was right.

Or, at least Harlow didn't know what was going on.

"I think she's got the hots for Knox, and Knox has the hots for her, and they won't do anything about it because Cap and I are together, and she's my best friend, Knox is Cap's best friend, and they're big, fat dorks," Raye shared.

Time to get my question in.

"Do you know why Knox was at Luna's Sunday morning?"

Raye shot me a baffled expression. "He'd come over to ours. Cap was going to make brunch then they were going to the shooting range."

Oh.

That wasn't very hot tea, or any tea at all.

Bummer.

"Knox was pretty up in her space while Mary was brandishing her knife," Harlow noted.

"Knife?" Stella asked.

"*Shh*, don't interrupt," Daisy whispered to her.

"I saw him get close, but I didn't see what happened when Mary whipped out that knife," I said. "Liam had pulled me out of the way."

"Knox put his arm around her belly and yanked her behind him," Harlow told me. "It was really sweet. And I thought it was weird that it looked like Luna's face would burn off, it got so red. But I figured she was ticked that he protected her when Mary wasn't going to do anything with that knife." Her gaze wandered to the restaurant. "Maybe it was something else."

Oh, it was something else.

We all looked to Luna, including Daisy and Stella twisting on their stools to do it.

Luna felt it, and without turning our way, yelled across the space, "Kiss off and die!"

Daisy's laugh sounded again.

"We probably should go back to work," Raye said.

We probably should.

"I'll check on your order," I said to Daisy and Stella.

"Thanks, sugar, you're the best," Daisy replied.

I headed back to the kitchen.

The order was up.

I brought it out to the girls, gave them cutlery and got them both sodas.

Then, except for Stella, once she finished the toad-in-the-hole, declaring she was coming back once a week for lunch before they left, nothing else happened all shift (apart from Tito barking out laughter on occasion while he read his book, something I decided to take as a positive sign).

This lull in activity was good, even if I didn't know how good it was at the time.

Because, as Eric would say, shit was about to spark off in a huge way.

We just didn't know that.

If we did, we would have wallowed in that quiet time.

Alas, we didn't.

EIGHTEEN

COPY THAT

At around 7:20 that night, we rolled up on Mary's door at the long-term hotel where she was staying.

Raye knocked.

We waited.

Raye knocked again.

We waited some more.

"She's not a spring chicken, maybe it takes her time to get to the door," Harlow remarked into our collective impatience.

"It's a glorified hotel room with a kitchenette and a baby living room. How much time does it take?" Luna asked.

I pushed in to knock again, but I didn't when we heard shouted from the other side, "I can see you! And I'm not answering because I'm mad at you girls!"

We all glanced at each other before I called toward the door, "Why are you mad at us? You barely know us."

We jumped when the door was yanked open, and Mary stood there in all her petite, old lady glory, complete with pink fuzzy slippers on her feet, glowering up at us.

I would never tell her this, but the glower lost some of its power due to the slippers.

"Because now all my kids *and* grandkids know I was sleeping in a tent, and they're all mad at me, *and* they're all scraping together the little extra they have so they can get me a nicer apartment," she explained, all crotchety.

"If my grandma was sleeping in an abandoned parking lot in a tent, I'd want her in a decent apartment," Luna pointed out.

"They already don't have a lot, now they're gonna have less," Mary shot back.

"No. Now they'll have peace of mind you're taken care of, which is worth more than anything money can buy," Luna returned.

Mary worked her jaw while she considered this.

We had the population of the whole homeless camp to get to, and I had a desire to get it done in time for Luna to be forced to spend even just a little bit of it with Knox that night, so I stated, "We're looking into these abductions from the camp. Can we ask you some questions?"

She focused her glare on me for a few beats before she stepped aside and let us in.

We all trundled in, and yeah, the place was no palace. It was small, but it was clean, even if her belongings were wedged everywhere there was space to fit them.

The tiger cat, who had assumed the high ground on a tall stack of boxes, took a swipe at Harlow's hair as she passed by. With a squeak, Harlow jumped out of range.

"Zuzu, quit that," Mary ordered.

Even though she had no hope of reaching her, Zuzu responded by taking a swipe at Mary.

"Her name is Zuzu?" Raye asked.

Mary looked at Raye like she had two heads. "No. His name is Frank."

We all looked at each other again before Raye pointed out, "You just called him Zuzu."

"I call him Zuzu, and King Catopher, and Cat Catofferson and Prince of His Domain, and Scallywicious," Mary shared. "He's the only baby I have left. He gets a lot of nicknames. Obviously, you don't have cats."

This reminded me, I was in the market for a pet. It was time. I had a guy to talk to now, so I wasn't talking to the sink anymore, but still.

Both Mom and Dad had no patience for animals, and both Jeff and I had always wanted one.

I wondered what Eric thought about cats.

"Actually, I moonlight as a pet sitter," Raye told her.

"Great. I'll take your card and call you the next time I go to the Caribbean," Mary retorted.

I was beginning to like this chick.

However, time was a'wastin'.

"So, Mary, about these abductions," I began.

She shook her head. "I didn't see anything, and I wish I did or I woulda told the cops all about it when they came around," Mary stated.

Damn.

"Have you heard anyone else talk about anything?" Luna inquired.

"No. That group doesn't talk much. But they'd talk about that," Mary said.

So, this was a bust and eating into Luna's forced time with Knox.

"Though..." Mary drew that out.

We waited.

She didn't say anything.

I sighed and said, "Mary, we have a lot of people to talk to tonight. If you have anything we can go on, we'd really appreciate you telling us."

"That boy was there. I saw him," she declared.

Boy?

"What boy?" Raye asked.

"He sells those pills. The bad ones. The ones that really mess people up," Mary said.

Oh no.

"Fentanyl?" I asked.

She nodded. "Yeah. That stuff."

"Why would you mention him?" Luna queried.

"Because he sells to some of those people in the camp, which is so sad. But also because I didn't get a good feeling about him when he did," Mary explained. "And not just the normal bad feeling of him doing what he was doing."

"What kind of feel did you get?" Harlow asked.

"Like he was there to do more than sell those pills," Mary told her.

"What else was he doing?" Raye pressed.

"Having a good look around," Mary stated.

Oh man.

Casing the joint.

"What does this guy look like?" I asked.

Mary turned to me. "Young. Real skinny. Shifty. Dark hair. 'Bout as tall as you, maybe a little taller, not much though."

"How young?" Raye kept at her. "Like, twenties young or thirties young?"

"Twenties young. Maybe just hit his twenties. He could pass as a teenager if you didn't get a good look at his face," Mary said.

"You said dark hair, is he white?" That was Harlow.

Mary nodded.

"Beard, mustache?" Again Harlow.

"No hair on his face. But the hair on his head is longish," Mary said.

"Did he come during the day or at night?" That was Luna.

"Always during the day. Most of those kinds of guys slunk in at night. Not him. Right in broad daylight, breaking the law and destroying people's lives, like he had every right to do it," Mary groused.

We all took a moment to mentally grouse with her before I asked, "Did you tell the cops about him?"

A quick nod. "I did. But I could tell they thought it was just another drug dealer. They get a lot of those in the camp."

I was sure they did.

"Would you recognize him if someone showed you a picture of him?" I questioned.

Mary brightened. "I would. You got pictures?"

"Not yet, but we're working on some things," I told her.

Or at least I hoped Tex and Duke were.

"You show me a picture, I'll tell you if it's the guy," Mary decreed.

And if we could get a picture, maybe I could figure out how to find Javi and, since he knew everyone on the street, maybe he'd know who this guy was connected to and why he might be getting the lay of the land at the camps.

"Thanks, Mary. This has been really helpful," I told her.

Her brows shot up. "It has?"

I smiled at her. "It has."

She seemed pleased with herself as we said our goodbyes.

Frank took a swat at me as we started to leave, so I stopped and pointed at his kitty nose.

"Be good," I ordered.

He curled a paw around my finger, gave it a good sniff then licked it.

"Good boy," I murmured.

He stopped licking and swatted at me.

I laughed and braved a head scratch.

Frank started purring.

"Scammer," I whispered.

"You got the touch," Mary noted. "Frank doesn't like just anybody."

I hoped I had the touch.

"Is it better to get them as kittens or cats?" I asked her.

"It's better they got someone who loves and feeds them," Mary answered. "No matter what their age."

She spoke truth.

She also followed us to the door.

"You girls be careful out there," she called as we walked down the hall. "This is serious business."

She wasn't wrong about that.

Raye tagged the elevator button.

I turned to Mary and gave her a salute.

She gave me a *shoo* hand.

We got on the elevator, rode it, got off, hustled out to the parking lot, into the Sportage, and then we rolled out.

Raye was parking outside the camp when I received a return text from Eric about my text asking, *Do you like cats?*

Yes. Prefer dogs. Why?

I think I'm getting a cat, I replied, hit send, grabbed my Taser and angled out as the other girls did.

I'd learned from watching Eric, so I shoved my Taser in my front left waistband.

Easier to get to.

I did this making a mental note to ask Arthur for holsters. But I needed to do research before that, because I wanted to pick the one I'd get so it'd go with my outfits.

My phone vibrated in my hand.

Want to go to a shelter this weekend and look?

To respond and do it expeditiously, I sent him about twenty smiley emojis.

We headed toward Homer's tent, with me watching Homer emerge from it to greet us, when my phone vibrated again.

I glanced at it.

Eric replied with a smiley, a thumbs up and a red heart.

All three were good.

Though, the heart was my favorite.

"Late again, Jessie," Homer noted when we made it to him.

It wasn't that late. It was just before eight.

But it was dark, already cold, and people were disappearing.

So I got his concern.

"Yeah, Homer. You remember my friends Harlow, Luna and Raye."

He looked between them while nodding.

"We wanted to walk around and ask a few questions about what's going on," I told him.

"Why? Your guy is here," he stated.

So he figured out Tex was ours, because I wasn't sure Tex would tell him.

"You're not telling everyone he's our guy, are you?" I asked.

He shook his head. "Nope. He came to me. Requested space. Shared what he was doing and asked if I was okay with it. When I said yes, he told me we had to keep it to ourselves. But I'm glad he's here."

Well, either Tex or Mace or someone knew how to navigate this, because that was how to navigate it.

"Tex hasn't been around the camp for very long," I remarked. "But I think some of the folks trust me, so I thought maybe I could ask."

"No one knows anything, Jessie," Homer said. "Only time the cops have come not to rustle us around was when they came asking about this. We're worried. If we knew something, we would say."

"I'd like to ask anyway. Is that okay?"

He nodded.

"Will you escort us?"

He nodded again.

I slid a glance through the chicks, and we headed into the camp.

A frustrating, slow-going hour later, we found Homer was right.

No one knew anything. Or at least not the ones who would talk to us, which was about half of the camp. Homer took over questioning about a quarter of the rest. The last contingent didn't talk to anybody, not even Homer, so we didn't approach them.

Though, one woman, her name was Connie, made a remark about the Fentanyl dealer and the worse-than-normal feeling he gave her, which I didn't think was a coincidence.

Tex avoided us by entering his tent when he saw us, something I wasn't surprised about. Being "new," he'd be edgy about outsiders, so he did it to keep his cover just in case someone was watching.

One thing of concern was that I noted the General wasn't among them.

We were back at Homer's tent when he said, "Seems like we wasted your time."

They didn't.

Though, it was close to time for Harlow to meet up with Brady, so it wasn't worth it for Luna to take her slot, which was a bummer.

"We have a semi-kinda lead we'll be looking into," I told him. "Maybe it'll pan out. It wasn't a bust."

He dipped his chin at me, at the chicks, and he was about to duck into his tent when I asked, "Where's the General?"

Homer gave me a sad look and said, "He goes out on what he calls patrol at night. Usually gets lost, rattled, holes up somewhere, and in the morning, we gotta go find him. By now, he's probably lost."

God, I hoped Scott, Louise and the guys found help for the General, and soon.

Homer waited to see if I had anything else, making me wish, not for the first time, that I could find help for him too. He was such a good guy.

Maybe I could talk to Scott and Louise about it.

Since we didn't have anything else at that moment, I smiled at him and said, "Thanks for helping."

He nodded, once, and finally ducked into his tent.

As we walked to the car, Raye said to Harlow, "We'll drive out like we're driving away, so I can make sure we don't have a tail. Then we'll come back and drop you on the other side of the warehouse."

"Cool," Harlow said.

We all got in the car. Raye drove away.

"Keep driving," an ultra-deep voice came from all the way in the back.

We all shrieked, and Raye drove up on the sidewalk.

I twisted in my seat and had to contort because Javi was pushing himself through the opening into the backseat with Harlow and me.

Somehow, he managed this miracle regardless of his size, and he planted his fine ass between me and Harlow.

"Quick draw. Impressed. But if you tase me, beautiful, when I come to, I'm kissin' you," he said, his head turned toward Harlow.

I leaned forward and saw Harlow staring up at him with her mouth hanging open and her Taser aimed at Javi.

"Harlow, put your Taser down," I ordered. "This is Javi."

"You're Javi?" Harlow whispered in her adorable grown-woman, little-girl voice that I suspected drove some men wild.

"In the flesh," Javi whispered back.

"Hi," Harlow breathed, yep, still in that grown-woman, little-girl voice.

Javi made a low, rough noise that I felt in my nipples.

Translation: he was one of those men who her voice drove wild.

Which meant I also felt my eyes bug out of my head.

I turned to Luna to see she'd twisted in her seat to stare at them, and her eyes were bugged out of her head.

I looked to the rearview mirror to see Raye had corrected us and we were back on the road. She was still driving, but she was also looking in the mirror with her eyes bugged out of head.

Their eyes could be like that simply due to all that was Javi, since this was the first time they'd seen him.

Though, I suspected it was only partly due to that and partly due to what was happening between Harlow and Javi.

I returned my attention to them to see I'd still ceased to exist and those two were the only people in the SUV.

I only had a split second to consider a Javi/Harlow hookup.

In that split second, I decided it both scared the shit out of me, and I loved it.

Then I had to move us along.

"Sorry to interrupt."

It took visible effort for Javi to turn his head to me.

Whereupon I smacked him in the chest and snapped, "Dude! You scared the shit out of all of us."

"We can't be seen talking, and your man would lose his mind if I broke into your house to get a brief," Javi returned.

Eric would indeed do that.

It was neither here nor there now.

"Raye drove off the road," I reminded him.

He glanced forward then back at me. "Woman's got quick reflexes. She got us right."

"That's not the point," I stated.

"I freaked you. You're fine. Now I wanna know what you found out from the community," he retorted.

I drew in a breath to get over all that had just happened, and told him, "Nothing. No one has seen anything."

"Fuck," he murmured.

"Though some dealer has been sniffing around," I said.

He refocused on me. "Lotsa dealers plague the camps."

"Mary and Connie both made note of him because they thought he had ulterior motives," I shared.

Javi cocked his head to the side. "They give a description?"

"Young, early twenties. Dark hair. White. Skinny. About my height, maybe a bit taller. No facial hair. And he deals Fentanyl."

Javi stared straight forward, clearly deep in thought.

I let him think then I poked him in the arm.

He looked at me.

"You know this guy?" I asked.

"Not a tight description, but sounds like it might be Lil Clown," he said.

"Lil Clown?" I asked.

"Lil Clown deals goodfellas."

"Goodfellas?" Luna queried.

"Opes. Blues. Dance fever. Apache. F. Fenty. Opioids. Fentanyl," Javi explained.

I made a mental note to brush up on my drug slang before deciding it seemed like maybe Lil Clown was who we were looking for.

"I'll take it from here," Javi declared.

He would not.

Not with Jeff in his posse.

"We've got this," I told him.

He turned again to me. "If this involves Lil Clown, you don't."

"We're working with the Nightingale team," I informed him grandly.

"They don't know who they're dealin' with either," Javi returned.

"Well, how about you have a sit down with them and share," I suggested.

Javi shook his head. "They can take care of their business. I got the street."

"Instead of pissing in corners, maybe we can all work together and get this shit done before anyone else disappears," I fired back.

"I don't work with anyone but my crew," Javi retorted.

"Well then, I guess we'll just have to hope, while we try to figure out what you already know, and you move forward not knowing what we might find out, someone else doesn't get..." I finished that by doing what Mary did and drawing my finger across my throat.

Javi's head cocked again. "You're kinda a pain in the ass, you know that?"

"Why do men always ask that when they know a woman is right?" I inquired.

Javi flashed his megawatt grin. "More proof you're a pain in the ass."

"Because I was again right?" I deduced.

He chuckled.

I heard Harlow sigh.

Yeah, his amusement sounded way nice.

"Tell us about Lil Clown," I demanded.

Javi's grin died. "He's in a crew that isn't gonna last long."

"Why?" Raye asked from up front.

"Aggressive expansion," Javi told her.

"Are we talking more product and more customers, or are we talking more territory?" Luna inquired.

"Both," Javi said. "That's the aggressive part."

"So they're not gonna last long because they're pissing off other players," I noted.

"That, and they're assholes," Javi stated. "And yeah, you can argue they're all assholes, and they are. These guys are just bigger assholes."

"Fantastic," I muttered.

"What do you think they're doing to the people they take?" Harlow asked.

Javi turned to her, and it might have been because there was so much of him to give off a vibe, or it might have been the strength of his emotion, but it felt the whole atmosphere in the car turned gentle when he did.

And...

Damn.

I needed to give more than a split second to this Javi/Harlow gig.

"No clue, lil' mama," he said softly. "But it isn't good."

"Yeah," she said softly back.

They lapsed into sharing another moment.

This moment was broken when Raye turned us around and headed back to where we came.

Javi noticed and said, "You can drop me anywhere. I'll make my way."

"We're going back to drop Harlow. She's on a surveillance shift in ten minutes," Raye told him.

"Which one is Harlow?" he asked.

So, Super Street Man didn't know everything.

"Sorry," I said. "I didn't introduce everyone. Raye, the driver. Luna, front passenger seat. And Harlow's sitting to your left."

Javi didn't even glance at Harlow.

He kept his gaze locked on the rearview mirror.

"Surveillance of what?" Javi asked Raye.

"The camp," Raye said.

We all silently suffered the tectonic plates shifting as he processed this before he said, "The fuck she is."

"I am," Harlow piped up cheerily. "It's my shift."

Javi slowly turned his head toward her, and my eyes bugged out at Luna, who was still twisted around in her seat.

They were thus at the pounding displeasure filling the cab. Luna's eyes were bugged out again too. A quick glance at the rearview mirror said Raye was having the same reaction.

"Chill, Javi," I said soothingly. "Knox is up there, and Brady's coming to relieve him. She's not going to be alone."

Just as slowly, Javi turned to look at me.

Mm-hmm.

Pounding displeasure.

"You sure you got this right?" he asked in a low voice.

"I'm sure Harlow's a grown-ass woman who can make decisions for herself, and one she's made is that she's an Angel. So I don't know why you're asking me that shit when she's sitting right next to you," I replied.

"Yeah," Harlow chimed in, and Javi turned back to her. "I don't know why you're asking Jess. I'm right here. And I'm an Angel. And I pull my weight."

Her voice was getting higher on the last few words, which sadly made them sound cute rather than I-got-this badass.

Then again, nearly everything Harlow did was cute.

Javi didn't have a chance to reply.

Raye decelerated, turned off her lights, and we were all silent as she crept into the abandoned, weeds-growing-through-cracks-in-the-pavement parking lot on the other side of the warehouse.

When we came to a stop, Javi leaned forward, tipped his eyes up and checked out the warehouse.

He sat back and looked at me. "You got a setup up there?"

I nodded.

"Respect," he murmured.

Apparently, they'd set it up without him knowing.

This made me proud, not knowing why, since I wasn't on the Nightingale team, and I had nothing to do with it considering the men had taken over that part. If it had been us, there was a good likelihood even the president would know of our maneuvers.

Still.

Harlow got out but stood there and girlie waved into the car. "Later, guys."

"I'm walking you up," Javi stated, forcing her out of the doorway as he got out.

"I can walk up some stairs," she told him.

"Woman. I. Am. *Walking*. You. *Up*," Javi stated very clearly.

"All righty," Harlow whispered, her head tipped way back so she could stare up at him.

She was at least a foot shorter than him, and I couldn't see all of him, since head and shoulders were cut off from view by the car, but I still thought they looked cute together, which was again terrifying at the same time awesome.

"Later," Luna and I called to get them moving along since we both sensed they could stand there all night, gazing at each other.

"Text when you're safely in position," Raye ordered. "We're not leaving until we get it."

"Gotcha," Harlow replied.

Javi shut the door carefully, so it didn't make a noise.

And we all sat and watched as they headed to the dark building, Javi with his hand at the small of her back, Harlow's jaunty step making her ponytail sway side to side...yeah, like she was a grown-up cheerleader.

"He doesn't know where they're heading, why is he guiding her?" Luna grumbled.

"Because his other option is to morph into a complete caveman, throw her over his shoulder and take her to his lair in order to both save her from a man's job of surveillance at the same time have his wicked way with her," Raye answered sardonically.

I gave voice to my feelings. "They're cute together, and terrifying at the same time."

"I think they're just cute," Raye put in her vote.

"I think they're terrifying," Luna said. "Jess already lost her brother to this shadow crew. I don't want Harlow needing to live off the grid or whatever."

We all pondered that point until all of our phones vibrated with a text.

I looked at mine.

I'm in. Brady's already here. Harlow.

Is Javi still there? Me.

He melted into the shadows when we caught sight of Brady and Knox. Harlow.

Rad. Raye.

Be sharp. Be smart. Luna.

Of course, silly. Obviously, Harlow.

Raye didn't move and we all kept watching the warehouse, even though Harlow was in place.

I knew why we did it.

We were waiting to see if we could catch Javi leaving.

But he must have found some exit not on our side of the building, because either he was sticking around, or he'd escaped into the night sight unseen.

Eventually, Raye put the car in gear and did a circle in the parking lot, pointing us toward the city.

"You're right. He's *muy guapo*," Raye stated.

"Yep," I replied.

"He's also *muy macho*," Luna put in. "Did you notice how he sidestepped the whole working together thing when, if he came onboard, we'd totally get this done faster. I mean, the man can't even troll the camps because they'd make him, and he had to wait for us to find out what we got from our questioning. And we didn't give him shit about asking, we just told him what we found out, even if it wasn't much. We all play a part in this. He needs to get with the program."

I couldn't argue that.

I looked down at my phone and texted Harlow, *Did you get Javi's number?*

I texted it to the string, and no one said anything, Raye just kept driving as we waited for a response.

Harlow's return text came in, and both Luna and I looked down at it.

"Jess asked if she got Javi's number," Luna explained to Raye. "And Harlow said, 'No! Why would you ask that?'"

Because we might need to get hold of him, I texted, and Luna recited it when it hit her phone.

"'Oh, I didn't think of that. Sorry!'" Luna again read Harlow's reply out loud, climbing way up on the last word in a great imitation of Harlow.

"I'll call Joshua. Get him to get a message to Jeff to get a message to Javi that we need to continue our talk," I said into the cab.

"And I'll email Arthur to see if he can get comms on this guy," Luna added.

"I know Harlow will probably tell Knox and Brady, but can

someone text Cap? Or Jess, text Eric, and let them know about this Lil Clown character?" Raye requested.

"On it," I said, and turned back to my phone.

I gave Eric the highlights, including Javi, and hit send.

Raye kept driving.

Eric texted back.

"He said, 'Got it,' and 'Good work,' and 'We'll get on it and give the heads up to Tex and Duke to keep an eye out for this guy,'" I told them.

"Well, at least the night wasn't a bust," Raye said on a sigh. "We got a possible lead, and Harlow might possibly get laid by an enormous but gorgeous vigilante."

I'd bet, with all that bulk, Javi had learned how to be gentle in bed.

Which reminded me, we'd already made plans and Eric was picking me up at 3:30 for our stakeout shift. And while we did that, the icebox cake would be sitting lonely in its pan in my fridge, and my vagina would be sitting lonely in my jeans.

"This guy better team up," I complained. "Because if his pride drags this out, and *I* don't get laid by a muscle-bound, gorgeous PI, and soon, it's gonna piss me off."

"Sounds like she's already there," Raye whispered to Luna.

"You have Cap. He gives it to you regular. How fun was it, the delay you two endured before you connected?" Luna replied.

"Copy that," Raye said.

I let out a breath, sat back in my seat and looked out the window at the city passing me by.

I did this wondering what drug dealers would do with a bunch of homeless people.

I came up with no answers, except the fact that, whatever the answer was, it was nothing good.

NINETEEN

EXPAND

Stakeouts sounded like they were all fun and games.

But let me tell you. They weren't.

First, I had to set my alarm for 3:00 a.m., which didn't seem like a big deal, until it went off at 3:00.

Then, I had to call out for my alarm to snooze, something I did. Twice.

At 3:14, I had no choice but to drag my ass out of bed, brush my teeth, wash the sleep out of my eyes, throw on some black clothes (at least that wasn't a problem), and drag my tired ass down the stairs to where Eric told me he'd pick me up. And true to his word, there he was waiting for me in an idling Denali outside the security gate.

I climbed in, stretched across the cab to give him a brief kiss, then I ordered, "QuikTrip."

He grinned and drove us to a QuikTrip.

We went in, got two giganto cups of coffee, and I abandoned my corn snack theme. On the fly, I created a donut snack theme by bagging two chocolate long johns, two cinnamon rolls, two old fashioneds and two cream-filled Bismarcks.

On Eric's part, he nabbed two Kind bars, which I ignored

because it made me question my dedication to falling deeper in love with him.

Eric butted in to pay, whereupon I shared, "Arthur reimburses us."

To which Eric said, "And so does Mace."

Okay then.

I let him pay.

We walked out, drove south, parked five blocks away from the warehouse and had to hoof it in, going out of our way to do so to be absolutely certain we weren't seen by anyone who might be watching.

Once we hit the warehouse, we had to climb up two flights of stairs.

By the time we made it to the area set up to surveil—which had two folding camp chairs (the pimp ones with the beverage holders built into the arms) and a camera with a long-ass telephoto lens on a tripod, and that was it, and thus this setup wasn't super welcoming—I was done with the stakeout.

Alas, it had just begun, and I had no choice but to get stuck in doing it.

We greeted Cap and Raye, who, for obvious reasons (and it wasn't the donuts I offered them), seemed really happy to see us.

Cap took a Bismarck, Raye took a cinnamon roll and handed me a set of funky-ass binoculars.

"Night vision," she explained the funky-ass part.

Oo.

Cool.

Night vision!

That was so awesome, things looked up.

Briefly.

They left.

I put the strap of the night vision binoculars around my neck and Eric warned, "It's strange at first, Jess. You gotta get used to it."

I went to the grimy window, and I could see, even in the mostly dark and through the aforementioned grime, it had a full view of the encampment. I put the binocs to my eyes.

Yes, it was weird, but it was also easy to get used to.

And when I got used to it, I noted all was quiet on the camp front. Not a creature was stirring.

Eric had his own binocs, and he came up beside me and had a look.

Then he turned to me and said, “Have a seat, sweetheart. It doesn’t take both of us to keep an eye. The way this goes is shifts within shifts. That means, on our shift, I’ll take the first half hour. You spell me. And so on.”

“Right,” I replied, thinking this made sense.

I let my binocs drop to my chest and sat down in one of the camp chairs to sip needed coffee and hork down a Bismarck.

I kept my eyes on Eric as he stood off to the side of the window, binoculars held to his eyes, scanning.

I munched into the cream-filled, chocolate-covered dough thinking I really loved the length of his body, how he naturally held himself so straight, and the width of his shoulders.

Okay, so I could forgive him the Kind bars.

“How was surveillance room duty?” I asked.

“Over, and good I don’t have to do it again for another week.”

I heard that.

I didn’t even know what surveillance room duty was, but if what we were doing now was anything close, I wanted no part of it.

“So, Javi and Harlow shared about a half dozen moments in the ten minutes he was in the Sportage with us tonight,” I informed him.

Eric’s head turned to me and he dropped the binocs. “Moments?”

“Instant attraction,” I explained. “Though, I think he might have blown it by going all he-man, macho alpha on her and questioning her ability to be an Angel.”

I couldn’t be sure. It was dark and we had zero light up in our little station (for obvious reasons), but I still thought I caught his smile.

"Not the way to go with you women," he remarked.

"Totally," I agreed.

"Somehow, I feel this is a good thing, at the same time I'm not so sure," he stated.

"My thoughts exactly," I agreed.

I munched more donut, chased it with coffee, and through this, he'd turned his attention back to the camp, before I asked, "Are you okay? You're not running on much sleep."

"I'm fine, honey," he murmured to the window.

I finished my donut and decided to let him concentrate, thankful I'd been smart enough to wear warm clothes, because it was damned chilly outside.

While I did this, my body decided to go back to sleep.

I knew this last part when I jerked awake, the coffee still in my hand sloshing, because I felt my phone vibrate against my ass.

I looked to Eric as I slid my coffee cup in the holder in the camp chair's arm and leaned forward to grab my phone.

He was looking at me, and I hoped I was only asleep for a couple of seconds (though, I could tell my coffee was no longer warm), thus, I hoped he didn't notice I fell asleep approximately five minutes into my first stakeout.

"You in dark mode?" he asked.

He meant my phone.

I nodded.

I mean, I was me. I was dark mode through and through.

I pulled my cell out, quickly processed the fact that Eric had to notice I fell asleep, considering my screen told me it was after 5:00 and I'd way missed my turn keeping my eye on the camp (which meant, along with processing that, I had to process how sweet it was he let me sleep), and then I focused on the number.

It was one I couldn't identify.

Not even marketers called at this time, and with all the shit going down, I couldn't ignore the call.

So I took it.

"Hello?"

"Jess?"

It was Jeff.

My heart skipped a beat.

"Jeff, are you okay?" I asked.

"No," he answered. "I'm at the police station. Javi and me have been arrested."

My eyes zipped to Eric.

Fuck!

No one ever thought racing to a police station because their brother was arrested was fun and games.

But let me confirm. It was not.

Matters were worsened because Eric had to make a call to someone to relieve us, which meant we had to wait to leave our stakeout until they arrived.

And once Liam showed, we then had to race down the stairs and jog to the Denali, and I'll take this moment to remind you I didn't do official exercise. So jogging what amounted to probably seven blocks (because, again, we had to avoid lights and not be seen on a direct trajectory of heading back to the SUV, or at all) made me reconsider my philosophy that living a generally active life kept me in shape.

I reconsidered it more when we both angled in the Denali and Eric wasn't even breathing heavy, but I was, and added to that, I had a wicked stitch in my side.

He didn't fuck around getting to the police station.

Once there, I was forced to explore the depths of my patience when I was relegated to a chair in a waiting room, and Eric disappeared into the bowels of the station accompanied by a uniform.

I wasn't sure why he was allowed in and I was not, but asking that question might be detrimental to exploring the depths of my patience, so I decided to keep my mouth shut.

About seven hours later (okay, it was probably maybe ten minutes), Roam strolled out from where Eric had sauntered in.

Even in the current circumstances, I took the needed moment to recover from how fine he was (as with all these men, he was just that fine) while he made his approach to me.

He sat down beside me and turned my way.

"Your brother and Montoya are being released," he announced.

I let out the breath I could have sworn I'd been holding since I heard Jeff's voice on my phone.

"They weren't arrested," Roam continued. "They were taken in for questioning because they brought two males who'd sustained gunshot wounds to an ER."

My heart stuttered to a halt.

"Gunshot wounds?" I whispered.

Roam's lips thinned before he shared, "One was DOA."

That was when my heart twisted.

"One of Javi's men?" I asked, my voice stretched tight.

He nodded.

Oh God.

Poor Jeff.

Poor Javi.

Poor unknown Shadow Soldier.

I put my elbows to my knees and dropped my head in my hands.

Roam rubbed my back, not invasive, not expansive, just right.

It felt nice.

Seriously, these were *such good guys*.

Then it hit me, and I sat up abruptly.

"What about the other guy?"

I didn't like the look that came over Roam's face, even before he explained it.

"He's in surgery. We don't know." He paused, studying me closely, then from whatever he read he made a decision and carried on, "But it's not looking good because he was shot seven times."

Seven times?

Seven?

"Fucking *fuck*," I bit off.

At this point, we both sensed motion to our sides.

We looked that way, and I saw Eric and Mace with a handsome Latino dude who wore a more-official-than-just-normally-official uniform coming our way.

The handsome Latino dude, who I'd never seen in my life, caught sight of me and then let out a visibly massive sigh like I worked his last nerves.

I didn't get that, but I also didn't have time to consider it.

Because with them were Javi and Jeff.

I stood, feeling both heartbroken and nervous, because I hadn't left things in a very good place with my brother, and now I knew he was suffering.

I should have known not to be nervous.

We'd had spats before.

We got over it.

We'd had one doozie of a spat, the worst ever.

And in that moment, my brother didn't hesitate to walk right up to me and wrap his arms around me.

I returned the gesture.

"I'm so sorry, honey," I whispered in his ear, my eyes on Javi's face, noting how his male beauty had turned to stone in his grief.

At my words, Jeff said nothing, but his arms did.

They got tight.

I let him leech what he needed from me for a while before I pulled a bit away. He lifted his head, I peered in his eyes, and I whispered, "Let's get to the hospital."

There was maybe one good reason to go to a hospital. That being because you were having a baby. All the rest, it was known by all and sundry, were clearly not fun and games.

I could confirm, of the variety of reasons you went to the hospital, the reason we did it sucked huge.

The news we received upon making it there sucked exponentially huger.

Javi's other soldier died on the operating table.

I wasn't sure how the men corralled Javi and Jeff into a Denali and to the Nightingale Investigations & Security offices (along with me).

I just knew, a half an hour after Javi and Jeff were dealt that second blow, we were there, in Mace's office, and Cap and Raye, Roam, Knox, Brady and Gabe were all there too.

And, obviously, Eric.

Raye and I sat on a couch in the back of Mace's super slick office.

She held my hand.

I couldn't tear my eyes from Jeff, who was sitting in a chair in front of Mace's desk, leaned forward, both of his hands wrapped around the back of his neck.

Javi was pacing.

No one said anything, and they were giving Javi loads of room, something I understood because the vibe he was emitting was terrifying.

Eventually, Mace decided it was time. I wasn't sure he was right, but I didn't have a choice.

Because he remarked to Javi, "I think you understand it's time we debrief."

Jeff shot straight, but I got wired when Javi suddenly stopped pacing and faced off against Mace.

"You wanna tell me why the fuck we're in your offices?" Javi demanded.

"Because I need you to tell me what went down tonight," Mace stated calmly. "And then we need to talk about how we're gonna navigate the future."

I jumped when Jeff surged out of his chair, and I was about to do the same, but Raye gave my hand a warning squeeze, so I sat still.

Tense and ready to intervene, but still.

However, Jeff just started pacing like Javi had done.

"You got your thing, we got ours," Javi belatedly answered Mace.

"Your team was nearly halved tonight, Montoya," Mace said quietly.

A muscle jerked up Javi's cheek and his gaze intensified on Mace.

I reckoned the first part was emotion at the mention of his lost brothers, the second part was surprise that Mace knew so much about Javi's crew (safe to say, I was surprised too).

Nearly halved meant it wasn't a very big crew, news I also found surprising.

Mace was still going quiet when he said, "Please tell me you did not order that raid."

Raid?

What raid?

"I'm not that fuckin' stupid," Javi snarled.

"Then explain what happened," Mace returned.

"I don't gotta explain shit to you," Javi shot back.

"We're on the same side, brother," Mace told him.

"You got a couple boys tagging Angel ass, so to keep those asses available, you waded in," Javi sneered, showing his hand about how much he knew about us, as well as how much he didn't. "You're about billing for services. Don't pretend this is your mission."

I could feel Eric and Cap's elevated tenseness, along with that same happening with all the men in the room, just not as much as Eric and Cap.

But Mace was the soul of composure.

"You don't know me or my men," he said, still calm and muted. "I understand your loss—"

"You don't understand shit," Javi spat.

Mace lost some of his calm.

"My little sister's head was blown off right in front of me, Montoya, so maybe also don't tell me what I understand."

My chest tightened at learning this horrid news about Mace.

Javi scowled, because at learning it, he was not only not afforded a comeback, he had to sit with that horrid news too.

"We can be allies," Mace stated.

"They went rogue," Javi bit out.

"What?" Mace asked.

"Joaquim and Jamal, they went rogue," Javi said.

Crazily, my mind noted that Javi seemed to collect people with J names. It did this in the fraction of a second it took Javi to continue.

"Joaquim has a sister who's hooked on Fenty. Lil Clown deals to her. Since he does, Joaquim has a serious beef with Clown." He shut his mouth and shook his head, and my throat got tight when he whispered, "Had. He had a beef."

Oh, Javi.

I turned my attention to Jeff.

His eyes were locked on Javi, and they, along with his nostrils, were red-rimmed from fighting tears.

"I gave them the intel the Angels discovered tonight," Javi went on. "Joaquim got jacked up about it. He was sure Clown and his crew were doin' their fucked-up business with whatever they're doin' with the community. He wanted to roll in. I told him we didn't even have confirmation it was Clown dealing in the community yet, much less his crew bein' behind that shit. I told him we had to get all the info, confirm it, and plan how we were gonna hit these motherfuckers. Because they're motherfuckers, they're strapped, they're organized, and if we didn't have our shit tight, they'd obliterate us. And as you can see, I was fuckin' right."

He was.

He was fucking right.

"So they went in," Mace murmured.

Javi nodded before he shook his head. "I thought I'd calmed him down. I was wrong. And Joaquim and Jamal were brothers before they joined the brotherhood. They'd known each other since they were kids. It was pure Jamal to take Joaq's back, even if he knew Joaq was leadin' him into a shitstorm. Jamal was not DOA at the hospital.

Jamal was gone by the time me and Jeff got to their location. Neck shot he had, he was dead at the fuckin' scene. Even shot seven times, Joaq still dragged his body out. So that meant Joaq died knowin' he killed his brother."

God.

This was such a tragic mess.

"We don't need the cops on our ass, Mason," Javi stated.

"You both said nothing while you were questioned, but I'll tell Alvarez this wasn't on your order," Mace assured. "That said, the cops are still gonna be on your asses. Just not about this."

Javi nodded and muttered, "Gratitude."

"I hate to ask it, but it's gotta be asked, did Joaquim share anything that we all need to know about this case?" Mace inquired.

Javi blew out a big breath before he shook his head. "They didn't get that far." His body visibly tightened before he added, "They sacrificed everything, for fuckin' nothin'."

On that desolate note, the room fell silent, and I wasn't sure what was going to happen next.

Since nothing happened for what seemed like a long time, I squeezed Raye's hand before I let it go, got up and went to my brother.

I wrapped my fingers around his and waited for him to look down at me.

"I'm not momming you," I said to start. "I'm just offering, because you lost people who meant a lot to you. Do you want to stay with me for a while?" I finished in a hurry. "I won't be mad if you say no. I'll get it."

Jeff looked to Javi, so I did too, to see him watching us.

Particularly our fingers wrapped around each other's. And it was the first time that night where he appeared pleased about something. Still broken and sad, but there was a little goodness there.

"You can come over too," I invited Javi. "I'm learning to cook. I can make you both breakfast."

Or I could try to.

How hard was it to whip up some scrambled eggs? I'd watched Ina do it at least half a dozen times.

"I gotta talk to Joaquim and Jamal's people," Javi said to Jeff. "But if you wanna hang with your sister, do it, brother."

My brother brought my hand up to his chest and pressed it in, so I looked at him.

"I gotta do that with Javi," he said softly.

I hurt for him, and I was proud of him at the same time.

To share this, I pulled my hand from his hold and hugged him.

He hugged me back.

So they could get on with their sad task, I let him go.

But I moved right to Javi.

And then I hugged him.

It took him a second, but his arms curled around me, and he squeezed so tight, I had to hold my breath so I wouldn't wheeze.

When he seemed to realize what he was doing, his arms loosened, but he didn't let me go.

I tipped my head back and said gently, "I'm so sorry you lost your brothers tonight, Javi."

"I am too, *hermanita*," he replied.

"If you need anything..." I let that trail, but I turned to my brother, so he knew what I hoped he already knew. The offer was for both of them.

Jeff's lips lifted up in acknowledgement and a smile he didn't feel.

Javi let me go.

I stepped away.

Roam stepped forward. "I'll drop you wherever you need to go."

"We can make our way," Javi replied.

"I wasn't questioning that," Roam returned. And he didn't stop there. "Something to know about me, I grew up on the street too. I get it. I get why you keep your crew tight. But don't make bad decisions when the offer is made to expand your world. I had one dead brother and one live one,"—he jerked his head to Cap—"and we were facing nothing good. Then we let our world be expanded." He lifted his hands to indicate the men in the room. "Not a lecture, just something to think about. Now, you want a ride?"

Javi didn't move, he just stared at Roam for a really long time.

I relaxed when he finally muttered, "That'd be good."

I gave my brother another hug before he left with Javi.

Raye got close when the door closed behind them.

"I called Luna. Luna called Harlow. Harlow is taking my shift this morning. Luna then talked to Tito, and Willow is taking your shift this afternoon. I'm taking Harlow's."

Willow provided our baked goods in the coffee cubby. Willow also acted as backup in the unusual event one of us needed to call off.

"I'm fine," I said.

"I'm not saying you aren't. I'm saying take some time. If you want to come in, come in. If you don't, it's covered."

God, I loved my chick.

I wasn't a hugger, but clearly hoarding most of my life's supply meant I had to clear out some space, because I gave her a hug too.

When we broke, Eric was there, and he took control of my hand.

"I have the rest of the morning free too," he said.

Decision made.

I wasn't going into work, at least not until later.

I said goodbye to everyone, made sure to thank them all, especially Mace, for intervening, then Eric took me down to his Tahoe that was parked in the garage under their building.

We got in, he drove us straight to the Oasis, and he gave me an amazing gift as he did so.

Our comfortable silence.

Not that I didn't have a lot on my mind. It was just, sometimes, I dealt with it better on my own.

And I loved it that Eric gave me space to do that.

Once home, I realized, even having a guy, it'd be nice to snuggle a cat. So I decided, even with all that was happening, we were so totally going to an animal shelter that weekend.

I might not get one, but I was going to get the lay of the land.

On this decision, I went right to the refrigerator.

I pulled out the icebox cake, my big, round platter and a table knife. I wedged the knife into the side of the pan and ran it around the cake. I then placed that fucker on the plate, released the spring mechanism, and pulled the pan away.

It was supposed to have shaved chocolate as decoration.

I was in no mood to shave chocolate (I could do that on something else down the line).

Thus, I did not hesitate to nab two dessert plates, grab my chef's knife and cut two enormous wodges and put them on plates.

Eric had leaned a hip against the counter in the kitchen with me and had watched all of this, which was good. He was right there when I shoved a fork into his wodge and handed it to him.

I then shoved a fork into my wodge.

After that, I cleft a massive amount of the creamy cookie cake onto my fork and rammed it into my mouth.

Absolute heaven.

Eric didn't partake.

"You okay?" he asked.

"No," I said around mocha cream and softened-by-cream chocolate chip cookies.

"You gonna be able to calm down enough to take a nap with me?" he asked while I shoveled more cake into my mouth.

"Yes," I answered, still with mouth full.

"You going into work later?"

I swallowed and said, "Tito gives what amounts to a week of personal or sick days every year. I usually use it as vacation because I don't often get sick. So I won't be out wages. But I need the tips, and it feels gross to ask my girls to cover for me."

"Two of your brother's friends were shot dead last night. It isn't gross to let your friends cover for you when serious shit goes down that you should take the time to deal with, Jessie. And I could tell by the way Raye arranged that, they won't mind."

"We'll see after our nap. Do you have to go in later?"

He nodded and finally forked into his cake.

I watched as he took a bite.

His eyes widened before going lazy, and after he swallowed, he murmured, "Fucking hell."

"Don't tell anybody," I warned him.

His brows drew together. "About the cake?"

"Yeah."

"Why?"

"Because Raye made the mistake of bringing her insanely delicious pudding to an Oasis shindig, and now she can barely show her face in the courtyard without someone expecting her to magically produce it. I can't say. I'm eating this now and don't have any of her pudding on hand for an on-the-spot comparison. But since I'm eating this now, I'll make the pronouncement it's better than her pudding, with the stipulation that I might retract that when confronted with a bowl of her pudding. To wit, if anyone knew about this cake, everyone would force me to make it all the time."

"It wasn't hard," Eric replied.

"How will I get practice making other shit if I'm always making this?" I asked, indicating with my fork the cake on my plate.

"Fair point," he said, his black eyes twinkling with humor, which masked his relief I wasn't losing my shit that my brother was facing the day after earning two very dead friends, how my brother's friends got dead, and the fact he was mixed up in that world.

We lapsed into silence and ate our cake.

When we were done, even though I was down for seconds, Eric took my plate from me, ran both of them under water, stacked them in the sink, came back to me and grabbed my hand.

"Let's go to bed," he murmured.

I loved those words coming from his mouth, even if what we were going to do there wasn't what I'd been hankering for from the minute I met him.

I selected an okay-ish, totally simple, black cotton nightie for this non-adventure.

And I learned quickly there was absolutely nothing better in the whole world than to have the fright of my life, followed by a prolonged witnessing of heartbreak, only to end that wrapped up in Eric's strong arms in a darkened room in my bed.

You would think it would take me a while to wind down after all of that.

It didn't.

Nuzzled close to Eric's heat and hardness, safe in his strong arms, I fell right to sleep.

TWENTY

A PLAN

My eyes opened, and I got an instant view of Eric's face, close-up and asleep.

How had I not noticed how long his lashes were and how many of them he had?

Now noting it, I knew it was something I'd never again miss. A thrill for the ages, or as long as we were together.

Something I was getting closer and closer to hoping would be forever.

The next thing I saw was, even in sleep, there was no boyishness or innocence left in him.

His mother dead before he hit high school, resulting in the loss of his brother and dad in different and painful ways, what he'd seen and done in the FBI—a dirty partner, a dead colleague—then a narcissistic wife.

Any kind of innocence had been stolen from him.

On this thought, I felt an almost overwhelming desire to smooth the black hair that had fallen over his forehead, and with my touch, take his past away, erase it like it never happened.

But I couldn't.

Like I couldn't take Jeff and Javi's pain away that day.

Or I couldn't give Jeff the mom and dad he needed. All kids needed patient and supportive parents, but kids like Jeff needed them more than most. And he'd never had that, not even close, not his entire life.

Or I couldn't get Javi's mom the help she needed so he didn't have to live his entire life vulnerable, exposed to a world no kid should even know existed, having to do this at the same time look out for her.

Or I couldn't make it so Stella hadn't met Mace first, so instead, she'd fallen in love with Eric, and he wouldn't have had to lose so much of his life to a woman like Savannah.

And that part was hard to think about because it meant, down the line, I would not be where I was right then with him.

But that was how deep my feelings had grown.

Because I knew I'd be happy if he was happy with someone else, loved by someone and free to love them, raising children together, without any of the shit he'd had to eat from his ex, even if that meant there'd be no shot for me.

All these thoughts tumbled in my brain and...

God.

I wanted to touch him *so bad.*

I didn't, because he'd had two nights with very little sleep, he was sleeping now. I couldn't give him the things that would have made his life smoother, filled with more joy than pain, but by God, I was going to let him get more rest.

Carefully, I slid away from him and started to turn to get out of bed before I checked the time and made my decision about whether or not to go to work.

I didn't get very far.

Eric's arm around me tightened, and he pulled me right back.

When I looked at his face this time, those beautiful eyes were open.

His voice was a rough, sleepy, sexy purr when he asked, "Where you goin'?"

"Go back to sleep," I whispered.

He pulled my nightie up at the back and then went into my panties with both hands, pressing me forward so my pelvis was tight to his.

Or more aptly, I was pressed to his hard cock.

"Where you goin'?" he repeated.

"Nowhere," I whispered.

His eyes got lazy, he looked to my mouth, then he kissed me.

I wasn't sure what to expect from Eric in this department... exactly. I just knew it would be good.

But, man, what commenced wasn't good.

It was life altering.

Deep, wet, unhurried kisses. Hands (both his and mine) roaming, exploring, discovering.

Eventually, he rolled on top of me, and his lips, tongue and teeth moved deep into the exploring mode, striking out along my jaw, neck, below my ears.

Down.

Across my chest, between my breasts.

He tugged the stretchy bodice of my nightie over one of my breasts, and, vaguely bummed that it wasn't in one of my good nighties, I whispered, "Sorry about the nightie. I wanted it to be a special one."

I licked my lips at how nice his warm hand felt covering my exposed breast. And it felt so nice, I didn't notice for a second that was all he did, and I didn't have his mouth on me anymore at all.

I tipped my chin down to look at him, only to note his gaze was on me.

The instant I caught his eyes, he whispered, "It's not the nightie, Jessie. It was never the nightie. It was always the woman in the nightie."

Hang on.

Wait.

Oh my God.

Did he just say that?

I stared into warm, black eyes.

He said it.

I squirmed under him to get back to his mouth. Mission accomplished, I kissed him, and with an almighty heave (which, granted, I think he allowed), I rolled him to his back.

After I broke our kiss, it was my mouth and teeth and tongue exploring his stubbled jaw (nice), his neck (yum), his corded throat (delicious).

Down.

His pec (amazing).

And I didn't dally. I scraped my teeth along his nipple before I suckled at it, testing if he was sensitive there. His hand sifting into my hair and the low noise he made told me was.

Excellent.

Turned on by this (or more turned on by it than I already was), I went after the other nipple, and God, what a journey across the furred hills and valleys of his chest (stupendous).

Then down.

I took my time at his boxed abs (Lord, *scrumptious*, especially the way they tensed and rippled under my attention).

I could do that for hours, days...

But I went down again.

And I pulled at his boxer briefs.

His thick, pretty cock sprang up, I got a good look at it, and...

Fuck yes.

It was just as perfect as the rest of him.

I grabbed hold, emboldened by his soft groan and softer, "*Honey.*"

I licked the tip, I stroked the shaft with my hand, I lifted my eyes to his burning ones, and once our gazes caught, I deep throated him.

That groan was so powerful, I could feel it in my mouth.

The wet between my legs got a whole lot wetter.

Better, his head fell back and the muscles in his neck tensed, veins popping out.

Oh yeah.

Giving head to Eric was gonna *rock*.

I sucked and bobbed and stroked, and sometimes gave myself a break to lick.

I was into it. I was feeling it. The low, sexy noises Eric made told me he was definitely feeling it. I loved how his big, strong body grew more and more tense around me. I loved what I was giving him, I loved how much he liked it, and I loved that he was all out there showing he did.

So I was squirming and wet and way getting off on what I was doing.

And then I wasn't doing it anymore.

I'd been pulled up his body, rolled...

In one blink, my panties were gone.

In the next, Eric rolled back, taking me with him, pulling me up, up and *up*, until I had to sit up or I'd go through the wall.

And once I did, I was sitting on his face, his hands at my hips bearing me down, and he was eating me out.

Yes!

"Oh God, baby," I whispered, my head falling back.

Men could be bad at this. Sloppy. Lazy. Going through the motions in hopes of getting the same in return.

Eric, my astonishing overachiever, strove for greatness, and make no mistake, he attained it.

He pulled me just off his mouth before he ordered roughly, "Lose the nightie, Jessie."

I broke records ripping off my nightie.

He kept bossing. "Now ride my mouth, honey."

I glided back down and gladly did what I was told while he licked and sucked and sometimes scraped.

The orgasm he was building wasn't flirting with me. This was no tease. It was ready to rumble.

But after a hard suck of my clit, it suddenly started to bolt in, and like he felt it coming, I was off Eric's face and on my back in bed.

No!

"Baby," I begged as Eric got off the bed.

"Condom," he grunted.

I watched him yank off his briefs.

I went still.

Man.

I'd been *soooooooo* right.

His ass was *insane*.

"Clean," I panted, pushing up to sitting. "The pill," I finished.

He turned to me, his cargos in his hands. "You trust me?"

"Do you trust me?" I asked back.

"This is a big step, honey," he said gently.

"I want only you," I replied, and those words were husky with feeling, and not simply the feeling that I wanted him to make me come ASAFP.

In an instant, my Mr. Smooth Move executed another one.

Because he'd entered the bed hooking my leg behind the knee, pulling it up at his side, forcing me back down on the bed at the same time covering me, and I felt his cock catch between my legs.

"Fuck you're wet," he murmured gruffly.

"Is that surprising?" I asked.

He grinned, wicked and wolfish. "No."

He gave me that grin, but he didn't move.

Seriously?

"Eric, are you gonna tease me forever or...*ooooooh*!"

My last was because he glided in, slow and steady and so, so deep.

He kept going until he was in to the hilt, and I was full of him.

It took me a second to accommodate his thickness (also, it must be noted, his length). I enjoyed that second thoroughly and only opened my eyes after I realized I'd closed them, but more importantly, he wasn't moving.

When I did, I saw he was watching me.

I was about to tell him to stop messing around.

I didn't get a chance.

Because he whispered, "Christ, Jessie. You're so fucking beautiful."

It happened then.

That was when I knew it was over.

I was done.

We could have unprotected sex not only because I was on birth control and I trusted that he was safe, but because he was the only man I was ever going to sleep with again.

I was in love with him.

And yes, as time went by, I would continue to fall deeper and deeper into that state.

I wanted to get a cat with him (and then maybe a dog).

I wanted to live with him.

I wanted to have babies with him.

And, if he insisted, I was going to marry him (though, he'd have to put up with a black wedding dress, no DJ, no dancing, no toasts, none of that traditional shit (however, I could do flowers), just him, me, a ceremony, lots of food and drink and a big party...because I was me and that was the only way I'd do it).

I didn't know how he knew where I was in my head. Perhaps it was the tears I felt shimmering in my eyes.

But this perfect moment became more perfect when he answered all my thoughts with one word.

"Yeah."

Oh shit.

I was about to sob, but fortunately I didn't, because he kissed me and started to move inside.

I dug sex, if it was good.

I liked to fuck, especially. And I was down with getting more than a little nasty.

But I didn't realize until that moment that never in my entire life had a man made love to me.

Braydon occasionally tried it, and I knew what he was going for.

But he always failed.

I knew that now for certain, because Eric was making love to me.

Kissing me then nuzzling me and whispering to me how beautiful he thought I was, how good I felt, how tight I clutched him, how much he liked it, how wet and hot I felt around him, how gorgeous he thought that was.

Through this, our hands were linked, fingers through fingers, as, with my free hand, I roamed the wonderland of the skin and muscles of his back and ass and let him love me with his body, his words, his movements.

Truth, I had never felt more loved than I felt in those moments with Eric.

Another truth, I'd never in my life felt precious, except right then.

So it was unsurprising when the gently lapping waves suddenly washed in with a tsunami of an orgasm, I wasn't expecting it. Not for it to happen yet, but especially not for it to be that all-consuming.

It was my world, and I was lost in it.

No.

Eric was my world.

And I was lost to him.

When I emerged, Eric's rhythm had increased, but his eyes were locked on me, there was a heated fluidity to the inky depths that was awesome, considering it showed openly how much he got off on making me come that hard.

But I could sense him holding back.

I got that, I didn't want this to end either.

Still.

"Let go, baby," I whispered.

He kissed me, but he didn't let go.

I bit his lower lip, dug my nails into his ass, and through his sexy groan and sexier growl, I repeated, "Baby, let go."

He buried his face in my neck, finally thrusting hard and deep (giving me a preview of just how fantastic fucking was going to be with Eric). I wrapped both my calves around him, and then he grunted, before he sunk his teeth into my flesh (fabulous), buried himself inside and poured himself into me (and that was phenomenal).

His big body gave a glorious shudder when it left him that felt so good, it was like he was starting foreplay again. Then he ran his lips along where he bit me before they glided up my neck, along my jaw, to my mouth.

This kiss was a return to long, wet and languid, with lots of hands roaming, a circling back to the beginning that felt like a promise.

That promise being, we'd just shared the most intimate thing two people could do, and it was over. But it was never really going to be over.

Because we were never going to be over.

Oh shit, I was going to cry again.

Eric broke our kiss and whispered, "Okay?"

I swallowed hard and nodded.

His eyes warmed, his face got soft, and he was still whispering when he noted, "So you felt it."

I nodded again and made a sobby noise deep in my throat.

His lips were twitching when he asked, "Are you gonna cry?"

"No," I forced out, but it was croaky, and it sounded like I was going to cry.

I felt his body move with laughter before I heard it.

So, obviously, I slapped his arm and snapped, "Turner!"

"Hardass, greet-the-day-by-flipping-it-the-bird-and-getting-on-with-it Jess Wylde, crying after her man makes her come hard," he teased.

"I don't greet the day by flipping it the bird," I denied.

He raised his brows.

Whatever.

"So I greet the day by flipping it the bird, metaphorically," I admitted. "A lot of the time the day flips me the bird back, so I gotta get mine in before it does."

"Right."

I didn't want to ruin the moment, so I didn't remind him that today hadn't given me an awesome greeting...or him.

I didn't have to say it.

He felt it coming from me, or he recalled it, because his amusement vanished and he said, "It didn't start out great, but it led us to finally having the time to connect in a way we both wanted, to take our time doing it, to do it right, and have time after so I could give you shit and you could shovel it back."

This was true.

And the doing it right part was especially true.

Though I'd never admit it aloud, the shoveling shit at each other was fun too.

"That's life, Jess. The shit hits. You deal. You keep going. And then sometimes, for your troubles, it hands you the perfect moment to make it all worth it. You know that," he reminded me.

Perfect moment.

Worth it.

"I don't want to freak you, but I do want to say that, even though that climax was pretty damned extraordinary..." I began.

He shot me a smug grin.

I ignored it.

"...just so you know where I am with this, it's deep, Eric."

"Good. Then we're on the same path," he replied.

Shit!

Verbal confirmation.

I was definitely going to cry.

Fortunately, Eric located his amusement, he made it visible, audible and physical, so instead of weeping, I started glaring.

"Important to note," I began, "you should feel free to do that to me whenever you want."

His, "Obliged," shook with his continued humor.

I ignored it again.

"But I also like to fuck."

More humor in his, "Fantastic. I do too."

"And I don't mind getting nasty."

That caught his attention, I knew, because the lazy went out of his eyes, the humor did too, a curious light shone in them, and he added a head cock.

"What does nasty mean to you?" he asked.

"What does it mean to you?" I asked back.

"I asked first."

"I brought it up."

"Nasty encompasses a lot of things, honey, so bringing it up is vague at best, a tease in reality."

I clicked my tongue. It was hardly a tease.

"You ditched the nightie, sat on my face and rode it pretty fucking fast when I told you to," he noted.

Mm.

Lovely memory.

"Fuck, how did life lead me to you?" he asked, and the way he did had me shooting right back to the present and staring at him.

"Eric—" His name was shaky.

"No." He cut me off, then touched his lips to mine. "We're not gonna analyze it. It's there. We both know it. We both felt it." He dipped close. "And I'll dominate you all you want, honey, because I get off on that too."

I shivered.

Eric smiled.

Then he kissed me, we took our time doing it, but we both knew why he stopped.

It was only that Eric murmured the reason. "I'm out and you're leaking. Let's get you cleaned up and have some lunch."

I was down with that, so I allowed him to pull me out of bed.

I grabbed my nightie and panties, and ever the gentleman, he told me to use the bathroom first.

I was in the kitchen perusing the contents of my refrigerator (we had icebox cake and leftover fettucine) when he sauntered in wearing nothing but his cargos.

After-sex bonus: I got an unobstructed view of his chest.

"We have fettucine, or I can DoorDash some Mad Greens," I told him.

I suggested Mad Greens for him. If it was only me, I'd do a chili-cheese Coney dog from Sonic.

"Mad Greens," he said (of course), then he pulled his phone out of his cargos. "I got it."

I shut the fridge door. "I can buy us lunch, Turner."

"You need to go to work to earn tips because you've been bringing jerky and water to a homeless camp, Jess." There was my overachiever, always figuring stuff out. "You also got all the shit for pastitsio, fettucine and icebox cake. I'm buying lunch."

"Are you keeping track?" I asked.

"Do I have a dick?" he asked back.

He did, and it was a lovely one.

I got lost in my memories of just how lovely it was, and how much I liked what I did to it, and how much more I liked what it did to me. Somewhere in the middle of remembering how full I felt when he was planted inside, I had his lips on mine and his tongue in my mouth.

When he broke the kiss, he didn't go far.

But he did say, "Just so you don't doubt it, you give great head."

"Just so you don't doubt it, you got serious chops eating a girl out."

I watched his eyes smile. "Good to know."

"Same," I replied.

"What do you want from Mad Greens?"

I had no idea. I knew it existed. But since I frequented Lenny's for my burger, shake and sandwich needs, QuikTrip for my on-the-go-needs, Raising Cane's for my chicken tender needs (you get the gist), I had no experience with Mad Greens' healthy-living menu.

I knew Eric knew this with just how much more his smile shone from his eyes before he bossed, “Go get your phone and pull up the menu while I pull up DoorDash and get the order started.”

“I live to serve,” I muttered as I moved away from him.

I got a vagina ripple when I heard his return mutter, “At times, you will,” as I walked to the bedroom.

I located my phone in my pants and started back to the kitchen, but stopped dead halfway down the hall when I engaged the screen.

I pulled up the first text from a number I didn’t know, sensing I knew what I was going to get.

I was right.

This is Jeff. My new number. And I just want you to know I love you.

I took a shuddering breath.

Then I pulled up the next text.

Hermanita, thanks for this morning. You now got my number. Store it and I’m there anytime you need me. J

Javi.

I texted Jeff: *Love you too. Thanks for your number. And try to keep your chin up.*

To Javi, I said: *I’m there anytime too, hermanito.*

I walked into the kitchen and saw Eric leaned into his forearms on my bar, his phone in his hands, but when I showed, his head turned my way.

And he caught my vibe because his voice was quiet and cautious when he asked, “What?”

I lifted my hand and shook my phone side to side. “Jeff gave me his new number.”

That was when his whole, gorgeous face went soft. “Good.”

“Javi gave me his number too,” I told him, coming in closer, a lot closer, so much so, my stomach was brushing his hip. Once there, I leaned my side against the counter.

I was pulling up the Mad Greens menu when Eric announced, “I’m gonna tell you something, sweetheart, and I want your okay on it.”

I turned my attention to him.

"I'm gonna suggest to Mace that we make moves to recruit Javi and Jeff to the team," he announced.

My breath stopped coming.

Eric kept talking.

"We have some intel on the last member of their crew. Not sure he'd be a good fit. The partners have a zero-tolerance policy about drugs, except marijuana. That said, there's no pot usage for twenty-four hours if you're going to be on duty or at all if you're in the middle of a case. This isn't an issue because none of us use weed. Javi does, only occasionally. Same with your brother. But the last member of their team, a guy named Cody, is a habitual user. To the point he might have a problem with addiction."

One, it seemed they'd made great inroads into amassing info about Javier and his crew.

Two, I was weirdly relieved the last member of that crew didn't have a J name.

"Cody is also much younger," Eric went on. "He's only twenty-three. As far as we can tell, Javi doesn't use him in the heavy shit. He's usually surveillance or their wheel man." A smile quirked his lips. "And since they don't have an anonymous benefactor, they all have jobs, and Cody doesn't do too badly. He's self-taught and designs e-commerce websites."

"What does my brother do?" I asked.

"He works with Javi at Sky Harbor as a baggage handler."

I knew to my bones this was a waste for both of them. No shade to baggage handlers. Their job was important, not easy and probably held no small amount of stress.

But even Superman didn't fit in his mild-mannered reporter suit, if you get my drift.

"So, I guess that one guy flipping on them opened the floodgates for you boys," I surmised.

"If we know your name, we can find out just about anything about you."

Fascinating.

"How long have you known all of this about Jeff?"

"Mace and Roam were digging into that crew, and I wasn't keeping anything from you. They're not done. I wanted to give it all to you, or at least all we could find, when we had it."

"I didn't think you were keeping anything from me, baby," I assured. "We haven't had a ton of time together since I met Javi."

"We had this morning, but you fell asleep five minutes into our stakeout."

I just *knew* he wouldn't let that slide.

I decided not to engage, something that was hard to do with the smug, playful grin he was shooting at me, so instead I looked back down at the menu.

Seriously.

How could normal people find anything to eat at this place?

"So?" Eric prompted.

"I think I might do a Spicy Bacon Hearty Wrap," I told him.

I mean, it had bacon. So it couldn't be bad.

Right?

"No, I mean about attempting to fold Javi and Jeff into NI and S."

I looked to him. "I sense what you do is not a lot less dangerous than what they do."

"It actually is a lot less dangerous, because we have vastly more training and experience, but also simply because most of our cases don't involve us dealing with drug peddlers, asshole pimps and gangbangers."

This was good to know.

"And I'd recommend Jeff for the surveillance room," he went on. "Knowing his diagnosis, we'd need to keep him in situations that have less stress."

This was sounding better and better.

"Javi would be in the field," Eric continued. "And Jeff might think what he's doing is less of a rush, or less important, but even if surveillance can be boring, it's vital. Not only is it a healthy line item in our income, when we're in the middle of a tactical operation, input from the control room and efficient, organized, informed comms is crucial."

"I have no issue with this, Eric. I just don't think they're gonna say yes," I warned him. "You were the one who told me they're in a blood pact brotherhood. And I've seen the tattoo on Jeff's arm. I wasn't in any position to inspect it, but he didn't have it before. And tattoo says permanency like nothing else."

I knew by the troubled expression that came over his face what was about to come next.

And then it came.

"You're right about their commitment. But things have changed. I don't think after what happened this morning he can say no. If he wants to continue to make a difference, do shit that's meaningful, with the bonus of making a lot more money, even if some of our cases will cut across the grain, he's gonna have to tap in. This morning means the cops are going to be dedicated to making certain the same thing doesn't happen to Javi and Jeff, and they'll be happy to put them in a cell to make that so."

He slid closer and kept his gaze glued to mine.

"And honey, in case you didn't put it together, this crew that those two men moved on could think it was on the orders of Javi. If he hasn't already put it into the grapevine they acted on their own, this is the perfect storm for an epic beef to kick off. And if they have the organization and firepower Javi mentioned, their crew against his decimated one is not good odds."

That thought had made many attempts to penetrate my brain, but until then, I'd kept it at bay.

I couldn't keep it at bay anymore, because Eric was right.

"So Javi needs you guys," I said quietly.

"If he was any other man, we would have put pressure on him to get them both in one of our safe houses. We know enough that'd be a wasted effort. But the man is far from dumb. He knows they're vulnerable, and he knows Joaquim made them a target."

"Do you think that means he'll lay low?" I asked hopefully.

I couldn't describe my relief when he nodded.

"Montoya was destroyed at the loss of his brothers. He's not gonna risk losing more. And if he's out of the picture, his mother will be exposed. If his bio dad doesn't have the pressure exerted, no doubt he'll tap out and fuck knows what'll happen to Javi's mom. What Javi does, he definitely takes risks. But what he said today proves this guy doesn't have a hot head that guides him to do stupid shit for the sake of his calling. I believe he takes a great deal of time to calculate the risks and knows, unless something entirely unexpected happens, he'll best them before he tackles them. He doesn't do this because he has an issue with failure. He does it because he's not about to lose a brother. He's not going to expose a man he's pulled into his mission to an undue threat. And he's not gonna stop being the buffer between his mom and the world."

"So it's the perfect time for your team to make their move to fold him in," I surmised.

"It's that, but mostly, he's exactly what we need on our team."

He totally was.

"Are you sure you're okay with me pitching this to Mace?" he asked.

Javi, who I'd come to like a lot, and my brother, who I loved, being welcomed to a team who made great money, garnered enormous respect, and did cool stuff to feed their hero complexes?

"Yes, I'm sure I'm okay with it."

Eric smiled, ordered, "Mouth," I gave it to him, and after I pulled back, he said, "So the Spicy Bacon Wrap?"

"Sure," I confirmed.

I could eat another slice of icebox cake after I shocked my system with veggies and grilled chicken and such.

He sent the order off and straightened from the counter.

"Are you going into work?" he asked.

I looked at the clock on the microwave. It was half past noon.

I really should go.

But since they had it covered...

"No," I answered.

"I'm glad," he said quietly.

I was too.

"Are you gonna be late tonight?" I asked.

He shook his head.

"I feel like mastering frying a burger," I stated. *I'll need it after a healthy lunch,* I did not add.

"Works for me."

"So lunch, fuck, you go to work, I go to the grocery store, you come home, I make us burgers. Then more fucking, pass out, get up and do our stakeout, and this time, I take first watch. Is that a plan?"

"Absolutely. And I like how much fucking you wedged into our schedule."

I smirked at him.

Then I continued planning. "Tomorrow, hopefully we'll have a normal day, outside early morning stakeout, of course. Then come home, pass out, wake up, another stakeout, and we can go look at kitties."

"Again, absolutely."

Oh yeah.

Earlier, we both felt it.

We were in deep and getting deeper every moment.

And we liked it there.

I smiled.

Eric kissed me again.

Yeah.

We liked it there.

TWENTY-ONE

PAIN IN MY ASS

My alarm went off, I told it to shut up, then I rolled to my back and stared at the ceiling, blearily trying to recall whose bright idea this stakeout business was, and if I could stop myself from murdering her.

Since it came to me it was Harlow, and then it came to me I loved her, I then came to the realization that I'd need to adjust my plans for the day to ones that were less homicidal.

It was the next morning, post-stakeout, and I needed to get up and get to work.

But first, allow me to catch you up from then to now.

After Eric left yesterday, I texted the girls (and Tito) that I wouldn't be in and thanked them for covering for me.

I then resisted the urge to text my brother and ask him how he was doing, because I knew how he was doing (rotten), I knew what he had to do that day with his friends' families had to stink, and I didn't want him to think I was going to get up in his shit now that I had his new number.

I then dove into research on how to fry the best burger and

discovered the mind-boggling number of philosophies regarding this concept (approximately 25,739—perhaps a slight exaggeration).

And I might have spent a few minutes (okay, it was more) looking at black wedding gowns.

Eventually, I morphed a few of the recipes together and realized, in all my kitchen accoutrement buying, I didn't own a cast iron grill pan.

So I took a shower, swiped on some makeup, went to the mall to grab a pan and the grocery store to get the food.

Eric came home, we ate, and he declared my burgers were fantastic. I thought they were only pedestrian and made a mental vow to try again.

Though, the roasted fingerling potatoes with rosemary were da bomb.

We went to bed early because we had to drag ourselves out of it to go to the stakeout.

Important note: twice in this time I discovered Eric could fuck just as good as he could make love. And my testimony to that was the fact, after the nighttime version (the afternoon version was a quickie, still good, but it only hinted at what was to come), I passed out pretty much right after I got back in bed from cleaning up, which I barely had the energy to do, the sex had been so physical, and I'd come so hard.

Mm.

Onward from that...

My early morning QuikTrip choice was a bacon, egg grilled cheese, and proving he could surprise a girl on occasion, so was Eric's.

We munched them on the way to the warehouse, and when we got to the stakeout zone, I saw Harlow and Brady there instead of Cap and Raye (she told me she was first up to spell their shitty timeslot, Luna and Knox were doing it tomorrow, and I hoped we'd wrap this case up before it became Eric's and my turn, because our timeslot already sucked, it was just that Raye and Cap's sucked more).

When we arrived, Harlow bounced up to me with ponytail swinging in an exuberant way that made me worry Eric and I weren't doing stakeouts right.

Harlow asked after Jeff and Javi, though I was pretty sure she was more interested in Javi.

I gave her the expected response that they were both not in a good place, and she told me to tell them they were in her thoughts (and I was pretty sure she was keener I get that message to Javi).

After that, they took off.

I took first watch.

While I did, Eric lounged in the camp chair with his long legs stretched out and elevated, his boots resting on the edge of the window (hot), and he sipped coffee (also somehow hot, then again, I thought everything he did was hot).

Sometimes we chatted.

I learned Eric's family never got another puppy after the one that died in the wreck with his mom, and Savannah didn't like animals, so after the dog Eric had when he met her sadly passed, he didn't get another one. I also learned he'd never had a cat. And last, I learned his favorite color was blue.

On the other hand, Eric had learned I took my photos with my phone, I'd never had a pet at all, and I confirmed my favorite non-color was black, my second favorite one was white, and I didn't have a favorite actual color, but if forced to pick one under threat of torture, I'd pick red.

Through this, all was quiet on the camp front, and I fell asleep after my third shift of watching, so Eric did the whole final hour (was my guy the greatest, or what?).

He took me home. We had another quickie. It was a good one. So I was passed out before he even left my room to go to work (I mean, how does the man do it? He's a machine).

Which brought me to now.

"Ugh," I grunted as I hauled myself out of bed.

I pulled on my stretchy cotton nightie, my undies, hit the

bathroom and loaded up my toothbrush. I was going at my teeth while heading into the kitchen to fire up the Nespresso when I screamed, jolted, my toothbrush went flying across the bar only to land on the floor in the living room, still vibrating and sending specks of toothpaste everywhere.

Javi, Jeff and Clarice, who were all standing in my living room, stared at the toothbrush.

I stared at them.

Then, mouth full of foam, I shouted, "What the fuck!"

They all looked at me. Jeff was laughing. Javi was smiling. Clarice put her hands on her hips like I'd personally wasted her entire morning.

I went to the kitchen sink, rinsed, spat, grabbed a towel to dab my mouth then headed to the living room to retrieve my toothbrush.

I turned it off, slammed it down on the coffee table, and instead of asking if any of them had heard of a telephone or knew how to ring a buzzer, I asked a more pertinent question of my brother.

"Are you okay?"

He pulled me into a tight hug.

"Man, I needed that laugh," he whispered in my ear.

Oh.

Well then.

Whatever.

Jeff let me go, and I was about to ask Javi how he was doing when Clarice butted in.

"You sleep late."

"Excuse me, but I was up at three fifteen to go stake out a homeless camp."

"Your man has been at work for the last two hours," she pointed out.

So, clearly, tabs were kept on the Nightingale men.

Hmm.

I wondered if they knew.

I socked that away to mention to Eric and addressed Clarice.

"That's because I think he's an immortal god who actually doesn't sleep. He's like Apollo or Zeus or somebody, existing among us mere mortals as a way to alleviate the boredom of eternal life. We just haven't advanced in our relationship far enough for him to confide that in me," I returned.

"I'd always wondered how that one was in bed," Clarice muttered. "Think I have my answer."

I wasn't going to verbally confirm, but...she did have her answer.

I caught my brother making a gaggy face.

I took no offense. I got it. I didn't want to think about how any woman he saw would be in bed either.

Moving on.

I turned my full attention to Jeff. "Not that I don't want to see you. But what are you doing here?"

"I didn't want you to worry, so I'm here to let you know we gotta vanish for a while," Jeff explained hesitantly, and the hesitance was probably concern I would lose my mind, which would be the precursor to me lapsing into a lecture about this Shadow Soldier business.

Since Eric suggested them laying way low was the way to go, I didn't.

And seeing as Jeff didn't want me up in his shit so much that he took a half a year break from me, that was another reason why I didn't.

That said.

I looked to Javi. "I take it you didn't get it into the grapevine that raid wasn't on your order."

He shook his head but said, "I did. They're just assholes. They went after our last brother. We got him safe. Now we gotta ghost."

This wasn't the best news in the world considering my brother had been ghosting me for a while. But since I had him back and didn't want some aggressive, illegal narcotics organization to take him away from me forever, I'd have to deal.

To do that, I drew in a breath and let it go before I looked to Clarice. "What's your part in this?"

She tipped her head to Javi. "I'm Javi's attorney."

Of course he had an attorney.

And of course she was his.

"And I have access to a safe house in the mountains," she finished.

Right.

Taking in the slick, winter-white business dress with matching blazer she was wearing, I wondered if her safe house had fur rugs, and Waterford crystal for all your beverage needs.

I didn't ask.

I went back to my brother. "Can we talk for a minute?"

He nodded, so I took his hand and led him to my bedroom.

"Gross, Jess," he muttered. "It even smells like sex in here."

I sniffed.

It smelled like rosemary, cedarwood, lotus blossom and pepper (the latter two were from my perfume) and...fucking.

Ah, happy memories.

"Jess," Jeff tore me from my happy memories.

"How did yesterday go?" I asked gently.

Surprisingly, sorrow didn't hit his face. Anger did.

"Jamal's people were wrecked," he shared. "They knew how it went down before they asked that first question, because they know Javi...and they know Joaq."

"Okay," I replied.

"Joaquim's people were assholes. All up in Javi's face that he killed their son and brother. Totally blaming him. Javi didn't say dick. Just let them pile it on him."

"Did you tell them it wasn't his idea?" I asked.

"I started to, but Javi gave me a look to shut me up." His head ticked angrily. "I get it. He's willing to shoulder the blame that isn't his when they're grieving. But Joaq spent half his time growing up at Jamal's house because his parents make Mom and Dad seem functional and loving."

Yikes.

I winced.

"Yeah," he agreed.

"I'm sorry that was even less fun than it was already going to be," I said.

"I am too."

Taking us out of that...

"Okay, not that I'm going to text you every hour, but while you're in the mountains laying low, can I contact you? Just to check in."

He looked uncomfortable.

"I don't have to," I said quickly. "I'm sure it won't take us long to figure this out, and then you guys can come back."

Or at least I hoped it didn't take long. I was so far over these stakeouts, it wasn't funny.

"That's not why I feel hinky."

"Why do you feel hinky?"

"Because I fucked us up."

I grabbed his hand again. "What? No. We had a thing. That thing is over."

"You texted me once yesterday, Jess."

I nodded. "I know."

"The old Jess would have called to ask how it went down when we talked to Joaquim and Jamal's people."

Oh shit.

"Should I have done that?"

He pulled his hand from mine to point at me and say, "That. Right there."

"What?"

"The shit I said made you think you have to back off. Made you think that offering to spend time with me after two of my friends were murdered is momming me."

"I just wanted to—"

"I was mouthing off," he declared. "I was taking it out on you how pissed I was that it took me finding Javi to understand my diagnosis was serious, but it's manageable. I didn't have anyone who said, 'Okay, he has this, how does he live the fullest life he can while having it?' Then get me to those things."

When I opened my mouth to say something, he hurriedly continued talking, at the same time showing he knew what I was about to say.

"And that wasn't your job, Jess. You were only nineteen when I got diagnosed. But for them, I was just a pain in the ass. I was 'mental.' I was constantly listening to them bitching because they had to shell out a co-pay they wanted to use to buy booze or smokes or whatever the fuck. Listening to them complain how I was a drain because they had to take time off to take me to see a doctor. How I didn't get access to some stuff I need, like CBT, something I've found can be really effective in reducing episodes, because it was too much money, too much of their time, too much of a hassle."

He tore his hand through his hair as I fought the urge to race to our mother's house and then to our father's to tear each of them new assholes.

And then Jeff kept going.

"That was it, Jess. They made me feel like a constant hassle. So much of one, it made me think everyone thought that way about me. You. Joshua and Kat. Everyone."

"I fucking hate them so much," I whispered, my voice trembling with just how much I hated our parents.

He shook his head and got closer to me.

"Now I know. I know I can hold down a job. I know that people can depend on me for important shit. I know I'm normal, I just have an illness. There are millions of people who live with illnesses every day. I'm just one of them."

I loved it that he figured that out. (I still hated our parents.)

"Even so, I can cool it with the big sis crap," I offered.

"Jess," he said quietly. "I was so into the life I was building, after cutting out everything from the one I had, I didn't realize I'd cut out a lot of healthy stuff too. I didn't realize it until you got in my shit. You weren't holding me down. I was lumping you in with 'That was when my life was fucked up.' When it wasn't you. It was Mom and Dad. Be you. Be my big sister. Give a shit." He cracked a grin. "Obviously, I need you around to spring me from a police interrogation at least."

I didn't know what was happening to me, but in that moment, I didn't fight it.

I hugged my brother.

"I don't have all day!" Clarice called from the living room.

I sighed.

We broke.

Jeff watched me roll my eyes.

I watched him smile after I did it.

Then we walked into the living room.

Javi was looking between us but stopped on Jeff.

"Cool?" he asked.

Jeff nodded.

Javi looked at me. "Good?"

"Don't make me be mushy. We just hugged. That's all I have in me for today."

Javi's face split into a grin. It warred with the melancholy in his amber eyes, but I was still glad I could make him smile.

"We're out," Clarice decreed, before she strutted on her stilettos to the door.

Jeff gave me another hug, and Javi waited until my brother was out the door before he followed.

But I hustled and caught his forearm before he could get away.

He turned back, looking down to his forearm before looking at me.

I let him go and whispered, "Thanks for introducing my brother to himself."

His handsome face grew gentle, and, man, it packed a punch.

"*Hermanita,*" he whispered.

"And don't shoulder the blame," I advised. "I'm not sure how you can stop yourself from doing that, but I really hope you try."

I knew from the dark look that passed through his eyes this would be impossible in the now, but I hoped I planted a kernel that might someday grow.

Javi lifted his chin to acknowledge he heard me, but he said nothing.

I couldn't do all this emotion. Days of it. Too much.

So I went on, "And Harlow is worried about you. She sends her thoughts."

"Pain in my ass," he muttered, but his mouth had softened the minute the name "Harlow" came out of mine.

Because it did, I made a split-second decision only time would tell if I'd regret. Though, with that gentle look I'd witnessed, I had a feeling I wouldn't.

"I could set that up," I offered.

"Total pain in my ass," he said as he moved away.

I shifted into the walkway and called after them, "See you on the flipside."

Jeff, on the stairs, jutted his chin to me. Clarice was already strutting toward the security gate. Javi, still on the walkway, didn't look back, just lifted a hand and flicked out a couple of fingers—Mr. Cool.

I stood out there until I lost sight of them when the security door closed behind them, and then I dashed into my house.

I nabbed the toothbrush to finish brushing (after I disinfected it with bleach since it'd hit the floor, my house was clean, but...gross).

Though, first, I went to my phone to report to Eric what I'd just learned.

It was ringing before I got to it on my nightstand.

The screen told me Eric was calling.

"Hey, I was just going to call you," I said as answer.

"I bet. What were your brother, Javi and Clarice doing at yours?"

I looked around, wondering if there were hidden cameras in my pad.

"How do you know that?" I asked.

"Because we hacked into the parking lot cameras of the Oasis so we can keep an eye on the three of you. Four, when Harlow moves in next week."

Oh.

And...

Rad!

I forgot Harlow was going to be moving in that soon. I needed to ask if she wanted help packing.

"Jess," Eric prompted in a growly tone.

Mm. Yum.

I shook off my pleasant reaction to his growly.

"First I will share how proud of myself I am that I've managed to curtail my homicidal tendencies twice today."

"Okay," he said slowly, like he was prompting me to go on, but he wasn't sure he wanted to know.

"My parents are assholes," I stated the obvious. "But Jeff and I worked shit out. I'll explain more tonight."

"Right. So the twice is both your parents?"

"No. I woke up wanting to kill whoever had the idea for the stakeout. Then I remembered it was Harlow, and I thus I determined I wasn't down for bestie-icide."

I listened to him chuckle.

Since I wouldn't hear that much if I was in prison, I was super glad I had such fantastic willpower.

I continued my brief. "Javi put the word out it wasn't his idea on the raid, but whoever this crew is doesn't care, and they went after Cody. Javi and Jeff took care of Cody, whatever that means, I didn't ask, but they did it. Though, apparently, Clarice is Javi's attorney, and she set up a safe house for them in the mountains. Before they vanished, Jeff wanted to say goodbye."

"Right," he murmured. Then he said, "This is good, Jess."

"I know," I replied. "One other thing of note, Clarice told me she knew you'd been at work for two hours. I don't know why, but I think that means Arthur keeps tabs on you."

"Whoever this guy is probably he keeps tabs on anyone who touches the Angels."

He didn't seem concerned.

"That doesn't bother you?"

"Since we're looking out for you, if he's looking out for you too, I don't give a fuck."

Great answer.

"Any word on this crew?" I asked.

"We've dedicated some resources to gathering intel, and we aren't liking what we're learning."

Damn.

"What's that?"

"Montoya was right. They're expanding aggressively. As much as we've learned so far, they've got three active feuds ongoing, adding the one with Montoya is four. The cops are putting out fires everywhere, and by that I mean draping sheets over dead bodies until the coroner can bring the body bags. These assholes have a burn-it-to-the-ground-then-go-in-and-plant-seeds mentality. In other words, if they want your turf, you back off it or they'll annihilate your crew and take it anyway."

This was not good news.

Seriously.

But still, it didn't answer why they'd be snatching unhoused people.

"Any theories on why they're grabbing people from the camps?"

"No good ones," he replied.

"Lay them on me anyway," I ordered.

"Bossy," he purred.

"Eric, don't try distracting me by being sexy," I snapped. Then I amended, "Or more sexy than your resting sexy."

I heard another chuckle before he let out a big sigh and said, "A guess? Free labor."

"You mean they're—?"

"Putting them to work sorting massive shipments into saleable-size merchandise? Yeah."

"Oh my God," I breathed, my mind flipping through the variety of ways you could force someone to work, who was so disenfranchised from society they lived in a tent without running water, available food, electricity, etc. And those were the ones who used shelter. Others might have a blanket and a prayer.

All of the ways my mind could conjure up were such that it wouldn't entertain them before expelling them, violently.

"It makes fucked-up sense if you're in that kind of fucked-up business," Eric noted. "They don't have to worry about quality control because they don't give a shit about it. They can use fear and pain as motivators. Though, they probably have to feed them, otherwise, they're free labor, so the profit-margin doesn't take a hit."

"We have to deal with these fuckin' guys," I clipped.

"We have to deal with these fuckin' guys," he agreed.

I glanced at my clock and groaned. "But first, I have to get ready for work."

"Come to my place tonight. Pack a bag. I'm cooking."

"You're on."

"Later, honey."

"'Bye, baby."

We hung up. I gave myself a moment to think about how sugary-sweet our goodbyes were and how I felt about that.

I quickly decided I not only had no problem with it, I loved it.

Then me and my toothbrush hit the bathroom (after, of course, we hit the bottle of bleach) so I could get ready for work.

TWENTY-TWO

SEX HAIR

Eric was fucking me missionary style, and I was totally down with it, seeing as I was close, he had a finger to my clit that was working magic, so I was about to get hit with what I knew from recent experience would be a rocket of an orgasm.

And then he pulled out.

I did not complain, because I was learning what would happen next, I just couldn't be sure how it would happen. Though, I could be sure I'd like it.

This time, Eric chose rolling me to my belly, hiking me up by my hips, then pounding in.

One could say I'd also learned that getting tossed around and positioned by a strong man who knew what he wanted and had some serious power in his hips was *the best.*

I reared back into his mighty thrusts, pressing my forehead to his bed and reaching for my clit.

I mean, *seriously*.

That big dick did some of the work, but mostly, my man could *fuck.*

"Don't touch yourself," Eric grunted. "Feel like fucking your pretty wet pussy for a while."

My vaginal walls clenched at the addition of his sexy talk.

Eric let out a growly purr.

My vaginal walls clenched again.

Mm.

Righty ho. I was cool with straight fucking for as long as he could do it.

His fingers trailed a tease along my skin over the cheeks of my ass, the small of my back, my spine and ribs, while I gladly took his fucking.

Until he squeezed my ass hard with both hands and murmured, "Work it, Jessie."

Oh, I was gonna work it, all right.

I met him, thrust for thrust, our flesh slapping violently, and I didn't think I could work it any harder.

Until he squeezed my cheeks again, the pads of his fingers pressing deeper this time, and he growled, "Sweetest ass on the planet. *Fuck*."

One could say my man was an ass man. Which was good, since I had an abundance to give to him.

But I loved that he dug that about me so much, I started slamming into him as he slammed into me.

I was close again, from just fucking, so of course he pulled out.

I was a wee bit less patient with it this time.

I lifted my head to share this but got stuck on watching him drop to his back and turning his handsome head my way.

"Climb on," he ordered.

I didn't hesitate.

I climbed on, impaled myself, and rode his thick dick, my eyes glued to the splendor before me. His tousled hair. The dark hunger in his gorgeous face. The liquid ink of his eyes. His wide, hairy chest, bulging pecs and defined abs.

God, how did I get so lucky?

For his part, Eric alternately watched our connection and my face before he locked on my face and put a thumb to my clit.

I knew by that he meant business this time, so I whimpered in anticipation, did it again (and a lot louder) when his thumb hit the spot...

And someone laid on the doorbell.

What?

No!

He pulled me down to full of him, his eyes aimed across the room toward the door, his lips whispering, "The fuck?"

He held me where I was while I attempted to process this devastating turn of events as he reached a long arm out for his phone on the bedstand.

He engaged it. We both saw no notifications on his screen, which meant this wasn't Nightingale business we'd missed while concentrating on fucking.

The person was still laying on the doorbell.

Gently, Eric pulled me off his cock.

And again...

No!

A quick peck on the lips, then he said, "Be right back."

He rolled off the bed, grabbed his cargos and was still yanking them over his superior ass as he sauntered to the door.

I scowled at the door after he disappeared through it.

I then curled thighs to tits on my ass in his bed, hoping this was just a really intent Jehovah's Witness that Eric could send on their way, and he would indeed be right back, because we'd had dinner (Eric made spaghetti, it had some heat to it, which made it awesome). Now all I needed was a mega-Eric-induced orgasm, followed by cuddle time, and then sleep, because we had to be up at 3:15 to hit the stakeout.

On this thought, I heard a woman shriek, "*You were fucking her?*"

I blinked at the door.

Holy shit.

Savannah was back in town.

I scurried off the bed, grabbed my panties, yanked them on, then hit up Eric's thermal.

Through this, I heard his low murmuring and her shouting, "Only because you gave up on us!"

I pulled on his shirt and hustled down his long-ass hall.

I hit the mouth of the hall and stopped to see they were standing by the dining room table, just in from the front door.

Eric had his back to me, but when her eyes scorched a path my way, catching me standing there in his thermal, while he was standing there without it, and we both definitely had sex hair (though, I'd bet Eric's was better), he looked over his bare shoulder at me.

His gaze dipped down, then up, he shook his head, but his lips quirked, and she didn't miss the last.

"You think this is funny?" she demanded. "You're fucking some other woman and it's *funny*?"

"I don't think it's funny," he said calmly. "I just like the view of my woman in my shirt."

Although that brought back that gooey feeling I'd come to know very well, I watched it make her face turn a violent shade of red.

I then gave myself a second to take her in.

And for sure.

Eric had a type.

Tall. Dark hair. Beautiful.

I mean, I knew I wasn't hard on the eyes, but I wouldn't describe myself as beautiful.

Though, Eric did.

I was a little surprised about her aesthetic, though.

Both Stella and I had entirely different vibes, but they were pretty casual.

Savannah had on crisp skinny jeans, a skintight tan shell, a lightweight, overlong (to her calves) matching tan blazer-jacket with gold buttons, a gold statement necklace, chunky gold hoops and high-heeled nude pumps. She was also carrying a stuffy, structured Louis Vuitton purse in the standard brown and tan design.

Now, I'd admit to a small amount of envy she could pull off such a fantastic eyeliner wing. But in my opinion, she went a bit overboard on the highlighter, at least during an ambush of her ex (however, it'd be perfect for a night out). And I didn't like to talk down about a sister—do you and work it—but it had to be said, her overuse of bronzer was practically criminal.

Or maybe it was fake tan since she had an orange-ish tint all over.

Eric took me out of my perusal by saying, "Savannah, it worries me I have to remind you we've been divorced for two years."

"A divorce I didn't want," she reminded him in return.

"We've had this conversation too many times, so you need to know, I'm not doing this," he warned.

"And I'm not doing this in front of *her*," she snapped.

"No, you're not doing it at all, because I'm going to put you out, and if you don't leave my property, you'll have to explain to the cops why you won't," he stated.

It was like he didn't speak.

"I had one simple request. You work on us. And you can't even give me that?" she demanded.

"He did, you just didn't show up at the counseling sessions," I muttered.

Eric dropped his head, though I was pretty sure I saw his shoulders shaking.

Hmm.

Even though it looked like he was silently laughing, from the expression on her face, maybe, as this rolled on to its conclusion, I should keep my mouth shut.

She stuck her arm straight out, finger pointing at me, and demanded, "You talked to her about"—she moved to flap that hand between them—"*us*?"

Eric's head had snapped up at her point (the man really had a thing about people pointing at me), and after she finished speaking, he bit out, "You point at her again, Savannah, shit is gonna go south."

Totally had a thing about people pointing at me.

"How much more south can it be?" she asked heatedly. "I'm currently standing in a home my husband doesn't share with me with the woman he's fucking."

"Ex-husband," he amended.

"Your choice, not mine," she fired back.

I could tell things were turning for Eric in a huge way even before he asked, "You wanna know how much more?"

"Yeah, *obviously*," she snarked.

But I could also tell by his tone she really, *really* didn't.

He told her.

"This much more south, Savannah. She's it. She's the one I've been waiting for. She's the one I would have left you for if I was still with you when I met her."

Savannah gasped, which was good, she did it a lot louder than I did, so maybe Eric didn't hear mine.

Though mine ended with that gooey feeling spreading, making me feel warm all over, and I reckoned hers didn't end like that.

"I cannot believe you just said that to me," she whispered.

I was right.

Hers didn't end like that.

"You made me miserable," Eric stated emotionlessly. "She makes me happy. And not only because, when I'm around her, I don't feel the need to exhaust myself by dancing attendance. It's easy. It's quiet. She makes me laugh. Our lives fit into each other's rather than Jess making me feel like mine is a burden and her life has to be my everything when she allows me a part in it. Every day, she does something to make me feel like I matter to her, or just matter at all. She's honest. She shares. She's not about bullshit. Shit is very real for Jess right now in a variety of ways, but she still asks about my day. She worries I'm not getting enough sleep. She gets in my space when we're just talking because she likes to be close to me."

My heart clenched because...

Wow.

None of what I did was very big. It was just what you did with anyone you cared about.

So...

Damn.

His life with her was even worse than I thought.

"Does she know about Stella?" Savannah sneered.

"Yeah. We're friends," I told her. "Stella is the shit."

"They used to be a thing," she informed me.

"I know. Fifteen years ago," I replied.

"If anything ever happened to her and Mace, he'll excise you before you can say boo so he can sniff after her," she declared.

At that, Eric dropped his head back to look at the ceiling.

Which told me he'd heard that before.

Maybe a lot.

So it was me who responded to her.

"That'll never happen, not Mace and Stella breaking up, and not Eric making a play for Stella. It's old news. Not to mention, he's with somebody."

"I—" Savannah started.

"*Fuck! Enough!*" Eric exploded, and both Savannah and I jumped when he did.

Me having that reaction wasn't a surprise. He'd never done that around me, to say nothing of the fact I didn't think he had it in him. He was a mellow guy. That said, we were very new.

It was Savannah having that reaction that told the tale. Because he'd obviously never lost it around her, and considering all that was her, that spoke volumes.

Her eyes were also wide in shock, which spoke volumes more.

"I cannot fucking *believe* I wasted over half a decade with a woman who doesn't listen, a woman who lays on a doorbell at nearly nine at night and then forces herself into my house in order to shove her shit down the throats of me and my woman," he gritted. "We're done, Savannah. Divorced. Finished. I moved to a different state to get away from you. Fucking *clue* the fuck *in*. We're *over*."

Her hand flitted to her throat. "My God, Eric, you don't have to be cruel about it," she said in a small voice.

I really should have found it in me to stop it, but I couldn't. This bitch was a total trip.

I busted out laughing.

She narrowed her eyes at me.

Eric was again looking over his shoulder at me, and a muscle was ticking in his jaw.

At the muscle, I forced myself to stop laughing, but it was hard.

"I see we want different things," Savannah said.

Good Lord.

"We do? You think?" Eric drawled sarcastically.

A snort escaped me.

Eric shot me another look.

I lifted my hand to him and nodded, sharing I'd be good.

"I don't need to be humiliated," Savannah declared.

"I didn't ask you to my house, or let you in, just pointing that out," Eric replied.

She looked at him, at me, back to him, lifted her chin and stated, "At least no one can say *I* didn't try."

God, Stella had this bitch *down*.

"Congratulations." Eric was still drawling sarcastically. "You worked hard, Savannah. I'm just not the man for you. Now, please, can you promise we're done with this shit?"

She huffed then shared, "You won't see me again."

"It took me forty-three years, and just yesterday it came clear I found the woman I've been looking for since I knew what girls were, and still, that vies for the best news of my week," Eric returned.

Aw.

I was feeling warm again.

She looked shocked. She then looked hurt. After that, she morphed to calculating. That was quickly edged out by hurt again.

She waited for Eric to respond to her self-inflicted wound, and when he didn't, she straightened her spine and announced, "I'll just be going."

"Excellent idea," Eric replied.

He sauntered to the door, opened it and stood there, holding it open.

Without looking at me, she moved that way and stopped to peer up at him.

She then either extremely belatedly reached for the high ground or made another play, it really didn't matter, he was done with her.

"Even with all this, I truly hope you have a good life and you're happy, Eric."

"Thrilled, Savannah, since I can confirm I got both..." his pause was so heavy, I braced in order to be certain I didn't start laughing again, "*now*."

Ouch.

Cripes!

Though, awesome comeback.

She walked out the door.

He closed it and locked it.

Then he turned to me.

"You okay?" I asked.

"I honestly think that's the end of it. No way she'd endure that humiliation and come back for more."

I bit my lip because, yeah...that was intense.

I stopped biting it to ask, "Does that mean you're okay?"

Something shifted through his face, and I recognized it.

He understood I got him because I'd asked the right question. Twice.

"It didn't feel good humiliating her like that," he admitted.

"I'm sure," I agreed.

"Unfortunately, she took it to a place where there was no other choice," he stated.

"Yes," I agreed again. "She one hundred percent did that."

"And it fucks me to lose my cool like that," he went on.

I knew it.

That wasn't him.

Really, totally, *such a good guy*.

"She took it to that place too," I reminded him.

"It still fucks me."

My poor guy.

"I'm sorry, baby," I said gently.

"Let's just hope it's over," he muttered.

I could do that with him, definitely.

"Does she spray tan?" I asked with curiosity since that didn't seem like his gig.

He shook his head. "No clue. She didn't when we were together."

"She certainly came decked out," I remarked. "Her eyeliner looked done by a professional."

"It probably was. She never wore makeup when we were together. She didn't have the time, and she'd sweat it off in the kitchen at the restaurant if she did."

So that was a big play coming from her.

I'd feel badly for her if she wasn't batshit crazy.

Now to get to the meat of it.

"You'd leave her for me?"

He shook his head again, but said, "This is one of the things I'm struggling with. I didn't think I was that man. And as amazing as you are, it wouldn't even occur to me if she was who she pretended to be in the beginning. Since she isn't that person, absolutely."

"You shouldn't struggle with it," I told him. "We didn't meet while you two were together."

"I know that, honey. But even if we did, I also know I'd end it with her so I could have you."

Ummmmmmmmm...

That made my gooey feeling hit such an overdrive, it was a wonder I wasn't a melted pile of Jess oozing across the floor.

"Wow," I whispered.

His brows drew down. "I thought we understood each other."

"Well, just to say, if by understanding each other you mean my telling you that I may have looked at black wedding dresses while researching the best way to fry a hamburger yesterday, and that doesn't freak you way the fuck out, then yes."

I wasn't quite finished talking, but since he'd started stalking, I didn't say more and instead started backing up.

"Uh..." I still didn't finish since he said nothing and was still stalking as I retreated.

He cocked his head to the side (yes, still stalking).

"Black wedding dresses?"

I nodded. "And no DJ. Or cake cutting. Or toasts. Or...*oof*!"

That last was because he rushed me, dipped down like a football player about to make a tackle when he got to me, then he threw me over his shoulder.

Another *oof!* escaped when he dropped me to my back on his bed and a third one happened when he landed on me.

There it was.

I didn't need him to give me an orgasm anymore. I'd just had three.

"We're not there yet," he said softly.

"No," I agreed.

"When we get there, I won't care what you wear. But you look amazing in black."

God, this guy was *the best*.

His hair had fallen over his forehead, so I smoothed it back then held his head in both my hands.

"Good," I whispered.

"You're not gonna have The Smiths and The Cure and Siouxsie and the Banshees and Nine Inch Nails and My Chemical Romance and Bauhaus piped into the reception, are you?"

I was impressed by his command of goth rock.

"You forgot Joy Division," I joked.

He grinned.

Then he kissed me.

When he broke it, he said, "Sorry you had to put up with that."

"I'm sorry you did."

"Yeah," he murmured, his beautiful eyes roaming my face. "That's you."

"What's me?"

"You think about me."

"Eric, baby, I hate to inform you of this, since it's clear you dig that about me, but I'm not unusual. Most everybody would be more concerned about how you reacted to what just happened than how it affected me."

"Jess, honey, I hate to inform you that you might be right, but there are also a lot of people who are completely self-involved."

"I'll give you that. But I feel the need to drive the point home that all the things you said I give to you are just normal things normal people give to people they care about. I'm not special."

A funny look crossed his face. "You're not special?"

I shrugged against the bed. "Not really. I'm way into you. I'm thrilled you're way into me. And we do click in all the good ways."

I still wasn't done talking when he said, "Jess, you spent six months scouring Phoenix to find your brother."

"A lot of people would do that."

"And you teamed up with your friends to solve cases in order to stop people from being hurt, the last two nights doing that meant you dragged your ass out of bed and hung out in a cold, abandoned warehouse keeping watch on a homeless camp."

"The first night I fell asleep through it," I reminded him.

His lips tipped up before he said, "My point is, you're not normal. You give a shit. You put your ass out there to make a difference. Homer doesn't touch anything without putting a plastic bag between it and him, but you've touched his heart. Mary would not be in a hotel room with a bed and a thermostat she can control if it wasn't for you. The General wouldn't have a place waiting for him in a facility in Scottsdale if it wasn't for you."

This was news.

"The General has a place?"

Eric shook his head. "I forgot to tell you. Yeah. We just need to figure out how to get him there. But don't change the subject. I didn't say I'd leave my wife for you, if she was still my wife, because you got a great ass and extreme talent in sucking cock."

I couldn't help my smug smile at hearing that.

Eric ignored it.

"It's because you're all that's you."

I was all that was me.

Shit!

I was either going to cry, or hug him, or both.

This had to stop.

"Great," I said smartly. "You're all that's you too, and it isn't all about your big dick and sexy bedhead. Can we stop being gooey now? We're here. We have our shit tight. Savannah's gone. Hopefully that's over for good. Now, we have to be up mega early. I just had three orgasms. But you haven't had one, so, if you're accepting orders, I'll take another one while you get yours."

His brows shot up. "You just had three?"

I took my hands from his head and counted them down on my fingers between our faces.

"The fireman's hold. Tossing me on your bed. Landing on me. One, two, three."

"You like to get physical," he murmured.

"Uh. Duh," I replied.

I got that out. And then about three seconds later, I was naked (and I didn't make myself thus). Less than three seconds after that, I was being kissed breathless. And a little bit later, I was fucked that way.

In the end, I got two more orgasms.

Eric got one.

Poor baby and his male biology.

But a big fat yay for me.

TWENTY-THREE

WE'LL TAKE HIM

Dawn was kissing the sky, and I'd switched out the night vision binoculars to regular ones.

The camp was waking up.

It was almost time to leave.

And my man was *out*.

I looked to him slouched in the chair, his feet up on the sill, ankles crossed, his arms crossed over his wide chest, his chin dipped into his neck, like he was the sheriff of a Wild West town, out on the front porch of the jail, catching some shut-eye between gunfights.

I was relieved to see he finally looked cute.

I thought this so I wouldn't do something girlie, like count my lucky starts that this guy was mine.

Since he'd fallen asleep, and I wanted him to keep doing it, I'd taken the last hour of watch.

I could report it still wasn't fun, specifically because it was super chilly that night. Eric had checked the forecast and gave me a heads up, that was why I was wearing a black knit cap with two huge pom poms positioned precisely so they would look like a certain mouse. When Eric saw me in it, he laughed so hard, I thought he'd injure himself. But I wasn't insulted, considering I was proud of my love of that mouse, not to mention, still laughing, he started making out with me, which felt really nice.

This shit was also unfun because it continued to be *mega boring*.

The camp was as quiet that night as it had been the night before and the one before that (I guessed, I wasn't awake to know, I just knew nothing happened outside my brother being taken in for questioning, but that didn't happen in the actual camp).

So Eric and I gabbed about the kind of cat I wanted (I didn't care, just as long as we vibed), the supplies I'd need and where I might put a litter box (I was going to buy one of those furniture-looking ones that hid it). Also my desire to make the perfect burger (I suggested mix-ins, like mustard, garlic and Worcestershire, Eric approved of this plan), my ideas on the signature cocktail for the Oasis Holiday Extravaganza (I was vacillating between a take on a French 75 with pomegranate juice, or some kind of mule that went heavy on the ginger, Eric suggested a seasonal switch up of a cosmo, which led me to learn he was a vodka guy, though he didn't turn away from gin), and what kind of safe house Clarice would offer (Eric chuckled at my fur rugs and Waterford idea, but he also admitted I probably wasn't wrong).

Of course, this led me to quizzing him on why an attorney would have a safe house at all.

"She likely doesn't. My guess, it's her summer place to get away from the heat," he'd replied.

That made sense, so that was undoubtedly it.

And that was the end of our discussion about it.

Then he fell asleep, and I returned the gift he gave to me the last couple of nights by letting him do it.

I heard a car door slam, which surprised me, since for hours I'd heard nothing but Eric's low, beautiful voice with the occasional whistle of wind through the warehouse, so I lifted my binoculars to have a look just as another door slammed.

I trained them at the road beside the massive lot where the camp sat and saw a handsome, middle-aged Black guy waiting for a pretty, same-aged Black lady to take his outstretched hand.

I felt Eric come up beside me (the car doors must have woken him), so I lowered my binoculars and looked up at him.

"Shit," he murmured, he dropped his binocs and looked down at me. "That's gotta be Johnson's parents."

"Johnson?"

"Chris Johnson. The General."

Shit.

I turned to the camp as Eric ordered, "Pack the shit, babe, we gotta try to head them off."

I looked back at him to see he'd already folded up a camp chair and nabbed the tripod with camera.

"I'll hoof it to the car," he said. "Gather the rest of this, I'll swing by and pick you up."

He didn't wait for my response. He took off.

Although I agreed we needed to intervene ASAFP (who knew how the General would respond to his parents suddenly showing?), and I was happy not to run back to the SUV laden with stuff, "the rest of this" included a couple of pairs of binoculars and a chair.

I was also mildly embarrassed that he knew I'd slow him down.

But only mildly.

I didn't dally in folding the chair, dropping the strap on the night vision binocs around my neck alongside the regular ones, and getting down the stairs.

I hid in a shadow in the doorway until I saw the Denali roll up. This took far less time than I expected, which told me Eric hadn't jogged back to the truck, he'd run. And he'd done it carrying a camp chair, tripod and long-range camera.

I headed out and wasted no time opening the back door, shoving the camp chair in and pulling the binocs from around my neck before I dropped them on the floor. Then I hauled myself up into the front passenger seat.

I turned to him while doing my belt as he circled out, and I expected him at least to be sweating.

He was not.

I mean, really.

Did Zeus have jet black hair?

We pulled up behind the General's parents' shiny, white Ram, parked and got out.

Homer had exited his tent and was standing, staring into the camp.

He turned to us when we approached.

I alternately smiled at him and scanned the camp looking for the Johnsons.

They were not to be seen, and this meant they'd wended their way deep into the camp.

I hated the idea that the General went on patrol, and why he did, but I hoped he was out of the camp now.

When we stopped by him, I greeted, "Hey, Homer."

"Are those General Grant's parents?" he asked.

I nodded. "Where did they go?"

He turned toward the camp. "They went in. But I don't think he's here. And I don't know if he wants to see them."

Yeah. As mentioned, I didn't know that either. And that was the worry.

I tipped my head back to look at Eric. "Were the boys planning an extraction today?"

He shook his head. "Don't know. Do know, when they figured out who he was, they reached out to his parents to see where they were at. But we didn't invite them to the party."

From what I could tell through the binoculars, where they were at was out of their minds worried about their son.

Which meant they learned where their son was and came looking for him.

Understandable.

But not optimal.

"I called Cap and Mace on the way to you," Eric told me. "They're en route."

I switched back to Homer. "Do you think you can find him? Bring him back? We'll handle his parents."

"It's time to go get him anyway," Homer said. "I'll grab some guys."

He took off, and Eric and I followed him into the camp.

Once our paths diverged from Homer's, I said to Eric, "I really want to talk to Scott and Louise about seeing if we can help Homer."

This made him stop, stopping me as well by catching my hand.

I looked up at him again.

"I get he's touched your heart too," he said carefully. "But you need to manage your expectations, sweetheart."

"I know," I whispered. "But it's worth a try, right?"

He squeezed my hand, said nothing, and set us again to moving farther into the camp.

We found the Johnsons deep in the bowels. Mr. Johnson was staring off into the distance, a haunted look on his face. Mrs. Johnson was staring at someone's grocery cart filled with junk, openly struggling with tears.

Mr. Johnson turned to us first, then he wrapped his arm around his wife to hold her close while we approached.

"Mr. Johnson, I'm Eric Turner. I work with Nightingale Investigation and Security," he said, holding out a hand for Johnson to take.

Johnson let his wife go and shook. "The firm that found our son."

They disengaged as Eric nodded and looked to Chris's mom. "Mrs. Johnson."

"Is he here? We can't find him," she said.

"He goes on…" I searched for a word that wouldn't trigger them, "walkabout at night sometimes. Some of the community are looking for him. Can we escort you back to your truck?"

"I'd like to see my son," Mrs. Johnson said.

"Let me rewind. I'm Jess Wylde," I introduced, glancing between them. "I was looking for my brother, which is how I became acquainted with the camp, and met Chris." I gestured to Eric. "This is my..."

Oh shit, was I going to say it out loud?

Oh yes.

I was.

"...boyfriend. He met Chris too, and one of their team is former Army, so they got the balls rolling to see if we could get Chris some help."

"We know. They told us they found him a placement," Mr. Johnson said. "But he doesn't have insurance. We stepped up, our families kicked in, but we couldn't find a facility that could keep him—"

"Nathan," Mrs. Johnson whispered as Mr. Johnson cut himself short. "Chris escaped," she put in quietly. There was pride tinged with sadness when she finished, "He's good at that."

The man cleared his throat and continued, "The VA should take care of this. They put a lot of effort in training them to kill. They order them who to kill. Then they come home, and they put no effort at all into helping them deal with killing people. It doesn't matter if those people were a threat. It doesn't matter if they'd done horrible things and hurt people. That obviously doesn't make my son feel okay about taking lives."

"No argument, they should," Eric replied. "But in the now, we have a relationship with a couple who work at a place that offers assistance to folks like your son. They dove into this situation. We've spoken to the administration of the facility they identified. There are funds available, which we've secured. His place is assured, the fees are covered, we just need to strategize how we're going to extract him from the camp and get him to help without causing any more damage."

I wondered if the "funds available" were from the miraculous slush fund NI&S seemed to have to pay Mary's hotel bills, as well as Chris's mental health facility bills.

If it was, then it was hemorrhaging money.

"And we don't know if seeing you will help or hinder that process," I said cautiously.

I didn't go cautiously enough. Mrs. Johnson's face got hard, as any mother's would at the very thought that her presence wouldn't be a balm to her child.

Her husband put his arm around her again and tucked her close, murmuring, "Shay."

"I'm sorry," I said. "That came out bluntly. I know how hard it is not to know where someone you love is and how they're doing."

"Did you find your brother?" Mr. Johnson asked.

I nodded and shot him a rueful smile. "He didn't want me to, but I did. It wasn't fun, but we worked it out. He got help. He's a lot better now."

At least he was in one important way.

Mr. Johnson looked beyond us, so we turned around and watched Cap and Raye walking toward us.

"These are the Johnsons," Eric introduced when they arrived. And to the Johnsons, Eric said, "This is Julien Jackson and Rachel Armstrong."

"Julien," Mr. Johnson stuck out a hand. "It was you I talked to on the phone."

"Yes, sir," Cap said (Julien, obviously, was his real name), taking Mr. Johnson's hand. "Nice to meet you."

They broke and he offered his hand to Mrs. Johnson.

She took it, they squeezed, and he stepped back and looked at Eric.

"Where's Chris?" he asked.

"They're finding him. We're uncertain he should see his folks, though," Eric told him.

Raye looked at me for guidance.

I shrugged and asked, "Scott and Louise?" as my suggestion of who would know.

"I called them on the way. They're coming. But I'll call again and see what they think," she replied and stepped away, pulling out her phone.

"Scott and Louise?" Mr. Johnson asked.

"The people I mentioned," Eric explained. "They run a non-profit that deals in affordable housing and the unhoused."

"Oh," Mr. Johnson mumbled.

"Mace is coming too, bringing Roam," Cap told Eric. "Scott said the best way to do this, is you and me explaining things to Chris, then escorting him to the hospital."

"Explaining things?" Eric asked.

Cap nodded. "In a way he understands."

"A mission?" Eric suggested.

"Or R and R?" Cap replied.

"What are they talking about?" Mrs. Johnson inquired.

I had to think quickly about how much I'd want to know if Chris was my blood.

Since I'd want to know it all, I shared, "Cap, or Julien, was the one who was in the Army. Eric was in the FBI. Your son senses that they've served in their ways, and as such, he views them as his superiors and accepts orders from them."

"Makes sense," Mr. Johnson said on a nod.

Mrs. Johnson turned her face away because it made no sense to her seeing as her son wasn't in the military anymore.

God, this was the *worst.*

"Maybe we can go and get some coffee somewhere while Jess and the men figure things out," Raye proposed.

Mrs. Johnson definitely didn't like that proposition.

Mr. Johnson dipped his head to hers and said, "Let's let them see how Chris is, darlin'."

Her lip trembled before she got a hold on it, and she told her husband, "Nathan, I want to see my son."

"I want to see him too, baby. But if there's even the slightest chance we're going to make this harder on our boy, harder for them to get him to people who can help him, I want no part in it."

Mrs. Johnson warred with this.

It took a while.

We all waited that while silently.

Finally, she turned to Raye and nodded.

I was careful not to make it noticeable when I let out a relieved breath.

Raye shot me a look then stepped to the side with a small smile on her face, an offer for them to precede her.

The Johnsons moved, but Mrs. Johnson stopped them when they came abreast of Cap.

"You need to know, we're proud of him. We're proud he served his country and did it bravely."

"Of course," Cap murmured.

"But we're also mad as hell," Mrs. Johnson went on.

"I'm the same for you," Cap agreed.

"Thank you for going out of your way to—" She stopped, swallowed, then forged ahead. "You didn't have to."

"Yes, I did. You know I did. You know if Chris was me, and I was him, Chris would too," Cap returned.

Oh hell.

That did it.

Tears sprung into her eyes.

Which meant I had to fight the same happening to mine.

Mr. Johnson huddled her close and moved her to Raye.

Raye led them through the camp.

Now Cap was staring into the distance.

I got near and bumped him with my shoulder, so he looked down at me.

"All right?" I asked.

He shook it off, put his arm around my shoulders, shook me too, then he let me go and turned his attention to Eric.

I decided to take that as he was. Or he was as good as he was going to be.

"We need to wait to get input from Scott and Louise, but I'm leaning toward mission. He seems stuck in that mode. I think he'd be wary of any mention of R and R," Cap remarked.

"Agreed," Eric said.

I tried to mentally calculate time.

Cap and Raye were the closest to the camp. Both Mace and Roam as well as Scott and Louise were at least twenty minutes more away, and making that worse, it was rush hour.

We headed back to Homer's tent to wait.

In the meantime, I got a text from Raye that said Scott and Louise told her they were close, and they'd talk to us when they got here.

Mace and Roam showed first. Scott and Louise showed about ten minutes later. And Scott confirmed there was no easy way to do this, and it was anyone's guess how he'd react. He simply cautioned that if Chris balked, they needed to back off immediately and get a professional opinion on how to reapproach.

The sun was up, the heat was coming on the day, my hat was shoved into my jacket pocket, which was shoved into the Denali, and we'd adjusted the stakeout equipment to the back. All of this by the time Homer and his boys returned with Chris, which was maybe about forty-five minutes after Scott and Louise showed.

Chris looked tired, like he hadn't slept all night, and perhaps that was what made what happened next go so easily.

Eric and Cap told Chris they were there to transport Chris to a new location. Chris got right into the Denali with them, and they drove away.

Homer took Mace, Roam, Scott, Louise and me to Chris's stuff, and I called Raye to let her know what was happening so she could tell the Johnsons.

Tex came out, and without looking into any of our eyes, silently helped as we packed Chris's stuff (it was meagre) and hauled it to the sidewalk outside the camp to see what Mr. and Mrs. Johnson wanted to do with it.

Tex slunk back into the camp, still not having fully looked at any of us.

I was impressed by his commitment to his cover.

When the Johnsons returned, they told us they wanted to take Chris's things with them.

So we loaded them in their truck. Mr. Johnson handed out handshakes. Mrs. Johnson gave Raye and me hugs, the men handshakes. They took off. Roam and Mace angled into their SUV. Louise gave us hugs and "Proud of you girls," whispered in our ears.

But before I got in beside Raye in Cap's kickass Porsche Panamera, I looked to Homer standing outside his tent.

He dipped his chin, lifted a hand to give me a salute, and then he disappeared behind the flaps.

That was his version of "Thank you for seeing to one of our own."

Raye set that baby to purring and drove us to the Oasis.

When we were going through the security gate, Martha was coming out.

She took one look at us and said, "Hells bells. You both look like you've been hit by a truck."

"We just took part in helping a man with severe PTSD be taken from a homeless camp to an inpatient psych facility," I stated.

Martha blinked before she said, "It's not even ten o'clock."

"We didn't get to pick the timing," Raye said.

Martha took us in.

She then declared, "I don't do hot chocolate. But I sure as shit do shots of whisky."

I appreciated whisky, even if it wasn't a fave.

Regardless, I asked, "Is that an offer?"

"The best one I got," Martha replied.

"Sounds pretty good to me," Raye said.

"Me too," I put in.

Whatever she was heading off to do, she abandoned it by marching toward the courtyard, ordering, "Follow me, girls."

Raye took my hand.

I held hers tight.

And we followed Martha.

"You don't have to do this now."

"No, I don't. But I think I need to do it. Though, you don't have to do it with me. I can come back."

"You're not picking a pet without my input."

We were sitting outside Halo Animal Rescue.

I won't get into what Eric told me happened at the psych facility. We could just say that getting Chris there was a whole helluva lot easier than getting Chris admitted. In fact, since he refused, they had to call the Johnsons back so they could admit him as members of his family.

The bad news for Mr. and Mrs. Johnson was that they still hadn't been allowed to see him and were told the staff needed a few days to evaluate and get him settled before he could have visitors.

The good news for Mr. and Mrs. Johnson was that they knew where their son was, it was safe, clean and there were people there who could help him.

So I decided to take that morning as a win.

"Let's do it," Eric said.

I nodded, we both got out, we went into the shelter, and we explained to the staff what we were looking for.

They asked us to complete a questionnaire. We did, they assessed it, and then they took us to the cats.

It was then I realized why Eric was hesitant about me doing this.

Regardless that they were double-decker and gave the fur babies room to move, just looking at the cages of unwanted animals that found themselves in their own homeless camp was so crushing in that moment, I took a step back.

Eric slid an arm around my waist and bent to me.

"We'll come back next weekend," he said quickly.

The staff member was studying me quizzically.

"No," I said. "Fuck no," I went on. "We're doing this now." I caught the staff member's gaze. "Which one has been here the longest?"

Her eyes lit, she beckoned with a hand and took us to a cage where a black cat lay, curled into himself. He had lovely thick fur and a chunky body.

I hadn't even seen his face, and it was love at first sight.

He didn't lift his head out of his fur, but he opened his big yellow eyes to look at me.

The staff member opened the cage.

The cat finally lifted his head.

Carefully, I offered my hand for him to sniff.

He sniffed it, then he stood and would have walked right out of the cage and fallen to the floor, if I wasn't there to catch him in my arms.

He curled up there and blinked.

"What's his name?" Eric asked the staff member.

"Homer," she replied, and I went still. "But we call him the General because, when he's in the community room, since he's been here the longest, he keeps the other cats in line."

My gaze shot to Eric, but he was staring at the lady in stunned surprise.

"You're shitting me," he said to her.

"No. Why?" she asked.

Eric didn't answer.

I did.

"We'll take him."

I SNAPPED a photo of El Generalissimo (I renamed him, for obvious reasons, and I was calling him Henny for short), who was lying on my chest, kitty nose turned in the air, eyes closed, purring.

I then sent it to Jeff with the text, *Meet El Generalissimo, Henny for short. My first child.*

It didn't take long before Jeff returned, *YOU GOT A CAT WHILE I'M STUCK IN A SAFE HOUSE!?*

Yes, it was in shouty caps.

Told you we'd both always wanted a pet.

The world keeps turning, my brother. I replied.

He looks bored. When I get home, he's coming over to Uncle Jeff's to play.

He's ten. Eric bought him 5,921 cat toys. He just sits there and follows them with his eyes as we jiggle them around. Then when I sit down, he crawls in my lap. He's a lover not a player.

We'll see.

Yes, we would.

El Generalissimo yawned, I clicked a quick shot and sent it to Jeff.

My baby has excellent teeth, I captioned.

He looks like he's roaring.

I checked.

It was true.

I also decided to print that picture and frame it, since it was awesome.

He wasn't. He was yawning, I told Jeff.

That's because you're boring.

I chuckled.

I also sent a middle finger emoji to my brother.

Eric came from cooking in the kitchen (we were having chicken tacos, the maiden voyage of my Crock-Pot) to stretch out on the other angle of my couch, his head close to my head, reaching to scratch between Henny's ears.

"Not sure all cats adapt to a place as quickly as this guy has," he murmured.

Henny had to sit with me in the car while Eric did an emergency pass through a PetSmart to stock us up on supplies. When we got him home, there had been some sniffing. We showed him his box when we got it set up. His food when we got that set up.

After that, he just jumped up on the couch, curled up on one of my throws, and fell asleep.

That said, he'd been at the rescue for eighteen months, so, I figured he knew home when he smelled it.

"Jeff's jealous," I told him.

"He can get his own cat."

"He's plotting on stealing mine."

"Then maybe you should tell him I own a gun."

That made me laugh.

Henny opened his eyes to share the vibrations were disturbing his rest.

I stopped laughing.

Henny closed his eyes again.

"He's got you wrapped around his paw," Eric noted.

"We're down with that, aren't we, Henny?"

Henny kept purring.

Oh yeah.

We were so down with that.

There was a knock on the door.

"Bets on who it is?" Eric asked as he angled up. He was definitely getting the hang of the Oasis.

"Raye," I told him. "She knows we were going to the rescue today, so she'll be all about meeting Henny."

Eric opened the door.

I was right. It was Raye.

Along with Cap.

Raye looked at me, and then Henny, but she didn't come to us. She and Cap just stopped once they were in enough to close the door.

I wasn't surprised about this, considering the feel they brought with them and the looks on their faces.

Eric felt it too.

"What's going on?" he asked Cap.

"We gotta go into the office, brother," Cap replied. "Someone in the camp got word to Mary. Mary got word to us. They took someone else." He paused and said, "Then Tex phoned in a report from the police station. He tried to stop them, but they shot at him, and he had to abort. Fortunately, no one was hit. Another bonus, Tex confirmed this Clown guy was with them. So we have confirmation on the crew we're dealing with."

My heart lurched, and I cuddled Henny to me as I shot to my feet. Henny didn't like the sudden movement, and he squirmed to get away, so I dropped him on the couch.

"The sun isn't down yet," I said to Cap.

"They're getting bolder," Eric noted darkly.

But Raye and Cap were both still giving off weird vibes, and I didn't like it one bit.

"What?" I asked.

"Oh, Jess," Raye whispered.

My lungs stopped functioning.

"What?" I wheezed.

"Honey," she kept whispering. "This time, they took Homer."

At this news, my heart flatlined.

TWENTY-FOUR

LEROY NEIMAN

I hadn't jumpstarted my heart in the second it took Eric to grab my hand and drag me to the bedroom.

Once he got me there, he bent so he was an inch in front of my face.

"I know you're gonna rally the women and go out," he stated.

Fuck yes, I was going to rally the women and go out.

I didn't get the chance to confirm.

Eric kept talking.

"Whatever you get, you feed to us. We know of this crew, but we don't know where their operations are. But they've got guns, Jessica, and you know they don't hesitate to pull the trigger. You get a location before we do, you feed that to us too. And then you back the fuck off."

I nodded, and I meant it.

I wasn't going to tangle with these motherfuckers. I didn't even want Eric to tangle with them, and I was half convinced he was an immortal god.

What I wanted was Homer back in his tent.

Then, in a voice I'd never used in my life, it was small, fragile and afraid, I begged, "Please find him."

I watched the fire burn in Eric's eyes, but he didn't respond verbally.

He didn't have to. I read him loud and clear.

He then caught me by the back of my head, pulled me to him for a hard kiss, let my head go but took my hand and dragged me back down the hall.

Raye was cuddling Henny to her chest (of course).

"We're gone," Eric grunted at Cap.

And then they were gone.

After the door closed, Raye told me, "I already called Harlow and told her to head over."

"Call her again and tell her to switch to the Sportage on the way," I ordered, moving to my Vans to put them on. "We're gone too."

I HAD separation anxiety from Henny after we headed out, and I honestly considered bringing him with us, in case he experienced the same. But I decided to wait to bring him out on operations after he was used to me and my chicks.

So, while Jinx rallied the crew to meet us at the diner, we swung by the Sun Valley Motor Lodge to have a conversation with Mr. Shithead.

He might not know anything, but he also might, and we were going to leave no stone unturned.

When he saw us approach the reception area, he didn't act like a dick.

Such were the powers of porn.

We swung in, and I could have kissed the girls for letting me lead it.

I dispensed with any pleasantries, as they'd be lost on him anyway, and asked, "Do you know a dealer named Lil Clown?"

"Where's my titty mags?" he asked back.

That was when it became clear I probably shouldn't be leading this.

This was because I launched myself over the counter at him, and with my hips balanced on it, my legs in the air, I caught him by the neck of his tee and dragged his face to mine while the girls all tried to pull me away.

"I asked...do you...know *a dealer*...named *Lil Clown*?"

"Je-Nat, come back," Harlow pleaded.

I shook him by his collar. "*Do you?*"

"Get off me," he demanded, testing the limits of his tee by pulling back on my hold even as he wrapped his fingers around my wrist to try to yank it free.

"*Answer me!*" I shrieked.

"I don't fuck with that shit, woman," he said. "I get mine legal by going to the dispensary. Now back the fuck off."

The girls managed to pull me away and Luna took my place—not accosting him, talking to him.

"As you can see, this is important to her," she began.

He jerked at his not-too-clean and now misshapen T-shirt. "Yeah, I can see that."

"So, I swear on all I find holy, those things being books, interior décor and really good vodka, that I'll bring you ten mags of your choice *and* ten movies if you have any information on this Lil Clown asshole or his crew," Luna bargained.

"I deal in hookers and rooms," he returned. "I see deals go down. I don't pay attention. They don't like people paying attention. It's just whores and beds by the hour and the occasional moron who wanders in thinking he's gonna get a deal while the spring training is on."

"Fuck," I bit off, turned on my Van and prowled out of motel reception.

The girls followed me.

When we got to the tail of the Sportage, Harlow sidled in close.

"I think you need to try some breathing exercises," she suggested.

"I think we need to get our asses to the diner," I retorted.

"I think we need to source a lot more informants," Raye muttered to Luna.

"I think you're right," Luna agreed.

"Can we go?" I asked impatiently.

Raye got in my space, which I didn't appreciate at that juncture, but I did nothing about it because she was speaking. "I love you. Heart and soul. I get it. It guts me that he's with them instead of in the world where he feels safe. But, babe, Harlow's right. You need to chill the fuck out."

This was true.

I needed to chill out.

I drew in an unsteady breath.

"Another one, please," Harlow requested.

I drew in another one. It wasn't any steadier, but I did it.

"We're gonna find him, or the men are gonna find him, Jess," Luna said. "Trust the process."

The Nightingale crew found Raye's sister who had been dead for nineteen years, *and* her killer.

They'd find Homer and the rest of them.

I took in another breath. It was a whole lot calmer.

Then I said, "Let's go."

We climbed in the Sportage, and we went.

When we hit the diner, the girls weren't inside.

They were loitering outside, all of them wearing non-sex worker outfits of jeans and sweaters or tees and jackets with the addition of sneakers.

Though, Divinity's sneakers were wedges.

And they were all there, that whole crew: Jinx, Persia, Divinity, Skyla, Lotus, Cameo and Genesis.

And standing with them were Bambi and Bambi's mom, Betsy.

Bambi's name wasn't Bambi, it was Christina. And Bambi wasn't a sex worker anymore. Bambi had been trafficked, saved by the Angels and the Hottie Squad, and then she spent a lot of time in counseling and attending support groups (and, the last I heard, she was still doing both).

Now Bambi was no longer Bambi unless she was in this environment, an occurrence, considering her history, that was rare and only happened so she could keep in touch with the crew, both ours and Jinx's. This happened over burgers at the diner.

Outside this environment, she was Christina and she was in beauty school.

But now, for some reason, she was here.

We got out and headed to them.

"Sucks you didn't bring the Merc," Skyla muttered, eyeing the Sportage.

"We don't have a lot of time, and we don't have a lot of resources," Raye declared. "So anything you got that we can go on would be appreciated."

It hit me then that Jinx and her chicks had somehow been fully briefed somewhere along the way. That meant one of my chicks briefed them.

God, totally worth a repeat at this point. I loved my girls.

"We know that, that's why we're goin' with you," Jinx stated.

Yeah, they'd been briefed.

"I don't—" Raye started.

"Listen, no denyin' you bitches get the job done," Jinx declared. "But you don't just roll up on these kinds of guys. You hear me? They see a familiar face, they won't blow it off. The other way around?" She shrugged.

This was good advice. I was freaked for Homer, but I didn't want my face blown off in the hunt for him, or any of my chicks' faces for that matter.

Jinx motioned to Bambi. "When she was in the game, Bambi here was dealers' choice."

That explained why Bambi was there.

And that really sucked for Bambi, and as much as I wanted all the help I could get, I wasn't sure about her state of mind wading back into this world.

"I knew Clown. I don't know who Clown is working for now," Bambi said. "But I know his old crew and where to find them."

Luna had the same thoughts as I did. "Are you sure you're up for this?"

Bambi lifted a shoulder but said, "I'm sure you and the girls had other things to do that didn't include finding me and the others and getting us out of that nightmare."

"What comes around goes around," Betsy piped in to sum things up.

Jinx got impatient.

"We're gonna roll out...together," she stated. "When we get somewhere, we'll tell you if you can get out of the car or not. No questions asked, you bitches do as I say. *Entendido*?"

She was kind of scary when she got bossy.

Though, that wasn't the only reason we all nodded.

"Bambi, you're in their ride," Jinx kept bossing. "We'll all follow." She turned to Betsy. "You go home."

"They helped my girl and me, I want to help them," Betsy said.

"This is time we don't have, mama," Jinx told her.

Betsy looked like she was going to be stubborn.

I fought screaming in impatience.

Betsy backed down. "Okay. You girls be super careful out there, okay?" Betsy asked.

We all nodded again.

Bambi hugged Betsy and we all went to our cars.

"Where they hang, if they still hang there, isn't far from here," Bambi told us, then gave Luna, who was driving, directions as we headed out of the diner's parking lot.

She was in the front with Luna, which meant Raye, Harlow and I were wedged in the back.

"What?" Harlow asked me.

I was a little freaked at how well she knew me.

"Nothing," I lied.

Bambi gave Luna more directions.

I looked behind us and saw Jinx behind the wheel of an older model Audi with some of the girls seated in her car, another car following them with the rest of the crew.

"What?" Raye asked, now watching me closely.

I faced forward, stretched my neck side to side and reminded them, "I know who knows where these operations are, which means they probably know where Homer is."

"Your brother," Harlow whispered.

"Jeff," I confirmed.

"And you're not calling him because?" Raye prompted carefully.

I looked to her. "I'm not calling him because, if he and Javi knew we were after these guys, they'd be down from the mountains in a shot. They also wouldn't tell me where these guys are. But they sure would drag their asses down here and intervene."

And by "intervene," I meant possibly get dead like Joaquim and Jamal did.

"Maybe they can work with the men," Harlow suggested.

"And maybe I don't want my brother in that line of fire. I don't want Javi in it either. Hell, I know how much experience the Hottie Squad has, and I'm in active denial that *they're* involved in this mess."

"I am too," Raye mumbled.

I jerked a thumb at her and asked Harlow, "See? And Raye's seen them in action."

"Let's just stay on target," Luna said from the front. "If we come up with nothing, we'll reconsider."

I pulled out my phone and texted Eric, *Anything?*

"Park here," Bambi said.

Luna swung into a spot on a street somewhere deep on the southside of the city when my phone vibrated.

Working on it. Stay cool. We'll find him.

I took in another deep breath.

"Wait here," Bambi said, then she popped out of the car.

Jinx and Persia met her on the sidewalk before they walked up to the house.

They went in.

We waited.

Nothing.

"This is torture. They've been in there ten minutes," I griped.

"They've been in there two minutes," Raye said quietly. "Chill, babe."

Ugh.

Twenty minutes later (or maybe it was four), they came out and Bambi took off toward the two cars behind us. Jinx came to the Sportage and got in the passenger seat.

"They don't know dick," she announced.

Fuck!

"But they say Sausage knows all about this shit," Jinx went on. "And Sausage likes me, which is good for me, and now it's good for you. Let's roll."

Luna pulled out.

I twisted to see that one of the cars followed, the other was doing a three-pointer.

"Gotta get Bambi back to Betsy," Jinx explained. "Cameo's gonna take her home. She good, but we don't wanna push it with flashback shit. We got this now."

I hoped so.

And I owed Bambi big time for courting flashbacks in order to help.

Jinx gave Luna directions, and we hit up a nondescript neighborhood with neat yards, middle-of-the-line, well-maintained cars and a lot of dead grass, since no one in this 'hood was going to spend money on water for fall seeding.

Luna parked at the curb.

The girls parked behind us.

Jinx twisted to all of us. "Sausage likes company. He also likes to hold court. But just know, he gets a look at you bitches, he's gonna beat his meat thinkin' about one, the other, or all of you."

Gross.

"Thanks for the warning," Luna muttered.

"Why's he called Sausage?" Harlow asked.

We all paused and looked at her.

"Oh. Eww," she said, then scrunched her nose, and the fact Harlow could be cute even in this situation was testimony to the awesome powers of her cuteness.

"Just to say, don't call him that to his face," Jinx advised. "We girls got that name for him, and he knows about it and thinks it's hilarious. But that's because no one has ever called him that direct. He wouldn't find that funny."

With the tone she used to speak it, I made special note of this advice.

None of us got the chance to ask what to call him before Jinx ordered, "Let's do this."

She then got out, so we all got out with her.

Persia, Divinity, Skyla, Lotus and Genesis met us in the driveway before we followed Jinx to a garage at the back.

She hit the side door, knocked, when someone bellowed, "I'm receiving!" she pushed through, and we came in after her.

The instant I hit the man cave that was Sausage's throne room, I made the decision to redecorate my entire apartment.

Black walls. Unfinished ceiling. Fantastic lighting. Glass-fronted beverage fridges filled with beer. A floor to ceiling rack of wine. A fully stocked bar made of padded black leather tufted in diamond shapes.

The space was shared by a pristine, gold-painted Camaro, its year, I wasn't sure, but my guess would be it was from the seventies. It was parked there, not because this was a garage, but because that car was so hot, it was a piece of art.

In a dope contrast to the black, two tan leather couches faced each other over a glass-topped coffee table that had some telltale leaves and buds on it, and if that wasn't telltale enough, someone had left behind their rolling papers.

And behind the man lounging in a massive tan leather chair that was set up on a plush, black-carpeted dais, was a portrait of said man, looking like it'd been painted Leroy Neiman.

It was kick...*freaking*...ass.

I wanted one.

No.

I *needed* one.

I forced my attention to the man.

He was Black. Even seated I could tell he was tall, and large, but not out of shape. Pure muscle. He was also bald. And he had a Mike Colter look about him that was *spectacular*.

He was smoking a cigar and had put aside a magazine when we entered, a look at which shared it was *Sports Illustrated*.

"Jinx," he said expansively, opening his arms wide. "You always bring me presents."

"Hey, baby," she replied, walking right up to him.

She gave his cheek a kiss.

She then stepped off the dais and to his side, saying, "You know the girls."

"Don't know all the girls," he said, eyeing my crew. Then he looked to Jinx's posse. "No love?" he asked.

They all marched up in a line with various "Hey, baby," "Hey, honey," and "Hey, sweetie," with one, "Hey, daddy," along with cheek kisses.

"These bitches are Jill, Kelly, Natalie and Dylan," Jinx introduced us, and we each raised our hand when she said our names like we were indicating we were present to our teacher.

I knew this was a grave errand, and I had the best guy in the world, but I hoped I got to give a cheek kiss to this guy.

His expressive eyebrows shot up, and he boomed, "The Angels!"

We all looked at each other, wondering if he guessed by the names or if our reputation had swung out that far.

"Fuck me, to what do I owe this honor?" he asked.

Whoa.

Our reputation had swung that far.

"Clown and his crew took one of Nat's boys, Titus," Jinx answered for us.

I shuffled back a step at the murderous expression that stole over his face.

Though, if his real name was Titus, he just got a whole lot better, because that was a kickass name, and he was already amazing.

"That little motherfucker," Titus growled. "Who'd he take, baby?" he asked me.

"My friend at the homeless camp. His name is Homer," I told him.

I was wrong.

The expression he had on his face before was sheer benevolence.

Now, he had a face full of murder.

"Those fuckers," he groused. "Pieces of shit, every one of 'em. Less than shit. Whatever the fuck that is."

"We need to find him, sir," I said.

Another swift mood change when he smiled. "Sir. That's sweet. But all my girls call me Titus. I make the pissants call me sir."

I nodded.

"You done good findin' those women and settin' that new crew of badasses on those dickweeds who snatched 'em," Titus declared (yep, our reputation had gone a lot farther than expected). "But you gotta give these boys a wide berth. They're no good. Until the other crews form an alliance to wipe them out, or a cartel gets wind of their shit, they just gotta do what they do."

"Homer doesn't touch anything without having a plastic bag over his hand," I shared. "I don't think he can wait while they do what they gotta do."

Titus stroked his chin in thought.

"We're not going in to get him," Raye piped up. "We're sending the new crew of badasses after Homer."

"That makes me feel better, baby," Titus replied. "And I asked around about that band of boys. Word is, they got their shit tight."

We all nodded to confirm the Hottie Squad had their shit tight.

"Even so, they got no idea what they're walking into with that den of snakes," Titus finished.

My heart took a hit with that, and I looked at Raye. I could tell the minute I saw her face her heart sustained the same.

"Javi shoulda known better," Titus muttered. "That shocked the shit out of me when I heard what went down."

"He didn't call the order," I told him. "Joaquim had a beef."

One of his brows drew down, the other went way up. "You know Javi?"

"Her brother is a Soldier," Jinx offered up intel I would rather not have shared.

That blew him away. "You're Easy's sister?"

Easy?

"She sure is," Jinx confirmed.

Wait.

Jeff's street name was Easy?

Wait again.

My baby brother had a street name?

And it was Easy?

"Man's solid. Why's he not here helping?" Titus asked.

Some of this wouldn't have been something I shared. But we were all in now.

"They needed to lay low because these guys went after them because of what Joaquim did," I answered.

He nodded. "Joaq, he was a fighter. He was also a hothead." Titus tapped his bald skull with fingers that were clenching his cigar. "He didn't think before he acted. Damn waste. Jamal...?" He shook his head. "Gotta give a brother props for loyalty, but...*shit*."

"Javi and Jeff are pretty busted up about it," I told him.

"Thicker than blood," Titus replied. "Doin' the good work. Or they were."

I pressed my lips together.

Titus turned to Jinx. "Been wantin' to meet this new crew."

Jinx looked at us in expectation.

"You mean, you want to meet the Nightingale men?" Luna asked.

"Can you arrange that?" Titus asked back.

"Will you tell us what you know about Clown and his people?" I parried.

"Darlin', I'll tell those boys anything they wanna know, they got the balls to clean up that shitshow."

Oh, they had the balls. I just wanted to keep those balls—all of them, but it must be said one set in particular—healthy and functioning. And for that to happen, they needed to know what they were up against.

"One second," I said quickly, and stepped outside the garage, pulling out my phone.

Raye came with me and huddled close as I made the call to Eric.

I put it on speaker.

He answered on one ring.

"How you hanging in there, sweetheart?" he asked as greeting.

"Hey, you're on speaker. And, well...okay, I'm here with the girls at the garage of a guy named Titus. I think his street name is—"

"Wait. Stop. You're at Titus's garage?" he asked.

I caught Raye's gaze. "You know Titus?"

"Everyone knows *of* Titus. But I haven't had the pleasure."

"Well, he knows Clown and I think a lot more, and he says he'll tell you guys because he wants to meet you."

No hesitation, Eric announced, "We'll be there in twenty."

Whoa.

Seemed Titus was the real deal, and I already kinda knew that with the Camaro and portrait.

"Wait!" I cried, thinking he was going to hang up.

"What?" Eric asked.

I took two gigantic steps away from Titus's door, Raye came with and huddled even closer, before I whispered, "Who is this guy?"

"Ex-dealer in his youth. Ran a big crew. He got tagged, did five years, got out, kitted out his garage with his drug money, and whatever part of the street Javi doesn't run, Titus runs it."

"Like, he's a vigilante?"

"No. Like, he's a negotiator."

"What does that mean?"

"That means he wasn't a big fan of doing time, or wasting years selling narcotics, and he's less of a fan of brothers killing brothers for stupid shit like turf wars and vendettas. He knows enough to know he can't stop people from committing illegal acts, but he does his part to make sure it doesn't get out of hand. In other words, he keeps the peace."

"He has that much respect?"

"I don't know the history. I just know that's how it works. I also know no one gets an audience with this guy unless they know him, or they've got an in. We've been trying for six months to get in front of him."

Thank you, Jinx.

"And last, he hasn't made it a secret he's pissed as shit this crew that took Homer is operating in his jurisdiction the way they are," Eric concluded.

"Do you know where his garage is?"

"Everyone does. We're en route now."

"Okay, baby. See you soon."

"Jess?"

This time, he caught me from hanging up. "Yeah?"

"We called Clarice who got us in touch with Javi. He and Jeff are coming down."

My stomach sank.

"We need to know what they know," Eric explained. "We tried to get it over the phone, but Javi refused. Demanded face to face."

Which meant he was also going to demand they be in on the takedown.

This also meant I was right.

Damn you, Javi!

"But they're at least an hour out," Eric continued. "So, if Titus can get us the intel, we can deal with this before they get here."

My stomach sank further.

"No one has anything good to say about these guys," I told him.

"Because there's nothing good to say," he told me.

"What I mean is—"

"Jessica, did I promise to get Homer for you?"

My breath was shaky again when I drew it in and let it out.

Then I said, "I think this is more than your average dangerous, Turner."

"And I think we're in a trust exercise we didn't expect, Jess. This is not all I do, but it's part of it."

Okay, trust.

I could trust him.

It was the bad guys I didn't trust.

"You with me?" he asked.

"Mostly."

"Jessie," he whispered.

"I'll get the rest of the way while you drive here."

"There's my girl. See you soon."

"'Bye, Eric."

We hung up.

"So there it is. They're coming," I told Raye something she heard herself.

"Great...and fuck."

My thoughts exactly.

"Yeah," I agreed.

We went to the door and knocked.

"If I know you're coming back, you don't have to knock!" Titus yelled.

We went in, with Raye saying, "Sorry. We didn't know the protocol."

Titus grinned, wide and white.

"They're coming," I told him.

"And here's me with my SI, waiting for the Suns game to start, thinking my night would be boring," he replied.

"We're not really good at boring," Harlow, for the first time, chimed in.

"I'm gettin' that, pretty baby," Titus cooed to her.

She blushed.

Good Lord, it was like she was collecting gorgeous, gigantic, morally dubious, but still sweet hot guys.

Titus stood, and we all watched, for my part, with my lips parted, as he demonstrated how gigantic he was.

I was understanding some of the respect now.

"I'm feelin' wine. A good red. Anyone feelin' wine?" he asked.

He got a chorus of "Me!" from Jinx's crew.

I stepped forward.

"I'm a mixologist, and I'm sorry to contradict, but if this situation doesn't say dirty martini, none do."

Another grin, an extended arm toward the bar, and an invitation of, "*Mi cantina es tú cantina*, darlin'."

Everybody's cantina was my cantina.

I moved behind the bar, got the lay of the land, and as I was in my happy place, I felt a little bit better.

Though, only a little.

When the knock came at the door fifteen minutes later, we were all lounged on the couches drinking martinis (except Jinx and Persia were lounged on the arms of Titus's chair, and Genesis and Skyla were sitting at the bar).

Titus looked to the screen on his watch, which told me he had a camera that showed him who was at the door.

"Enter!" he bellowed.

The men entered.

Not just Eric and Cap with Mace thrown in.

All of them.

Eric, Cap, Mace, Roam, Liam, Knox, Gabe and Brady.

I wasn't prepared for the onslaught of hotness, so I had to blink rapidly to assist my brain in not shutting down due to overload.

"Well, fuck me, it's *The Expendables*, the early years," Titus remarked.

I wanted to laugh, because it was funny, but I was too busy taking in Eric staring at me, lounging on a killer tan leather couch, drinking a martini.

"I think they do this investigative shit a lot better than we do," Mace muttered.

I bit my lip.

Harlow let loose a giggle, then swallowed it.

Titus stood again, saying, "The ladies are comfortable. Let's take this outside."

I stood too.

Titus instantly stopped moving.

Eric said quietly, "Jessie."

It messed with my head, but I sat down.

The men moved outside.

Once the door closed, Persia advised, "You gotta give 'em room to swing their dicks."

"Even if they don't know you're givin' 'em room," Genesis chimed in.

"They'll think they claimed the space." That was Skyla. "They never figure out you cleared it for them."

"You got Javi, you got Titus, you tapped a direct vein to the street, bitch," Jinx said. "You get that, you play the game the way they make the rules."

I didn't like being left out, but I took in their wisdom.

Then I sipped my martini.

Genesis did too, before she said, "Girl, I don't know what kinda magic you got." She lifted her martini glass. "I mean, it's vodka and olive juice, so how can it go wrong? But you make it so, *so* right."

"Thanks, sister," I said.

"I'm feeling peckish," Persia announced. "I hope, while those boys go kick ass, Titus lets us order a pizza."

"Indian," Genesis put in.

"Shit, now I want both," Persia complained.

I wondered how our chicken was doing in the Crockpot.

I wondered how Henny was doing all by himself in a new space.

I wondered if Homer was hanging in there.

A vision of the last time I saw Homer outside his tent assaulted my brain, and a sharp stab of pain went through it.

The door opened, and I peered over the back of the couch to see Titus entering, and Eric, hand on the door handle, torso swung in, eyes on me.

"We're moving out," Eric said.

I stood again. "I need to go with you."

Eric did a slow blink along with his brows going up, but he said nothing.

"Homer might need me when you get him out." I shook my head. "No. He's going to need me, Turner. I don't want to go in, but I want to be close."

"Babe, we're putting together an approach on the fly, and we're gonna need every man."

"Just close. A block away. I'll be safe. I won't move a muscle, I swear. You can call me when you're done."

"You're not anywhere near unless we have a man on you, and all we got is Tex and Duke, and it'll take either of them at least half an hour to get here, and you know, we don't have that time."

"I'll take her," Titus said.

I whipped around to him, nearly spilling martini, and gave him a happy smile.

"No offense, man, but I just met you," Eric said.

"None taken. I'd feel the same if she was my baby. So understand, I'll take care of her like she's mine," Titus retorted.

Luna stood. "One goes, we all go."

Raye stood. "Angels unite."

Harlow stood. "There's gonna be a bunch of homeless people who are gonna need a soft touch, so we all have to go."

"Shit, can't fit you all in the Camaro, we'll have to take the Jag," Titus decreed.

Awesome.

The situation warranted it, and until that moment, I wouldn't have thought I had it in me.

But I guessed I did.

I channeled Harlow and turned girlie, *pretty please* begging eyes to Eric.

"Fine," Eric bit off.

Damn.

That shit worked.

"You go, we'll follow," Titus said.

Eric scowled at him, doing some silent badass brainwave communication.

"I got this," Titus said impatiently. "Go."

Eric looked at me, he did it hard, and I could tell he was leaning toward changing his mind.

"I'm falling in love with you," I blurted.

His eyes went dark, his face went soft, he dipped his chin and said, "See you soon, honey."

Then he was gone.

I jumped when an arm was slung around my shoulders.

I tipped my head back to see Titus smiling down at me.

He smelled like fresh raked leaves and bergamot, with the barest hint of patchouli.

In other words, awesome.

"Well played, baby. Well played," he said.

I sucked back the rest of my martini.

Titus busted out laughing.

Once he got control of his humor, we headed to his garage behind the garage, got in his amazing, black Jaguar SUV and headed out.

TWENTY-FIVE

CHICKEN TACOS

I'd been patient a long time.

I really had.

So it wasn't untoward when I snapped, "Oh my God! This is agony." I turned to the girls in the backseat and asked Raye and Luna, "Did it take this long when they cleared out those traffickers?"

"No, it didn't take this long," Luna said quietly, holding Raye's hand.

"I see the martini wore off," Titus remarked.

I sat straight in my seat, crossed my arms on my chest, knowing Raye was freaking just like me and I didn't need to make it harder on her, so I only thought to myself, if Eric gets dead doing this for me (and Homer, and all the rest of them, and everyone else those assholes were fucking over), I was going to kill him.

"Well, shit," Titus murmured.

He was staring in his rearview mirror.

I turned around and that was when I saw the police lights. And within a few seconds, heard the sirens.

They were heading our way.

The two patrols shot past us, and it didn't take a genius to know where they were going.

"Is this good or bad?" I asked unevenly.

"I know one thing. If those motherfuckers put holes in your boys, they aren't calling the police after they did it," Titus answered.

My heart started thumping, and I turned again in my seat to look at my chicks.

"This is the clean-up crew," Titus concluded as another police car shot past.

I smiled at Raye.

She smiled at me.

My phone vibrated at my ass, I whipped it out and engaged the screen.

Text from Eric, *Tell Titus to bring you in.*

Thank you, God, thank you, God, *thank you, God*!

"We can go," Raye and I said at the same time, this meaning she got a text too.

Titus started rolling forward, but it took a while to get the three blocks to where all the police cars with their lights still flashing were angled around because Titus had to pull to the side twice for more patrols to pass us.

In that time, I texted Eric, *Coming!*

When Titus parked as close as he could get, he said in a voice he hadn't used yet, one that was not to be denied, it was also another indication of why he was who he was, "You go only when I tell you to go."

Not in the mood to see what would happen if I tried to deny Titus, I texted Eric, *We're here, but Titus won't let us get out until he knows it's okay.*

After that, we waited.

An ambulance came screaming in.

"Oh God," I whispered.

And then we heard the horns of a firetruck before we saw a

couple of cops angle their cars out of the way so that big, red behemoth could get in.

The firemen dropped down practically before that thing was fully parked and started hustling.

That was when I noticed the smoke billowing up from the house one down and across the street from where Titus parked.

"I'm thinkin' your boys don't mind mess, which I'm also thinkin' with this crew they were up against is a little bit of all right," Titus observed.

It seemed so. We only had to hope none of them were part of the mess.

I twisted again in my seat and asked Raye, "Cap texted, right?"

She nodded.

"There!" Harlow cried and pointed.

I looked there and saw Eric doing his beautiful saunter through the mess of first responder vehicles, heading our way.

He didn't have any blood on him, thank God, but he did have a gun holstered at his hip, as well as one in a shoulder holster.

"You can go now," Titus allowed.

We all jumped out of the car.

But only Raye and I raced across the street. Me to Eric, and Raye to Cap, who was trailing Eric by about five feet.

I hit Eric like a dart, if his *oof!* was anything to go by.

After I hugged him tight, I touched his head, his shoulders, ran my hands down his chest, while asking, "You all right?"

"Fine, honey. We're all fine."

Thank you, God, thank you, God, *thank you, God*!

I looked into his eyes. "Homer?"

"Come with me."

He took my hand and walked me to the sidewalk. We had to dodge a bunch of people, and a cop started to say something to us, saw Eric and stopped, when Eric led us into the yard of a house, the back of which was on fire.

To the side of the yard, well away from the melee but being guarded by some cops, was a gaggle of scruffy people.

One of them was Homer.

I pulled my hand free and raced to him.

Eric called, "She's with me," to the cop who moved to block me.

I came to a rocking halt in front of Homer.

He looked unsettled, undone, and seemed to have trouble focusing on me.

"Hey, Homer," I greeted. "You okay?"

When my voice sounded, it appeared as if some of the confusion cleared.

Therefore, I kept talking.

"Do you need me to go get some plastic bags so we have everything to get you home?" I asked.

I watched the confusion completely clear, and he focused on me.

"You're here," he whispered.

"Yeah, big guy," I whispered back. "I'm here."

He stared at me.

I lamented my decision to study cocktails and not psychology.

Then I held my breath as he walked up to me, got toe to toe, bent his neck, pressed just his forehead to mine, and repeated, "You're here."

Good Lord.

I was going to lose it.

"You're my friend," I said huskily.

"You're my friend too, Jessie," he replied.

Totally going to lose it.

"I'm so glad," I choked out.

We looked into each other's eyes.

Then he stepped back and the spell was broken.

"Can I go home?" he asked.

"As soon as we can manage it," I answered. "Promise."

He nodded and shuffled away to get close to the others. They didn't look good, mentally or hygienically, though at least they looked fed.

Harlow and Luna were cautiously approaching the huddle when I turned and nearly bumped into Eric.

The look on his face aimed right at me took my breath away.

I powered through that and requested, "Can we get them home?"

"Don't ever again tell me you're not special," he said as reply.

Oh God, I was holding it together, and he was going to send me over the edge.

"I can't now, honey," I warned him.

He nodded sharply and shared, "We're working on it. The cops obviously need to interview them. Mace is trying to tell them that'd go better if they got them where they feel safe."

I looked across the bustling space and saw Mace in an intense conversation with that man who wore a more-official-than-the-normal-official uniform.

Then, after I got over the shock of them all standing together (seriously, it was like staring at the sun), I also saw Liam, Brady, Knox, Gabe and Roam hanging. They were chatting like they were discussing how they thought the Cardinals would do tomorrow, and not like they were in proximity to a house that was ablaze, firemen working to contain it, nearly a dozen cop cars with the cops from those cars hustling around, and (cripes!) paramedics rushing an occupied stretcher to the ambulance.

Gabe had some blood on his Henley, but it was clearly not his.

Time to stop looking at the guys.

I turned back to my guy.

"Copy that," I said to Eric.

"I'll go check and see how that's progressing," Eric said. "Stay right here. I'll be back."

I nodded.

Harlow and Luna got close to me. Raye wandered over when Cap was called to talk to a uniform. We stood together, with me glancing often to Homer and the others to see if I could take their temperature (I couldn't).

Though, they were openly tweaked and restless, but who wouldn't be?

I felt something funny and looked the other way.

Titus was leaning against the fender of his Jag, arms crossed on his wide chest.

When he caught my eyes, he dipped his head down and to the side in what I understood was a unique salute.

He pushed away from his car, went to the door, folded in, reversed out.

And he was gone.

A COUPLE of not-so-fun things happen when you spring a bunch of abductees from unpaid, forced labor in a Fentanyl, heroin, cocaine operation.

Yes, it was confirmed that was why they took Homer and the rest of those people.

Allow me to explain...

THE FIRST NOT-SO-FUN thing was watching your man, who prided himself on keeping his cool, lose his ever-lovin' mind, at the same time you watched your friend's man do the same, when the dude with the more-official-than-the-normal-official uniform told a couple of cops to round the four of us Angels up, put us in police cars and take us to the station.

I shared a car with Harlow, and before we were whisked away, I watched Eric being *very* in the face of the big kahuna cop. Cap, his entire body so tight, it was a visible ticking time bomb, was right at his back.

The rest of the guys were fanned around them, and I couldn't tell from body language, should the situation escalate, if the Hottie Squad would pull Eric and Cap off or join in.

Though, it seemed like they were veering toward the joining-in scenario.

That was scary, and after all we'd just been through, I didn't want Eric to get arrested for assaulting a police officer, but it was also all kinds of sweet (not to mention sexy AF).

As we drove away and lost sight of them, I took stock of my girls' and my current situation.

On the good side, we hadn't been handcuffed.

On the bad, we were in the back of cop cars, somewhere I'd never been, and I couldn't say much for the experience.

And after I asked what this was about, and the cop who was driving said, "Chief wants you, that's all I know, so don't ask any more questions," I was no closer to knowing why I, as well as all my besties, were in cop cars on a mandatory trip to the station.

More on the good side, when we got there, we weren't printed, nor did we have our mugshots taken, which was fair, I thought, seeing as we hadn't committed a crime (that I knew of).

Instead, all four of us were taken to an interrogation room, we were given cups of really bad coffee and told to sit our asses down and wait.

And wait we did.

For two hours.

(Okay, maybe it was more like half an hour, my sense of time was skewed seeing as I would rather have been procuring plastic bags and whatever the others needed to feel safe going back to their spaces.)

Eventually, fancy uniform guy walked in.

We were seated, two on one side of the table (me and Harlow), two at each end (Raye and Luna).

He took the only open chair on the other side of the table from Harlow and me.

"I'm Jorge Alvarez. Phoenix Chief of Police."

He didn't offer his hand, so none of us did either.

"Now, my guess is, you girls know about the Rock Chicks," he went on.

Okay.

I could call myself a girl. And my girls could call me a girl. And other girls could call me a girl. And Eric could call me his girl.

But I was a thirty-three-year-old woman.

To this dude, I was not a girl.

My eyes narrowed.

He didn't miss it.

"Shit. Women," he muttered his correction.

Better.

I kept my eyes narrowed.

I also spoke. "I'd really like to see how things are going with Homer."

"We have psychologists who are going to assist in questioning the victims and returning them to their...places," he replied. "I can tell you that all of them seem healthy and fed, even if a few of them have clearly been roughed up."

Not good news.

My narrowed eyes got narrower as my always lacking patience began to run out.

"What I'm saying is, we're looking after them," Alvarez asserted.

"I'd still like to see for myself," I stated.

"Yes," Alvarez retorted. "And you can do that as soon as I inform you that Phoenix is not gonna be the car bombs exploding, high-speed chases on city streets, haunted houses being shut down, cars getting plastic wrapped, quarterly kidnappings, apartments obliterated, assassins dispatched nightmare that Denver became when the Rock Chicks were active."

Cars getting plastic wrapped?

Assassins dispatched?

No one mentioned anything about any assassins.

"Now," he said sharply and turned to Raye. "I know about your history, and I'm truly sorry for your loss and what your family went through." He looked to me. "And I know you were searching for your brother, and although I'm glad you found him, I wish you'd tell him to stop doing fucked-up shit, like right now I'm telling you to stop doing it." He then looked between Harlow and Luna. "And I don't wanna know what you two might get up to." He took us all in. "And that's the reason why you're here." He lifted a hand and circled a finger to the table. "This, whatever it is you women are tied up in, ends tonight."

The last was a proclamation.

Before any of us could say anything, Harlow tentatively raised her hand.

"What?" Alvarez clipped at her.

"Well, first, only Jess got kidnapped, and it was by her brother, so it kinda doesn't count," she said.

Alvarez looked to the ceiling.

"Well, it doesn't," Harlow pressed.

I was of a different mind. A girl gets hooded and zip-tied, it doesn't matter her brother did it to make a point.

But I wasn't going to slow Harlow's roll.

"And second," she went on and lifted her chin when Alvarez aimed his steely gaze at her. "We've semi-kinda helped solve two cases without any high-speed chases or that other stuff. I mean, barring Jess's kidnapping, which we already agreed doesn't count."

"Right. And you're hooked up with Montoya, and I saw you women with Titus tonight," Alvarez began. "So you've managed to make connections in a matter of months that every cop, investigator and criminal has tried to make, with most of us failing, for years."

Interesting.

"But there's no reason to be hooked up with those two men except reasons you shouldn't be hooked up with them," Alvarez concluded.

"We haven't hooked up with Javi," Harlow declared.

"*Yet*. For one of us," Luna mumbled.

Raye chuckled.

Harlow turned on Luna. "I'm not hooking up with Javi. He didn't even ask for my number." She swung her attention to me. "And did he ask after me when you saw him before he went to the safe house?"

"I mentioned you," I told her.

"And what did he say?" she demanded, a super curious look in her eye.

"He told me I was a pain in his ass," I shared.

The curious light died, and I felt like a bitch.

"He was literally walking to the car to head to a safe house, Lolo," I reminded her. "And he just lost two friends. I don't think that puts a man in a romantic mood."

"So there's one thing in the negative column of the when-do-I-gotta-get-me-some list for when the opposite sex doesn't have a mind to get him some," Luna chimed in.

"Speaking of getting some, we've been waiting, since it's clear you and Eric broke the seal, and you've said nada. Zip. Zilch." Raye aimed this accusation at me.

She was right.

How did I miss doing that?

"Okay. I can confirm you're correct. We broke the seal," I said, and then I smiled hugely. "Since, we've ripped it to shreds and set it on fire."

"Right on," Raye said, grinning at me.

"Which nightie did you go for?" Luna asked.

I frowned. "It was a dud. A cotton stretchy thing. Which makes me glad this is over, and I have tomorrow off. I can go shopping and get new ones. Eric said it wasn't the nighties, it's the woman in them, but still. I know he gets off on them. And now I have to one-up my best ones, which is going to be a challenge."

"He said it's the woman in them?" Harlow asked. At my nod she smiled. "That's so sweet!"

"I don't have anything on tomorrow. I can go shopping with you," Luna offered.

"I have to pack for the move," Harlow put in.

"Plan," Raye announced. "We bring Bosa and coffees to Harlow in the morning to help her pack. And in the afternoon, we go sexy nightie shopping."

"I'm in," Luna said.

Harlow clapped. "Ohmigod, guys! That would be so helpful!"

"I need to talk to Eric," I told them. "Henny's home alone and I don't want him home alone all day tomorrow. I'll see if Eric can hang out while we do girl shit. Speaking of..." I looked to Alvarez, who was staring at all of us like we'd just beamed down from our spaceship. "Are we done here? I need to check on Homer *and* I got a new cat today, he's home alone, and he needs his mommy."

Alvarez didn't answer my question.

He muttered, "I am so screwed," got right up and walked right out.

A couple of minutes later, a uniform swung in to tell us we could go, and Eric and Cap were waiting to take us home.

By the by, on the way to go check on Homer, Eric confirmed that he'd look after Henny for me so I could help Harlow pack and then go look for nighties (I didn't tell him that part, just said "shopping," after which, even driving, his eyes glazed over).

Totally.

He was the best.

The second not-so-fun thing that happened didn't last as long and wasn't as annoying (though, it was close, with the annoying part).

What happened was, after we checked Homer was all right and got home to find Henny curled up in one of my throws, sleeping and clearly not traumatized by us leaving, Eric started breaking up the chicken in the Crockpot to get the tacos going, and thinking ahead, I changed into lounge pants.

I was walking down the hall when the hammering came at the door.

I headed toward it while Eric scowled at it, and I said, "One guess. Martha."

I opened the door and immediately scooted back because my brother stormed in, followed by Javi, who was followed by Titus.

I shut the door behind Titus, looked to Eric and inquired, "Do you think there's any point to that fancy, new security gate my landlord installed?"

It appeared Eric was trying not to laugh, but otherwise he made no reply.

Suddenly, I only had eyes for Jeff because he'd put the pads of his fingers of both of his hands to his forehead, snapped them out, and shouted, "*Have you lost your mind!*"

Henny's head came up.

"Quiet down, you're upsetting Henny," I returned, going to my cat, picking him up, cuddling him to my face and cooing, "It's all right, baby. Uncle Jeff is loud and mean, but we just ignore him when he gets that way."

"Don't turn your cat against me, Jess," Jeff warned.

"Don't come in here shouting at me, Jeff," I shot back before I pulled out the big guns. "Or I'm showing him your picture, then taking away his wet food at least three times every morning to condition him to avoid you."

"Stop joking around, this is serious," Jeff said low.

I sighed, because sadly, he was right.

"Homer's fine. We need to buy a couple of folks new tents because they got bullet holes in theirs. And everything else is copacetic. Chill."

"*Chill?*" Jeff thundered. "Do you know what your band of badasses did to that crew?"

My eyes drifted to Eric who was calmly whipping up a batch of guacamole.

"I haven't had a debrief yet. We just got home," I said to my brother. "Do I care? The bad guys are out of commission. That's kinda all I need to know."

I glanced at Eric after I said that, and his attention was off the avocado and on me.

He winked.

My clitoris tingled.

I turned back to my brother to see Jeff was opening his mouth, but then Titus was there, stealing my cat from my arms while murmuring, "Give me this guy."

I watched as Titus hoisted Henny up to his face, hot guy and cute cat went nose to nose, they came to an agreement, and then Titus cradled Henny in his arms, Henny blinked a few times, closed his eyes and started purring.

"Brother. Not cool. We're barely in the door, and you made a play for the cat," Javi groused as he made his way to a stool.

"Snoozing is losing," Titus said as he went to my couch and assumed it like it was his throne.

"I have a feeling it's good we cooked all four chicken breasts rather than just the two," Eric muttered.

I had a feeling he was right.

"What are we having?" Javi asked.

He was right.

"Jess!" Jeff called my attention back to him.

"No, again, I don't know what they did," I snapped. "All I know is that all the people who were reported taken were found. Homer being one of them. And he's back in his tent. He's discombobulated, but he's back where he feels a sense of rightness and purpose. And right now, that's all I need to know. If Eric wants to tell me, I'll listen. And that's the end of it. So maybe now we can talk about how the Nightingale men asked for your help, and you refused it so you could horn in on the action..." I put a lot of weight in my pause before I finished, "*Easy.*"

Jeff made a frustrated snarly noise when I used his street name.

"She doesn't want to know how you earned that, brother," Javi remarked.

"She really doesn't, but I'll tell you," Titus said to Henny, then bent his neck to where my cat lay on his chest and whispered something in his pointed ear.

Since Henny had no reaction, I sensed he was unimpressed by this news.

But they were right.

I really didn't want to know.

However.

I turned my gaze to Javi. "You're in this too, *hermanito*."

"No, I'm not," Javi said, taking a pinch of grated cheese from the bowl Eric had put it in and sprinkling it in his mouth. He swallowed that and said, "If someone was gonna roll on them, we were going in with them. Those boys took care of business before we got there, and I don't blame them. That shit had to end. It did. Done." He then popped a black olive in his mouth.

"Instead of eating it all, you can help Eric by slicing those olives," I stated.

Not missing a beat, Eric got a knife and put it in front of Javi.

At this juncture, I noticed my guy hadn't waded into any of this, not at all.

It was like he was inured to crazy.

And I loved him for it.

Javi got up, walked around the bar, repositioned the cutting board while corralling the rolling olives, and got to work.

"Speaking of olives," Titus said from the couch. "I wouldn't say no to another one of your martinis."

Now someone was speaking my language.

I headed straight to the bar cart.

"Jess, we're not finished discussing this," Jeff declared.

I picked up the kickass shaker Javi bought me and turned to my brother.

"Yes, we are. Everyone I love is alive, breathing, healthy. I don't have to do stakeouts anymore. And I've got a new mission of finding sexier nighties than the off-the-chart sexy ones I already have, because Eric has seen all those."

Jeff raised a hand. "TMI."

"You came in, mouth a'blazin', you deal with the fallout," I returned.

"Lucky man, honcho," Titus said from the couch to Eric.

Eric just smiled at the guacamole he was forking together.

"To end," I continued, "you also don't have to be in a safe house anymore, another plus. Now, fortunately, before another shitstorm hits, I'll have time to find the perfect Taser holster. Life is good. Take a load off, stop distracting me from my cocktail shaker, and let it be good, Jeff."

He glowered at me.

I took it.

He kept doing it.

I kept taking it.

He kept doing it.

I got over it and turned to Javi, lifting the shaker. "This is pure class, Javi. I don't think I thanked you."

Javi winked at me.

His wasn't as good as Eric's, but it was still nice.

Jeff got on the stool beside the one Javi had used, asking, "Please tell me you have chips."

I turned to the counter, grabbed the bag of tortilla chips, and tossed them at my brother, who caught them.

Then I opened the freezer to grab my vodka.

As I was closing it, I felt a touch on the small of my back and looked to the side and up at Eric.

"Life *is* good," he whispered.

Him standing right there?

"It sure as hell is," I replied.

His onyx eyes were twinkling as he bent his head and kissed me.

And there it got better.

He went to the kitchen bar, slid the bowl of guacamole to Jeff and moved to the stove to start warming up tortillas.

I should have been making margaritas, but that wasn't requested.

Anyway, martinis went with everything.

Though, in the end, it was just me and Titus with a fancy glass.

Eric, Javi and Jeff drank beer.

Everyone was gone.

I was brushed, cleansed and moisturized, looking forward to a good, quick fuck and bed, as I walked into the bedroom.

Eric was coming out of it, and I moved to step out of his way, when he caught my hips.

I dropped my head to catch his eyes.

"Now," he said.

"Now?" I asked.

"The men are gone. The case is closed. The day is done. Now, you're safe to do it, Jessie."

I stared at him, having no clue how he knew.

But he knew.

I then allowed myself to feel the ghost of gratitude and fondness and the precious gift of human connection pressing against my forehead.

That was when I did a faceplant in Eric's chest, my shoulders heaved, the sob scored my throat, and the tears came.

Eric held me while I got it all out.

And when I was done, he lifted my face with his hands cradling my jaw and used his thumbs to wipe away the tears.

"Better?" he asked tenderly.

So *falling in love with this man.*

I nodded. "Though, I think I have to reapply moisturizer."

He smiled a sweet smile, touched his lips to mine, and said, "I'll bring it with me from the bathroom."

He headed that way, and I turned as he did, calling to his back, "That might have been a tender moment, but I'm not in the mood for gentle sex. We're fucking."

"Copy that," he shouted from the bathroom.

I grinned and climbed into bed.

"Babe?" Eric called from the bathroom.

"Yeah?" I called back.

"Just closing the loop, I'm falling in love with you too."

That gooey feeling suddenly overwhelmed me, and straight up...

I didn't mind at all.

"Okay then!" I shouted in reply. "You win. We can have gentle sex."

Henny jumped up on the bed and had a sniff around.

I watched him and thought Eric and I were wrong.

Life wasn't good.

Oh no.

It was *awesome.*

Eric showed at the door to the bedroom and leaned against the jamb wearing only his cargoes and holding my tub of moisturizer in his hand, his magnificent chest on display.

"Too late, babe. The decision was made. We're fucking," he said.

Oh yeah.

Life was *awesome.*

TWENTY-SIX

CHRISTMAS BLESSINGS

Eric rolled us from missionary to cowgirl, except once he got us in that position, he angled up and swung my legs around him so we were in lotus.

As I moved on his cock in his lap, I watched as he glided his hands over the silk at my sides, his head angled so he could see them roam.

That day, out shopping with the girls, I'd found a humdinger of a nightie. And I believed him when he said it wasn't about the nighties.

Still, he seriously dug the nighties.

He tilted his head back to look at me, and I had no more thoughts about nighties.

As was becoming us, he didn't need to say anything. I didn't say anything either. But I hoped like fuck my expression was communicating the same thing his was.

I would know it did when he slipped a hand up my spine, into my hair and tipped my head down for his deep, wet, thorough but still tender kiss.

Last night after the whole thing went down, we fucked.

Tonight, we were oh so totally making love.

And honestly?

I had no preference. I adored doing both with him.

But right now, this was giving me life.

It was about him, me, kissing, intimacy and connection.

So many kinds of connection.

The orgasm Eric eventually gave me was slow in coming, and not explosive when it arrived. It was sweet and sultry and lasted a really long time.

After I had mine, and then watched Eric have his, he shifted me to my back in the bed with him resting down my side, his long legs tangled with mine, and his eyes went back to his hand which was skating over the charcoal gray silk at my belly.

"Admit it, Turner, it's partially about the nighties," I teased.

His gaze came to me, lazy and sated and so fucking bedroom, I felt an orgasm aftershock.

"You outdid yourself, sweetheart," he replied.

I smiled.

"But...pink?" he asked.

"Pink?" I asked back.

With the very tip of his middle finger (yep, another aftershock), he traced the delicate lace at my bodice. It slashed a bit into the cleavage at an angle under my breast, and it adorned my left hip just at a little slit with the lace riding up nearly to my waist.

"This lace is pink," he said.

I frowned. "It's neutral."

He looked to be fighting a smile. "It's pink."

"I don't wear pink," I declared.

Clearly not in the mood to fight over stupid shit, he said, "Okay."

Though he said it in a manner where two things were clear. One, he didn't want to fight over stupid shit. And two, he was humoring me.

I was saved from a retort by Henny jumping up on Eric's bed.

My cat (or I liked to think of him as *our* cat) spent the day with his daddy at his daddy's house.

Before this happened, Eric and I had had a half an hour discussion about it, along with us both huddling over my laptop researching articles about stressors for cats, and if we should move him to a new location so soon.

Everything said no. But in the end, since Henny would be going back and forth anyway depending on where Eric and I would be for a night, we decided to give it a go and see how Henny responded. If he seemed to have an adverse reaction, Eric would just bring him back and hang with him at mine.

Henny, who'd lived a bumpy life and sensed accurately that rough ride was over, took it in stride.

Best.

Cat.

Ever.

I'd spent the day helping Harlow pack then out shopping with the girls.

Eric had spent the day with Henny, leaving him only to head back to the pet store to double up on bowls and toys and litterboxes.

Best.

Guy.

Ever.

After Henny checked we were okay, he collapsed on a hip, lifted his hind leg in the air, rested his front paw on his side then commenced cleaning his belly.

As for me, I used a finger to slide Eric's hair off his forehead (it just dropped back, but whatever) and regained his attention.

"You think Homer's doing okay?" I asked.

His gaze softened (or it did this more, it was already soft and warm and sweet) and he replied, "Tex visited him today and said he was hanging in there. And Tex wouldn't lie. So...yeah. I think he's hanging in there."

"You think maybe we should ask your dad to Phoenix for Christmas?" I blurted.

Now that things had settled down with all Jeff's and my

shenanigans, my mind had turned to my man, the upcoming holiday, and the fact that I had Jeff and a lifetime in Phoenix that gave me an abundance of found family, and Eric had none of that.

Eric had done his FBI thing, then spent time in Denver and lived in LA, but he was originally from Michigan, and both his dad and brother still lived there.

His brother...I wasn't going to go there. He sounded like a dick.

His dad, though...

I mean, Christmas was coming, I had Jeff, and all my girls.

He had no one.

Except me.

"Honey," he murmured.

"Okay, hear me out," I began.

He took his hand from my nightie to cup the side of my face, then he bent and got close to said face.

"I know you want good things for me," he said quietly.

"I do," I replied.

"And I love that," he stated. "But we're looking at a thirty-year commitment to his illness. I'm not without empathy. He lost his wife and the mother of his children, and he carries some earned guilt around that, because he deemed his work more important than sharing the responsibilities of being a parent. I know addiction is a chronic illness. But with any kind of illness, you have to commit to treatment. If you don't, there comes a time for the people in your life to be forced to make a decision, because your illness, and the decisions you make around it, affect the people who love you." He stroked my cheek with his thumb. "I made that decision a long time ago, Jess."

"Okay," I whispered.

He sighed, and it was such a big one, I wished I hadn't ruined our moment by mentioning it.

"I haven't cut him out of my life," he said. "I don't talk to my brother, but I do talk to Dad. What I also do is keep firm to my boundaries."

Smart. Healthy.

And I was such an idiot for bringing it up.

"I shouldn't have mentioned it," I replied.

His face got hard. "Don't ever, babe, not ever think that."

"We were having a moment," I pointed out.

"I'm still having that moment, being with my woman and our cat—" Tremendous, he thought of Henny as *ours* too—"and she gives a shit enough about me to want me to have my family close during a holiday."

"I'm glad you look at it that way," I mumbled. "Instead of me fucking up by bringing it up."

"With the holidays coming, we were bound to have this conversation, and there would never be a good time," he noted. "I can't say it doesn't fuck with me that at one point in my life I had a family. And then one night, I didn't. But I can say I've learned to live with it."

I rubbed my lips together to stop myself from replying.

He watched me do it, and when his eyes came back to mine, he whispered, "Fuck. It messes you up too."

The lip rubbing failed when I went back to blurting, "She died on Christmas Eve, Eric. And I haven't even mastered frying a hamburger. I don't know how to—"

I stopped talking when the pads of his fingers dug in, and he dropped his forehead to mine, his nose resting atop mine, and I felt like a total bitch, mentioning it and making him feel what I felt coming from him, blasting into me.

He slid his nose down the side of mine, lifted away, and said softly, "You learned I lost her last week. I've been living with it for decades. Do you honestly think I'm not looking forward to whatever dress you're gonna wear to that holiday party at the Oasis and sitting around for five hours on Christmas morning while you unwrap all the presents you bought Henny?"

Awesome!

We were having Christmas together!

"My tree is white with black and silver baubles," I warned him. "And we're putting it up tomorrow night after I get home from work. Which is no biggie, since it's super narrow, though it's tall."

His lips tipped up. "Copy that, Wylde. My Christmas tree is massive and we're decorating it this weekend with Luke and Ava and the girls."

Oh yeah.

Right.

He'd told me about this. Luke was first up to fill in at NI&S due to their short staff situation here in Phoenix. He was arriving the next day, staying with Eric while it was his turn in the rotation, but his wife and kids were coming to spend the weekend with them.

I grinned. "We have a plan. Now, I have to create a menu. Tree-trimming finger foods. Shrimp cocktail. Chicken satay. Meatballs. And some kind of Christmasy dessert that has ginger in it. And with the girls there, we'll have to have an after-trimming activity. I'm going to have to think about that, but a Battle of the Best Christmas Song might be in order. I just have to figure out how that's gonna go. And find time to buy some posterboard to create brackets."

His deep chuckle rocked my body.

I wasn't sure what was funny.

"What?" I asked.

"Babe, it fucks with me I'm gonna live a life of boredom with you in it. But I'm down to make that sacrifice."

Even though the words "live a life…with you in it" made me feel all gooey, I rolled my eyes.

He kissed me.

Obviously, while he did it, I stopped rolling my eyes.

Then, since I was leaking, I had to get up to clean up.

Henny, who had anointed himself the Official Bathroom Visitor, came with me.

Henny and I went back to Eric.

Eric and I turned off our lights, snuggled in, Henny curled at our feet.

And our little family went to sleep.

In our short relationship, Eric had never insisted on anything.

But the next morning, when I told him I was going to swing by the camp to see how Homer was doing before I went to work, he insisted on taking me.

Then again, I didn't really fight him on it.

When he rolled the Tahoe to a stop across the street from the entrance to the camp, or more precisely, across the street from Homer's tent, and we both watched Homer duck out, Eric said quietly, "I'll wait for you here."

I turned to him and nodded.

Then I got out.

I was halfway across the street when Homer put his hand over his heart.

He looked beyond me to Eric in his SUV, back to me, where he dipped his chin.

And with that, he ducked back in his tent.

I stopped moving.

Homer never ducked away from me.

I knew next to nothing about Homer, but what I did know was not to push this.

Feeling wrong—dejected, worried, maybe a little scared at what might be going on in Homer's head—I turned around and got back in Eric's car.

"He needs more time," Eric said.

"Yeah," I mumbled.

I heard him snap, looked down at the armrest between us and saw his hand extended, palm up.

I put mine is his. He curled his long fingers around.

After he did that, Eric took his foot off the brake, crept forward, found a place to turn around, and we drove away from Homer and the encampment.

As we did, one could say, I was really happy Eric insisted on coming.

"UNCLE ERIC!" Maisie shouted, hands on her little girl hips, pretty face screwed up in disapproval. She was standing among the open boxes of ornaments awaiting to be put to use. "This is *such* a *boy tree*."

Luke and Ava's second and final child, who was seven years old, had her father's dark hair and her mother's light-brown eyes.

She was also a bossy little miss.

The minute I met her, it was instalove.

"Yeah," her father agreed. "I like it. We're switching our tree to that next year."

Ava, working beside me in the kitchen, snorted, this stating plainly not only was this a tease, but even if it wasn't, no way Luke would make the effort to follow through with it.

I'd already sensed Luke was not a Christmas décor kind of guy and was only involved in the current sitch because it included hefting, assembling and mounting. Once the ornaments came into play, my guess was, he'd be out.

Maisie, along with her older sister Gracie, were horrified at their father's statement, even though I'd noticed this happened a lot in the short time I'd been around them since their arrival the evening before. It nevertheless seemed lost on the girls it was a tease.

Luke would have a pink tree in a Barbie themed house if it made all his girls happy.

Though, he wouldn't go out and buy it.

Sensing that was when I fell in love with Luke Stark.

"Daddeeeeeee, *no*!" Maisie screeched.

"Daddy!" Gracie cried in the horror a budding Victorian lady would use, lifting her hand to her throat and everything.

Cue the instalove with Gracie when I met her too. She had her father's hair and dark-blue eyes, and it was clear she took her big-sister duties seriously. Therefore, we bonded on that score.

The two girls couldn't be more different, with Gracie being quiet, observant, much more mature even if she was only nine, but having a talent with delivering understated dramatics that garnered deep respect from me.

On the other hand, Maisie was exuberant, talkative and had been given the gift I hoped she'd someday come to understand and appreciate: being the youngest, and as such, getting away with a good deal of shit.

It was borderline hilarious how *GIRL!* these two were when their father was the epitome of alpha masculinity.

That said, Ava was all girl too, in a womanly way. She was knockout gorgeous, with a curvy body, a head full of thick, blonde hair and a blatant attitude that sparked off Luke's to such an extent, the sexual chemistry was thick in the air (that being theirs mingled with Eric's and mine, obviously).

Though, I couldn't say Maisie was wrong about Eric's tree.

His actual tree was massive, both tall and very wide, and it was clear he'd hit a Michael's or some such and bought every box of matte baubles in various manly shades of blue, some green, with gold and bronze thrown in. The ornaments were different sizes, so at least there was that. And there were a lot of them. As in, *a lot*.

But that morning, once Eric and Luke had dragged all the stuff out, and Ava and I took a look at what we had to work with, we'd loaded the girls up and did a run JoAnn's and Michael's where we scored some corresponding plaid wired ribbon with a thin gold trim and some sparkly-gold branches to spruce the thing up.

And Maisie had thrown a fit about that too. She was of a mind purple was a better contrasting color and declared we had to do "*Something!*" to save Eric's tree, and plaid ribbon wasn't her idea of what that *Something!* was.

We'd managed to quiet her down by purchasing some matte-gold moose (momma, poppa and baby) that had fake brown fur mufflers around their necks and some fluffy lit boughs to drape around his built-in TV unit (which necessitated us grabbing the rest of the plaid ribbon to make them match).

However, now that this was all about to come together, it seemed it didn't appease little Miss Stark.

I stopped mid-arranging shrimp around the cocktail sauce I'd made, when Maisie pulled out the big guns, went to Eric, leaned into his side, reached up, grabbed his biceps beseechingly, and begged, "Uncle Eric, *pleeeeeease*, can we go to the store and get some of that purple ribbon I saw? It'll be *so perfect* on your tree."

Without hesitation, Eric stepped away from her but only to grab her hand and look at Gracie.

"Wanna come?"

Holy shit.

Gracie stopped petting Henny where they both were lounged on the sectional, popped to her feet and cried, "Yeah!"

Eric held his hand out to Gracie, she took it, and with all three of them attached, they headed to the door to the garage, both girls bouncing excitedly, and Eric looking through the adults as they moved out the door, saying, "We'll be back."

They disappeared, and not long later I heard the garage door engage and Eric's Tahoe fire up.

"Get used to it," Luke said from where he'd come to stand at the side of the island, taking me out of the stupor induced by what I just witnessed. "He spoils the shit out of them."

"All their uncles do, it's supremely annoying," Ava groused. She stopped scraping the meatballs off the baking tray and onto the serving platter and looked to her husband. "Luke, that purple ribbon is not going to work on Eric's tree."

Luke stared at his wife like she was speaking a language he didn't understand, and he was trying to decipher what she was saying through inflections and micro-expressions, before he noted, "Do you think Eric gives a shit?"

"That's not the point," Ava returned.

"What's the point?" Luke shot back.

"Your daughter shouldn't be allowed to dictate every proceeding she's a part of," Ava retorted.

"Why not?" Luke asked.

Oh yeah.

Totally loved this guy.

I could tell Ava was getting heated when she responded, "If you, and all the Hot Bunch, don't stop spoiling them, they'll be impossible when they grow up."

Luke nabbed a shrimp, popped it in his mouth, chewed, swallowed and only then replied, "She'll be impossible to everyone but us. Works for me."

"Are you...are you...?" Ava spluttered while blinking feverishly at her husband. "Are you spoiling our daughters to make them unbearable to be around so no man will touch them with a ten-foot pole?"

Luke didn't respond, outside of one side of his mouth hitching up in a half-smile.

"Oh my fucking God," Ava whispered scarily. "They're not even close to dating age, and you're already making them undateable."

"Start early, make sure the job gets done right," Luke drawled.

Ava seemed fit to blow, but even as hilarious as this conversation was, I had some things to say about the situation.

"Although this is clearly something you two need to work out," I began, and they both looked to me. "But did I just watch a little girl say she needed purple ribbon, and without even blinking, even though we're about to start trimming, we've been cooking for the last two hours, and everything is ready to create the spread so we can eat and decorate, he put her in his car with her sister to go get said ribbon?"

"That is precisely what happened," Ava confirmed irately.

My eyes wandered to the door as my lips tipped up, and I didn't even care they were standing there when I whispered, "I'm so freaking in love with that guy."

I felt something coming from Luke, it felt nice, but I didn't have the opportunity to bask in it because Ava's hand was on my arm.

I focused on her.

Her expression was deadly serious.

"Listen to me, Jess," she stated in full Rock Chick Advisory Mode. "Do not let them boggle your mind with their good looks and healthy rationing of orgasms. It doesn't *seem* those orgasms will wear off when they're happening."

Luke chuckled.

Ava shot him a death glare and came back to me.

"But they do. The haze clears. And then suddenly you realize you let them get away with a whole bunch of shit they never should have attempted in the first place." The death glare went back to Luke. "Like spoiling your daughters, allowing all your buds to spoil them too, and as such, ruining their plans for future happiness."

"Ava," I called, and she returned her attention to me. "I think you know this, but just to say, first, they're giving your girls indication they shouldn't settle for anyone who doesn't listen, doesn't take their wishes into account, and doesn't move mountains, when it's within their power, to see to them. And second, when they find that guy, he's not gonna give that first shit she's got an overbearing father and a dozen uncles who are the same. He'll win her heart and Luke and the Hot Bunch will just have to find it in them to deal."

Luke grunted unhappily.

Ava shot me a winning smile.

As for me, with two parents who treated me and my brother like heirlooms they didn't want, but couldn't give away, and Eric, who'd had his family disintegrate one hideous Christmas Eve, what I just watched boded beautiful things for our future.

A man who considered a child's opinion was not only worthwhile to listen to, but act on immediately, was going to be a great dad.

Obviously, I didn't want to be around spoiled brats, and definitely not raise any, but there'd come a time at Michael's where Ava was done, and she'd said a quiet, "Enough, Maisie," and Maisie let it go.

Clearly, she was a kid who had been taught she was free to be herself, but when she pushed it too far, all Mom had to do was say two words, and she'd also been taught to mind.

I believed every kid should be spoiled a little bit, they should feel safe to express themselves at all times, and in a matter as unimportant as purple ribbon, a good man in their lives they loved and trusted taking them to the store to buy it was a precious thing.

Luke moved back to finish positioning the boughs around the television and Ava edged closer to me.

"The guys and girls are pretty excited about what's happening with you and Eric," she whispered.

How sweet!

I looked at her with a smile on my face.

But her face grew stone-cold.

"We've waited a long time for him to find a good woman who makes him happy. But, if you hurt him, you are dead to us forever."

She said these words like she really meant them, and more, the Rock Chicks might actually make me dead if I hurt Eric.

Therefore, I blinked.

The doorbell rang.

"Got it," Luke said and moved that way.

Ava shifted from me like she didn't just little-sister threaten me about Eric.

"Where are my babies?"

At this demand, my attention hit the door to see most of the rest of our party was arriving. That being Shirleen, Moses, Roam, Cap and Raye.

Jeff was also coming, but since I got a text from him twenty minutes ago asking Eric's booze preferences, I figured he was at Total Wine for a host gift.

Cap was carrying a bottle of wine, so was Roam, but Moses was carrying a foil wrapped platter.

Moses and Shirleen didn't even live in Phoenix yet (though, the offer they put on that condo was accepted, which meant they were officially moving down early in the new year), so how they had a platter, I didn't know. But I suspected whatever was under that foil was made in Raye's kitchen, seeing as Cap relinquished it to his mom every once in a while.

"Eric took them to Michael's to buy more ribbon," Ava said, walking out from behind Eric's island direct to Moses.

I watched Shirleen take in the tree, the opened boxes of ornaments, the three cute, but lonely moose on his coffee table, then Ava.

"Are they hitting Pottery Barn and Home Goods too?" she asked as she gave Ava a hug.

"I hope not," Ava replied, heading for more hugs from Roam, Cap and Raye.

She did this as Shirleen was pulling her phone out of her purse.

She stopped doing it when she noticed Shirleen engaging her phone to send a text.

"Do not tell Eric to take my girls to Pottery Barn," Ava commanded.

"I'm getting my bearings, girl, and Pottery Barn is literally five minutes away, so it's no skin off his nose to do a drive-by," Shirleen retorted. She tipped her head to the island. "I see you got the food ready. I also see no pigs in a blanket, which is why we brought some, and the last thing I see is this house is woefully under-decorated."

"It's fine," Ava replied.

Shirleen turned on her. "The man has a woman and a cat, he needs more than a tree and three moose."

I agreed with her.

However, I didn't think buying Christmas decorations for his home was something I could do without Eric there. The bough wasn't a thing, men dug greenery, but the moose with fur mufflers were pushing it. Though, Eric had just smiled when Gracie and Maisie had put them out. That said, I thought he did that solely because Gracie and Maisie were the ones who put them out.

Ava opened her mouth to say something, but Shirleen put up The Hand right in front of her face, and added, "Stop! What is that racket?"

Everyone listened.

We heard nothing but Christmas music turned low.

Shirleen walked to Eric's smart-home unit, bent to it, and demanded, "Alexa, stop. Play. Nat. King. Cole. Christmas."

The Jonas Brothers stopped playing and Cole's *The Christmas Song* started.

So much better.

"There." Shirleen swiped her hands together like she'd just completed a taxing job. She then divested Moses of the tray, whipped off the foil, put it down on the island with all the other food (I was particularly proud of the ginger cake with brown butter icing Ava and I had thrown together). Shirleen then decreed, "Now it's a party."

"It's a party when I have a beer," Roam muttered.

"Word," Cap agreed.

They headed to the fridge.

"Oh my God, that cake looks amazing," Raye said as she came to my side and bumped hips with me.

Ava lifted her martini glass. "Wait until you taste her cocktail."

"It's a wet run for the holiday extravaganza at the Oasis," I told her. "Pomegranate gimlets."

"Are you shaking?" Shirleen asked me.

"Always," I answered, taking her hint and heading toward the cocktail shaker.

She hiked her ass on a stool.

"Men, over here, I think we're off by a quarter of an inch on the left side," Luke, standing behind the couch, arms crossed on his chest, was studying the placement of the now lit bough with a critical eye.

Roam and his opened bottle of beer went to stand next to him. "It's so thick, how can you tell?"

"Yup," Moses, also having gone to look, agreed. "Quarter of an inch on the left side. I got it." He then moved to the bough.

"A quarter of a—?" I started to ask after something that was obviously unimportant.

But Shirleen giving me a look and shaking her head stopped me.

Her look said, *As a woman's thing, it's totally unimportant. As a man's thing, it's the end of the world and has to be fixed immediately. Leave it.*

I processed this wisdom and left it.

An hour later, Jeff had showed with a bottle of Grey Goose, he got intros all around, and we were all on the sectional with drinks (Roam, by the way, had claimed Henny), when Eric and the girls trudged in laden with bags.

While Eric greeted the not-so-newcomers, Maisie dragged her bag right to Ava. "Look, Mommy! We went to Pottery Barn and Uncle Eric got these!" Whereupon she pulled out two toss pillows.

One was in the form of a snowman with a top hat and a red scarf, the other was much the same shape, but it was a red Santa with his hat pulled over his eyes and a fluffy beard.

"*Aren't they perfect?*" Maisie shrieked.

"Absolutely," Luke answered, and Maisie shot her father a dazzling smile.

"I'll get the batteries," Eric murmured.

"I'll help!" Gracie cried and skipped along with Eric's long strides as they headed to the pantry.

"Batteries?" I asked.

"For the trees that are gonna sit with the mooses!" Maisie told me.

She then tossed her spent bag aside and raced to the Michael's bag Eric had set on the floor.

"We got the ribbon, and we got some purple ornaments to match, and we got these!" She yanked out some stocking hooks that had gold stars.

After showing us those, she set them on the coffee table then went to another bag that Eric had brought in, this one Pottery Barn.

"And a stocking for you." She tossed a white, honeycomb faux fur stocking at me. "One for Uncle Eric." She tossed a bright red cable knit stocking at me. "And one for Henny!" she brandished the last above her head.

From what I could tell through the movement, it was a brown velvet stocking with black embroidered pine trees and black trim.

"I think they got things covered," Moses murmured, humor in his tone.

"Whose idea was Pottery Barn?" Ava asked suspiciously.

"Uncle Eric's," Maisie replied. "Gracie told him the mooses were lonely, and Uncle Eric said mooses live in a forest, we had to find trees. So we looked at the trees at Michael's, but they'd been picked over. Then Aunt Shirleen texted Uncle Eric about Pottery Barn, and he said we should try another store, and that's when we got the *pillows* and *stockings* and *trees*. And this!"

She went to the last bag and pulled out a creamy, thick throw that was fake fur on one side, and had the forest design with deer and mountains in black on the other side.

I made a mental note to steal that for my house while Eric came back with Gracie and a packet of AA batteries.

They got to work unboxing three glass trees of varying heights that looked great with the moose, and even better when they got the batteries in and lit them up.

I got to work on trying not to sigh like a grown-up Victorian lady at how adorable they were with all their dark heads bent together putting batteries into glass trees.

I'd turned into a total sap.

I didn't care even a little bit.

"Can we eat now?" Roam asked.

"Meatballs!" Maisie shouted and raced to the kitchen.

Ava sighed and got up. I got up with her, since everything was in the oven keeping warm so we had to respread the spread.

In the end, the food was great, and although the extra touches to the Christmas décor weren't splashy, they definitely upped the ho-ho-ho factor. Better still, they'd always remind Eric of Gracie and Maisie. Huge bonus.

And I was thinking Maisie had an eye, because the deep purple she picked provided the perfect pop of color and looked really good on the tree.

Most of all, through this, I was struck by three things.

Christmas blessings, if you will, of the early variety.

The first, the present company made Jeff instantly comfortable. The getting-to-know-you portion pretty much ended at introductions, and then it was all about football, strategizing how to hide all the cords (Jeff pulled that off with some bough placement magic and a slight adjustment to the tree) and an in-depth discussion about Phoenix's shooting ranges.

The second, Henny loved the girls. Henny loved the adults. Henny could give two shits about cat toys, but he loved batting ornaments along the floor, even if they broke and necessitated me finding Eric's broom and dustbin to sweep them up.

Henny was having the time of his life, perhaps literally.

Henny was finally home, and Henny had a family.

The last, I didn't have to worry anymore, because Eric had the same.

He had a lot of brothers. He had sisters. He had nieces.

And they were all the best kind. The ones he chose for himself, and the ones who would take a bullet for him (definitely literally).

I was thinking this thought as Eric and I were in the kitchen, cutting pieces of cake to pass around.

I felt his hand come to rest on the small of my back and looked up at him to see he was very close.

"Hey," I whispered.

"What's got you looking like that?" he whispered back, tenderness in his eyes as they moved over my face.

My gaze wandered to the living room, the sectional filled, the girls on the floor with some leftover ribbon playing with Henny, people talking, laughing, drinking, spent plates and napkins everywhere, Bing Crosby crooning, and the tree, boughs and décor glowing.

"How I cope," Eric stated, and I turned back to him.

"What?"

"With losing Mom. I don't know what I believe about life after death. If it's possible, or if it's just hopeful. But what I think is, if it's real, and Mom can see what I earned in my life, she'd be happy for me."

Liking this thought a whole lot for him, I forgot all about the cake and leaned into my guy. "Yeah."

"She'd be a lot happier recently," he remarked.

Oh God.

"Yeah," I repeated, but his time it was husky.

He bent and touched his mouth to mine.

Really, really loved it when he did that.

After he lifted away, though not very far, he said, "Those meatballs were insane."

I grinned at him, "I know, right?"

"Ugh! Mommy! Uncle Eric and Aunt Jess are like you and daddy!" Maisie complained.

We looked to the living room.

Shirleen was coming our way, saying, "I'll help pass those around."

But my eyes had gone to Ava.

She was cuddled into Luke but twisted to gaze over the back of the couch at me.

She was smiling.

She approved.

Oh yeah.

I didn't have to worry.

Eric had a ton of family.

I noted Jeff turning his head away when my eyes caught on him, but that didn't hide his smile.

And Eric's family was only going to get bigger.

And as things like this were wont to be...

Better.

For your edification, the Battle of the Best Christmas Song was hotly debated.

In the end, it became a girls versus boys thing, with the finalists being Bruce Springsteen's "Santa Claus Is Coming to Town" versus Taylor Swift's "Christmas Tree Farm."

Jeff, Roam and Cap were blindsided when Eric, Moses and Luke switched teams at the last minute so Gracie and Maisie's favorite song would win.

Listening to, singing with (and sometimes dancing) then ribbing each other through the voting process of all the songs was a blast.

But the best part was in the beginning, when I pulled out the posterboard brackets I decorated with red, green and gold glitter and Christmas stickers, something Eric hadn't seen yet, and something that delighted Gracie and Maisie beyond imagining (they got to use the fat gold and silver markers to write in the songs).

That was when I caught him looking at me a lot like I suspected I looked at him when he and the girls were putting the batteries in the trees.

So...yeah.

It had been an amazing night.

But that was totally the best part.

TWENTY-SEVEN

I KNOW

We were the Avenging Angels, they were the Hottie Squad, with a dash of Rock Chicks and a rumble of Hot Bunch thrown in.

Therefore, even after we solved the case of the missing homeless folk, the month of December was far from boring.

Allow me to sum up:

During the week before Ava and the girls were in town, Eric and I, the Angels and the Hottie Squad, with Javi, Jeff and Cody, attended Jamal's funeral (by the way, Cody shocked the crap out of me because he didn't look like a computer dweeb, but instead was a blond-haired, green-eyed Adonis, not as buff as Javi or Jeff, but he was taller than Jeff (not many were taller than Javi)).

Jamal's family were wrecked, but they were lovely.

The rest of it totally sucked.

The next day, with Javi, Jeff and Cody, me, the Angels and the Hottie Squad hung at the back at Joaquim's memorial service and disappeared before it was over so Javi and Jeff wouldn't cause Joaquim's family any distress.

That sucked more.

Harlow came to both of these, and Javi and Harlow circled each other like predator and prey each time, though for the life of me I couldn't tell who was predator and who was prey. That said, it wasn't the time to take it there, so nothing came of it.

But we would see.

The Monday I went back to work after our tree trimming party, Luna told me Tito was calling a staff meeting.

This did not bode well seeing as Tito had never called a staff meeting.

Tex was still in town, and since he was no longer undercover, he was also in the coffee cubby.

At the tree trimming party, I got the news from Shirleen that Tex's wife, Nancy, was still in Denver. Nancy's daughters and sons-in-law, Eddie and Jet and Lottie and Mo, were helping her get their house ready to put on the market.

Tex was sticking to Phoenix, considering his Rock Chick experience started at the beginning with Indy, so now that the Angels were on the move, he wasn't leaving anything to chance. That being leaving Phoenix in case he might miss some action.

Thus, he was also at the staff meeting.

In fact, we stood in the employee break/locker room with Tex and Tito standing in front of us like a deranged Penn and Teller, and precisely like Penn and Teller, Tito didn't say a word.

But Tex did.

"Shit is gettin' real here, so there's gonna be some staffing changes," he stated. "Shanti is moving from evening shift to afternoon shift with Harlow and Jess. Willow is coming in full-time. She'll be baking in the morning in the kitchen with Lucia, and then working with Raye and Luna until one. We're hiring someone else to help with the evening shift and we're hiring a daytime and nighttime busser slash dishwasher so you women don't have to clear the tables and load the dishes along with everything else."

We glanced at each other because this was all *rad*.

Truth told, things had been getting busier and busier. Fortunately, our crowd was pretty chill. Equally fortunately, busier meant more tips.

But it was beginning to get hectic, and it was never fun to do any kind of dishes (even if Tito had one of those industrial sprayers on his faucet in the dishwashing area, and that had its times when it could be fun, though that fun didn't involve rinsing dishes).

"That's it," Tex said. "Any questions?" Before anyone could even begin to open their mouths to ask a question, Tex clapped his hands and boomed, "Great! Get back to work!"

He then lumbered off.

Tito shuffled after him.

We all milled about for approximately two point five seconds before Tex bellowed from the restaurant, "Do I have to explain getting back to work?"

Lucia was already gone, Otis and Hunter wandered out, me and my chicks came up the rear.

"Did he become a boss without that being added to our two-minute staff meeting agenda?" Luna asked as we all headed through the kitchen toward the main area.

"I don't care if he's boss, I don't have to do any more dishes," Harlow spoke aloud my thoughts.

Tex was at the doorway to the restaurant, and as we girls came through, he stopped us.

"You, you, you, and you," he said.

With each "you" he tossed army knives at us so we had to hop to in order to catch them before they fell to the floor.

Everyone caught theirs except Harlow. Her pink version

clattered on the tiles, but she swiped it right up and shot Tex a sunshiny smile.

I noticed Tex had scored an orange one for Luna.

Rad part two.

"This is also for you," Tex said, pulling an envelope out of the back pocket of his jeans and handing it to me.

It was thick, but wasn't sealed, so I opened the flap and felt my eyes bug out at what I saw inside.

"Reimbursement for supplies for the camp from Tito and me," Tex explained what had to be at least two thousand dollars in cash in the envelope.

I looked up at him. "You didn't—"

"Shut it," he ordered. "I didn't request a convo. I handed you reimbursement."

I didn't really want to shut it. This was too much.

But the thing was, after all that spending, including adopting Henny and all that entailed, I was running low on Christmas funds.

Now, I was not.

I didn't get the chance to get another word in, however.

"Uh, are you our boss now or something?" Luna asked.

"Yeah," Tex stated without hesitation, and we all stared at him even before he went on to share, "Nance and me bought into The Surf Club. We now own a third of this joint."

That had us all blinking at him.

"You think maybe that was worthwhile to share during our staff meeting?" Raye asked.

"Why?" Tex asked in return.

"Because it's news worthy of the first-ever SC staff meeting?" Raye suggested.

"Why?" Tex repeated.

Raye had nothing more.

"I told you four," Tex pointed out. "You'll blab it to everyone else. News shared. Done."

He wasn't wrong about that.

And he was definitely done, considering, without another word, he trudged back to the coffee cubby.

We all huddled.

"I don't know what to say," Harlow started it. "Seeing as I'm totally okay with all of this so I don't have anything to say."

"Me too," Raye said.

"Totes," Luna added.

Before I could add my affirmative, I heard, "Hey."

I turned my head and saw my brother there.

"Sorry to interrupt, but can we talk?" he asked me.

The girls moved away, but not too far, because they were my girls, and we took care of each other that way (and other ways besides).

Jeff got close.

"You want a coffee or something?" I asked him.

"No, I don't have a lot of time. I just wanna run something by you."

I nodded.

"Javi and I just got done with a meeting at Nightingale Investigations and Security."

Oh boy.

Eric hadn't given me any heads up, so this could mean anything.

"Yeah?" I prompted.

"They offered us jobs."

Okay then.

Eric had kinda given me a heads up.

I sucked my lips between my teeth.

My brother watched me do this before he asked, "You knew they were gonna do that?"

I let my lips go to use them to state, "Eric had mentioned he thought it was a good idea and he was gonna run it by Mace."

"And you didn't stop him?"

I was confused. "Why would I stop him?"

A beat went by and then Jeff was hugging me really, really tight.

As his arms squeezed me, my heart squeezed itself. It didn't feel bad in the slightest.

Nope.

It felt great.

He let me go and said quietly, "I really wanna take the job, and not just because starting salary is three times as much as I make now."

Whoa!

I mean, I knew those guys made bank, but...*wow*.

"Okay," I said, because I didn't know what else to say.

"Jess, I'll be working with your boyfriend."

Ah.

I saw his concern.

"Well, I mean, that's the loose description of what he is to me," I shared. "He's more like the love of my life. But since we're not even a month old, I'm not making that official at least for another week."

Jeff grinned. "Just so you know, I'll be working in their control room. I might go out in the field occasionally, but they need help there the most. Since they know about my illness, I don't think I could push that, and I really want to work with those men."

I nodded.

I got that.

"Is Javi going to work with them?" I asked.

Jeff cocked his head to the side. "Blew my mind, but after they left us to discuss, we talked for about five minutes, and he was all in. They're taking on Cody too, though they told him he has to lay off the weed, and Cody won't have a problem doing that. He's good with computer shit, and other tech. He'll be doing night shifts in the control room. I'll be working days."

So NI&S was making moves to completely fold the Shadow Soldiers into their operation, tapping a direct vein to the street and scoring themselves two really good men in the process (probably three, I didn't know Cody that well, though he seemed solid).

I took my brother's wrist and pushed up the sleeve of his thermal.

Doing this, the tattoo of a shadowed horse that looked like it was running directly toward you was bared.

I covered the tat with my hand and looked at my baby bro. "You boys going to be good with working with another crew?"

Jeff let out a melancholy sigh.

"Our crew included Joaq and Jamal," he told me. "It's not the same. We'd already talked about it. We didn't want to stop, but we didn't know how to go on. This is a way we can go on. We're together, but we're different. We've moved on. You know?"

So, Eric had been right.

I nodded to tell him I got it.

"Is Javi still—?" I started.

"Yeah." Jeff confirmed before I even had to say it. "Joaq was a good guy. The best. But he could do stupid shit. Javi was trying to help him work on his control. His temper could spark, and shit would get out of hand. This makes Javi see it as his failure. He knew Clown dealt to Joaq's sister. He thinks that's his mistake. He thinks he shouldn't have told them, because Joaq hadn't locked onto his control."

"He's not responsible for another man's actions," I noted.

"I told him that. Cody told him that. Jamal's momma told him that. He isn't letting it sink in."

"You should probably share that with Eric," I advised.

"I don't think any of those men are missing it," Jeff informed me. "But yeah. I'll share. There's time before we're totally active. They got a hella training schedule that might last two years after Mace does an assessment of us." A smile spread on his face. "But it sounds pretty cool, and I think we're gonna surprise them."

I loved this. I loved it for him. I loved it for the NI&S team. And I loved it for Javi.

I smiled back at him.

"Mace also told us part of our jobs was to watch you and your crew's asses, so bonus is I get to keep an eye on you."

My smile turned upside down.

My brother started laughing.

Whatever.

"Are we done? I have to get back to work," I reminded him.

"You know the coolest thing in the world?" Jeff asked.

I had a feeling I knew several of the coolest things in the world, and Jeff was going to be working with all of them.

Still, I asked, "What?"

"They're assholes. They're wastes of space. But you and me didn't just make it out from under their bullshit, we got out and we thrived. I'd say, 'So fuck them,' but I don't care enough to say it. They're dust. And we're concrete. I'm that because I had you, and you never let me down."

He was talking about our parents.

And why were people always trying to make me lose it?

Really, I wanted to know.

"You never let me down either," I replied, trying to hide my voice was croaky.

He grinned. "I know. I'm the shit."

That got me over it.

I rolled my eyes.

He socked me in the arm a little too hard.

I socked him in the arm harder.

He busted out laughing and walked away.

I got back to work.

That night, all the girls met up at Raye and Cap's because Raye had gotten a message from Arthur and from what was in this message, according to her (and Luna, and Harlow), we had to do a ceremony to bless our new army knives and the Taser holsters Arthur had gotten us.

Even though this was ridiculous, I participated because first, I was outvoted, second, I got to pick which shot we did during the blessing ceremony (I selected kamikazes), and last, it didn't take that long, then we went out to were Cap and Eric were hanging in the living room, drinking beer.

There was some small talk.

I made a fresh batch of kamikazes so Eric and Cap could have one.

Then it was time for Harlow to start her bed preparations (this had a different slate of activities every night including but not limited to bubble baths, herbal tea or hot chocolate, facials, do-it-yourself mani/pedis, and a variety of other things), therefore, she left.

Luna had to take Jaques for his evening stroll, so she left.

And Eric and I had to fuck, thus, we left.

"You survived," Eric observed as we made the short trek to my pad.

"Barely," I answered.

With a smile on his face, he let us in, locked the door behind us and took my holster from me to inspect it.

"Tactical. Hardshell. Nice," he decreed.

It totally was. I could tell Arthur didn't scrimp.

"Ever see a fairy wearing a taser holster?" I asked.

Eric's eyes cut right to me.

"She'll be naked, except for her wings," I continued, and with that, I smirked.

He wiped the smirk off my face by tossing me over his shoulder and carrying me to the bedroom.

He brought the holster with us.

Once there, though, it was me who dug out my fairy wings. They were black with opalescent netting.

I learned in short order that Eric had never fucked a fairy.

But he liked doing it *a whole lot.*

THINGS at the Oasis were always hopping.

With the help of the Hottie Squad, moving Harlow in had been a breeze. She scored a unit across from Raye and me, on the bottom floor, about two doors down from where Luna was on the top.

I helped her unearth all her new decor, and if a power tool was needed, between Eric and Cap, they had assisted.

Now, we were all in at the Oasis.

And it was awesome, even if half the time, Henny and I were over at Eric's.

The pool and pool deck were done in time for the Holiday Extravaganza, and the new, kickass pool light had been set to cycle through red, green and blue.

I'd already set up the bar and premixed the gimlets so all anyone had to do was transfer into a shaker with some ice, shake them up, pour and garnish.

Eric texted that something he and Brady were doing meant he was going to be a little late, which was good, because I couldn't decide what to do with my hair. Middle part and long, or side bun?

I eventually decided to go whole hog with side bun and was putting the finishing touches on it when I heard the front door open and Eric call, "Babe?"

"Almost ready," I called back.

I turned my head when I felt him in the doorway of the bathroom.

"Jesus, fuck," he whispered, his eyes on my dress.

I knew what he was talking about, but not the dress.

He was wearing a dark blue, three-piece suit, white shirt open at the throat, burgundy pocket square. Ah-freaking-mazing.

"Will I do?" I asked after I tore my eyes off my hot guy in his suit.

"I'd marry you in that dress."

I stood completely still.

"We're already late, there's people all over the courtyard. How much later can we be?" he asked.

"I don't even care if we go now."

He gave me his wicked sexy smile then said, "After. The mood I'm in, I'll mess up your hair."

I'd just spent forty-five minutes on my 'do.

"I do not give two fucks about my hair."

He came to me, slid a hand from my midriff around my ribs to my back and put his lips to mine, not for a touch or a brush, but to whisper, "After." He then let me go and walked away, ordering, "Hurry up. I'm hungry. And Raye's pudding is already half gone."

Seriously?

"You are such a tease!" I shouted.

I heard him chuckle.

Guh.

Though, if Raye's pudding was already half gone, I had to hustle.

When I got out of the bathroom, I found Eric in my living room staring at my new PhotoShare frame on the kitchen bar.

He didn't even look at me when he said, "You're not supposed to buy yourself presents before Christmas."

Oh crap.

"Did you buy me one of those?" I asked.

He finally looked at me. "No. But if I'd known you wanted one, I would have."

I shrugged. "Don't want to spoil the surprise, but this is a sharing frame. You can send your pictures to it, and I can send mine to the one wrapped and under your tree."

I saw his lips curl up before he turned back and watched the photos cycle.

"These are all of Henny," he noted.

"There's one of us," I said as the selfie Eric had taken at the bar at Steak 44 cycled through. We'd gone early for our reservation to have a drink before we sat at our table.

It was our first "official" date. Something I told Eric was unnecessary (Steak 44 was hella expensive).

It was the second time Eric insisted.

Again, I didn't put a lot of effort into fighting him about it.

That had been a great night.

That photo cycled out to another of Henny. Which cycled to another one of Henny. And then to another.

They were all black and white. They were all perfection.

Eric turned to me and raised his brows.

"So I'm a cat lady now. I have no regrets," I said.

Eric laughed as he hooked an arm around me and pulled me to him, finally giving me a brush on the lips.

"Ready to party?" he asked when he was done.

I nodded.

With his arm still around me, we headed to the door.

"Be good," I said to Henny, though I didn't know why. He was asleep on the black fur Christmas skirt I had under the tree. He was also always good.

We walked down, and with all the fab Christmas décor, and everyone decked out (even Martha was wearing a shimmery sliver number), the place seemed more like a holiday wonderland.

When I'd set up the bar, I'd seen there was a drum kit, a set of keyboards, an upright piano, and some microphones and amps on a portable stage, so I was expecting a band. But instead, there was Christmas music playing from some speakers Bill and Zach had set around.

Eric went right to the drink table to shake our cocktails.

I went right to the food table to get us some pudding.

"Uhhhhhh..."

I turned my head to see Raye in a red, off-the-shoulder, to-the-knee bodycon dress with long, puffed sleeves sidling close.

"What's going on there?" she asked.

I aimed my eyes at her, then to where she was looking, and I saw

Luna, in a glittery gold, plunge-front, floor-length dress standing behind the striped baubles with Knox.

They were both face to face, or more aptly, nose to nose.

Even from where we stood, halfway across the courtyard, it appeared they were also significantly ticked.

"Whoa," I muttered right before I shoved some pudding in my mouth.

"I'll say," Raye agreed. "Then there's that."

She nodded her head toward Javi, who was smiling at Shanti, who was saying something. And about ten feet away, Harlow, in a seriously sparkly ice-blue number that looked like something Elsa from *Frozen* would wear, was standing with another resident, Jenn, and she was glaring daggers at them.

"Hmm," I mumbled.

"I will note, Cap and I have been here for half an hour, and Javi tried unsuccessfully three times to make an approach to Harlow, and she instigated evasive maneuvers each time."

God, my bestie could be a dufus sometimes.

I turned back to Raye. "Then she's getting what she deserves."

"It's like two live-action Hallmark movies," Alexis said as she came to stand with us.

She wasn't wrong.

We all turned back to the baubles in time to watch Luna poke Knox in the chest before she stomped to Harlow's apartment, entered it and slammed the door.

Knox watched this, then he stalked in the opposite direction and out the security gate.

Man, it had to be said, Knox was nearly as good at stalking as Eric was at sauntering.

Our attention shifted when Shanti's musical laughter could be heard.

Javi was still smiling down at her.

Harlow, though, had a face that was crumbling, before she

dashed across the space with almost as much grace as Alexis would do it, right into her apartment.

When her door closed behind her, I looked back to Javi.

He had his his eyes on Harlow's door.

Shanti did too, and she looked concerned.

Javi looked contemplative, but he morphed to pissed, at who—himself for playing games, or Harlow for doing it—I didn't know.

"He screwed the pooch on that one," Eric muttered as he handed me my cocktail.

"Absolutely," Cap said as he showed and offered a fresh one to Raye.

"Raye said she was avoiding him," I noted. "He went the flirt-with-another-chick route."

"Not a good call," Jacob, also joining us, grunted, then he shot a flinch toward Alexis who leaned into him and put her hand on his chest in a nonverbal *I'm over it, baby*.

Oh yeah.

Right.

Jacob had pulled that shit with Alexis too.

"If you only got eyes for her, you should only have eyes for her," Cap gave us some man wisdom.

"Yep," Eric agreed.

Shanti showed at our group. "Is Harlow all right?"

"She's into Javi," I told her.

"Okay," Shanti said like she didn't get it.

"And he was flirting with you," I pointed out the obvious.

Her eyes got big. "We weren't flirting. We were just talking. He's funny. He's gorgeous. But really, he wasn't flirting. I saw how he looked at Harlow, and it totally wasn't that, not only because it wasn't because he wasn't taking it there, but because Harlow's my girl, and I wouldn't take it there."

Good to know that about Shanti.

"Well, she doesn't know that," Raye said.

"And it looked like flirting," I semi-repeated.

"Should I go talk to her?" Shanti asked.

I searched for Javi.

He was now chatting with Jeff, Linda and Rhea (Raye's next-door neighbor) like he hadn't just blown it huge, the big oaf.

"Let them figure it out," Eric advised.

"I feel bad," Shanti mumbled.

"Don't," I said. "It's not on you. Really."

"All right," Shanti agreed, but I could tell she wasn't committed to it.

Ugh.

Javi and Harlow both needed a kick in the ass. If they wanted to play games, great. But collateral damage wasn't cool.

The music from the speakers cut out and the piano intro to The Pogues' "Fairytale of New York" started playing from the direction of the stage.

We all turned to where the drums and amps were set up only to see Stella freaking Gunn at the piano with Buzz, the Blue Moon Gypsies' bass player standing at a microphone ready to sing.

"Holy fuck," I said.

"Holy shit," Raye said.

"Oh my goodness," Alexis said.

"Fucking hell," Jacob said.

"Good Lord," Shanti said.

Cap and Eric had nothing to say.

But Eric threw his arm around my shoulders, and when I tore my gaze from the makeshift stage to look at him, I saw his eyes on Stella and a huge smile on his face.

It only got bigger when Buzz began singing.

The rest of the band—Pong, Hugo and Leo—showed with their instruments and started playing just before Stella jumped in on the Kirsty MacColl part.

The Blue Moon Gypsies—*all of them*—were playing an apartment complex Holiday Extravaganza.

This was *insane*.

It was also insanely beautiful.

Man, Stella totally was the shit.

We all wandered closer to them as if pulled by an invisible rope.

As for Raye, Alexis, Shanti and me, we were swaying, dancing and singing with them.

Tex sat on top of one of the outdoor tables, a bottle of beer in his hand held up high swinging back and forth, his head bowed, his torso moving with his hand. Linda was clapping with the beat. Bill and Zach were whirling around with arms hooked at the fast parts, and swaying side to side in each other's arms on the slow parts.

When the song ended, Hugo went to the keyboards, Stella got up from the piano, grabbed her guitar and moved to an unused mic.

"This one is for Kai," she said to someone offstage.

I looked that way to see Mace standing close to the bar, arms crossed, shaking his head but smiling, his eyes locked on his wife.

This happened before the band dropped right into Stevie Wonder's "What Christmas Means to Me."

That did it.

I handed my drink to Eric, and Raye, Shanti, Alexis and I gave up on the swaying and went into straight up dancing.

Within seconds Luna and Harlow had joined us.

So had Martha, Linda, Rhea, Patsy, Bill, Zach, Jenn, half the other Oasis residents and Tallulah and Walsh, Stella and Mace's two kids.

And just to say, Walsh was barely out of toddlerhood, but the kid could cut a rug.

"Angels get up here," Stella ordered after "What Christmas Means to Me" was over.

We all glanced at each other before we headed up.

I mean, when Stella Gunn, multi-platinum artist and Rock Chick, tells you to get onstage, you do it.

Right?

While we did, things got concerning as Tex handed each of us a microphone, and Tito moved to the front of the stage with his iPad facing out in front of him.

We barely got there before the Gypsies jumped into The Waitresses' "Christmas Wrapping," and I got a bad feeling that was confirmed when the karaoke words to the song scrolled on Tito's iPad.

I hated karaoke.

I mean, seriously.

The worst.

But it was Christmas.

So...

What the hell?

Right?

Wrong.

I'll tell you, if there's a karaoke song to cut your teeth on, this wasn't it.

We were a disaster.

Catastrophic.

But we went for it, everyone was laughing with us, dancing in front of us, and the best, Mace had joined Eric, Cap and Jacob, Javi and Jeff did too, Knox reappeared, and Brady, Gabe and Liam joined the crew, and they were all smiling at us.

Fortunately, Hugo could play a damn fine horn, and everyone out in our audience was screaming the words with us (or trying, seriously, that song was *hard*), both mostly drowning us out.

Topping that, Tito's Santa-hat-topped head was bouncing to the beat, his beard sometimes obscuring the words on the screen. Tex was stomping around the pool deck dance floor in some bizarre version of dancing. Tallulah had joined us girls in singing onstage, while Walsh seemed to be attempting to break dance by his mom where she was playing the guitar, and that was hysterical.

And I was up there with my girls, doing stupid shit, my stomach hurting because I had to sing and couldn't do what I needed to do:

bust a gut laughing. My chicks all looked gorgeous. They looked happy. And it was nearly Christmas.

So I was oh so very wrong.

It wasn't a total disaster.

With Eric standing with his phone in front of him, videoing this mess, a huge smile on his happy, handsome face, his gaze on me, watching me make a massive fool of myself with my chicks, what it was, was one of the best memories I'd made in my entire life.

And spoiler alert.

It always would be.

By the way: I got Jacob's name to be his Secret Santa. He was totally jazzed by the bottle of McCallan 12 I gave him.

See?

I had this shit down.

Martha was mine. She gave me a box filled with a dozen different colors of edible glitter.

Some mixologists might set those aside for sole use in their cocktails.

I might use some of it in cocktails eventually.

But when Eric and I got back to my place after the Holiday Extravaganza, we had other ideas.

"Right, it's officially not Christmas anymore, so I'm out," Jeff stated as he pushed himself up from the recliner angled beside the one Eric and I were cuddled in.

We were in Eric's man cave, and it was now seventeen minutes after midnight, the day after Christmas.

Somewhere along the line, Eric had strung multi-colored

Christmas lights around the edges of the ceiling, and that was our only illumination.

The room smelled of movie theater popcorn, and we'd just finished *Violent Night*.

This was after our movie marathon that started with *Lethal Weapon* then moved into *Die Hard* and finished with Santa kicking ass and taking names.

Jeff had Henny cuddled to his chest. "Great day, sis. Eric. See you two in the morning."

FYI: Eric had insisted on yet another thing. Jeff spending the night Christmas Eve so we could all wake up and start the day together, as well as him staying that night, so he didn't feel he had to leave, and he didn't have to be alone at all on Christmas Day.

That afternoon, we'd all hit up Mace and Stella's for an open house Christmas buffet that Stella, Cap and Raye had put together, and the gang was all there.

So all day, our Christmas was about family.

Thought I was crazy for falling in love with this guy in about a week?

As you could see, you were wrong.

"You can leave Henny," I told him.

"Henny's coming with me," Jeff replied.

I opened my mouth, but my brother was out the door with our cat.

I glowered at the door.

"Babe," Eric called.

I shifted my attention to him and stopped glowering.

"Thanks for not giving me my Christmas present of porn comics in front of my brother," I said.

He started chuckling.

And...yeah.

Eric had run across my stash of porn. He'd thought it was hilarious, but clearly hadn't thought it was a turn off, considering that day, he'd augmented it.

In front of Jeff, he'd given me a Disney Villain Maleficent heart-shaped onyx pendant with a vine of diamond thorns.

It was sheer perfection.

So much so, I was never taking it off.

"Thanks for waking me up with a phenomenal Christmas blowjob," Eric replied.

I grinned at him.

That had been present number one.

The biggie had been a kickass, decorative firepit for his yard.

He'd loved it.

Henny, by the way, did not get thousands of cat toys for Christmas, but he was allowed to scatter the spent wrapping, bat the bows and squeeze into the boxes to his heart's content.

"It's not Christmas anymore," he told me something I knew.

"Okay," I replied, not sure how I felt about how his expression had changed.

"You'll want to know," he murmured. "But I hope you'll get why I delayed it until after the big day."

"Know what?" I asked.

He blew out a breath.

Then without a word, he righted the recliner, put us on our feet, took my hand, led me to the door and out went the lights.

He then guided me to the bedroom, turning off more lights along the way.

Once he got us there, he gently pressed me to sitting on the side of his bed. Only then did he open the drawer on his nightstand.

I knew this was no Boxing Day present when he pulled out a plastic bag.

"Getting on their radar, especially how they did, the cops cleared out Homer's camp," he said.

My throat closed.

I'd been to the camp twice since the first visit after his abduction, and Homer had not come out of his tent either time.

Due to that, I'd been giving Homer space.

But I had to admit, things had gotten hectic, what with Christmas and all, and the last couple of weeks, I hadn't checked in.

"They were all moved, to shelters or other accommodations, or they scattered," Eric told me.

"Oh my God," I whispered.

"Homer has disappeared."

My heart stuttered to a stop.

"Oh my God," I whimpered.

"We've looked for him, and we can't find him. We'll keep looking, honey. But in the meantime, a woman named Connie gave this to a shelter worker saying it had to get to me, so I could give to you," Eric concluded.

He then handed me the bag.

Uncertain, I took it.

There was no weight to it. It just seemed to be an empty bag.

"There's something in it," Eric said.

I looked up to him, before I opened the bag and peered in.

A photo was in there.

Even more uncertainly, I reached in and took it out.

This time, my throat convulsed when I saw it was a picture of a much younger Homer standing behind a beautiful woman, his arms around her, his hands on her very pregnant belly.

They were both smiling huge.

"Sweetheart," Eric called gently.

I looked up at him again.

He was wavy through the tears in my eyes.

"We've also looked into him."

I knew I didn't want to know, but I nodded anyway.

"She died of postpartum preeclampsia."

I swallowed a sob.

Oh, Homer.

"The baby lived," Eric went on. "Then she got leukemia and passed when she was four."

I made a pained noise.

Oh, *Homer*.

I couldn't hold my head up anymore, so I let it drop.

Eric curled a hand around the back of my neck and put his lips to my hair.

"Let's get this done for you," he muttered into my hair. "Look at the back, honey."

To get it over with, I flipped the picture. I had to blink several times to clear my eyes, but I read:

> *This is home, Jessie.*
> *I'm glad you found yours.*
> *Hold on to it.*
> *As long as you can.*

I couldn't swallow that sob, my whole body bucked with the power of it.

Eric kept his hand on my neck, his lips to my hair as I allowed the tears to come.

When I started to pull my shit together, I felt Henny jump up beside me, start kneading my thigh with his paws, and that was when Eric moved away.

It was also when I watched him open his nightstand again to commence giving me my last Christmas gift.

He took out a beautiful silver frame.

At this point, he slid the photo from my fingers, and I watched him put it in the frame. I then watched him walk around the bed and rest the frame on the nightstand at my side.

He came back around, gently removed Henny from my thigh, took my hand, pulled me off the bed and into the bathroom.

He made me brush my teeth standing beside him at his basin.

After I changed into a nightie, and Eric had put on his sleep pants, when we were about to get into bed, I put my hand on his abs.

"Stop looking for him," I requested.

"Sweetheart," he murmured.

"I don't want him to feel hunted," I said.

His curled a hand around the side of my neck. "We aren't doing it that way."

"I know. But he might feel it's that way." I leaned into him. "If he needs me, he knows where to find me."

Eric gazed into my eyes a beat.

Then he nodded.

And when we were in bed, he tucked me close, and Henny tucked himself close to my back.

In the dark, I whispered, "I love my pendant."

"I know," Eric whispered back.

"But weirdly, Homer's present was the best one I've ever got."

Eric pulled me closer, and Henny adjusted so he didn't lose contact.

"I know," Eric said.

"Merry Christmas, baby."

"Best one I've had for thirty years."

Fuck!

Seriously!

Why was everyone making me cry?

"I take what I just said back, *that* was the best present I ever got," I husked.

Eric pulled me even closer.

And Henny adjusted.

So neither of my boys lost contact.

TWENTY-EIGHT

CURVED COUCH

Three months later...

WE WERE IN TWEETY, Raye's bright yellow Juke, on our way to the storage units, and I was getting the third degree from Harlow.

"So, are you moving in with Eric?" she asked.

Move from the Oasis?

Not until there was a ring on my finger.

"No, we're a dual household family," I answered.

"You're at his more than you're at yours," she accused.

I looked to her. "That isn't true." And it wasn't.

"Yes, it is," she retorted.

"No, it isn't," I replied.

"Yes. It. Is!" she cried.

Whoa.

At the drama, I narrowed my eyes on my bestie.

"Oh my God, bitch, dial down the sexual frustration already," Luna ordered from the front seat. "Jess isn't at Eric's more, but even if she was, who cares? Get over yourself and jump on Javi, for all of our sakes."

And...

Yeah.

Three months and that hadn't gone anywhere except to make Harlow be very un-Harlow on occasion.

That was my nice way of saying she could act like a bitch.

As in...now.

"Pot, say hello to kettle," Raye said under her breath.

Oh shit.

Luna's head snapped to Raye behind the wheel. "What's that supposed to mean?"

"Harlow is in a game of hide and seek with Javi, but every time he finds where she's hiding, she hides somewhere else. We all got that down since we've been watching it for three months. But I don't know what you and Knox are playing at," Raye returned.

"Mortal Kombat?" I suggested.

"Nothing is playing between Knox and me," Luna asserted (or more accurately, *lied*). "We're just friends."

"You two fight a lot for just being friends," Harlow pointed out. "You act like Luke and Ava, except without the marriage and babies, but with the sexual tension."

It must be said, Luke and Ava could bicker.

It was cute.

Knox and Luna?

It would be, if they were jumping each other's bones after, which they weren't.

So...

Not so cute.

"That's because he can be annoying," Luna fired back. "And there is no sexual tension."

"He's almost as mellow as Eric," I stated. "And we pretty much choke on the tension anytime you two are around each other." I turned again to Harlow. "It's suffocating if you and Javi are there too."

Harlow crossed her arms on her chest and pouted, "It's the man's job to make the moves."

"Oh my God, are you serious?" I asked.

"How many moves does he have to make before he gets himself some?" Raye asked right after me.

Harlow looked out the side window, which meant this conversation was over.

Okay then.

Moving on.

"All right, does anyone know why Arthur told us to go to the storage units?" I asked.

"I don't," Raye answered. "Clarice just dropped a key at SC this morning and said we needed to hit unit number fourteen. Tonight, and together."

Number fourteen meant our cache of units had grown by one.

"I hope it's a pink Hummer," Harlow mumbled.

I wouldn't pick pink, but even so, a pink Hummer for the Angels would also kinda kick ass.

"Do you have any idea how much of a gas guzzler a Hummer is?" Luna asked, clearly not over her attitude.

"Maybe they have electric ones," Harlow retorted.

It was hard, but I managed not to bust out laughing at the thought of an EV Hummer.

Personally, I didn't care what it was.

We'd had three months of chill.

I was down with that.

Henny was settled in.

Eric and I were settled in.

I'd mastered the perfect burger (yes, the Dijon, Worcestershire sauce and garlic was the ticket).

Eric had heard through the grapevine that Savannah had

abandoned her plans to open a restaurant in Phoenix, and even better, he hadn't heard a single word from her.

Javi, Jeff and Cody were all deep into training with the NI&S team. And they'd also recruited Jacob.

Even so, men from the Denver team were still cycling through as they got the new guys trained, so we'd all come to know Lee, Luke, Vance and Hector, as well as their respective wives, Indy, Ava, Jules and Sadie, pretty well. Fortunately, Daisy also came down on the regular, as did Ally, Lee and Hank's sister, and another Rock Chick. So we'd met Daisy's hubby Marcus, and Ally's man, Ren.

Shirleen and Moses had moved to the Valley of the Sun, and Moses had joined the team, taking over managing the control room.

Roam had found a pad, and he was all moved in too.

Tex and Nancy had sold their place in Denver, but as yet had not found a home to buy in Phoenix, because apparently, (always full of surprises) Tex was picky. This meant they, along with all their cats, were living with Mace and Stella, in the casita at their massive compound in Paradise Valley.

But even as awesome as all this was, we needed a case.

What could I say?

I hadn't known him long, but I missed Titus.

And doing deeds to stop people from suffering was a serious high.

Raye swung into the storage facility.

But it was Luna who whispered, "Whoa," when we all saw Shanti standing outside her car that was parked outside our units.

Raye parked bumper-to-bumper with her vehicle, and we all got out.

"Hey, girl," Raye called guardedly to Shanti. "What are you doing here?"

Shanti looked confused. "I don't know. You texted me and told me to meet you here. You said it was urgent."

"I did?" Raye asked, which meant she did not.

Though, somehow, Arthur did.

Seemed we had a new recruit.

The question was...why?

We met up with Shanti and huddled around her phone.

Sure enough, there was a text from Raye asking her to meet us there. Urgently.

"Does this have to do with Willow?" Shanti asked.

Uh-oh.

"Willow?" Luna asked in return.

Shanti nodded, and it was then I remembered Shanti and Willow were super tight.

"She's got a bad ex," Shanti explained. "He's a supreme dick. He comes and goes out of her life, leaving a mess in his wake. She hasn't said anything, but she's acting weird, so I think he's back."

We looked among each other.

"Has she talked to you guys about him?" Shanti asked.

"Ummmm...." Harlow didn't answer.

No one else said anything because she hadn't.

This lasted a long time, so to end it, I made a decision.

"Raye, open the door and let's see what's up. We can explain to Shanti after."

"Good idea," Raye said and turned to the lock.

She unlocked it, threw up the rolling door and hit the lights.

"Holy...*what*?" Harlow breathed.

None of the rest of us uttered a word or sound.

We just stared into the unit that had thick, white carpeting throughout. At the back, there were two gold standing lamps on either side of a curved red couch with black piping that faced a baronial black desk, which had one thing smack dab in the center of it.

An old-fashioned speaker.

The walls had been paneled and covered in wallpaper that was a swirl of red, pink, orange, and black on a white background, that would normally seem too much, but somehow, it totally worked. Though, the wall behind the desk had a large, built-in screen.

There was a delicate secretary desk angled toward the unit close to the door, on top of which was a keyboard, and in an arched display along the outer edges were four computer screens.

Opposite that, there was a life-size marble statue of a woman in a Grecian gown with two slits up her legs. She had gold leaves adorning the front of her gown and her hair. She had gold angel wings at her back.

But she was not angelic.

Exactly.

She was in attack stance, one of her arms straight out, holding a golden bow, the other arm was bent, but up, as if she'd just let loose the arrow.

Oh yeah.

And along the walls were Andy Warhol inspired portraits of Raye, Luna, Harlow, me, plus Shanti, and oh fuck...Willow.

It was a far cry from Titus's setup (there was no bar or beverage fridge).

But it was a start.

And that angel was kick-freaking-ass, but those prints were *everything*.

Morgan Freeman's voice came from the speaker.

"Come in and close the door, Angels."

"What the holy hell?" Shanti whispered.

Mm-hmm.

We had a lot of explaining to do.

Raye took Shanti's arm and guided her in. "I think Arthur's going to share a few things with you."

Shanti looked at Raye with wide eyes.

Luna, Harlow and I stepped onto the carpet.

And I turned and closed the door.

The End

The Angels Will Return in...
Avenging Angels: Tenderfoot

AUTHOR'S NOTE

Back in the day, when I lived in Denver, I decided to adopt a just-mine, I'm-now-an-adult cat.

I went to the shelter and met Oscar.

After being homed, he'd been "returned" to that shelter by another family because he was "too much trouble."

This trouble took the form of an upper respiratory infection that isn't awesome for anyone to have, especially cats. But the vets who serviced the shelter did not give up, they took care of Oscar, and he beat the infection.

But the cat I saw was *rough.* He had fur shaved for IVs and medicines, he was skinny…

But honest to God, if he had an opposable thumb and a tin mug, he would have been dragging that thing across the wire of his cage, demanding freedom.

He was a mess, but I was in love. I took him. And one could say Oscar had a pretty intense personality. This intensity centered around the fact he was 100% not an indoor cat. And yet his momma was 100% a keep-the-cat-indoors kind of mom. We clashed. He won.

I kept my window open above my bed, and he came and went as he pleased.

He was so happy. We were so happy.

And then my knowledge of why I wanted him inside hit him in the form of a car and took his life.

I was devastated. I felt guilty.

But in the end, I could have kept him inside, and he'd have been miserable. Instead, he was the king of the world...for a while.

My devastation was such, the house felt hollow, empty, and I had to have another cat immediately.

I went to the shelter again, a different one this time, and I selected another black cat. But I shared with them how Oscar had died, and they had a policy they couldn't adopt a cat to people who let them outside. They had to get board approval, and if the board approved, I'd have to sign a contract that stated I wouldn't let my next cat out.

I did so readily.

But in the meantime, they adopted the cat I'd selected earlier. I'd gone to pick him up, and he was not there because he was (I hope) in a loving forever home.

This was tremendously upsetting, until they told me they'd had a black cat dumped on their doorstep a few days before.

His name was Homer.

They took me to him.

He was obviously scared and overwhelmed by all the cats around him and had tucked himself up in a cat box in an act of self-preservation.

I fell cross-legged to the floor and cooed to him.

I believe I cooed for approximately two-point-five seconds before he slunk out of that box, curled into my lap and started purring.

I was his.

And he was mine.

I took him home and he didn't even do a cursory sniff. The

minute I let him out of his carrier, he jumped up on my lounge chair, curled up and fell asleep.

He knew he was home.

Because he was.

I renamed him Cedric. You know him in an earlier book as Boo. I took him to England with me. And years later, driving in a panic, I felt his presence leave this world as Mark and I tried to get him to emergency care in Bristol after he had surgery at a local vet during which he crashed repeatedly.

He was no longer young, and he'd been riddled with cancer, so as much as it gutted both of us, it was his time.

I miss him to this day.

And I'm so glad that other cat went to another home, so I could have my Cedric. I'm thrilled I could give Oscar the full, free life he needed to live before it was over. I'm immensely proud of this love I've given, and forever grateful for what I received in return.

I share all of this with you as an insight into some of the stuff I've written in this book.

I also share it because, if you've been thinking about adopting an animal, but are on the fence, I hope this book, and this note, pushes you off and you find a shelter near you, and an animal to love.

There are too many lost souls out there without a home.

If you can find one, and give them your home, your rewards will be endless.

I promise.

One last note: Halo Animal Rescue is a real place in Phoenix. If you live around here, and are looking for a pet, hit them up. If you love animals and have a few dollars to spare, hit up their website and donate: www.halorescue.org.

CAST OF CHARACTERS

AVENGING ANGELS SERIES

Avenging Angels

- Rachel "Raye" Armstrong
- Willow Knightley (to be inducted)
- Luna Nelson
- Harlow O'Neill
- Shanti Winston (to be inducted)
- Jessica "Jessie" "Jess" Wylde
- Clarice Davis
- "Arthur"

Hottie Squad
Phoenix Branch: Nightingale Investigations & Security

- Knox Chambers
- Brady Houston
- Julien "Cap" Jackson
- Roman "Roam" Jackson
- Gabriel "Gabe" Stark

- Liam Clark Tucker
- Eric Turner

OG Rock Chicks

(In order of Rock Chick books)

- India "Indy" Savage Nightingale – owner, Fortnum's bookstore (Denver)
- Jet McAlister Chavez – barista, Fortnum's bookstore
- Roxanne "Roxie" Logan Nightingale – self-employed website designer
- Juliet "Jules" "Law" Lawler Crowe – social worker, King's Shelter (Denver)
- Ava Barlow Stark – self-employed graphics designer
- Stella Gunn – world-renowned rock star
- Sadie Townsend Chavez – owner, "Art," a gallery
- Alison "Ally" Nightingale Zano – Owner/Partner, Private Investigator - Rock Chick Investigations
- Daisy Sloan – Owner/Partner, Office Manager - Rock Chick Investigations
- Shirleen Richardson – Partner, Nightingale Investigations & Security, ex-Office Manager Denver Branch (by end of *Avenging Angel*)
- Malia Clark Tucker – Paralegal

OG Hot Bunch

(In order of Rock Chick books)

- Liam "Lee" Nightingale – Partner, Nightingale Investigations & Security, Managing Partner Denver Branch
- Eddie Chavez – Denver Police Detective
- Hank Nightingale – Denver Police Detective

- Vance Crowe – Partner, Nightingale Investigations & Security
- Luke Stark – Partner, Nightingale Investigations & Security
- Kai "Mace" Mason – Partner, Nightingale Investigations & Security, Managing Partner Phoenix Branch
- Hector Chavez – Partner, Nightingale Investigations & Security
- Lorenzo "Ren" Zano - Businessman
- Marcus Sloan – Businessman
- Moses Richardson – Corrections Officer, Juvenile Detention (Denver)
- Darius Tucker – Partner, Nightingale Investigations & Security, Managing Partner Los Angeles Branch

Shadow Soldiers

- Javier "Javi" Montoya
- Jeff "Easy" Wylde (also Jessie's brother)
- Cody
- Jamal
- Joaquim

Luna's Family

- Dream Nelson - children: Dusk and Feather
- Louise Nelson
- Scott Nelson

Informants

- Betsy and Cristina "Bambi" Markovic
- Cameo
- Divinity

- Genesis
- Jinx
- Lotus
- Persia
- Mr. Shithead
- Skyla
- Titus

Oasis Square Residents

- Alexis
- Bill and Zach
- Jacob Brewer
- Jenn
- Linda
- Martha
- Patsy
- Rhea
- Sally

Phoenix Police Chief

- Jorge Alvarez

The Surf Club

- Tito – Owner
- Byron – Regular
- Hunter – Staff/Barista
- Lucia – Head Chef – husband: Mario
- Otis – Staff/Barista
- Tex MacMillan – Guest Barista, wife: Nancy

KristenAshley.net
NEW YORK TIMES BESTSELLING AUTHOR

Two broken hearts find love and healing
in each other in this spin-off from
the Rock Chick and Dream Man series.

Dream Maker
the story of Evie and Mag.

READ MORE FROM KRISTEN ASHLEY

Dream Maker

From New York Times bestselling author Kristen Ashley comes the first sexy, contemporary romance in a brand-new, spin-off from the Rock Chick and Dream Man series, in which two broken hearts find love and healing in each other.

Evie is a bonafide nerd and a hyper-intelligent chick who has worked her whole life to get what she wants. Growing up, she had no support from her family and has only ever been able to rely on herself. So when Evie decides she wants to earn her engineering degree, she realizes she needs to take an alternative path to get there. She takes a job dancing at Smithie's club thinking this would be a quick side gig, where she can make the money she needs. But with her lack of dancing skills and an alpha bad boy who becomes overly protective, Evie realizes this might not be as easy as she thought.

Daniel "Mag" Magnusson knows a thing or two about pain, but the mask he wears is excellent. No one can tell that this good-looking, quick-witted, and roguish guy has deep-seated issues. Mag puts on a funny-guy routine so he can hide his broken heart and PTSD. But when Evie dances her way into Mag's life, he realizes that he needs to come face-to-face with the demons of his past if he wants a future with her.

DREAM MAKER

DREAM TEAM SERIES BOOK 1

Chapter One

I Can't Even

Evie

"I...can't...*even*," I snapped at my windshield as I slammed on the brakes when the car started to pull out in front of me, and I knew it wouldn't stop because they could care less I was only three car lengths away and going five miles (okay, maybe ten) over the speed limit.

"Stupid millennial!" I shouted when I noted the age of the clueless person driving.

Of course, I was a millennial.

Which meant, obviously, I could call my own people stupid and clueless.

Some Gen Xer said something like that, it'd tick me off.

But right then, I had visions in my head of ramming him from behind just to make a point à la Evelyn Couch in *Fried Green Tomatoes*.

Sadly, Evelyn's insurance was great, but mine wouldn't take another bust-up, of which I'd had many (and this might have a *wee* bit to do with me going five, more like ten miles over the speed limit on more than the regular occasion—then again, I was always in a hurry and it was no lie that wasn't hardly ever my fault).

Another reason my insurance agent was going to blackball me to all insurance companies happened right then.

My phone rang.

And I looked to it instantly.

What could I say?

I'm a millennial.

The call was from my mother.

Normally, it was a very good possibility, to the point of it being a probability, I would avoid my mother's call.

Today, I could not.

So, I snatched up my phone and engaged, hopeful to the last (in other words, delusional) that maybe for once, I might have backup in the current situation I was going to have to handle. A situation, like all of them, that was not mine.

"Hey, Mom," I greeted eagerly.

"Evan, darlin', please tell me you're going to see your brother."

Oh, I was going to see my brother all right.

In lockup.

Again.

I was Norm from *Cheers* at Denver County Jail.

"Of course I'm going to see him," I replied.

"Okay," she said, sounding relieved.

I understood her relief.

And my heart sunk.

Because it was not about the proud mother of a good little sister looking after her big brother.

It was a good little daughter doing what a mother should be doing and thus the mother didn't have to do it, which was good, since she wouldn't do it anyway.

Again.

"Tell him his momma sends her love and if he needs anything..." She trailed off.

Call your sister, Evan, I finished for her in my head.

"Mom, I gotta say, this is the last time—"

"Okay, honey, good chat. I gotta go. I gotta get to work."

She did not.

She was unemployed.

Again.

"Talk to you later," she went on. "Come over for dinner. Your stepdad and I miss you."

With that, she hung up, not setting a dinner date, not staying on the line long enough for me to share with her I was D...O...N...E *done* with sorting Mick's crap and not ending the conversation saying such as, "I love you, you can't know how much. You're so responsible, I've no idea how you got that way, but we're so lucky you did because I don't know what we'd all do without you."

No, she did not say that.

I tossed my phone to the seat, drove to the jail, and as I was pulling in the parking lot, I heard it buzz with a text.

I glanced at it, looked back out the windshield, and muttered, "Oh boy."

I found a parking spot, shut down my car and snatched up my phone again.

I went to texts.

I read the latest and then, because I was clearly in the mood for self-flagellation, I scrolled up and read it from the top.

The tippy-top stating the text string was with DANIEL MAGNUSSON.

Hey, this Evan?

Yes, is this Daniel?

Mag. And yeah.

Mag.

Who called themselves *Mag*?

Hi.

Hey, we doing this?

"This" being going on a blind date because our mutual friend Lottie (who'd set us up, like she'd set up all my girlfriends at the club where we worked with friends of her fiancé, Mo) would not let it go even though I got the impression both of us consistently, and for some time, tried to put her off.

For my part, I knew I did just that.

And his "we doing this?" solidified the impression he did too.

Sure.

You climb?

Climb?

Indoor climbing. Rock walls.

Rock walls?

Was he insane?

No.

I did not climb.

I owned eight pairs of Chucks in eight different colors.

But I did not own a single item that might be construed as anything that had anything to do with physical activity.

This was partly because I stripped for a living, which was physical enough.

This was also partly because, when I wasn't stripping, I was so busy doing everything else, I didn't need to work out.

How about we go for ice cream?

That got me about two full minutes of continual dot, dot, dots, which did not turn out to be a textual opus.

It turned out to be three words.

Right. Sounds good.

Such a lie.

I knew he thought it didn't sound good.

He probably had protein shakes for breakfast and lunch and an unseasoned chicken breast for dinner.

What could I say?

He was Mo, Lottie's fiancé's former roommate, and Mo was a commando.

And so was *Mag*.

That was what I'd guess commandos ate.

That and rations.

You open Tuesday?

Yeah.

How about 6:00?

Liks. In Capitol Hill.

I know it.

See you there.

Great. Yes.

See you there.

This had all happened last Thursday.

It was now Tuesday and my hope was that his latest text would be about canceling.

It wasn't.

It was,

Hey, we still on for tonight?

Because Mac won a gift card to a restaurant.

It expires tomorrow and if someone doesn't use it, it'll be wasted.

She's offered it to us.

Mac, by the by, was what some people called Lottie, seeing as her last name, for the time being, was McAlister.

And considering she wasn't close with her dad, she was totally going old school and taking Mo's name when they got married.

"Yes," I said out loud to my phone. "We're still on, after I go in, see my brother, listen to him beg me to post bail while I try to find the courage to tell him this will be *the* last time *ever* I post bail for him or get his ass out of whatever jam he's gotten himself into. Then I'll fail to find that courage. I'll then go to my second most often visited hotspot in Denver. Saul Edelstein, bail bondsman. But I actually do not want to have dinner with you, alpha male, probably toxic male. Though Mo isn't toxic, he's very sweet, but Lottie warned me you had 'issues' and needed someone to settle you down, and apparently, she thinks I'm that person."

I stopped talking to *Mag*, who Lottie told me was actually called Danny, who wasn't there.

And I stared at the phone thinking that the issues Lottie didn't share with me, but the girls at the club did, were that some woman had broken Daniel Magnusson's heart, and like a definitely toxic dude, his strategy for curing it was sleeping with everything that moved.

However, to be honest, although this appeared to be one more project I didn't need, even if Lottie hadn't been entirely forthcoming, my sense was that mostly Lottie seemed like she wanted to fix us up because she liked us both a lot, thought we'd be good together, look out for each other, and in the end, be happy.

I could not imagine what she was thinking.

A commando was *so* not my style.

A manwhore?

Totally not.

My last boyfriend was shorter than me by two inches, weighed twenty-five pounds less than me and his skin had not seen the sun for probably five years and not because he was a vampire.

Because he was a gamer.

I liked him.

We shared a lot of the same interests. He was funny, he could be gentle, he listened, he wasn't all that great in bed, but he gave it his best shot, and he felt safe.

Of course, his eventual utter lack of interest in anything but gaming led to the demise of our relationship.

So now, I missed him.

Or the him I'd had before I lost him to gaming.

My thumbs flew over the bottom of my phone screen.

Sounds good.

When and where?

I was folding out of my car when I got back,

I'll pick you up.

At six.

Pick me up?

For a date?

What was this?

1987?

I'll meet you there. Where is it?

And 6:00 is good.

I was nearing the door when I received,

Picking you up, Evan.

Six.

I don't think it's fancy.

But I don't think it's T and jeans either.

Then,

Mac gave me your address.

See you at 6:00.

Of course she did and of course he was old school too.

No one got picked up for dates anymore.

And now I was stuck for a whole dinner.

It was easier to feign a headache, or better yet, period cramps and duck out if I had my own ride.

"Damn," I whispered, standing outside the doors to the jail.

I texted,

See you then.

Looking forward to it.

I got back an unconvincing,

Yeah.

Me too.

Now I had to spend at least a couple of hours with this guy rather than snarfing down a quick cone while we mutually agreed we didn't suit, shaking hands, then I'd go home and give myself a facial or watch some Japanese anime or repeat a binge watch of *Fleabag* or something.

Ugh.

I entered the jail, did the rigmarole check-in, and while doing it, caught up with Officer Bobbie behind the desk (bad news for Bobbie: her kid had the flu so bad, they' had to hospitalize him, good news: he was okay now, and mental note: stop by the jail and give Officer Bobbie something fun to give to her recently very sick kid).

Then, I was sat in front of a video screen and I waited for Mick to appear before I grabbed the handset.

But when he appeared, I didn't grab the handset.

My heart started beating in a strange way I'd never felt before.

It was like there was nothing in my chest cavity, it was hollow, save my heart, and my heart was thumping in there, all alone.

I snatched the handset so fast, my hand was a blur.

And I nearly came out of my skin listening to the warnings about how the police were recording our visit.

When it was done, his name jumped out of my throat.

"Mick?"

"Hey, Evie," he said, his voice wrong, wrong, *wrong*.

Tentative.

Trembling.

Scared.

My cocky, criminal, wastrel, good-time, bad-decisions big brother didn't get scared.

I leaned forward. "Mick—"

"You're gonna get a text, honey. Take it, and...you know. Just take it and do right by your brother."

Oh God.

"What?" I asked.

He leaned toward his screen too.

"You...are gonna...get a *text*, Evie. *Take it*. And...do *right*."

What did that mean?

Before I could find some words to ask him to share in ways that wouldn't get him into trouble, or later be used to incriminate him, he kept talking.

"I'm counting on you."

"Mick."

And then he did not ask me to go to Saul.

He did not say the reasons for his current accommodations were all a mistake.

Or he'd been in the wrong place at the wrong time.

Or they'd brought him in on nonsense to lean on him to rat on someone else.

Or one of the hundred other excuses he used.

He did something that sent ice splinters tearing through my veins.

He pressed his middle three fingers to his lips, then pressed them to the screen, hung up his handset, stood and walked away.

Dream Maker is available for purchase in all formats.

ACKNOWLEDGMENTS

A shout out first to my readers. Thank you for taking another adventure with the Angels. I hope you had as much fun with them as I did.

This is also my opportunity to give props to my fabulous team: Amanda Simpson, Kelly Brown, Tanaka Kangara, Grace Wenk and Stacey Tardif. You can't know how much your talent, support and hard work is appreciated. Just trust me, it totally is.

Rock On!

NEWSLETTER

Would you like advanced notification about Upcoming Releases? Access to exclusive content? Access to exclusive giveaways? The first to see a new cover reveal? Sign up for my newsletter to keep up-to-date with the latest from Kristen Ashley!

Sign up at kristenashley.net

ABOUT THE AUTHOR

Kristen Ashley is the *New York Times* bestselling author of over eighty romance novels including the *Rock Chick, Colorado Mountain, Dream Man, Chaos, Unfinished Heroes, The 'Burg, Magdalene, Fantasyland, The Three, Ghost and Reincarnation, The Rising, Dream Team, Moonlight and Motor Oil, River Rain, Wild West MC, Misted Pines* and *Honey* series along with several standalone novels. She's a hybrid author, publishing titles both independently and traditionally, her books have been translated in fourteen languages and she's sold over five million books.

Kristen's novel, *Law Man*, won the *RT Book Reviews* Reviewer's Choice Award for best Romantic Suspense, her independently published title *Hold On* was nominated for *RT Book Reviews* best Independent Contemporary Romance and her traditionally published title *Breathe* was nominated for best Contemporary Romance. Kristen's titles *Motorcycle Man, The Will*, and *Ride Steady* (which won the Reader's Choice award from *Romance Reviews*) all made the final rounds for Goodreads Choice Awards in the Romance category.

Kristen, born in Gary and raised in Brownsburg, Indiana, is a fourth-generation graduate of Purdue University. Since, she's lived in Denver, the West Country of England, and she now resides in Phoenix. She worked as a charity executive for eighteen years prior to beginning her independent publishing career. She now writes full-time.

Although romance is her genre, the prevailing themes running through all of Kristen's novels are friendship, family and a strong sisterhood. To this end, and as a way to thank her readers for their support, Kristen has created the Rock Chick Nation, a series of programs that are designed to give back to her readers and promote a strong female community.

The mission of the Rock Chick Nation is to live your best life, be true to your true self, recognize your beauty, and take your sister's back whether they're at your side as friends and family or if they're thousands of miles away and you don't know who they are.

The programs of the RC Nation include Rock Chick Rendezvous, weekends Kristen organizes full of parties and get-togethers to bring the sisterhood together, Rock Chick Recharges, evenings Kristen arranges for women who have been nominated to receive a special night, and Rock Chick Rewards, an ongoing program that raises funds for nonprofit women's organizations Kristen's readers nominate. Kristen's Rock Chick Rewards have donated hundreds of thousands of dollars to charity and this number continues to rise.

You can read more about Kristen, her titles and the Rock Chick Nation at KristenAshley.net.

facebook.com/kristenashleybooks
instagram.com/kristenashleybooks
pinterest.com/KristenAshleyBooks
goodreads.com/kristenashleybooks
bookbub.com/authors/kristen-ashley
tiktok.com/@kristenashleybooks

ALSO BY KRISTEN ASHLEY

Rock Chick Series:

Rock Chick

Rock Chick Rescue

Rock Chick Redemption

Rock Chick Renegade

Rock Chick Revenge

Rock Chick Reckoning

Rock Chick Regret

Rock Chick Revolution

Rock Chick Reawakening

Rock Chick Reborn

Rock Chick Rematch

Rock Chick Bonus Tracks

Avenging Angels Series

Avenging Angel

Avenging Angels: Back in the Saddle

The 'Burg Series:

For You

At Peace

Golden Trail

Games of the Heart

The Promise

Hold On

The Chaos Series:

Own the Wind

Fire Inside

Ride Steady

Walk Through Fire

A Christmas to Remember

Rough Ride

Wild Like the Wind

Free

Wild Fire

Wild Wind

The Colorado Mountain Series:

The Gamble

Sweet Dreams

Lady Luck

Breathe

Jagged

Kaleidoscope

Bounty

Dream Man Series:

Mystery Man

Wild Man

Law Man

Motorcycle Man

Quiet Man

Dream Team Series:

Dream Maker

Dream Chaser

Dream Bites Cookbook

Dream Spinner

Dream Keeper

The Fantasyland Series:

Wildest Dreams

The Golden Dynasty

Fantastical

Broken Dove

Midnight Soul

Gossamer in the Darkness

Ghosts and Reincarnation Series:

Sommersgate House

Lacybourne Manor

Penmort Castle

Fairytale Come Alive

Lucky Stars

The Honey Series:

The Deep End

The Farthest Edge

The Greatest Risk

The Magdalene Series:

The Will

Soaring

The Time in Between

Mathilda, SuperWitch:

Mathilda's Book of Shadows

Mathilda The Rise of the Dark Lord

Misted Pines Series

The Girl in the Mist

The Girl in the Woods

The Woman by the Lake

Moonlight and Motor Oil Series:

The Hookup

The Slow Burn

The Rising Series:

The Beginning of Everything

The Plan Commences

The Dawn of the End

The Rising

The River Rain Series:

After the Climb

After the Climb Special Edition

Chasing Serenity

Taking the Leap

Making the Match

Fighting the Pull

Sharing the Miracle

Embracing the Change

The Three Series:

Until the Sun Falls from the Sky

With Everything I Am

Wild and Free

The Unfinished Hero Series:

Knight

Creed

Raid

Deacon

Sebring

Wild West MC Series:

Still Standing

Smoke and Steel

Other Titles by Kristen Ashley:

Heaven and Hell

Play It Safe

Three Wishes

Complicated

Loose Ends

Fast Lane

Perfect Together

Too Good To Be True

Printed in the USA
CPSIA information can be obtained
at www.ICGtesting.com
LVHW042328051224
798478LV00006B/17

* 9 7 8 1 9 5 4 6 8 0 6 4 7 *